DARK WITNESS

REBECCA FORSTER

DARK WITNESS
A Josie Bates Thriller
Book 7
By
REBECCA FORSTER

Dark Witness
E-book Edition
Copyright © Rebecca Forster, 2014
All rights reserved
Cover Design: Createspace

GET A SPECIAL GIFT FREE

FOR
My husband whose vision is always clearer than my own
My son, Alex, who is grandly fearless
My son, Eric, who is gloriously curious
Thank you for lifting the dark and
lighting my way with your affection, counsel, and humor
I love you all beyond words

ACKNOWLEDGMENTS

As always, there are many people to thank for their help and encouragement when a novel is completed. Those individuals know who they are and know they are appreciated. With the publication of **Dark Witness**, I would like to acknowledge those who might not know how important they are to the process: **my readers**. Thank you for writing to let me know you were worried about Hannah and Billy. Thank you for wishing Josie and Archer happiness. Thank you for insisting that Max-the-Dog be cared for and kept safe. Thank you for hoping that the next Josie Bates adventure would be told sooner than later. Thank you for reading my other books while you waited for this one.
Thank you.

"O comfort-killing night, image of hell! Dim register and notary of shame! Black stage for tragedies and murders fell! Vast, sin-concealing chaos! Nurse of blame! Blind, muffled bawd! Dark harbor for defame! Grim cave of death! Whispering conspirator with close-tongued treason and the ravisher!"

—William Shakespeare

1

———————

"Hannah. Come on, Hannah! We've got to go now."

I stand with my back to Billy, and I barely hear him. When I turn my head to look over my shoulder, I don't really see him. All I see is the phone booth; all I want is to hear Josie's voice. I take a deep breath and answer him.

"In a minute. I'll be there in a minute."

"I really think we should go now," he insists.

He's right, of course, but it's not as important as he's making it out to be. We can go now or later because running away is easy. I've been doing it all my life.

My mom, Linda Rayburn, turned running away into a high art: a sleight of hand that dipped into someone's wallet for a little stash, sweet lies to reassure a man of her undying love right up until the minute she left. A quick step. An open door. Done. Gone. Travel light. Turn on a dime. Smile, smile, smile because the next opportunity is in front of you. Grab it. Milk it. Run again when it goes south or you get bored. A bird in the hand isn't half as cool as the two in the next bush. If I was as good as her I wouldn't be standing on this hard-packed dirt, hungry, tired, and freezing my ass off. I wouldn't be eyeing a falling down old phone booth like it was the Taj Mahal. Yeah, running away is easy; it's staying gone that's hard.

I raise a hand and dismiss Billy as he huffs in frustration. He calls out to the truck driver who's waiting on us.

"Give us a minute. Just hang on."

Billy kind of dances my way while he does this. When he's at my side, he lowers his voice even though there's no one within a hundred yards to hear or a hundred miles who might care what he has to say.

"Hannah. If we don't go now he might leave us. It's so cold, Hannah. What are we going to do tonight if he leaves us?"

"He's not going without us." I say this even though there's a fifty/fifty chance it's a lie. I can't help myself. I want to make a call home so bad I can taste it.

The other part of his argument – the part about the cold – is something else again. We are as far from Hermosa Beach as we can get. We traveled through Oregon and Washington. We turned left at the Canadian border and made our way to Alaska on a fishing boat.

When I asked the captain for jobs he wasn't even curious about how old we were or why we looked half starved. He just asked if we got seasick and then put us to work: me in the galley and Billy hauling nets all the way to friggin' Alaska. When we got off that boat Billy asked:

"Where do we go now?"

Home.

That's what I wanted to say. Then I wanted to say:

How should I know?

I almost said that because I was scared, and I'm just a kid, and it was time for him to have some ideas. I didn't say that, of course. Billy doesn't have a home to go to. His sister is dead, and there is a crazy guy who wants to kill him because of a fifty-year-old blood feud that happened in Albania. We'd never heard of

Albania or blood feud, but that's why his sister is dead and that's why we're running. It seems a blood feud never ends until the one they want dead is dead. When we got off the boat I just shut up, and we started walking again. We ended up here at this truck stop, and Billy is worried about all sorts of things. Missing our ride is one; me getting in that phone booth is the other one.

"Hannah, please. Don't do this. It's not good for you. It's not good for anyone."

"I won't do anything stupid."

I don't push him out of the way really. I just start walking and Billy steps aside. If the trucker leaves us, so be it. I'll find us somewhere to sleep. Not that it matters to me where we lay our heads. A doorway, a flophouse, a farmhouse, or a ditch, I dream about Josie. No, that's not exactly right. I dream about that dock in Malibu where we made a stand against Gjergi Isai. He wanted to kill Billy. He would have killed me to get to him. Josie got in the way, and every night I dream it was her he killed.

In my mind's eye I see her floating in a calm ocean, tall and lean, her arms out like she's been crucified face down. If there were waves to wash her toward shore I would go into them and pull her out even if it meant me dying. That's how much I love her. Archer isn't in my dreams. I'm sorry about that because I came to like him a lot. Max isn't there. He's probably sleeping in his doggie bed in Josie's house.

Luckily, I know positively that the man from Albania didn't kill Josie. If she were dead, Faye would have erased the message on the office answering machine and she didn't. I've heard it once before. Now, I need to hear it again even though making a call probably isn't smart like Billy says. I guess sometimes I'm not smart because I leave Billy turning circles in the dirt and get into the booth.

The glass is so dirty I don't want to touch it, but I do. I slam it shut and a miracle happens: a light comes on. I never did need more than a little bit of light to make me feel safe and now that I've got it I take stock. There a big, black, box of a telephone on the wall with a receiver attached by a fraying cloth cord. A phone book hangs in shreds from a rusted chain. Cold seeps through a crack in the glass that people have etched bad words on. It doesn't take long to figure out how this thing works, so I dig in the back pocket of my jeans and come up with two quarters, drop them in, and pick up the clunky receiver.

Nothing.

I do what actors do in old movies. I click the little silver thing up and down and curse.

"Come on, dammit."

I hit the box. Then there is movie-magic in the middle of Alaska. I get a recording. The box wants two more quarters. Luckily, I have them. I dial Faye's office. It's Saturday. Josie won't be there, so when I hear her recorded message I smile, lean my forehead on that dirty glass, and leave a message of my own.

"We're still okay. We'll be okay."

I don't say I miss her even though I want her to know that. I don't say I am afraid because I know she suspects it. I hold the phone to my ear long after the machine on the other end beeps that my time is up. Billy knocks on the door, but I press that receiver close like it has the power to suck me in and fly me over the wires to Faye's office or maybe even to my own bed in Josie's house.

When Billy inches into my line of sight, I can't pretend anymore. There is no magic; there are no miracles. I don't change into anything in that phone booth. There is no big red S on a blue jumpsuit for me. I'm sure not a super hero; I'm just sort of Billy's hero.

I hang up and put my hands on the glass doors, but for the first time since all this started I can't move. I am not wise beyond my years, or an old soul, or strong. Adults just assume I am all of those things because I am mostly silent. When I'm not, I talk tough to cover up. Adults want me to be wise so they don't have to be; they want me to be self-sufficient so they don't have to be responsible for me. I have spent years trying to tell them that the way I look is not what I am; the way I talk isn't what I know.

I look up through my lashes at Billy and my shoulders fall a little. His faith in me is heavy, but if I give up and we go back to Hermosa Beach Billy will go into foster care. He doesn't deserve that. If I leave him alone, he'll make a mistake and someone will kill him. He sure doesn't deserve that. If we keep running like Josie told us to do, there is a chance we'll be safe. I think we both deserve a shot at that.

"Can we go now?"

The glass muffles his voice, his nose is red and his cheeks are white with the cold. He keeps moving because he is anxious when I am gone from him too long, even if all that is between us is dirty glass. My fingers drum against the booth – once, twice, three times. I stop that as soon as it starts.

Touching and counting are things the old Hannah did, and all that fumbling never accomplished anything. There aren't any doors for me to guard any more. Everyone who has come into my life is gone except for Billy. I don't count the seconds until those people return. It's me. I'm the one who will have to go back; I just won't go back now.

"Yeah. I'm coming."

I push open the door, but it only goes so far. I have to squeeze out. In that one second when I am caught half in and half out of this little box, while the light flickers off and on, I think of all the things I want.

I want to put my fist through this glass booth; I want to rip the phone off its cord; I want to scream for someone to come help me.

Me. Hannah Sheraton.

I want to see Hermosa Beach again.

I want to take Max for a walk.

I'm a teenager.

I want to paint.

I want my hair to be long again.

I want to see Josie and Archer and Faye.

I am frightened.

I want. . .

"Hannah, what are you waiting for?"

"Nothing," I say.

I push my way out of the booth. Billy bounces from one foot to the other. His arms wrap around himself. I had a chance to pack stuff when we left Hermosa, but he didn't. I had the money I made from selling my paintings; Billy didn't have a dime. The captain on that boat screwed us out of our wages.

"What are you going to do?" he asked when I demanded that he pay us. "Call the cops?"

He was smarter than I gave him credit for which is more than I can say for most adults. When we left Hermosa the idea was to get Billy somewhere safe until the adults figured things out. I didn't think it would take this long or that we would have to go this far. I thought we were safe in Oregon, but when we heard a big man was looking for us I figured it was Gjergy Isai. We never laid eyes on him. We ran with all we had, and at that point we didn't have much. We have less now.

"You need warmer clothes. You need different shoes," I say.

"Yeah. Who knew Alaska would be so cold?"

He laughs at his own joke. It kind of ticks me off that he doesn't complain. I seem to be mad at him a lot. Mostly I'm sorry for it, so I don't say anything. Billy touches my shoulder, and I flinch. He seems sad when he says:

"Come on."

Billy motions toward a bunch of trucks pulled up near the

giant gas tanks. Two of the operators are in the shop having coffee. Billy caught the third guy in the john at the back of the building and hit him up for a ride while they stood side-by-side peeing. I can't decide if I don't like the looks of the guy, or I'm just not happy that Billy didn't consult with me before arranging this. Either way I am not happy, and Billy is trying to figure out how to get my rear in gear.

"The shop guy isn't going to let us sleep inside."

He's right. Nobody wants two homeless kids anywhere near their stuff overnight. You never know what we might do. Of course, they never think of it from our perspective. We never know what the adults will do. Still, we can't stay out in the open Even sleeping bags won't be enough to keep us from freezing to death in another few weeks.

"Okay." I say this like I've made a choice even though we don't have one.

"We're coming." Billy waves at the trucker, flashing him a brilliant smile. He's so relieved he glows. Even from this distance I see the trucker glower. Then I make Billy crazy again.

"I've got to use the bathroom." I duck off into the little store while Billy hollers.

"She's got to pee!"

I roll my eyes. It's a good thing I don't embarrass easily. I open the door, and I am in and out in less than five because I didn't really have to pee at all.

"Here."

I give Billy a puffy fleece jacket that is the most god-awful screaming yellow color. It was the only thing they had close to his size. Billy takes it like I just handed him the Golden Fleece. He wants it in the worst way, but says:

"I'm taking it back. We need the money."

I set my jaw, rip off the tags, tear them up, and toss them.

"Now you can't return it. Come on."

Grabbing my duffle, I walk away from the light and through the late afternoon dark of Alaska. It will only get blacker the further north we go and that is perfect for hiding. The bearded guy who's going to give us a hitch stands in a puddle of light cast by a single bulb strung on a wire above him. He wears a hat with earflaps. It takes a certain kind of guy to wear a hat like that the right way. He's not that guy. Billy pulls up beside me. The screaming yellow fleece jacket is even grosser when it's on him. He's got it zipped up to his chin, his hands are buried in his pockets, and there's a bounce in his step. He is so grateful for every little thing – even an ugly jacket.

In the next minute, I flatten my gaze and forget Billy. The trucker is watching us. Only he's not really watching us, he's watching me. I've seen too many men look at my mother like that, and I know it's not nice. The good news is that I'm not my mother. I stop in front of him. His dirty fingers wrap around the door handle.

"There's only room for one up front." His voice is like his beard: stubbly, sketchy and unattractive.

"It's okay. You ride up front, Han–" Billy begins to talk, but I cut him off. He's so clueless.

"We'll both go in back."

I cut my eyes to the container he's hauling on the flatbed. It reminds me of the place Josie was imprisoned. I flash on doors shutting, chains threading, locks ratcheting, rotten air, isolation, death and madness. I just know all of them are already comfortable in the cave-like corners of that metal box. I look back at the driver. He is just a stupid man, not a crazy maniac. I've seen a lot of crazy people up close and personal. Not everyone is a friggin' crazy person. I have to remember that.

I know that my stare shames him because of what he's thinking. Hitchhikers have to pay: ass, grass or gas. It's not Billy's ass he's after. I pull a twenty from my pocket and hand it to him.

8

"Gas."

"Suit yourself."

He scowls and leads the way to the back. As he passes, I smell beer on his breath. When we get to the rear he unlocks the container and pushes one tall door back. The metal groans and the inside yawns like the passage way to hell. I feel sick, but I toss the duffle in and then grab the side of the door. If I go in fast it won't be so scary. Then the guy in the dork hat puts his hands on my butt, and his touch is like a cattle prod. I jump down and square off.

"Don't touch me," I growl.

I've got a fist up and my feet planted like I could really take him on. Billy isn't so sure I won't try, so he puts his arm between us. I can feel his whole being begging me not to make trouble. I hate trouble, too, but I didn't start it. Billy should do something so I don't have to. Then again, he's done as much as his good nature will allow. Finally, the driver shakes his head. He spits on the ground.

"I was helping, you little black bitch."

I ignore the slur. It could have been worse. He could have left us there. Instead, he waits until I climb in. Billy scrambles after me. We stand together, seeing our breath blow ice-white in the grey of the interior. The thing is half filled with boxes. The inside smells of something but it isn't food. The metal floor is buckled, and it pops under our weight as we shift to get the feel of our surroundings.

"Don't touch nothin'," The driver warns.

I look back at him. I want to say that we won't. I want to say thanks to make up some. He slams the door before I can. I thought I knew what dark was, but until that second I didn't have a clue how black the world could really be.

When I hear the latches bang and a chain run its course, the crazy-making itch of uncertainty, fear, and despair runs through me. I need a razor blade in the worst way to slice myself and bleed it out. This tight and nasty thing makes me feel like I did when my mother took hold of my shoulders and shook me, her face close to mine as she spit out words that made no sense except to her.

My last chance to have something good . . . you're a good girl
He needs to like you . . . men don't like kids
How can I take care of us. . . I'm saddled with you

"Hannah, I'm here," Billy calls, but I don't pay attention. That's what happens when I think of my mother. I only hear her voice.

The scars on my arms swell as if blood is pumping through them but that's impossible. None of them are new. There is no life in that ugly little map of mutilations on my forearms, but the fear is alive, writhing, and its tentacles are deep. I push out a hand, my fingers crunch into my palm. My nails are short now, but they still bite into my skin as they keep time with the numbers flashing behind my eyes. I am so afraid I can't speak. Funny that a slamming door can do me in when Gjergy Isai and the old judge, Fritz Rayburn, should have been far more frightening. Maybe they weren't as scary as this because I could see them coming. Suddenly, Billy is beside me, a young man wrapped in a ball of yellow fleece.

"I got you, Hannah." It's true. He has my hand. He squeezes it. I'm not real happy he's done this, but for now it's all good. "It's okay. Dude, it's okay."

I laugh because he calls me dude, because he comforts me in the same voice he uses to talk about everything. That voice is tinged with awe and sweet faith. Some things never change. Even though we can't see each other, I know he's smiling because my laugh is a relief to him. It means that I am not mad at him, and I am okay. As long as I'm okay, so is he.

The truck starts up with a deep rumble of an engine that

sounds out of whack. We lose our balance, drop to our knees, and crawl to the side of the container. We laugh as the floor pops under us like metallic bubble wrap and then scramble between stacks of boxes to settle in. The cardboard will steady us and help us stay warm. The container lurches and shakes a little. The cargo is strapped; it's the truck that is unsteady. I wonder if the bumper has one of those 'how am I driving?' stickers on the back and if someone will report this guy. I hope not because we are on the road again, and we need to get to the end of the world. I don't know where that is, but I think we're pretty close to it in Alaska.

I am so deep in thought that I jump when Billy touches my head. Being touched gently in the dark like that always feels creepy. Someday, maybe, there will be someone I love and I'll welcome the touch that comes out of nowhere, but now I duck away. Billy doesn't take offense. He just stays on his own track.

"Cutting your hair was massive, Hannah. Really. It was awesome."

I smile even though I've heard this almost every night before he sleeps. What he really means is that he misses the Hannah he knew. The one with style, with a diamond pierced through her nose and a stutter of gold rings through her ears. He doesn't know this Hannah, the girl with the halo of kink and curls, dyed blond with a box of Clairol swiped from a sale table in front of a beauty supply shop back in Sanger. It was too dangerous to go in to pay for it when we were that close to home. I left a few dollars. I hope the girl from the counter found it. I touch the scrub of hair on my head and say the same thing I say every night:

"Yeah, I guess."

I don't point out that we've both changed. Billy's hair has grown past his shoulders and he parts it in the middle or pulls it back in a ponytail. It is beautiful, straight and sandy brown instead of beach-bleached white. I don't think he misses the beach after what he's been through but strangely I do. It was never the ocean that bugged me anyway; it was the people living near it who made me crazy. They were so happy. I've never been real comfortable with happy when it skims the top of a person and doesn't sink further than a white-toothed smile. That kind of happy is like the froth on a latte; deceptively sweet and easily overpowered by the bitter drink beneath.

Thinking of Hermosa brings hot tears to my eyes, but I'm more angry than sad. Life isn't fair, and I'm so done with that. It's time for life to at least give me and Billy an honest-to-God break. I put my head on the floor, curl into the boxes on my side, and close my eyes.

"We should try to get some rest," I say.

"You look more like a black chick now." I hear him settling in against the boxes on his side. He's sleepy, but he keeps talking. I found that out about him early on. He talks himself to sleep. "Even if your hair's blond, you still look like a black chick. When your hair was long you looked Indian. From India, you know?"

"Yeah, I know." I truly do know, but he's not talking about what I look like. He wants to know if I will stay with him. I wish he'd just ask straight out, but he doesn't. It doesn't matter, really. I don't have the energy to reassure him when he never can be reassured. I can't even be truly honest with myself. Maybe some of my mother is in me – the part that eventually bolts for greener pastures.

"Do you miss it, Hannah?" he asks dreamily. "Your hair? Do you miss it?"

I shake my head. No, I don't miss my hair as much as I miss what might have been if I was still in Hermosa with Josie.

"You okay, Hannah?"

"I'm good. It's nice to ride. I was tired of walking. I didn't like the boat."

"It is nice to ride." Billy echoes me. Then there's a minute and he adds: "Yeah, you look more like a black chick now."

Billy Zuni stops talking. He sleeps. My eyes are open, and I stare straight ahead seeing nothing. His words echo in my head. *Black chick.* That's what I am. I am getting darker by the minute. But this black has nothing to do with the color of my skin and everything to do with my heart and my mind.

I am afraid of myself just a little bit.

2

_____

The truck is sliding. Skating. Sledding over the road. I reach for Billy. He has slipped down and is lying on the cold floor of the container with his back to me.

"Billy?"

The truck lurches, scrapes, and brakes.

"Billy!"

I bolt upright and scoot past him on my butt, but he sleeps like the dead. I sit cross-legged in the middle of the floor with my hands flat on the buckled metal to see if I'm being paranoid. The truck is moving the right way again. My heart beats a little more slowly. I was dreaming. Having a nightmare. Maybe we're almost there. Maybe we'll get out of here soon. I convince myself that we will.

As I'm thinking this good thought, the container sways to the right and then left again. I slide backward. The boxes shift, straining against ropes that tie them into towers. A second later the container swings once more, and my stomach drops like it does when a Ferris wheel stops your car at the very top on a windy day. The car swings, the guy at the controls stares up. You don't know if he will let you down, and he's the only one who can. You don't know if he's a crazy person.

I take a deep breath and beat myself up.

Not everyone is a friggin' psychopath.

I know that's true, but I can't help myself. I assume the freakiest worst, horror movie worst, the tenth level of hell worst, the no-turning-back worst because that's how afraid I've been for so long. I am the only one I can trust. I am the only one who will not run away from me. I almost laugh at how stupid that thought is, but the container moves again.

"Billy! Billy!"

My voice catches as the gears grind with the most god-awful sound. He doesn't hear. He doesn't feel that we aren't just on a hill anymore. We are driving over a mountain, the road isn't good, and it's tossing this tin can we're sitting in with a vengeance. I remember the beer on the driver's breath, and now I'm really freaked. This isn't the scared of what may happen, this is the terror of knowing something is going to happen.

Kneeling, I put my arms out as the back wheels slip. I'm thrown over and hit my shoulder hard as I tumble. I grab for Billy. My fingers scrape against the sole of his shoe. He's awake, and he does what comes naturally. He looks for me.

"Hannah? Where are you? Hannah!"

"Grab the rope! Grab the ropes on the boxes." I scream orders as I crawl back to him. The sounds are horrific: the floor popping under my hands and knees, the gears screaming, the towers of boxes groaning as they sway and strain.

"Find our stuff. We have to get out." I'm as close to hysterical as I've ever been, so I huff and puff and count the seconds between each breath to calm myself. I grab his leg; he grasps my wrist.

"What's going on?" He pulls me up so that I am in his arms for a split second.

"I don't know. I don't know."

I turn away from his embrace and start slapping at the wall of cardboard boxes until my palm hits the hemp. Like a blind girl, my fingers run over and around that knot as I talk.

"It sounds like he can't get traction."

"Where are we?" Billy kneels beside me.

"How should I know that, Billy? How?"

I scream at him to keep from crying. Before he can say another word there is a terrible sound – metallic screeching and wailing. The truck moves in slo-mo like it can't decide where it wants to go.

"Billy, the boxes are coming loose. Pull the rope!" I have no idea if what I'm saying is right or even possible, but we are not going to get crushed to death by a bunch of stinky boxes if I can help it. "Tighten it. Lean back against the boxes where I am and put your feet on the ones that you were near."

"Okay. Okay."

He grunts, giving it all he's got. My hands run up and down the ropes and flutter over the series of knots as I try to visualize what I feel. My heart sinks.

"Never mind. I don't think you can tighten it," I tell him. "Can you get up?"

"The whole thing might come down if I let go," Billy cries. He hollers, "What the hell is he doing? Stop the damn truck. Stop!"

"Billy. Billy! He can't hear you." I put my hands over his. He's got hold of the rope so tight that his fingers are like stone. Even when I touch them, they don't relax. "Billy, listen. We have to get away from these things. Okay? You have to let go. Hurry. I'll keep my back up against the boxes, and you get on the side. We'll take them down together so they don't fall on us. Okay? Okay?"

"Okay." He sniffs. He sniffs again like a boxer and wills his fingers loose.

Billy lets go of the rope, turns in the small space, and crawls between my legs. We play leapfrog in the dark, and the seconds seem like minutes, and the minutes like hours. I move tentatively. The boxes don't fall. I turn fast and put my hands up, but the top one is too high for me to grasp. Then Billy is up and his hands are next to mine. Between the two of us we manage to lift the top box down and put it on the floor. With my foot, I push it toward the end of the container.

"There's two more," Billy breathes. "Two more on this stack."

"Can you get those two on your own?"

"Sure, just don't get in front of me," he warns.

"Okay."

I drop down again. My duffle is still stuck between my tower of boxes and the skin of the truck. Everything we own is inside that duffle. I pull it hard just as I hear a second box hit the floor. The truck fishtails. Billy cries out.

"What happened?" I'm half on my knees.

"The edge of one of them hit me. I'm good. I'm good."

I take him at his word and go back to trying to get my bag.

"Soon as I have this, we'll push these down near the door and make a wall–"

The truck comes to life again and cuts me off. A box falls and the inside of this metal prison reverberates like a gong. Billy groans. My mouth goes dry and my head pounds. I know what's coming.

"Come on, Billy. Come away – " I beg, and then it doesn't matter what we do any more.

The truck has crested the hill and in the next blink we are in free fall, shooting down the other side. We are a ten-ton luge. We are bullets fired out of a defective gun barrel. That's how fast and out of control we go. The container swings, finds its path, and then it's running out like a fisherman's reel, away from the truck bed. I am thrown forward into Billy. We connect for only a second before he is tossed one way and me the other. I hear his grunt as he hits cardboard while I slide between the stacks only to be slammed against metal.

"Billy!" I scream.

"Hannah!" he shouts back.

Both of us are afraid for ourselves and for each other. There is nothing I can do to make it better. No one can make this better especially not the guy in the dork hat who puts his hands on girls' butts and drinks beer before he drives.

Some of the boxes break free, others slip and slide against their restraints. Now we're rag dolls tossed into a toy chest with outsized blocks. I try to throw my arms over my head, but then I put them straight out and grab for something, anything that will stop my slide.

Then I'm levitating.

I am free.

The weight on my shoulders lifts. Worry is a thing of the past. Fear is replaced with awe. I am flying. When the driver opens the door, when I come to ground, when I can see the damage done, I will be fearful, and grateful, and probably be one of those crazy people I always worry about. But now I am flying and happy and then Billy cries out in anguish. He knows what's going to happen a split second before I do.

The container is hit in the middle and folds like a big guy sucker punched by a coward. The edge of the flatbed hits the same hard thing a second later. The boxes break free completely. My hands go over my head. I tuck as best I can into a fetal position. In the blackness I don't know where the danger is coming from; in the next instant I do. Danger is coming from everywhere: down, up, around us, inside and out. Boxes filled with heavy things fly at us, the container surrounding us is no longer formidable; it is only a skin as easily cut through as that on my arms. We bounce around like pinballs; we slide away like air-hockey pucks. We try to grab ahold of one another to keep from smashing into things, but things smash into us. Our hands never meet. Our voices rise and fall. The sounds we make are nothing compared to the awesome sound of metal crushing. The heavy cab of the truck gets the best of the trailer and is now racing downward, front first, pulling us with it. We careen. We crumple. We roll and bang. I scream and scream. Billy calls out my name one last time and then all is silent.

All is still.

My mind goes dark.

Billy Zuni is no more, and neither am I.

―――――――――

Nell kept the plane steady on its course for ten miles before dipping down to check out a particularly promising place, in the seemingly endless forest, where she might be able to put down some weekend warriors who didn't want to hike from her usual drop point.

Idiots.

What were they coming all this way to do if not hike?

Still, the customer was always right so here she was scouting as the day wore down. When she found a clearing that would do, Nell made the turn and headed home. Her heart really wasn't in this gig. The season was over, she had worked steady, and her bank account was solid. The last thing she wanted was to be responsible for a bunch of fat cats who would panic at the first white out and then blame her for not being able to get in to pick them up.

Nell checked her headings and then veered off course a few

degrees, flying low and tight to the mountains just for the fun of it. She started to sing *Some Enchanted Evening* in a voice that would never be ready for prime time as she drummed a beat over the sound of the engine. She was almost on the second verse when she thought she saw something out of whack below. She was too tight to circle, but kept her eye on it as long as she could as she fired up the radio.

"This is Beaver 220," she said.

"Hey there," came the response. "Whatcha doing up this late in the day?"

"Scouting," she said. "Listen. Is there some major logging going on out north of my location?"

"Not that I know of," came the answer. "What are you looking at?"

"I'm not sure. Looks like a big hole in the universe down there." She laughed. "Like all the trees are missing just below an old road."

"That's weird," came the reply. "No construction or logging that I know of. Any vehicles on that road?"

"Not that I can see," Nell answered. "Back at you if I figure it out."

With that, she signed off. She was home forty minutes later, but it was twenty-four hours later that she decided what she saw might actually be worth a closer look.

Duncan double-checked to see that he had logged the list of verses Pea had given him correctly. When he was satisfied, he closed the Bible and put his fingers to his eyes. He had been holed up for hours interpreting the word of God. It was a laborious task – and one he was blessed to do – but it was a pity it must be done in secret, in this cold little room. Still, order must be preserved. His followers believed that his divine interpretations were as mystical as Pea's prophesies, so the concealed room and secret Bible were a necessary invention. If they got it into their heads that anyone could interpret the Book, the community would crumble.

Of course, Duncan was grateful for the help he got from his radio, too. That was almost as important to his flock's wellbeing as the holy book. Now that radio was spitting and spatting and wanting his attention, so Duncan took up the headphones and adjusted them over his ears.

He tuned it to the proper channel, and jotted down the pertinent information he heard between the bush pilot and the State Troopers' office near Denali. It was a short conversation, but he heard enough to know there was an opportunity to be had. Scavenging in God's name wasn't scavenging at all. It was a chance for folks to earn a few blessings by sharing what they had. If there were loggers out there making a 'hole in the universe', it was a sure bet they had brought along some fine supplies. Not that things were dire in their little community, but every little bit helped.

Setting aside the earphones, he left his work, and went to look for Robert. There might be time to catch him and share this bit of news before he cast off. Taking care to bend so that he didn't hit his head on the low ceiling, Duncan left his private room, went out the back that was almost hidden by the overgrowth of brush, climbed over the rock wall, and walked down the path toward the dock. The only sound was that of Glenn's ax hitting wood; the only smell, besides that of the great outdoors, was the faint scent of something cooking in the main house.

Everything was ordered, as it should be. Duncan's soul was at peace as, he was sure, was everyone else's. He turned onto the path that led to the river and smiled. As usual, his timing was perfect.

"Robert," Duncan called out. "A minute of your time."

Robert turned at the sound of his name. He blinked, wiped his sleeve across his nose, and waited for Duncan to come to him. When the tall, slender man was onboard the boat, he put his arm around Robert and said:

"I have received a message just for you."

3

God spoke to Robert just as Duncan said He would. He had
expected it sooner, but God had been quiet for the two days he
had spent in town buying and begging supplies. He had been
just as quiet when Robert started home, so he was surprised
when the good lord finally made himself known.

It was so surprising, in fact, that Robert nearly fell over the
side of the boat and into the great Yukon River. Had he done
that, he would have been in trouble because he was positive God
did not know how to work a powerboat. God also wouldn't know
how to stock the store with all the supplies even if He did
manage to get the boat back where it belonged. Not to mention
the fact that it would be bad for Robert if he fell in the river
since he couldn't swim. All in all, it was a good thing he didn't
fall over.

At first, Robert thought he was imagining things, but
Duncan had assured him that would not be the case. He would
know the voice of God in the same way he knew Duncan's voice
and he knew that pretty darn well. Everything Duncan said was
true or wise or both, so Robert kept his ears out for God.

Now, here he was driving the boat and it was like God was

sitting on the cargo, picking at his nails, having a little conversation pretty as you please. A couple of times Robert turned around thinking it would be polite to talk to God face-to-face, but He was quick. He disappeared himself really good only to come back and start talking again when Robert turned his back. God, Robert deduced, was a practical joker or shy or something. Maybe God didn't really look like his pictures – which were all pretty awesome – and was ashamed to be seen. Didn't Robert just get that one for sure? But God was a real good talker. He sounded so normal, chuckling a little, offering a tiny suggestion, a cosmic push that eventually made Robert turn the boat toward shore, tie up, and get off. In fact, God directed Robert to the shore just about where Duncan said he would. Duncan and God were very close.

God wanted Robert to go look for the hole in the universe. That's what He said. Look for the hole in the universe. When Robert found that, he would find something good. It might be treasure. First, though, he had to relieve himself.

Robert tied up, got off the boat, and trudged a little ways away from the riverbank. He snapped the safety pin that held his pants together, unzipped his zipper, and whipped it out.

"In front of God and everyone," Robert said aloud, in his slightly high and nasal voice.

He thought this was quite funny because, as he deduced, there was no 'everyone' in the forest, and God had already seen his 'equipment' since He had made it in the first place. Robert was concluding that his deduction was correct – that there was nothing to be ashamed of by peeing in the forest when – Bam! Wham! Bam!

God screamed in Robert's left ear so loud Robert poked his substantial tummy with the safety pin before he clasped it shut, and then he forgot to zip up his pants. That's how much of a rush he was in to do God's bidding and find the hole in the universe.

Looking around all he saw was forest and more forest. Left and right, behind him and in front of him. God and Duncan had given him directions by the compass so he took it out, considered it, and then started walking north and a little east.

It was hard to go as fast as God wanted because Robert was a big boned man. That's what Duncan said. Big boned. Not fat. Not obese. Not grotesque. Big boned. No matter what he was, he couldn't hurry very long so he walked some of the way and then stopped at an outcropping of rock. He steadied himself by putting an arm on a ledge and thinking both God and Duncan had got the whole thing wrong. He didn't see a road. All he saw above him were the mountains rising to dizzying heights. Before he could look closely, he was distracted by the sound of a plane. Or at least he thought he heard the sound of a plane

In the years Robert had lived in this place, he had only actually seen one plane. It landed in the river with its motor sputtering and coughing. That day Robert stopped what he was doing, sat behind a stand of trees, and watched the pilot work on the motor. Then the man sat on the pontoons for another hour and napped. If Robert had a gun he could have shot that man dead or wounded him and taken him prisoner or just, well, shot him. Robert could also have taken the plane.

But Robert had no gun.

And Robert didn't know how to fly a plane.

And Robert wouldn't have done either of those things because that wasn't how things were supposed to go. Duncan was very keen on how things were supposed to go. God told Pea, the prophetess, who told Duncan, the interpreter, who then told Robert and Melody and Glenn and Teresa and the others how things were supposed to go. That's how order was done, so that was why Robert didn't hurt the pilot of that plane. Because no one told him to.

It was just interesting to Robert that he had been so close, and the man never knew he was there. In Alaska, keeping yourself apart was as much a choice as making yourself known. That's the way it was in heaven, too. Apart. Together. Known. Unknown. Within. Without. Face your sins, make up for them, be forgiven, be healed, be peaceful, and be whole. That's what Duncan said.

Easy Peasy.

Robert listened harder for the sound of a plane, but there was only ungodly stillness – or godly silence – all around. Robert chose to think of it as godly silent. Duncan said you had to choose how to look at things. Like a glass half full or half empty. Like Robert's face. Half . . .

He flinched when snowflakes hit his lashes. He blinked and he forgot what he was thinking. The wind skated through the branches of the fir and pine and birch. There had been ice already in the river. Animals were hiding and hibernating.

Maybe God was hibernating, too, because Robert couldn't hear Him anymore. Maybe he had run so fast he left God behind. Or maybe he'd gone so slow that God had gone on ahead. Either way, Robert was a little worried because Duncan said God would guide him, and now He wasn't talking. Tired and disheartened, Robert deduced he had been stupid to think God was talking to him.

He sniffed really hard and took a deep breath. He didn't like being on the river when it was very, very dark. He hoped Glenn would have the fire going strong and that Teresa would have something good to eat when he got back. He hoped Melody would fix the button on his pants for him. He hoped Duncan wouldn't be sad that he had failed to find the hole in the universe. Robert raised his head as if he could smell the bread baking, but all he smelled was snow and frost. Then he saw a little miracle. Not a hole in the universe, but a pretty little fawn with a white flick of a tail and eyes that looked afraid even though he hadn't done anything at all to make her afraid.

If Foster were with him, he would kill that deer and that would be sad. Robert loved a good hunk of deer meat, but he didn't want to kill a big-eyed deer to get it. He would like to pet her, though. He would pet this one if he could get close enough, but the wind shifted. When she smelled Robert, she bounded off on her matchstick legs. Deer were like people in that respect. If they smelled something on you like weirdness or ugliness or stupidity they just took off. Even the one person who was supposed to love you forever didn't like that smell.

Ah, well.

The deer was gone.

The snow was falling.

God was silent.

Robert's nose was running.

He was ready to go back to the boat, but he looked around once more just to be sure he hadn't missed something. He even looked up again in case he might see God hanging out in the sky pointing the way. He didn't see God, but he saw something he missed the first time. Oh, yes he did. Robert narrowed his already narrow, close-set eyes. He tilted his large head one way and then it flopped to his other shoulder. He pursed his full, pink lips.

Some of the trees had no branches. It sort of looked like there was a hole in the forest. He could see the granite colored mountains. He could see the dark sky. He could see a road. He shouldn't be able to see those things from where he was standing. Yes, there was a hole in. . .

Oh, God!

Robert shouted out in his head.

27

Oh, God!

A hole in his universe.

He was so excited that every layer of him wiggled and jiggled as he minced over the slick, flat rock. He balanced his massive person on the smaller rocks as he climbed right and then left. He teetered once and almost fell. That nearly stopped his heart. Falling out here, breaking a leg or spraining an ankle could mean death. He didn't want to die in the forest; he didn't want to die at all. Still, he was excited and because of that he tumbled the last few feet but landed more or less upright. What he saw made him let loose with a big "Oooh!" of amazement.

Robert climbed over limbs that were the size of a man, stepped over smaller branches and sunk into tufts of dead, snow-covered pine needles that made the ground squishy. Finally, he stood in front of a wreck of metal: a crushed container, and a flatbed truck. Two of the chains that were supposed to secure the load had snapped. No surprise. They were rusted and should never have been used. Even Robert knew that and, as people used to point out, he didn't know much of anything.

Cupping his hands over his nose, Robert breathed in and out to warm up his face as he poked around and climbed until he finally got to the cab. He stood on a rock that had slid down after the truck went over the side of the road. He looked into the empty cab. He drew his head out. He called:

"Hello! It's me, Robert. Duncan and God sent me."

When no one answered, he got down on his stomach and inched up the rock so that he could look over the side. When his head was hanging down between the rock and one of the giant wheels, he laid eyes on the dead person.

"There you are."

Robert took a huge, huge breath of cold air because this was not a pretty sight and he was afraid he might throw up. He hated to do that. He didn't hurl, though, because he was trying to figure out how the man had managed to fall underneath the cab and behind it all at the same time. Not that it mattered. He was deader than dead. Robert could only see the man's legs, so he slid off the rock, hunkered down to look into the little tee-pee space the crumpled metal had made, and looked at the rest of him. The man had done a number on himself. One arm was gone and the look on his face – once Robert got past all the blood and the hole where his cheek should be – was one of astonishment.

Robert wondered who he was, if he left anyone behind, and if he had any idea that he was going to die that day. Receiving no answers or directives from God, and certainly none from the dead man, Robert bit down on the fingers of his glove. He pulled it off, set it aside, and put that hand right on the man's stump. Even though it felt weird, he let it rest there while he thought about God, and the end of life, and all that. He did this because it was pretty much a sure bet nobody was going to be bringing this guy back home anytime soon. Robert for sure wasn't going to be letting the authorities know about this mess. He'd already been down that road and a lot of no good had come of it. The only authority in heaven and on earth was God like Duncan said. Well, and Duncan was an authority, too.

Tired of doing what he was doing, Robert climbed back up on the rock, side-stepped his way up to that toppled over cab, leaned in, and teeter-tottered on his substantial stomach to see what he might salvage. The inside of the cab stank of cigarettes and liquor and that answered the question of why the window was open. Robert wouldn't want to sit in that stink and neither did the driver.

Robert grunted, grabbed the keys hanging in the ignition, slid out again, dropped to rock's surface and got himself back on the ground. He rubbed his big tummy and wiped his perpetually running nose. He checked out the keys. There were three.

One had been in the ignition. One was probably for a house, and the other one had to be the key to a lock on the back of the container. Now he knew why God and Duncan had sent him here. Whatever was in this truck was something that Duncan needed. Robert hurried to the back and tried the key on the container lock. Sure enough, it swung open revealing a treasure trove of boxes.

Pushing one door open as wide as he could, Robert put his hands on the container and wobbled back and forth to make sure the thing was stable. It was at an awkward angle, but there was no doubt it was tight up against the trees. Twice he tried to lift his great bulk into the back. When he finally made it, his head was spinning from the effort and from seeing that there were about a zillion boxes of something inside.

When his eyes acclimated to the dark and his breathing was even, Robert opened his penknife, slit the tape on the box nearest him, and ripped the flaps open. There was bubble wrap on top and under that was a grid of corrugated cardboard. Nestled inside that were small bottles that had labels with lots of writing that Robert couldn't read. He was disappointed he hadn't found food or candy, but Robert filled his pockets anyway. If Duncan liked this stuff, Robert would come back with Foster and Glenn and they would get it all. Every last box. Maybe they would sell it in the store. Maybe it was something Duncan needed to do the healing. If that were the case, Robert would be a hero. Robert would be healed first and he he would get new pants, girls would like him, and life would be good.

When his pockets were full, Robert realized he had room on the boat for a few more boxes. He lowered the open box to the ground and then seized another. He tossed three more out of the truck with a 'whew' and an 'ugh' and a whistle. He was about to go for one more when he froze. His ears pricked. Slowly, he let go of the box he was holding. He peered into the dark thinking an animal had found its way inside. If it was an animal, it might hurt him. It might launch itself at him. Then he deduced the truth by considering one thing at a time as Duncan suggested he do.

First, how could an animal have gotten in the truck when it was locked?

Perhaps the animal was very small and found a little opening. That's why it made a very small noise.

That was as far as Robert's deducing went.

Still hunched over, Robert peered past the mountain of boxes as he unhooked the flashlight from his belt. He pushed the switch expecting to see something scurry away under the sudden light but nothing did.

He ran the narrow beam over the boxes. There was nothing to see but tumbled cargo and crushed metal. Still, Robert didn't think he was crazy. If he could hear the voice of God on the river, certainly he couldn't be mistaken about a noise inside this truck.

Inching forward, he put out his free hand, touched a box, and paused. The front of the container lay lower than the back and the angle was getting steeper. As he started to take his next step, he slipped and fell. His rump hit the floor so hard the sound was thunderous. The flashlight flew out of his hands and rolled away. Robert turned onto his stomach, groped for it, and kept his eyes on the shaft of light that was shooting upward. With a 'harrumph' he got his hand on the flashlight and was pushing himself into a sitting position when he heard:

Here

He froze. His bizarrely small eyes widened as much as they could, and the light in his hands shook just the littlest bit. He craned his neck. He said:

"I'm here. I'm here. Where are you?"

Here

"Keep talking," Robert said.

He got to his feet, all the while wondering 'what would Duncan do?'. Then he wondered what would God do? Then he decided if Duncan/God led him here, then whatever was here must be for him to discover. All the while he thought and deduced and waved the light around and the voice called out like a drip from a faucet:

Here

Here

Here

"Okay. Okay. Okay," he responded.

Sweat soaked through Robert's undershirt and his shirt and his sweater until it made stains under his arms and got stuck between his sweater and his jacket. Sweat rimmed his brow where his hat was pulled low. He licked some of the salty stuff off his upper lip. Finally, miraculously, he saw a small space between two of the boxes where he could wedge the end of the flashlight. When it was secure, he started to work in earnest.

"Are you in there?" His meaty hand pounded on one of the boxes and he heard a groan. Assuming that was a yes, Robert shoved two boxes to the side and pounded on the next one.

"Talk again!" he shouted.

Here

Robert felt like a sausage on the coals, hot on the inside, ready to burst through his casing on the outside. It was hard to breath. His arms were tired. He would like to quit and go back to the boat and go home. His tummy was telling him that this whole situation was nothing but trouble; his head was telling him there was glory to be had.

"Hello! Hey!"

Three more boxes were set aside. When he picked up the fourth he saw a foot, and then a leg, and then a bloodied knee poking out of a ripped pair of jeans. The foot moved. Robert's heart leapt to his throat.

"There you are! There you are! You're all hurt. My name is Robert. My name is Robert. Here I am!"

Carefully, Robert lifted another box and there he was; a whole human being with a head and legs and a hand that didn't quite look like it was put together right. Robert reached for the last box that would show him this person's face.

"I'm going to take this one down, but I don't know if the side ones are going to fall. Be ready in case it bangs your head. Okay, here I go."

Robert lifted the box and the others did not fall. The person gasped. He sobbed. The person was crying.

"Don't move. Don't move," Robert cried out joyfully.

Oh blessed be the Lord that he had not killed this person with his good intentions. Turning, he grasped the flashlight, swung back and held it high. In the light he saw a young man not much younger than himself. His long hair was matted with dried blood. There was blood on his very nice yellow jacket. There was blood on the boxes. Tears rolled down his dirty, bloodied cheeks. But it was the boy's maimed hand that Robert found most interesting. It was resting on top of a head so bloody there was no way to tell what color the hair was or what kind of human being that hair belonged to. The boy must have seen him looking because he sobbed:

"She's dead, dude. Hannah's dead."

4

―――――――

"Help! Help!"

Robert started calling the minute he tied up the boat. He lumbered up the path, huffing, puffing, and screaming. His voice was hoarse because he had actually started screaming for help a half a mile down river. One by one the people he was calling paused in their chores and prayers, raised their heads, and tried to pinpoint where the cries were coming from.

Glenn was the first to react. He dropped the heavy headed sledgehammer to the ground and took his first slow, cautious steps toward the sound. He well knew that panic was the devil's tickle and made a person act irrationally. When he was sure that Robert was in need, Glenn left the split in the log, and the hammer on the ground, and went to render assistance.

Teresa was next.

Even though it was cold outside, she had cracked the window because the kitchen was hot. When she was sure she heard Robert, Teresa wiped her hands on a hopsack towel and left the chicken stewing. She walked past the table that was set and through the front door. Outside, Teresa took the stairs in a goodly, measured fashion. She was a practical sort who looked at adversity with the same level gaze as good fortune.

Upstairs, Melody set aside her mending and looked through the window in time to see Glenn disappearing down the path with Teresa following. Melody took the stairs quickly, her step so light that she floated over the uneven wooden floors, the steep rise of the porch stairs, and down the slippery path that led from the main house to the river.

That left six more people in the compound: two who were in *Hours,* the dedicated time of prayer, and Pea who was so extraordinarily blessed that she was *Within* and communing silently with God. Those people would not be expected to come running when Robert called because *Hours* and *Within* were sacred. There was also Foster who was with little Peter. The boy took advantage of Foster's distraction to run out of the schoolroom. Even Melody, who liked just about everyone, would not want to be stuck all day inside with Foster, so she couldn't blame Peter for trying to escape. Foster, though, managed to catch him and herd him back inside.

The only one who didn't run was Duncan because it was Duncan's job to wait. He waited to see which way the wind blew, he waited for those who needed guidance to ask for it, he waited to be served at meals and to be wished goodnight. He waited for enlightenment and for discourse with Pea who imparted God's plan to him. Duncan kept order for them all.

Still, Duncan was human and curious. Even he could not resist Robert's call or the commotion it caused. He left his time with Pea and came down the stairs just as Melody flew out the door.

He went only as far as the porch, stopping at the top of the old wooden steps, leaning casually against the post, his hooded eyes trained on the people on the path. One hand was in the pocket of the jacket he favored and the other rested on his thigh. One booted foot was crossed over the other.

Some took his calm for disinterest and others for arrogance. Some believed his eyes were covered intentionally to hide his slyness and his posture was a disguise to hide his dangerous nature. To some he was a curled snake resting under a rock coiled and waiting to strike whoever came within range. To others he was a stalking cat. To some he was a reptile with a poisonous, stinging tongue. To his followers, he was none of those things. He had rescued them, gathered them up, brought them to this place where they would face their sins, prove their worth and be healed. His half-mast eyes were like a confessional grate, obscuring the sinners as they poured out their pitiful hearts. They would never see judgment reflected in Duncan's gaze.

Duncan watched them disappear into the woods. They were so like children, eager for an adventure, happy to forget their trials. Soon they would be rushing back up to show him what they had found. Duncan didn't even care what it was, as long as they brought it back to him.

Melody looked back at Duncan. She thought their eyes met and that his softened. It was hard to tell, but sometimes Melody felt that Duncan did not want to be the one left alone. Still, he gave no sign that he wanted her to wait with him, and the lure of Robert's call was even greater than her longing to be important to Duncan, so she ran on. Melody was the last to reach him, but she heard Robert clearly when she did.

"I have a girl. I have a boy. They're hurt. I carried her all the way. . .the boat. . . From the forest. . .God helped. . .but I saved them. . ."

"Oh, my," Teresa said as she quickened her pace. "Robert you didn't."

"Yes. All the way." Robert's big head threw itself forward and was almost too heavy to throw back again but he managed one huge nod. "I did...Maybe...She's dead...I carried her...."

"A girl and a boy?"

Glenn asked this in the same way someone would voice amazement that twins had been born. But that was Glenn. He had long since stopped asking questions; now he only sounded as if he were asking them.

"Who are they?" Melody's voice was not far above a whisper. Still, it was easily heard by those who had grown accustomed to it.

"I don't know. I don't know!" Spittle flew from Robert's mouth, and his hands waved. He was missing one glove, and his exposed skin was raw with cold.

"Where did you find them?"

Teresa called over her shoulder as she moved ahead. Melody half skipped to catch up with her. Glenn kept pace. Robert, realizing he was going to be left behind when it was his right to show off what he found, tried to run. But he could not run and talk, so he talked loudly and walked briskly.

"Four miles down river. They were in a truck smashed all to hell..."

"Robert, don't swear," Glenn admonished, but Robert was beside himself and didn't hear.

"... hurt so bad...one might be dead..."

And so they went, the four of them, rushing down the road toward the dock: Teresa measured, Melody lightly, Robert lumbering, and Glenn skirting from side to side as if he hoped to find an opening that would allow him to take a lead he didn't truly want. Finally, they reached the boat that was piled high with boxes and bags, and things covered with tarpaulins.

Some of it would be sold at the store to people who would arrive from somewhere and melt back into nowhere after doing their business; some would see the congregation through the winter.

"There," Robert called from the rear and everyone stopped. "I didn't think the boat would make it. It did. There. There."

One by one they saw what Robert was pointing to. They shuddered. They crossed themselves. They closed their eyes and opened them again.

"Do you think you should have brought them here?" Glenn asked.

No one had an answer to that question, if indeed it was one. The fact was that they were here, on the boat, at the dock. Teresa took Melody's arm:

"Come along."

Teresa got on the boat, turned around, and offered Melody a hand up. The younger woman gathered her long skirts and grasped the older woman's hand. Once on deck, Teresa hunkered down and pulled open the blanket around the boy.

"Dear God," she exclaimed.

She looked at the girl and her face went pale. Teresa had been a nurse's assistant in her life before this place and knew that the girl was in a very bad way.

"He shouldn't have brought them here."

"Where else would he bring them?" Melody asked as she crouched beside Teresa.

"To the city. To a hospital," Teresa answered.

"Robert couldn't have done that. It wouldn't have been good for him even if he knew how to do it." Melody lowered her voice and stole a look at the big man standing on the dock. "There would have been so many questions."

"What about when these two are missed and people come looking for them? What if one of them dies and we have to bury them here? Nothing to be done about it now," Teresa said, and then she spoke to the boy. "Can you stand?"

The boy said, "Take care of her . . ."

"We'll take care of your friend. Just do what I ask. Do you understand? Do you hear?"

He nodded. Teresa took his arm knowing that he didn't understand at all.

"Take his other side, Melody," Teresa directed.

Teresa put her free arm around the boy's waist. Melody did her best to do the same, but it was more difficult for her. They bent their knees, the boy rallied, and when Teresa gave three counts they rose up. He cried out, and Melody almost screamed herself.

"Sorry, my boy. Can you walk?" Teresa asked. He nodded and Teresa turned him slightly. "Melody. Melody. Step slowly. Stand as straight as you can, girl."

Melody did as she was told and they began their slow progress. Glenn and Robert helped them all to the ground, holding them upright until the boy was as steady as he could be.

"Listen up, young man," Teresa said. "You're going to have to go up a ways. Do you understand? Do not faint on us."

He nodded. He made noises. Teresa gave directions to Glenn and Robert.

"Take the girl under the arms and at her knees. Always at the joints. Don't bounce her or pull her. Watch her head. We don't know if she has internal injuries or broken bones. We don't know about her neck."

Eyes forward, Teresa gave the signal. She and Melody and the boy began to make their way back to the house: stopping, stumbling, and starting again. The boy's eyes rolled back in his head. He fought them a little because he wanted to stay with the girl, but that didn't last long. He was weak with hunger and pain.

The men went faster with the girl because she was small and

unconscious. When they were halfway to the main house, Duncan's hand came out of his pocket and he splayed his legs as if to protect the entrance. This cargo was not what he had expected.

The men stopped. The girl was slung between them like a felled doe. The side of Duncan's mouth twitched. He looked at her for what seemed like an eternity as he tried to make out what this all meant. He couldn't. He needed time. He needed Pea. He said:

"Take her all the way up."

"Near Pea?" Glenn asked. "You want her near Pea?"

Duncan nodded and stood aside. The men went up the steps and he called after them:

"Lay a fire, Glenn. Make it a good one. She's near frozen."

Teresa and Melody came to the porch with the boy, stopping as surely as if Duncan had blocked their way but all he had done was look at them squarely. His eyes went over the boy, top to bottom. His jaw set. Duncan listened to the boy's mumbling.

Hannah

Hannah

Hannah

"What's your name?" Duncan asked.

"Hannah. . . okay?" The boy muttered.

Duncan, came down the steps, the only sign of his impatience was in the sound of his boots hitting hard on the old wooden steps. Only Teresa noticed his mood, but that was not unusual. She was most familiar with his moods. Melody was overwhelmed when he put his hand on her shoulder and leaned closer to look at the boy. When Duncan reached for his broken hand, she was faint with the anticipation that the healing was about to begin. First this boy's hand would be healed and then Duncan would touch her arm, and then Teresa and. . .

"Your name?" Duncan asked again.

"Billy," came the answer and Duncan released him. It was only then that Billy Zuni moaned. He rolled his head, and his weight became almost unbearable for the women. He was not healed at all. His hand was still broken, and Melody was sorely disappointed.

"He's going to pass out, Duncan." Teresa held tighter. Her arms were shaking; her back was sure to crack in two.

"He'll be better in my house," Duncan said and stepped away.

"Bless you, Duncan," Melody murmured. In all this time only she had been allowed in Duncan's house but only to clean. No one had ever been a guest.

The two women and the hurt boy stumbled through the gloom of the early evening toward the small house while Duncan stood and watched. When he heard the door close, when he saw the women through the window settling the young man, Duncan put his hands back in the pockets of his jacket and shook his head, amazed at this turn of events. Then he looked up toward the third floor and realized he shouldn't be surprised.

"The lord works in mysterious ways," he muttered.

He would see the boy first.

5

I see a bright light, a blinding white light, and a silhouette at the center of it. It undulates, fading and struggling back, unable to take shape. I would think this is heaven except that I'm pretty sure it's not. A loved one has to meet you at the Pearly Gates, and my list is short. Josie, Max, Faye. Archer or Burt might be good stand-ins, but I think it has to be a loved one who has passed and not just some you like a whole lot. This could be Billy except this person I see standing in the light is busy and seems to know what they're doing. Billy doesn't move like that. Still, if anyone's going to be dead I suppose it would be him. Then again, I doubt this is Billy because I don't love him. Not enough to meet him in heaven anyway. I love him just enough to watch over him on earth.

I wish I could wake up. I would pray to wake up if I knew how to do that, but I don't. Not for myself, or for Billy, or anything. The busy angel beside me talks. I wonder if she's praying. If she's taking to God, I hope she asks him to just let me go. I'm kind of done with all this.

The light is too bright.

I close my eyes.

It's dark.

I am gone again.

Maybe to heaven, but I doubt it.
That would be too easy.

"She's a colored." Melody held Hannah upright as Teresa washed her back.

"She's mixed. It doesn't matter," Teresa muttered.

"But it might matter, Teresa. How are we to know? We've never had a colored."

"She's hurt, that's all that matters right this minute."

Teresa sponged the blood encrusted cuts across Hannah's shoulders and the angry scrape at the small of her back. It was the injury to the back that worried Teresa most. If this girl's back were broken, it would be better if she died. Even Duncan couldn't heal that. Not that Teresa was truly convinced he could heal anything.

"It's hard to tell what's blood over on this part of her shoulder what with that tattoo," Teresa said.

"I've never seen anything like this," Melody whispered. "Not like this, with all the colors. Why would she defile herself this way? Do you think her soul is lost, Teresa? Is that what this means? Does she worship the devil?"

"Pay attention, Melody. Hold her tighter," Teresa ordered, tired of Melody seeing the devil in everything.

Melody readjusted her grip. Her arm hurt, but she didn't complain. If she complained, she would be chastised; if she didn't complete her task, she would never earn her healing. They were all so close to it that no one could afford to mess up now. Still, it wasn't as if she couldn't talk and do her chore all at the same time.

"Do you think it's wrong? Do you think it's sinful to do that to your body? I mean, we are God's temple, aren't we?" Melody asked. "Then again, if that's true, why would he have made us the way we are?"

"Lower her down." Teresa directed. "Gently, gently. Good. You're doing well."

"You'll tell Duncan I did this as well as anyone, won't you?"

"If he asks," Teresa said.

Melody slid her arm from under Hannah, happy that her skin was warm now. This room was never used and when they stripped away her clothes she had shivered so violently that Melody was sure she was in the death throes. But Glenn had laid his fire, Teresa massaged her, and Melody held her until it seemed the worst was over.

"Well, do you?" Melody asked. "Do you think it's sinful to do that to your body?"

"It's not for me to judge." Teresa looked up sharply. "It's not for you to judge. Do you hear me, Melody? It is not for you."

"Should we worry that she hasn't opened her eyes?" Melody pressed.

"Maybe. I'm surprised either of them are alive," Teresa muttered.

"I think the boy is going to be fine. Do you think he loves her? He didn't think of anything but her. They must be lovers. I think it's wonderful . . ."

"Melody! Please. There's more to do." Teresa lifted a thick cloth she had hurriedly put around Hannah's head wound. The blood started instantly. "Quick, quick, another towel."

Melody rushed away and came back with two towels: one to put over the ragged gash in Hannah's head and one to tuck over the pillow. She would rather wash one towel than bloody bed linens.

"Now the heavy thread and the curved needle," Teresa ordered.

Melody ran off again. The older woman pressed hard against

the deep and jagged tear in Hannah's head, but it was no use. When Melody returned, she held the needle out to Teresa who merely glanced at it.

"Thread it," the older woman said. "A good long length."

Melody fumbled with the needle and thread. Once she managed, she offered it to Teresa again.

"There's no knot, girl," Teresa snapped.

"Teresa, I can't," Melody objected.

"Alright. I should make you, but alright." Teresa motioned her over to hold the towel while she took the needle and thread.

Melody scurried around the bed. Teresa took a deep breath, pinched Hannah's skin and put the needle against the wound.

"Wipe away whatever comes out best you can. I need to see. The light in here is no good for something like this," Teresa ordered. Melody steadied herself, towel in hand, but Teresa just stood there.

"Teresa?" Melody prodded.

Teresa blinked. Thinking that this girl's life might be in her hands had paralyzed her. She pulled herself together and said:

"I'm sorry. Keep it clean, Melody. Very clean. I'm worried about infection."

"Maybe we should call Duncan to lay hands now," Melody said, "He could heal her."

"She's done nothing to deserve that kind of healing," Teresa muttered.

"We don't know that, but Duncan would. Wouldn't he?"

"Melody. The cloth. I can't see for all the blood and such."

Melody wiped at Hannah's temple with swift, precise motions. "I'm sorry. I just think–"

"Don't, Melody. Don't think," Teresa warned. She, herself, had done too much of that lately, and it only led to discontent. "It does no good to think. It's not as if Duncan has healed anyone yet. We don't even know if it's possible."

Before Melody could take Teresa to task for such blasphemy, Teresa stabbed the needle through Hannah's skin.

Pop.

One stitch in.

Pop.

One stitch out.

There were fifteen stitches. All were done as neat and tidy as Teresa could do which was not as neat and tidy as Melody would do. Melody's cloth soaked up the blood and the palm of her hand became a map of pink tinged lines and crevices; Teresa's fingernails grew half moons of the sticky stuff. All the while Hannah lay still, barely breathing.

When it was done Teresa held out the needle and dropped it into the soiled towel Melody held out. Wasteful as it was, Melody would throw that needle away; she never wanted to stitch with it again. She would throw the towel away; it would never be clean again. Teresa rinsed her hands in the bowl of water near the bed and then dried them on her apron.

"We've done what we can. Let's get her dressed."

Teresa held Hannah up, one strong arm around her back and the other on the girl's shoulder. Melody unfurled the nightdress and took Hannah's arm to thread it through the long sleeve. It was then that Hannah's eyes opened, big and bright and green like glass. Those eyes stared into Melody's. Hannah's lips moved. She said:

"Don't."

"I can do it, dude. I can."

Billy swatted at Duncan's hand, but it was Glenn, not Duncan, who gasped and made an awkward move for the boy. Duncan raised a finger.

"It's fine, Glenn. He's afraid is all. He's like a hurt animal."
Duncan's gaze stayed on Billy, but he shot a quick smile at
Glenn. "Why don't you see if you can find something for Billy to
eat."

"Will you be alright?" Glenn asked.

"Of course, my friend. I'll be alright won't I, Billy?"

Duncan looked down on the longhaired boy. He sat on the
small stool, his back up against the wall, his legs splayed, his
swollen and misshapen hand in his lap. He was covered in grime
and blood, and his face was bruised and scraped. He was
beyond hunger, crazed with sleeplessness, and terrorized by his
ordeal. He was a cornered mouse and it was laughable that
Glenn should be concerned for Duncan's safety, but Duncan
didn't laugh easily. Smiles were another matter. He had a reper-
toire of smiles a politician would envy, so he laid a particularly
beatific one on Billy.

"I guess he doesn't feel much like talking, Glenn. Go on now.
Find something hot for him to eat. And water. He'll need a lot of
water. Oh, and have Melody give you soap and some of her
sleeping liquid in a cup of tea."

When Glenn had gone Duncan knelt down in front of Billy,
but the boy wouldn't look at him. Duncan tilted his head one
way and then the other, trying to catch Billy's eye. As he did, he
spoke in the way only Duncan could.

"Billy. Billy. How long has it been since you've eaten? How
long since you slept?"

Billy shook his head and pulled his legs up, swinging them
away from Duncan. He didn't want this guy close to him. He
didn't want to hear his voice. He didn't want to eat. There was
only one thing he wanted.

"I want to see Hannah. I need to see Hannah, dude."

"I know. I know," Duncan soothed. "But she's being cared for and we need to get you fixed up, too. Your hand. It's in bad shape. You'll need to rest."

"Now, dude," Billy pulled his legs into his chest and bent over. He waved his good hand. "I just need to know she's breathing. Come on. Just for a minute."

"I'm afraid you're going to have to–" Duncan began, but Billy shot off the stool and dashed for the door before his sentence was finished.

Duncan turned to catch him, but he didn't have to try too hard. Billy's knees buckled before he got half way to the door. Duncan got up, walked across the room, and stood over him. His hooded eyes saw so much: the dried blood in Billy's hair, the way the part in it was not quite centered, how the boy's neck was long and slender in contrast to his broad shoulders. The yellow jacket was too big for him. He wore no belt with his jeans. The way he had fallen pulled the jacket up and his denims down just enough for Duncan to see that he was golden skinned everywhere.

"You are a beautiful, broken being," Duncan said. "And soon you will be visited by such pain that you will not remember who Hannah is."

"Bull," Billy shot back.

Duncan wasted no more breath on him. He put his hands under Billy's arms and tried to lift him up, but he was dead weight. Duncan dropped him back on the floor, and that's when Billy Zuni began to shake. He crossed his arms and buried his face in the nest they made. Duncan knew that hand of his should have caused Billy Zuni to faint with the pain of it, but there was an even deeper pain in the boy. It was a pain of the heart and the soul. Billy Zuni cried and his cries became wails and the wails became a long shriek. Within it all there were words of self-recrimination, pleas for forgiveness, and the name Hannah. Duncan slid down beside him, and put one hand on his back, and his other across his heart as he listened. He took Billy's sorrow for his own.

"My fault. . .If she dies. . .Because of me. . ." Billy wept.

"She won't die, Billy. Hannah is in God's hands. He is merciful. He meant for you to be found and be delivered to us. We'll figure it out, and when we do you will be made whole. You might even be healed. But for now, you are safe. Do you understand? You are safe."

Duncan spoke in his Goldilocks voice: not too harsh, not too soft, just right. Soothed by that voice – or simply reaching the end of his grief – Billy fell silent and so did Duncan. But still Billy's tears fell, and the preacher continued to rub his back through the dirty yellow jacket. When he had stopped shaking and moved his head so that his cheek lay against his arms, when he gave up and gave in to his shock and weakness, when his eyes stared lifelessly at the door, Duncan put his arms around Billy.

"Come on. Find the strength and raise yourself up. I'm here to help you."

Billy blinked. Duncan tightened his grip and finally the boy got up, unsteady and dazed. Duncan had seen this kind of trauma before, these psychic wounds, this delayed alarm, this sudden realization that someone you love is in jeopardy. He would heal this boy. He would heal this girl. Not just their bodies, but whatever ailed their souls. Perhaps that was why they had been delivered to Duncan, to test him. Slowly, he guided Billy to the daybed that served as his couch and planned for what glorious things were to come for these two souls who had literally been lost in the wilderness.

"Dude," Billy mumbled. "Please. Please."

"My name is Duncan, Billy."

Duncan sat the boy down. He took one of Billy's legs and put his other hand on Billy's shoulder. He pushed and pulled until Billy lay on the mattress, the fight gone out of him.

"Time to clean you up." Duncan unzipped the yellow jacket. "We can't afford to waste anything here, and I just can't bring myself to cut this fine jacket off you. I'm sorry, Billy, this has to be done."

Duncan took hold of one cuff on the jacket. He pulled fast and sure over Billy's broken hand. The boy howled and writhed in pain, but Duncan went on with his chore. He pushed the jacket under Billy and then took the other sleeve down. Still he talked.

"By the way, I answer to brother. Duncan is fine, too. I just want you to know that we have rules here. Courtesies."

He squared Billy's shoulders. He found a pillow and put it under his head. When that was done, Duncan pulled the stool over and sat close to the bed. He put his hand on Billy's head and petted it.

"We are a very small group here, Billy. We are orderly and your arrival has not been orderly. We are coming upon a great moment in our history. A baptism of faith that is so profound we – all of us – are going to have to focus on that. So, I want you to listen to me very carefully. Are you listening?"

Billy nodded, but it was a reflexive action. The world was crashing down on him. The fear he had held at bay through those hours in the container was devouring him, and the exhaustion of watching over Hannah weighed so heavy on him he could barely breathe. He wasn't sure what he was hearing; he didn't know what he was supposed to say. All he knew was that Hannah was gone, and that he hated the sound of this man's voice. When Duncan put his hand on Billy's shoulder, he felt as if he had been branded.

"God was with you in that horrible place 'cause it's a sure bet you weren't going to be able to save either of your sorry rears, wasn't it, Billy? God called Robert to find you. It is sort of amazing that he called Robert, but there you have it." Duncan pressed harder on Billy's shoulder, his face came closer, and his hooded eyes swung toward the ceiling as if he saw God hovering over the bed. "Yep, Billy, God is watching you now. He will reach out His hand the way I have reached out mine. He will press down hard – even harder than I am pressing now – and he will touch all your wounds and it's going to hurt. I'm telling you this to prepare you. It will hurt bad, inside and out. But when he sees you are worthy, when you prove you've got something worth saving, He will heal you and your friend. There will be no hurt."

"We don't do religion," Billy muttered.

"Of course you do, Billy. Everyone does religion. They do it alone, in the dark, and when they're desperate." Duncan sat back. "I bet you prayed some when you thought you were going to die in that truck. Come on. Admit it. Don't lie now. Tell me you didn't beg for God to save you and heal you. You probably offered everything if he would just save Hannah. 'Oh, God, take me instead,' or 'I'll give you anything you want if you let her live." Duncan chuckled, amused by his mocking. "Tell me you didn't call on every prayer your mother taught you."

"You don't know anything about my mother."

Billy turned his eyes to the ceiling. He didn't want to explain about his mother, and he didn't want this man to see that he was right about praying. Billy had bargained for Hannah's life. If it was God who heard him then it was God. That wasn't religion. That was a low percentage shot.

"Oh, I think all mothers are the same," Duncan went on. "They teach you when you're small, and then leave you when you're big. One way or the other they leave you. If that weren't the case you wouldn't be here. Truth be told, I wouldn't be here either."

Duncan started to open the buttons on Billy's shirt as he talked, but Billy clamped his good hand over Duncan's wrist. His eyes blazed, but his hand shook and his grasp was weak.

"Take your hand away, Billy," Duncan said this as if his limit-less patience was being sorely tested. "Take your hand away, now."

They stared at one another. Billy and the man with the half-mast eyes whose calm was frightening and cold, who was stronger than Billy, who spoke as if there was no question but that what he wanted was right. Still, Billy resisted. Duncan raised his brows and pursed his lips.

"You can't help Hannah if you're weak, can you? And you must think highly of her because you didn't think of yourself first. That's a Godly thing to do. So, since we are both Godly men and want the best for those we care about, let go of me. Or," Duncan went on, "is it that you are weak, and Hannah is the Godly one. Could that be it? Could that be why you need her so much? Is Hannah the one God has blessed with strength?"

Billy's hand trembled, his grip loosened.

"That's right. That's good. " Duncan slipped the next button open and the next. "You close your eyes. You rest. You are in good, good hands. The best, really." His eyes flicked over Billy's smooth chest. Duncan unbuttoned the last two buttons and pulled the shirt wide. "Now, I will get you cleaned up. I'll do it myself. I'll even wash your feet, Billy, because that's what I have been called to do. Is that acceptable?"

Billy stayed still, and Duncan paused.

"You should say, 'Yes, Duncan'. That's only polite. To acknowledge me. Isn't it?"

"Yes," Billy answered.

"Duncan." He leaned closer to Billy. "Duncan." And closer still "Say yes, Duncan."

"Yes . . . dude."

6

"She's awake."

"Let go of her arm, Melody," Teresa directed.

"What?"

"Her arm." Teresa nodded toward it.

"Oh my God. Oh, my God, Teresa." Melody saw the cross-hatch of scars on the girl's dark skin and dropped Hannah's arm as if it were a hot poker. "She's for me, isn't she Teresa? She's for me to prove myself. I think I'm going to be sick."

Teresa closed her eyes. It pained her to hear the despair in Melody's voice. They had all thought Pea was Melody's trial to atone for her sin, but this changed everything. Or it seemed to. They wouldn't know for sure until Duncan made a judgment. Melody would be no good to anyone if she panicked so Teresa soothed her.

"No. No. She did this to herself. That's different, Melody. No one did it to her, so she can't be for you."

"And it's not her face, is it? I can't tell if she has a beautiful face. I think she does, but it's hard to tell the way she's beat up." Melody's voice trembled. "What if she has demons? That must

be why she cut herself, right? She has demons. Or, what if. . ."
Melody's eyes widened in horror. "What if she's the devil?"

"Hush," Teresa said. "We don't have time for nonsense. Pick
up her hand. Pick it up, Melody. It can't be what you're thinking.
Pick up her hand, put on this nightgown without holding her
arm. It distresses her. Go on. Do it."

Melody hesitated, shot one more pointed look at Teresa, and
then threaded the nightgown over Hannah's arms, trying not to
touch the scars.

"Good girl," Teresa mumbled. "Now, over her head."

When that was done and they were working the gown over
her body, Melody said: "We need to tell Duncan before Pea
does."

"Pea won't have anything to say about this."

"You're wrong, Teresa. Pea has a say in everything. But you
might as well tell me now. What is it you think I should know?"

The women looked toward the door to see Duncan standing
there. Neither of them had heard him come up the stairs or into
the room. Melody blushed and buttoned the high neck of the
nightgown, moving her own body to shield Hannah's nakedness
from him.

"She's scarred, Duncan. Teresa says she did it to herself. It's
different because she did it to herself, isn't it?"

He was so close that Melody rushed to finish her chore,
pulling the long gown down over Hannah's feet. Before she
could arrange the bedding, Duncan put his hands on her
shoulders.

"It's alright for me to see her, Melody. Haven't I seen you and
Robert and all the rest? Haven't I looked upon all your infirmi-
ties without judgment? If Hannah is in need, I should know." He
squeezed Melody once, twice, a third time to coax her to his way
of thinking. "Show me what you've seen. Please show me, so I
can help her."

"It's her arms, Duncan. She's cut her arms. There are scars and she doesn't want them touched," Teresa said.

As she spoke, Duncan put Melody behind him and moved closer to the bed. His eyelashes fluttered. He took the tips of Hannah's fingers between his own and raised up her hand as though he might kiss it. Instead, he unbuttoned the cuff and slid the sleeve up gently. Hannah did not open her eyes. She did not tell him to stop. He rotated her arm and looked at the scars.

"How sad," he sighed.

"If she has demons, Duncan, why didn't they save her?" Melody asked.

"They would be no match for Robert's faith," Duncan answered. "But I think her demons are long gone. These scars are old. I think she is for you, Melody. Don't you think so Teresa?"

Not wanting Melody to carry a heavier burden then she already did, Teresa chose her words carefully "Possibly. Maybe you should ask Pea."

"Pea spoke of upheavals and tests. Isn't that why we are all together? To test our resolve, and our faith, and earn our way back into God's good grace? I would say what happened today is an upheaval. I would say this girl is particularly suited as a test for Melody."

"You might be right." Teresa agreed, albeit reluctantly. In this flock, they were all impressionable, but Melody was a kind and sweet soul. She was the most impressionable of all and there was only so much she could take. Still, Teresa had no right to tell Duncan anything. She had no rights to Duncan at all anymore.

"What about the boy? What about Billy?" Teresa asked.

"Perhaps he's for me," Duncan said. "I'm thinking he's my challenge."

"But, what is your sin?" Melody asked.

Duncan shook his head. "I have no idea. I suppose Pea will

tell me in good time. But, Melody, Hannah is for you. Teresa can help, but she'll be your responsibility."

"I'll see to her," Melody promised, sad that there was now another test for her to pass. No one else had two trials. Still, if Duncan said it was so then it must be.

"But how is the boy?" Teresa asked again, wanting Duncan gone from this room. It wasn't right to have him here, not when the girl was at such a disadvantage.

"Hurt, beside himself with worry, exhausted. He's skin and bones. They both are. This will take some nursing, won't it? Do you think you are up to it, Melody?"

"I can sit up all night with her if you think it best," she answered.

"I do. I'll make sure Billy stays put," Duncan said, before adding. "He shouldn't be in this room, do you understand? I think he came to a bit of madness locked in that truck. We will have to be on our guard." Tired of talking about Billy, Duncan smiled at Melody. "You've done a good job."

"Teresa, too," Melody answered, sure that he would admire her more if she shared this small glory. "She did the stitches."

"You are clever, Teresa. Come to think of it, she might be for you, too. She's just a child, after all. We'll know soon enough what her purpose is. Now that we've done everything humanly possible to help them, we'll pray."

Duncan held out his arms, but only Melody walked into them. He wrapped his arms around her and took both her hands in his. Melody's eyes closed. Her head fell back against his shoulder. She could feel every breath he took as he spoke.

"Pray for her recovery, Melody. Pray that the scars she carries fade to nothingness and that whatever tortured her in her previous life is left behind. Pray that she is resurrected in the light of our love."

Lulled by the sound of his voice and the feel of his skin

against hers, Melody prayed as hard as she could. She prayed so hard, and believed so deeply, that she was sure she would not only find Hannah healed, but herself transformed when Duncan released her.

He gave her hand one last squeeze and passed her back to Teresa. Duncan cast down his gaze upon Hannah. Teresa looked into space of her own making. Melody bowed her head, preferring to look at the wooden floor than a face she knew would soon be beautiful.

"For behold," Duncan prayed. "The day is coming, burning like a furnace. And all the arrogant and every evildoer will be chaff; and the day that is coming will set them ablaze. . ."

Duncan lowered his hand. He put his fingers beneath Hannah's chin.

". . .so that it will leave them neither root nor branch. . ."

One finger hooked under the high neck of the gown.

". . .but for you who fear My name. . ."

Hannah's neck arched as he pulled on the material and lowered his face toward her.

". . .the sun of righteousness will rise with healing in its wings; and you will go forth and skip about like calves from the stall. . ."

Melody looked up from beneath her lowered lashes. Duncan's voice had changed the closer he got to the girl. When their lips were a breath apart, Melody's flushed. Frantically, she looked at Teresa, but the older woman's eyes were closed tight and she didn't see what was going on.

"You will tread down the wicked," Duncan whispered. "For they will be ashes under the soles of your feet on the day which I am preparing. The day that I am preparing, Hannah."

Melody closed her eyes tighter and listened harder, but she could still see him touching the unconscious girl. When she opened them again, Duncan had let go of her collar and taken

the hem of Hannah's nightdress between two fingers. He
lifted it.

"Dear God." This seemed less a prayer than an exclamation
of awe. "Let our sister feel no pain. Let her dream no dream."

He exposed her knees.

"Let her lie in this darkness which is the ultimate peace. . ."

With every inch of brutalized skin he exposed, Melody's
heart beat faster. Teresa opened her eyes and raised her clasped
hands toward him as if pleading for him to stop. Duncan paid
her no mind so lost was he in his prayer.

"And in the dark, let her remain as a seed that sprouts only
when the true light shines bright. Your light. . ."

The nightgown went above Hannah's knees and the girl was
still as stone.

"Duncan!"

Teresa barked his name. The man paused as if he had
suddenly come upon a surprising thing and didn't know what to
make of it. A muscle across his back rippled and another
chorded in his neck.

"Yes, Teresa?" He swung his head her way.

"I'm thinking this isn't seemly," she said.

He pinched the fabric between two fingers, lifted it higher,
and then pulled it back down past Hannah's knees.

"I'm thinking you need to examine your thoughts during
Hours, Teresa. This woman is under my protection now. I need
to know everything about her pain."

"They aren't part of us," Teresa reminded him.

"'He will command his angels concerning you, to guard you.'
Isn't that what God has directed?"

"Melody is her angel," Teresa said. "Not you."

"True. Melody is an angel, and I put this girl in her hands."

Duncan smiled as he stepped away. Melody moved around
him and rearranged the nightgown with her trembling hand.

Before she could pull the covers over Hannah, Duncan stopped her.

"Her leg is broken," he said.

"I don't think so, Duncan," Teresa said.

"Come, see for yourself. Come on in here." Duncan held out his hand, took hers when she was close enough, and placed it on Hannah's shin.

"Feel that? Deep down, Teresa," he urged. "It's broken. Press your fingers into her bone. That's it. To the bone. Yes. Yep, there it is."

"I'm not sure," Teresa said.

"I am. There it is." Duncan pressed down on Teresa's hand. "Broken."

"Yes. Yes, I suppose. It could be," Teresa began.

"We have to take every precaution. Isn't that right?"

"I'll put on a splint and tape it. She should have a doctor to set it properly," Teresa said and he shrugged.

"If only we could get a doctor here," he sighed. "But there we have so little fuel, there is ice on the river. You know the boat is in need of repair. Besides, neither of them could make the journey even if the boat could. It's up to us to watch out for this sparrow fallen to the ground. Make no mistake. He has seen her. And Billy. And He's watching you, too. This is your greatest test, Teresa."

Melody's murmurs were background music to Duncan's tune.

We'll pray.

We'll watch.

We won't cause more harm

As always, Duncan shamed Teresa with his judgment and his sense. They could not get these young people to a doctor until they were stronger. Duncan ran his hand over Teresa's shoulder and down her back. He said:

"That leg needs a cast, Teresa. Do you understand?"

"I'll try," she promised.

"Treat her as if she is your daughter," Duncan said and then he chuckled. "I mean, the way you would treat your own daughter now."

Teresa's jaw locked. He took one last long look at Hannah and went to see about Robert and Glenn and the all the rest to make sure the house was once again in order. Teresa went in search of what they would need to cast Hannah's leg.

Melody stood alone in the twilight room trying not to think about how beautiful Hannah would be when she was well. But then she had a second thought. Hannah wouldn't be quite as beautiful as she probably was before. Teresa's stitches would leave an ugly scar.

That, Melody thought, would be a pity.

Sort of.

Duncan opened the door of Pea's room and found her as he always did, bowed in prayer, waiting for God's call. He walked across the room and knelt on the large pillow directly opposite her. It had been like that since they were children: Pea *Within* herself and he waiting *Without*; Duncan listening to Pea; everyone else listening to Duncan.

"So, Pea, it has happened. I expected something a little different. Heaven opening up. Seraphim. You know, like that. A big sign that it was time for me to, well, you know, heal everyone. That's what I expected. Ah, well. This is interesting, isn't it?"

She remained silent and still, but Duncan knew she heard him. His voice was her link to this earthly world and hers, when she used it, linked him to heaven.

"I don't know what to make of it. This is beyond me, Pea. Not my faith – I've always had that – just my understanding. That's all, Pea. What am I to do with them? Really? What? What, indeed."

To pass the time, he picked at the carpet. He reclined, his long legs spread out to his side, his elbow on the pillow. When he got tired, he lay down with his hands laced behind his head and stared at the ceiling. He considered the walls and his handiwork. He hoped the room was warm enough for her. He stared at her and wondered about her face. It had been so long since Duncan had seen her face that he had forgotten what it looked like. It must be so different now, womanly and not girlish. He couldn't remember a time she was upright. He wondered if she could even stand upright any longer.

The hours bled away. He may have slept or dozed, but at some point he began to think that there would be nothing for him that day. He was on his own, and he didn't like that one bit. Just when he decided to leave, just as he was about to stand up, Pea made herself known.

Her legs did not quiver under her gown.

Her feet did not move.

Her fingers remained tented on the rug.

Her head stayed down, her face hidden by her fall of hair.

From her throat came a trill, followed a balloon of sound, and a trill once again. Duncan got on his knees, clasped his hand, bowed his head, turned his ear her way to hear her clearly. When she spoke, the words and numbers tumbled out so quickly it was all Duncan could do to stick them away in his head.

Hebrew: 13:2
Galatians 5:14
Leviticus 25: 35-38

Jeremiah 22

Jeremiah 22

Jeremiah 22

On and on Pea went. When there was a final trill and swelling and trill again, Duncan's shoulders fell. He sat back on his heels, filled with awe and gratitude.

"Thank you, sister," he whispered.

He rose, took her head between his hands and leaned down so that his lips rested upon her hair. He breathed her in but could not smell her scent; he kept his eyes open but could not see her. One day, when they were all worthy, after the healing, all would have the pleasure of Pea and God.

He went on his way as he always did after his time with Pea. If Melody or Teresa had come out of the room next door he would not have noticed them. If Hannah had appeared on the stairs in front of him he would have passed through her as if she were a ghost. If Robert's great person had blocked the front door, Duncan would have simply raised a hand and disappeared him into the darkness. If Billy challenged him, he would swat him out of the way. That was how Duncan always left Pea: entranced and empowered.

Duncan went down the stairs and out the front door. He walked through the freezing cold with only his light jacket. When Duncan walked past his own house, Glenn, who was sitting with Billy, got out of his chair to watch until he was past the stand of saplings. Duncan went by the old outhouse and finally came to the store where he veered off the path, climbed over the rock wall, pushed through the brush that almost covered the back door, and let himself inside the building. He flipped the switch and a bare bulb was illuminated. There were boxes stacked against three walls. He moved some of them and pushed open a panel in the wall that led to his private and sacred room.

He sat down at a very old table that had been fashioned from the bow of the Ark, and had come to him by way of a trader he had met on his journey to this place. There were books on a small shelf along with his drawing tablets and paints. On the desk was the Bible that had been Duncan's mother's bible. She had not been worthy of it. It took him a long while to understand that the tradeoff – a good mother for the word of God – was not a bad one.

Duncan put his hand upon the Bible, gave thanks for Pea's guidance, and prayed that he was a worthy servant. He wrote down the verses exactly as he heard them, set the paper aside for reference, and opened the book.

Hebrew 13: 2

Do not forget to show hospitality to strangers, for by so doing some people have shown hospitality to angels without knowing it.

Leviticus 25: 35-38:

If your brother becomes poor and cannot maintain himself with you, you shall support him as though he was a stranger and a sojourner, and he shall live with you.

Jeremiah: 22:

Do no wrong or violence to the foreigner, the fatherless or the widow, and do not shed innocent blood in this place. For if you are careful to carry out these commands, then kings who sit on David's throne will come through the gates of this palace, riding in chariots and on horses, accompanied by their officials and their people. But if you do not obey these commands, declares the Lord, I swear by myself that this palace will become a ruin.

. . .

Duncan didn't know how long he had been studying the book, but suddenly he was aware that the cold in the tiny room had become tortuous. He shook himself like a wet dog, envying Pea her constant state of *Within*. How wonderful it would be to never feel anything. Duncan shut the Bible just as he heard the crackling and buzzing of the ancient radio. He smiled more broadly and put on the headphones. God and the radio were both chatty today.

He heard nothing more than a trucker talk to his dispatcher about the meat he was carrying to Anchorage. Pity he was so far out of the way. Duncan would have liked steak. He took off the headphones and made a mental note to ask Robert what else was in the truck. Surely it was more than human cargo. After all, that was why Duncan had sent him out to look in the first place.

Duncan left the backroom of the store the same way he had come. He walked across the compound, through the cold, the light snow and the wind. All the while, the words he had read were like neon in his brain, like a dry bush burning bright, like lightning striking: *hospitality to angels. . .if a brother becomes poor he shall live with you. . .do no harm to foreigners and the King will ride through the gates . . . harm them and God will ruin this place.*

By the time Duncan went into the main house his step was lighter. He always felt better when there was something important to do. He felt better still when he saw the congregation gathered around the dinner table waiting for him.

Waiting just for him.

7

The seven-dog team pulled Andre Guillard's sled smoothly across the early snow that blanketed Denali Park. In the distance, Denali, the mountain itself, rose majestically. It, too, was covered in white. The weather had turned mid-September, which was unusual but not strange. Most of the people who had won lottery tickets to drive the one road that wound through the great park had not made it as far as Savage River because of the unseasonable snowfall. Andre needed neither permit nor car to travel here. Every inch of Denali – and then some – was in his care. He was an Alaskan State Trooper whose job it was to keep peace in what appeared to be a perpetually peaceful land.

Which it was not.

Dark days of winter made people fickle and fearsome or just downright crazy. Some were happy to hibernate and wait out the snow; but some were gripped with cabin fever and massacred each other over how the fire was stoked. Add to that the problems with poachers, subsistence hunters without licenses, and rescue missions, and winter was a trooper's challenge. At the moment, though, Andre wasn't challenged at all. It was almost sinful that what he was doing was considered work.

"Gee!" he called to the dogs and they turned right at his command.

"Haw!" he called again and they went left, landing back on track, responding as if they and the sled were one living thing.

Andre had not been raised in Alaska. He migrated there when he was twenty-two because he was no more comfortable in Florida's humidity and heat than he had been in the midst of his large family of brothers, sisters, aunts, uncles, first, second, and third cousins. He grew tired of his mother wondering if he would ever get married and his father telling him that marriage was not all women cracked it up to be. He was unnerved by his sisters' squealing babies, their complaints about their husbands' lack of attention, or the fact that grown women seemed to cry for the sake of crying. Andre was befuddled by his brothers who thought a car engine was beautiful yet had no use for a clear blue sky. His one brother's two ex-wives were scary as were his other brother's parade of girlfriends teetering on very high heels and wearing very short-shorts. It wasn't that Andre didn't like women; he just liked women of a different sort. So he left Florida behind, confident that he was now more a part of his family than he ever had been. His life in Alaska gave them something to talk about while they grilled their steaks and drank away their Sundays.

Andre leaned forward, calling out to let his huskies know he was still part of the team. They had covered ten miles and had another three to go before they made it to the field, and they still ran as if they were morning fresh. He pedaled the sled. The cold air was like champagne fizzing against his skin. A fringe of ice had formed on his mustache and beard. There were deep lines around his blue eyes, earned in the hours spent straining to see the point just beyond the furthest point on the horizon. Andre hoped he never saw it, but he kept trying. His jaw was square under his trim beard and his cheekbones were high. He was tall.

He was broad of chest, slim of hip, and comfortable in his skin. He was twenty-nine years old and the summer campers or winter visitors who came upon him often took pictures so they could show people at home the beautiful man they had come across in Alaska. The criminals he apprehended, the abusive husbands he confronted, the poachers he tracked down more often than not simply gave up when Andre showed up so impressive was his appearance. Andre, though, was oblivious. However handsome he might be, his looks paled in comparison to the wilderness around him.

Today's sky, for instance, reminded Andre of Boris' coat. A true Siberian husky, the blue-eyed dog was white on the belly and black and grey on his back and ruff. His coloring was as dramatic in contrast as the deep and threatening colors of the sky above and the bright white of the snow below. Andre pedaled once more, and the dogs pulled faster to please him, and all too soon they arrived at their destination where Nell was waiting. She called out as he came close. She beamed at Andre, but threw her arms out to the dogs as the sled came to a stop. First Boris and then all the others in turn, talking as she would to well-reared but excitable children.

"You're happy aren't you? Yes, you are. You had a good run." She ruffled their fur and unhitched them one by one. "I thought maybe you'd mushed your way to Russia, Andre."

"I would have if I could have." André joined her and together they managed the rigging.

"I hope you would have at least stopped for a chat on the way," Nell laughed as her work-worn hands buried themselves in one dog's dense coat.

Andre admired those hands. They were as rough as any man's and aged beyond their years. The fact that Nell wasn't ashamed of them was damn sexy. She didn't notice him looking and soon the team was free, sent off for their food and a well-deserved rest. Andre released the straps on his gear and slung his backpack over his shoulder. Nell put her hands on her hips and gave him the once over.

"You look like you had a good run yourself, Andre."

"Can't complain." He swung his pack forward again and dug into the side pocket for her mail. "By Pass Service, ma'am"

"Thanks."

Nell took the stack of envelopes, but showed no interest in the mail. She had no family, her friends were in Alaska, and her charters were picked up online or through the state offices. Any news that came by mail could wait. She was more interested in Andre.

"I think God made Denali just for you, my friend. You look good, but then what else is new?" She chucked him on the shoulder. "Come on in. I'm not sure we'll get you all warmed up, but we'll take the chill off."

"Do I have time for a cup of coffee?" he asked.

"A short one. I'm not liking the looks of that sky."

Andre glanced up. He loved the look of the sky, but said, "You're the boss."

They walked toward the cabin, their boots sinking in the deep, soft snow. He noted the pile of wood up against the side of the house and was satisfied that Nell was good for the winter. He stomped his boots on the wooden porch before stepping across the threshold of the log house. When he was inside, Andre peeled off his gloves and slid his hat back. His dark hair was cut short but still waved and curled. Nell had more than once told him that any woman would kill to look as good as just one of Andre's parts did. She shut the door, and then swiped at the ice on his beard. Andre unzipped his jacket .

"Nothing ever changes here, Nell," he said.

"Everything just gets a older," she answered. "Including yours truly."

"Not so you'd notice." He gave her one of his mega watt smiles and she gave one right back.

"You must have brain freeze, buddy," Nell laughed. It was doubtful Andre would notice her blush, but she turned from him anyway. "Glad they sent you. It's been way too long. Hope this isn't a wild goose chase."

"If you think it's worth checking out then it is," he answered.

"Help yourself to that coffee while I get my gear. It's fresh." She nodded toward the two-burner stove. "Much as I'd like to chat, I think we better get going soon as."

Andre dropped his pack and chuckled as she disappeared into the back. He was still laughing when he raised his voice: "I planned a little lay over just for that on the way back."

"Nice of you, Andre. Real thoughtful." Nell's voice was muffled, and he knew she was rooting around in her closet, so he gave up on trying to converse.

The front room was neat as a pin. Her desk was up against one wall with the shortwave, satellite phone, and two computers on top, file cabinets underneath and maps on the wall. Her living quarters were a room in the back. To Andre's right was a small kitchen and Nell's pantry that would sometimes have to see her through a long winter without being restocked unless Andre made a trip out. To the right of the front door was Nell's gun rack.

Sure that he wouldn't be caught, Andre pulled a can of candied nuts she fancied out of his pack and put them into one of the cabinets for her to find. He poured himself a cup of coffee. When she returned, she was decked out in full gear. Andre hadn't bothered to sit down, and she didn't either when she roused the Denali station.

"I have Trooper Guillard, Denali. I'll check back around fourteen hundred after I drop him."

The radio was a good one. It didn't crackle or fade in and

out, so both of them could clearly hear that it was Cressi on the other end.

"You get Andre back in one gorgeous piece, Nell. I'm holding you personally responsible," she said knowing full well that Andre was within hearing distance.

"Shaking in my boots, Cressi. Don't worry. I'll make sure every hair's in place when he gets back. Promise." Nell signed off and said to Andre: "Let's do it."

Andre took one more gulp, put his cup in the sink, grabbed up his gear again, and followed her out. The gun rack was locked, but her door never was. They walked the hundred feet or so until Nell broke off and did a quick check of the skin of 'the beaver', the workhorse of bush planes that would take Andre where he needed to go. Even in the few minutes they had been inside the house, the sky had grown blacker and the heavy clouds looked as flat and thick as carpeting rolled out wall-to-wall. A wind kicked up, and it was suddenly warmer than it should be.

Andre raised his face to catch it.

It felt like summer and fall had joined forces in a last ditch effort to make winter back off. Still, that wasn't what caught his attention. It was something he heard; a sound that signaled something coming their way. Then he laughed a little. He shook his head slightly. There was nothing. It was his imagination working overtime; it was the warm coffee coursing through a still chilled body; it was the time of day that made him uneasy. He looked into the cockpit. Nell was going about her business.

Still, Andre couldn't shake the feeling that somehow the wilderness had expanded and that the plane was going to be too small to traverse it. He shuddered like the freaked out nine-year-old he had been when he saw that episode of the Twilight Zone where a plane took off from one place at one time and put itself down in the same place but another time altogether. Funny he should think about that; funny he should be getting goose bumps when he thought about that.

"Andre! Come on, buddy. We gotta skedaddle."

Nell raised her voice just as she threw the switch and started the engine.

"Yep. I'm ready," Andre muttered.

He tossed in his gear. She put on her headphones and flipped a few more switches. He grasped the side of the plane to hoist himself into the cockpit. Pausing, still fighting the feeling of being out of place and time, Andre Guillard hesitated. He didn't want to strap himself in a seat. He didn't want the door to close. He turned his noble head and raised his handsome face when he heard the howling of his dogs over the churning of the engine. The wind ran across the land and the snow became a billowing haze that obscured the horizon.

For the first time since Andre Guillard had come to Alaska, he didn't want to go further into the wilderness, he wanted to stay with Nell and have that chat.

8

Andre watched until the little plane was a pinhole of silver against the clouds. When he was sure that Nell was well on her way, he hiked until night was only an hour ahead of him and set up camp: a one man tent, a fire, a quick meal and clear water from the river that was about a half mile to the east. He washed, rolled out his bag and went to sleep more easily than if he had a real roof or bed. His work would take about a day and a half. If worse came to worse and Nell had to wait out the weather, he had provisions for three days. In his daydreams, Andre could imagine living off the land forever, alone, and at one with Alaska. Luckily, he was also extremely self-aware. He had run across a couple of those old recluses and there was a fine line between a man at one with nature and a man who was certifiable. Andre knew he was definitely not the latter.

The next morning he woke to a dishwater-dawn and lazy snow, made his coffee and sat in the great forest with nothing on his mind other than wondering how strange it was that the word content was so similar to contempt. The next thought he had was to wonder why the first even entered his mind.

Andre finished his coffee, cleaned his camp, slung his pack

and headed toward his destination which was not so much a place as a point on a compass, a cross-hair of longitude and latitude deep in grand, unmapped rough country.

Along the way, he kept his eyes open for evidence that someone was killing Muskox and leaving the meat to rot on the carcass in favor of the trophy boss and horns. He looked for deer antlers discarded at a kill site. As expected, he found nothing. It would be pure happenstance should he stumble across poachers this far out. Of course, this far out no one considered a clean kill poaching. They considered it a necessity.

At the foot of the mountains, he climbed easily across stones and rocks, as sure footed as the Big Horn sheep. He paused atop a boulder to check his compass and, an hour later, found what he was looking for: the 'thing' Nell had spotted on a fly over four days earlier. The 'thing' was a truck – or it had been a truck.

Andre went for it, glancing at the road cut into the mountain above him as he did so. God only knew who had carved it or why. From his vantage point, it seemed barely wide enough for a car which meant that the trucker had to be hauling something he shouldn't be and didn't want to chance a border, checkpoint, or traffic stop. Alaska folk weren't afraid of much, but that road should have been on the driver's short list.

Andre put his foot in the crotch of an outcropping of stone, balanced briefly and then launched himself. He landed solidly, the snow puffed up prettily, and he dropped his pack as he called:

"Andre Guillard, Alaska State Trooper. Hello!"

Not even an echo came back at him. Andre dug out the tools of his trade and went about his business. He checked out the boxes, noting that at least a few had been cleared out manually. He swept the snow from the top one, opened his knife, and cut through the tape. Andre ripped it open and pulled out the packing material. He used two fingers to extract one of the small bottles. The fine print was nearly impossible to read, but read it he did. Pure, liquid Nicotine. Do not ingest. Do not allow contact with skin. Contact poison control if any of the following symptoms occur: nausea, coma, seizure. Can cause death. Dilute before using.

Charming.

A load of poison was being transported to who knew where by who knew who, and now it was lying at the bottom of a cliff in the middle of nowhere. It was going to be a bitch to get this stuff and the truck out of here.

Andre put a couple of bottles in his pack, took out a marking pen, wrote the date and time and the word DANGER! on the box. Finally, he put his name and claimed it for the Alaskan authorities. He took pictures. He took more pictures of the back of the truck before checking out the container itself.

"Jesus," he muttered.

There was enough of the stuff to kill everyone in the state. He noted the key in the lock of the chain. Someone had been walking around long enough to use that key.

Andre moved on to the downward slope and photographed the truck from that angle. He pointed the camera at the trees then moved uphill taking picture after picture. All of these would be filed and that file would be shared with insurance company wonks, forest department personnel, transportation department folk, the HazMat specialists, and commerce bureaucrats.

He focused on the cab from the outside then climbed up to get a good look at the mess of beer cans, chip bags, and cigarette butts inside. Andre tried the passenger door. Opening it was a no-go so he reached through the open window and collected everything in the glove box: a hauling permit, a class three license with a picture of a man that looked more like a mug shot than an I.D., a couple of maps that hadn't been used in a good long time, and three condoms in the same condition. Considering the picture on the I.D. it did not surprise Andre that the driver hadn't seen much action with the ladies.

A chill wind blew. The sky darkened and the day shortened. He went back to his pack and put the things he found in a larger plastic bag, logged them and then walked around the length of the truck again. Just as he was wondering where the driver had gotten himself off to, the question was answered. He had gotten himself off to either heaven or hell, both of which Andre fervently believed in.

Andre got on his stomach, rested his chin on a rock as cold and smooth as marble, pointed his camera at the mutilated corpse – barely recognizable now that so much of him had been eaten away – and took five pictures. Just as he got up Andre's attention was caught by a glove sticking out of the snow. Worn but still serviceable, he assumed it belonged to the dead man. Since at least one of the poor cuss' arm was probably in the belly of some animal by now there was no way to match it to its mate until his other arm was dug out.

It didn't bother Andre that nature had taken its course, what distressed him was that this man died for nothing. If you're going to take risks, if you're going to give your life, then do it for something worthwhile. He got up and took a small tarp from his pack and put it over the remains. Someone would be back to get him. With no more to discover, Andre Guillard now attended to the niggle wobbling around in the back of his brain. He did a half turn.

There were the boxes.

Another quarter turn.

There was the cab.

He stared at the ground.

There was a man's body.

That man was pinned and his lower extremities crushed, so

it was highly unlikely that he got up after the accident, opened the back of the truck, and squished himself under the cab again to die. That meant someone else had been along for the ride. That meant they had survived. But why open the back? Why take only a few boxes out of the truck? And where in the heck were they now?

Andre walked to the back of the truck again, stopping only long enough to grab a plastic bag from his pack, drop the glove inside and note the time and date. This was the scene of an accident, and there was no evidence of foul play. These were regulated goods, and if they were in the back of this truck, then they sure as heck weren't being regulated by any system Andre knew about. He would be curious to find out where the vials had come from, where they were headed, and who hired the driver, but it was the lock and key that truly intrigued the trooper.

Andre unhooked the flashlight from his belt and hoisted himself into the container. A wide wedge of the interior shimmered under the broad beam. He poked through the boxes. None of them were open. He was about to wrap it up when a canvas bag caught his eye. He moved a few boxes to get at it, hunkered down, and shined his light inside.

Women's clothes. A man's shirt. Socks.

He swung the light across the dark dried stains on the floor, rested on one knee, and inspected it more closely. It looked like blood, but he couldn't say for sure. He got up, took a picture of the dark patch, zipped the duffle, and that was that.

When he reached the door, Andre tossed the bag to the ground and got down after it. He stashed the flashlight and secured the duffle to the top of his own pack. If anyone had been in the back of that thing, it sure hadn't been a comfortable ride. And if the lock had been secured, there was no way out without help. It was a mystery and one that wouldn't be solved now.

Adjusting the harness on his huge pack, he secured the hip

belt and gave the truck one last look. The person who unlocked that truck was long gone, and the fresh snow covered any tracks they might have left. He could wonder all he wanted, but odds were he'd never know what really happened up here. Still, it wasn't a wasted trip. A crew would be sent back to confiscate this stuff. It was off whatever market it was headed to. Andre took out his satellite phone and raised Nell.

"I'm done. Heading back. Yeah, kind of interesting." He told her what he'd found and then listened as she ran through the weather and let him know that Boris was off his food.

"He misses me," Andre laughed. Before he signed off he had one more thing: "Nell, do a fly over about five miles northeast and then come back and get me. Keep your eyes open."

"What am I looking for?" she asked.

"A passenger from this wreck. Might be a woman. She'd be on foot."

"Injured?" Nell came back.

"Not even sure if she exists, but a look-see won't hurt. Watch for any encampments," he said.

"Got it. See you in the a.m. my friend."

Andre Guillard *Rogered that* and started his hike back to the place where Nell would pick him up. This time instead of looking for signs of poachers, Andre kept his eyes open for any indication that someone had walked away from that crash. All he saw was snow and trees and a moose the size of a mini-van. Soon Andre Guillard was thinking what a lucky man he was that life in this part of the world was pretty darn simple.

When you were dead you were dead, and when you were alive it was glorious.

―――――

Mama Cecilia wore the moccasins her son had given her on her birthday. The moccasins were a little too big and were made to look like they were caribou but they were not. They were plastic. Cheap beads of yellow and pink were stitched onto the top of them in a flower pattern. The leaves of the flower were iridescent green. Mama Cecilia had never seen that color on a leaf in all of the years that she had walked on the earth. Her son had given these moccasins to her, remembering her birthday the year he was sober, and buying them with money he had taken from her wallet. As with all of life, Mama Cecilia knew there were happy things and unhappy ones. She was happy he remembered her birthday and unhappy that he had stolen from her to buy a gift.

But what could she expect from a drunkard except big sadness and small happinesses?

Her son did not hunt, he did not fish, and he did not have a job. He had a woman once, not his wife. Together they had a daughter, but even the daughter was not enough to make him want to live in the world. In the end, Mama Cecilia had to believe what Oki, the shaman, told her: her son's spirits were bad spirits. She did not, however, have to accept what he told her.

Today, the sound of the cheap moccasins on the cracked linoleum floor was like sandpaper as Mama moved back and forth, washing the dishes, drying them, putting them on the open shelves in the kitchen of the small and silent house. She used her foot to move aside the washtub that would catch the drip that would come through the ceiling when the heavy snow came and melted and came again. Three steps across the kitchen, she opened the back door and walked down the old wooden steps, holding onto the handrail that wobbled when she leaned too hard upon it. The wind blew as she stepped onto the hard packed ground that had a goodly amount of snow. Mama Cecilia didn't pull her sweater closer because it would not warm her quickly enough to bother. She was only taking the clothes off the line that was strung between an old metal pole and an even older wooden one. On that line, her son's underwear and jeans danced in the wind like clothes on stiff-legged ghosts. She unhooked the wooden pins and put them in the bucket near the post. Carrying the near frozen clothes, she retraced her steps, and held a little tighter to the rickety handrail as she went back up the stairs and into the house.

She folded the jeans over her arm and even folded the underwear in half as she went through the small living room, past her own bedroom, and to the door of her son's room. There was no knob to turn or lock to lock. There was only a hole where the knob and the lock had once been so the door opened sound-lessly. Inside, a little bit of light bled through the high window, but it was like the light in the eyes of a dying man, flat and faded and difficult to see through. The curtains she had made for her son when he was a child still hung there. The cowboys and the horses they rode upon had faded so that the horses looked like stumps and the cowboys like mushrooms.

"Go away."

Her son always knew when she was there. He always ordered her away. He moved as if he was agitated. Even though his legs were short, they were too long for the narrow bed. His shirt crept up his back and she saw his smooth skin. The black hair on his head was bent in many directions. She could not see his face, but she didn't have to in order to see his anger. His anger was dull and black like coal inside the belly of a cast iron stove.

Mama Cecilia was not startled when he spoke to her nor was she hurt by his admonition. Her son was always awake enough to know when someone living was close, and he was sure to send the living person away before he caught their condition. Most people were afraid of his gruffness, and the smell of his breath, and his wild hair, and his red eyes, but she was not.

"You should get up. I have food."

Mama Cecilia laid his clean, cold clothes on the wooden chair. She wanted to sit beside the metal bed, smooth his hair, and lay her hands upon him, and share her good spirits.

"Leave me alone."

He muttered and swatted at an imaginary mother because Mama Cecilia had not sat beside the bed. She stood there, her squat body unmoving, her chubby hands by her side. She said, "I am going for a while. I am going to the lodge about Susan, your daughter."

He made noises, not words, and that was disrespectful. She wanted to call sharply to him but she had no real name to call him that felt right on her tongue. Calling sharply without a name would not be the same. He liked to be called Cole like his white father who had left them, but she could not say that name. He would not answer to his native name, so she shuffled away without calling sharply or saying a name.

She closed the door, went to her own room, and sat on the bed that was neatly made up. She did not turn on the light because she found the gathering grey comforting. It did not hide her from the world the way her son's dark room hid him, it embraced her gently so that she could become one with the changing season.

Mama sat with her back erect and folded her hands in her lap. She saw that her lap was large and wondered when she had grown so wide. There were times that she still believed herself slim and quick and beautiful. Mama Cecilia loved when those moments came, but then they were gone. She was herself, an old woman with long grey hair to braid and small dark eyes that no longer saw much even of her own village. Her high full cheeks were soft, but they were wasted. There was no one to kiss them, no husband or grandchildren or even a dog to love her enough. The wrinkles around her eyes were deep and furrowed more from closely held sorrow than shared joy. She was sad to be old, but to be old was no excuse for sitting down and weeping.

Finally, Mama Cecilia leaned over. Her stomach folded, pushing the breath out of her as she removed the cheap moccasins. She picked up the ones she had made from the hide of a caribou with the fur turned inside. Plain as they were, these moccasins were her treasure. She had stitched them together with a length of hide that she had tanned herself when she was a young bride. The shoes were softer than the day she had first worn them. Her sharp and practical brain had not changed with the passing of the years and neither had her feet. They were still small although everything in between her head and her feet had gotten bigger and softer. Her heart was the biggest and softest of all. If it had not been, she would not be putting on her good moccasins and going to the lodge.

When she was done, Mama Cecilia stood up and her long skirt fell to her toes. No one would know that she wore proper moccasins, but she would know. She took off her house sweater and her apron and hung them on a hook next to her good sweater. The good sweater she took down, put on, and buttoned up to her chin. When that was done she went to her small closet and took out her parka, her *amaut,* made of seal and fox and wolf. It was too early in the season for this coat, but it was good to wear it to the lodge.

In the hall, Mama Cecilia cast a look at her son's room. She heard nothing, not even snoring. She went back through the small house and took the paper from the table by the door. This she put in her pocket, and then she opened the door and stepped outside. Mama Cecilia did not bother to lock the door behind her. There was nothing to steal inside her house. If someone were so desperate that they must steal nothing then she would not begrudge them.

She did not pause between the closing of the door and

beginning her journey. She looked neither left nor right. Soon she had walked down to the road that was not paved, her arms at her sides, her chubby fingers hanging loose, and her narrow dark eyes on the straight path. The breeze could not find even a single strand of her hair to toy with so tight was her braid. Her cheeks did not flush with cold because they were the color of polished mahogany and a blush could not shine through.

Mama Cecilia walked one mile and some feet and then she was at the lodge. She opened the door and ducked her head to enter. Inside, Mama Cecilia straightened, standing only a little taller than she was wide. She breathed in through her short, flat nose and her old eyes looked slowly around the big room. The benches lining the walls were empty, but then she saw that someone was at the far end of the long hall sitting at the table where the chief usually sat and spoke about important things. But he was not sitting there often since he, too, had moved to the city.

"Mama Cecilia."

"Hello, Priscilla Wolf Skin." Mama greeted the woman who was very much younger than she, which didn't mean she was young at all. Priscilla Wolf Skin did not greet her back in the old way because she was very excited about things that seemed big to her but which were not.

"I'm putting the report in order. The chief is coming in a few weeks, and we need to have an accounting of us all. There are so few of us, but it is still a chore that must be done correctly," the young woman chirped.

Mama nodded and kept her eyes on Priscilla who had not asked her or her son to make an accounting of themselves. It seemed to Mama Cecilia that she should make an accounting before Priscilla could make one to the chief. But Mama did not speak. She just looked at Priscilla who was forty years plus five. She was old enough to know that the chiefs did not care about the people here but Mama Cecilia didn't want to make Priscilla feel sad, so she didn't point out that the chiefs had been making promises for all the eighty years Mama Cecilia had been alive. Nothing got better; everything got worse.

"Are you alright?" Priscilla asked.

This was a kind question; still Mama Cecilia was a little disappointed that it was Priscilla asking it. She had hoped for someone with years to speak to her.

"Are you alone?" Mama asked.

"Yes."

Mama nodded. Without a telephone to call to the village she had to take her chances. Now that it was only Priscilla Wolf Skin, Mama Cecilia assumed her spirits meant for her to find this woman.

When she decided this, she put her hand in her pocket and withdrew the paper she had so carefully read over the last few days. She unfolded it and put it on the table in front of Priscilla.

"I have this letter from my granddaughter."

Priscilla rested her eyes on Mama Cecilia for only a flicker before she took the paper, opened it, and read it. Then she read it again. Mama Cecilia waited, knowing everything came in its own time including what Priscilla Wolf Skin would have to say. While she waited, Mama looked with her eyes here and there but did not turn with her body. She saw the dust motes clinging to the weak light coming through the glass in the lodge windows. That glass was melting from the top down because that was what happened to ancient glass. She saw the wooden floor and felt her feet upon it. It felt good to stand on something older than her feet.

"Your granddaughter is in Eagle, Mama. That is so far away."

"Not too far," Mama answered with some authority even though her chubby hands were still by her side, her voice flat and practical, and she made no motion to indicate she had any authority. "She doesn't give me a phone number or an address, but she says to send money to that place. I would like to go find her and bring her back to help her father. I would like to find out if the people at that place know how I can find her."

"I think that would be hard without a phone number or address. I think this is just an office to wire money."

"She won't be far away if this is where I send money," Mama assured her. "But I cannot go alone. Will you come with me, Priscilla Wolf Skin?"

"Mama Cecilia," Priscilla lamented, as her brow knotted. "I have my children. My husband hasn't worked in so long. I couldn't get the money. And look, it says your Susan wants money. I don't think you have enough to send her some and to pay for a trip to Eagle, do you?"

Mama Cecilia took the letter back, folded it, and remained silent. Priscilla's concern deepened because it seemed clear now that no matter what she said, Mama Cecilia was determined to do this thing. Priscilla wanted to tell the old woman that her son was not worth saving, but that would not be kind. So she said:

"Does your Cole know? He should know. He should be the one to go find her, Mama. Or, at the very least, he should go with you if you are determined."

Mama Cecilia nodded. All that Priscilla Wolf Skin said was true. Her son should go, but he would not even if Mama begged him. She could die, and he might not notice. That's how sure she was that Cole would not go to Eagle. But if she could bring her granddaughter back to this village, Cole might see her and want to be a good man for her. When Mama died, she would have someone to mourn her. Mama was almost certain that she was not enough to inspire her son to be a good man so she would put another person in his way. That person would be Susan.

"Do you want me to talk to Cole?"

Priscilla Wolf Skin was calling after the old woman who was

now leaving. She did not answer Priscilla who, Mama knew, thought she was helping just by asking the question. She was not. That Mama Cecilia left dissatisfied was not a bad thing. It only meant that the way to where she needed to go would not be straight.

The old woman walked out of the lodge and then the mile and some feet back to her house. When she had put away her *amaut* and good moccasins, hung up her good sweater and put on her apron, Mama Cecilia sat on her bed with the letter in her lap. She closed her eyes and considered that the girl might be no better than her father because she asked only for money and not after Mama Cecilia. Then she thought that perhaps Priscilla Wolf Skin might be wiser than Mama gave her credit for. Perhaps a journey together would be good for her son. They would know one another again. If he was walking with her then he could not drink.

She would go tell him. She would smile and help put things in a case for him. She would do everything that needed to be done, and all he would need to do would be to put his feet on the ground and hold her hand.

Mama got off the bed. She went down the short hall to tell her son of these plans, but even before she went into the room Mama Cecilia saw that things were different. The door to her son's room was open wide. Mama looked in and saw that the clothes that had been there were gone.

She made no exclamation of surprise. Instead, she went to look in the wallet that she kept beside her bed in the drawer. Her money was gone. Her son was gone. Mama sat on the bed again because the weight of her heavy heart was too much and she could not remain upright.

After a minute, Mama Cecilia raised her legs and lay down on her neatly made bed. She stared up at the ceiling, crossed her hands over her chest and clasped the letter from her granddaughter beneath them. She listened in case her son should come back and have a cheap present bought with her own money instead of running away to nowhere.

The door did not open.

He did not bring her a present.

He was gone.

Mama Cecilia closed her eyes and slowed her breathing. Soon it looked as if she were dead. But she was only waiting for her good spirits to guide her. When they did her good moccasins would take her where she needed to go.

9

Andre Guillard sat up in bed, the sheets and blankets falling away to reveal his wondrously naked body. Nell's house was chilly, but for a man used to sleeping out in the open it felt downright toasty. The fire in the potbellied stove in the corner of the room was still burning and Nell was giving off a goodly amount of body heat herself.

She rolled over, opened her eyes, and pushed herself up. She wore a t-shirt, more out of habit than necessity she told Andre the first time she suggested that they indulge in a little 'chatting' when he was in the neighborhood. Andre thought colleagues-with-benefits was not a bad idea; benefits with Nell were special, indeed. Of all the women he had ever met, it was Nell he admired most. She was older than he but that was part of her charm. She was funny, not frivolous; she was thoughtful never overbearing; she could fix a plane or please a man; she knew what she wanted and wasn't afraid to ask for it. He would trust her with his back out in the wild, and he treasured her affection within these walls.

The only annoyance between them was the way they looked. Nell was far too aware of her age and far too clueless about her true beauty. He had never really seen what all the fuss was about. His face and his body were what they were. It wasn't like he'd done anything to earn them so he couldn't take credit. For her part, Nell just wanted to make sure he had an out – which he never seemed to want. She loved Andre Guillard because he was simply Andre, and she assumed he must love her a little just because she was plain old Nell.

"Morning." Nell touched him lightly, somewhere between his last rib and his hip. He put his hand on her head and mused her hair.

"I didn't mean to wake you," he said.

"What time are you taking off?"

"An hour. Maybe two."

"I'll get you some breakfast." Nell pushed off her side of the sheets, swinging around to kiss him and then back the other way so she could get out of bed. She said: "You are welcome."

Andre laughed as she took her robe and left the room. He showered but his mind was still unsettled. He had been restless in the night, and he still was when he sat down to bacon, eggs, and toast.

"You shouldn't have used 'em up on me, Nell," Andre said even though the scrambled eggs were just what he needed.

"Next time you're out bring me some or you'll be on the powdered stuff."

"I'm not picky," Andre answered.

"I could take that the wrong way, my friend," Nell said.

"Don't." He closed his eyes as the first forkful went into his mouth and gave her a 'yum'. She laughed, which pleased Andre to no end.

"By the way, thanks for the nuts. I found them after you left. Didn't save you even one." She got up and poured herself a fresh cup of coffee, leaned her hip on the counter, and looked out the window. "It's a good thing I got you out when I did. It's going to be brutal in a while. I can't remember the last time we had weather like this so early."

"HazMat won't be able to get that stuff any time soon, then." Andre glanced toward the window.

"No one else will be able to either, so at least you don't have to worry about it." Nell turned away and mumbled into her coffee. "I'm going to be grounded all week. If you don't get your rear in gear, you're going to be stuck here with me."

"There are worse places to be snowed in." Andre picked up his plate and put it in the sink. He filled his cup. "Unfortunately, my team could get me home no matter what, much as I wouldn't mind telling the boss I was stuck."

"You're a sweet talker, Andre. You should think about writing poetry," she chuckled.

Andre set his cup aside, took her around the waist and pulled her close. Nell held her cup high, and he flashed her a bright white smile.

"Roses are red, violets are blue, if I'm stuck in the snow, it better be with you."

Andre nuzzled her neck and Nell's throaty laugh dissolved into giggles as his beard tickled her skin. For a guy who didn't care much for people, he sure had a way with them. She threw her arm around his neck, pulled back, and grinned.

"It's a good thing we've got you tucked away out here. Unleashing your charm on the rest of the world would cause riots."

Andre let her go, took his coffee, and sat down at the table again. "I'd be in the loony bin if I still lived out there."

"Are you all packed up?"

"Yep."

They made lazy conversation before it petered out completely. The small talk never lasted more than a few minutes so Andre's silence was nothing new to Nell, but this time his quiet was telling.

"What's on your mind? You didn't sleep well."

"I keep thinking about the back of that truck and the dried blood. And the duffle; that duffle doesn't make a whole lot of sense. What do you make of that?"

Nell shrugged. "Could be the driver's bag and he threw it in the back, but it's got women's clothes in it. Maybe that was for his wife or girlfriend."

"Could be, but there were some guy's shirts, too," Andre answered.

"Half the time I wear men's clothes. I don't even own a dress." Nell sat down with him. Her robe was wearing thin. He made a note to pick one up for her next time he got into Fairbanks.

"I'd like to see you in a dress," Andre said. "You'd look great."

"Maybe in my next life," Nell answered. "Still, if someone was hitching why toss her stuff in the back? There was plenty of room up front. And if she had the duffle, why toss her in the back? And, if that's where she was, where is she now?"

"I think she was a passenger. The passenger window was open. She could have survived the fall and crawled out that way," Andre speculated.

"Any blood in the cab?" Nell asked.

Andre shook his head. "Only in the container."

"I don't know what to tell you." Nell twirled her cup on the saucer and played along. "Somebody was around because that padlock didn't open itself. I didn't see anything from the air. I suppose someone could have picked her up – if she exists. It's a mystery for sure"

"River's not too far away. Still, you'd have to know that. Someone who didn't could get lost real easy. Far as I know, there's not even a hermit out there to help. There isn't a lot of boat traffic now, so even if she made it to the river who would pick her up?"

They both thought about that for a while and the silence between them was still lopsided. Nell wasn't curious and Andre was bothered. As far as she was concerned, there were things on heaven and earth she would never figure out. It seemed like a waste of energy to try. She didn't think about why she'd been born or how she'd die, she was more curious about why things happened over and over again. Why the human race didn't learn from the past was beyond her. Why a duffle bag with clothes in it was in the back of a container truck was not a real worry.

"You're right. It all probably adds up to nothing." Andre pushed his cup aside. "Do you want me to leave it here? Maybe there's something in that bag that you can use."

She shook her head. "You should take it back with you. It's logged, and you have to turn in your report. Given the stuff you found in those boxes, that duffle might be some kind of material evidence." There was a beat and Nell asked, "Did you go through the whole thing?"

"Not really," Andre finished off the last of his toast.

"Maybe there's some I.D. If he was carrying a passenger, there might be family who would be awfully grateful to hear what you've found."

Nell got up. Her slippers flapped on the hard wood floor, went silent on the rug, and gave one last slap as she stopped at the desk, reached underneath, and grabbed the bag she had stashed near Andre's gear. She unzipped it as she brought it back to the table, pulling things out as she went.

"Whoever these belong to must never eat. What is this?" She laughed and fumbled with the shirt she had pulled out as the bag landed on the table. "A size two? Who in the hell is a two?"

She tossed the t-shirt on a chair and brought out a blue

sweater, another t-shirt, and underwear. The latter she held up
for Andre to see.

"Expensive even if they aren't fancy and about five sizes too
small for me. I think your driver was taking this stuff back to a
little sweetie somewhere. Nell tossed out a man's t-shirt. It was
worn and faded but the logo of a surf shop was still visible. She
added a pair of boxer shorts, a brush, and a thin blanket to the
pile.

"What have we here?" Nell held up a sleek and expensive cell
phone.

"Is it charged?" Andre pushed back his chair. Nell poked at
the buttons.

"It's charged. No passcode." She tapped the phone a few
more times. "Hannah's phone. No last name."

"Does she have any messages?" Andre asked.

Nell tapped the screen. "Three from the same number. The
most recent was a month ago. Shall I call it?"

Andre motioned for her to go ahead, and Nell's eyes
sparkled as if she was doing something naughty. She hit redial,
put the phone to her ear, and listened.

"It's ringing."

She held it toward Andre. On the other end a woman picked
up. She said:

"Hannah?"

Andre Guillard, Alaska State Trooper said:

"To whom am I speaking?"

"Robert, give it to me. Seriously. Right now. Nobody can stand
looking at you in it anymore."

Melody tapped her foot as she waited outside Robert's room,
calling through the closed door. The arrival of Hannah and Billy

had been so exciting a few days ago, but the excitement had worn thin. Duncan's directive that those two be catered to did not seem exactly right to her. She had no problem caring for them, but Duncan had spent their community *Hours* preaching about their angelic nature. Even though Melody had bowed and raised her voice in praise, she knew that this time he was wrong. Those two weren't angels. They were very hurt people and would heal on their own unlike the rest of the congregation.

Not that Duncan was untruthful, he could never be that, but he had been led astray. Pea had led him astray, or he had not heard her correctly, or something. And Duncan had not spoken of the healing since Hannah and Billy had been found. They had been promised healing when the weather turned. Well, it had turned and now there wasn't a peep about when she – they – would be made whole.

Melody couldn't think about it anymore. She had chores to do. Regular chores and more chores for the two 'angels.' It all just made her so darn angry and that was the last thing she wanted to be.

"Robert! Robert!" she called and pounded on the door until it was flung open. There he was in all his gigantic glory wearing a sweater pulled out of shape and still too small for him; a sweater soiled from food droppings.

"Don't call so loud, Melody. I'm in *Hours*."

"You're never in *Hours*," she scoffed. "You think I don't know what you do when you're supposed to be in *Hours*? I've seen you through the window. You make faces at your reflection. You don't pray."

Robert looked behind at the small window in his very small room. Desperately he tried to deduce what he might have been doing in front of that window, and exactly when Melody had been outside to see him do it. He whipped his head back to her.

"I didn't mean to, Melody. I didn't. I just try to see what I would look like," Robert insisted, near tears as he pleaded. He hated when Melody was upset because her voice wasn't so pretty anymore. She sounded like she hated him. She sounded like his mother, and that made things so very difficult. He just wanted to smash her face in when she sounded like that. Instead, he said: "Don't tell Duncan. He won't believe you, anyway. I found the angels and brought them here, so he won't believe you. He said I was blessed."

"Be quiet. Be quiet," Melody snapped. "I won't tell, but give me your jacket. I have to try to clean it. Give it to me now."

"I'm supposed to go to work after *Hours*. Can't you do tonight?" Robert whined.

"No. I don't want to work all day and all night."

Seeing that fighting with her was useless, he lumbered over to the one chair in the room. He picked up his jacket, came back, and shoved it at her.

"You shouldn't care if you work a lot. That's how you'll get healed. You tell Duncan I wasn't quiet in *Hours,* and I'll tell him you were complaining about working."

"I'm not complaining. I just have a lot to do and there isn't enough time each day."

Melody took his jacket and tried to soften her voice. She did not want Robert telling Duncan anything. She looked at the streaks of blood that had soaked into the outer shell.

"I'll have this back tonight before the meeting. Then you can wear it outside tonight."

"Are the angels going to be there? Are they coming to the meeting?" Robert asked.

"They aren't angels, Robert." Melody's shoulders slumped. He could be so stupid.

"Duncan said–"

"It was a lesson, Robert," Melody snapped. "A lesson. Treat people as if they could be angels."

"I don't think so, Melody. . ." Robert began, but she was gone, taking the steps lightly, crossing Duncan's path, and giving him a smile when she did. The smile must have been particularly beautiful because Duncan actually returned it, stopped, and put his hand to the side of her face in blessing.

"Look at you, Melody. Always keeping us pulled together. Thank you."

His hand slipped away. He was leaving and she didn't want that.

"I would like to be the first, Duncan," she blurted out. It was so wrong to be that selfish, but she couldn't help herself. This waiting was wearing on everyone. "I try so hard, and I would like to be the first to be healed."

"We'll see, Melody. We'll see how it goes. The new arrivals change things. We must figure out what God's intent is. If we have to live with our afflictions a little longer, so be it."

He continued up the stairs, book in hand. Melody was sure he was going to read to Hannah. Duncan believed the girl could hear him in her unconscious mind, but Melody thought that was nonsense. For all they knew, she was brain dead. Still, all Duncan thought about since Billy had told him that Hannah was an artist was getting her to wake up. He longed for artistic conversation. Well, it was easy for him to wait for the healing time because he was perfect. The rest of them pretty much didn't care if Hannah woke up or not.

"I don't understand how kindness toward them should mean that we can't have what was promised."

Melody clutched Robert's jacket tighter. She moved from foot to foot, leaned up against the bannister and then away from it again in her agitation. Duncan just watched her and his silence created a void she felt compelled to fill.

"Billy and Hannah will heal on their own, but we can't. And

they don't believe the way we do; they haven't sacrificed the way we have."

"They are outcasts, Melody."

"They left civilization to survive. They weren't cast out," she insisted.

"True," he said. "But I'm not sure healing should be done in front of those who don't believe."

"Do the healing so that they will believe." Melody begged. "If they see a miracle, then they would be part of us, and we could call them brother and sister."

Duncan came back down the stairs slowly as they debated.

"Do you think God wants us to flaunt a miracle to impress these two people?"

Melody hung her head and shook it. She was wrong as always. "No, Duncan. I don't, but I don't think it's all about them."

"I don't either, but that isn't for me to say," he assured her. "Pea will say when we begin. Somehow these people are part of the plan, and we need to figure it out. Be patient, Melody. " Duncan looked at the jacket. He smiled and plucked at it. "It looks like you have your work cut out for you, Melody. Robert's jacket is big enough for three people."

"Yes, Duncan. But how much easier would it be to clean if I were healed?"

She turned around. For once, Melody wanted him to see her back, to feel her frustration, to think about what she had said. She was thirty-one, a virgin, a kind person, a loving person who had never been loved and that was unfair. If God couldn't be merciful, he should at least throw her a bone. Short of that, Duncan should give her hope. But what had he really said? Nothing. She was beginning to think he would never heal any of them. She was beginning to think. . .

Melody stopped herself before she blasphemed. He had

provided for them. He had found this home. He had made them equal and worthwhile here; away from a world that had no use for them. Hadn't Duncan done everything he said he would?

Yes.

Yes.

Yes.

Yet he didn't heal them and that was what he had promised.

Melody threw Robert's jacket on the wash table and pulled at it to get it straight. All the logic in the world couldn't make her feel better, so she reveled in her ugly thoughts and the ugliest was about this jacket. God only knew who had worn it before Robert, but she couldn't imagine they were any happier than he had been in the outside world. It was a cruel place, and none of them had lived well there. Even Duncan had not, of that Melody was sure. If he had, why would he be there with them?

Melody dug in the bin next to the large tin sink. She took out a scrub brush and the lye soap. She ran the water as hot as she could but also put some on to boil in case she needed to scald this fabric. She slammed the big pot down and muttered her annoyance when the flame didn't light the first time.

Melody bit down on her lower lip and tightened her upper. She closed her eyes, took a moment, and put her mind in the proper place. It was taking longer these days to convince herself that service to God was not servitude to the congregation.

When she tasted blood, she pulled herself together. Biting a hole through her lip wasn't going to make anything better, so Melody attacked the blood and dirt stains on Robert's jacket. But the first swipe of the scrub brush caught on something in the pockets.

"Good grief," she muttered and dug into the outside pockets, sure she would find half eaten food, or lumps of sugar or something else Robert had taken one too many of. He was always so sure there wouldn't be enough for him to eat. Melody didn't think Robert should work in the store but Duncan was adamant that each of them would do work that would put them square in front of their greatest temptation. For Glenn it was the woodpile, for Melody it was to be in the presence of beautiful Pea and now Hannah. For Robert it was to stock the shelves with the food they canned, grew, hunted, and cured along with the supplies he brought back from the city. He had to do it all alongside Teresa. Teresa had to face Robert. It was all so simple, and yet so difficult.

Finding nothing in the outer pockets, Melody flipped open the jacket to see what he had stashed inside. He probably bought something in the city just for himself, with community money no less, and hidden it to eat later. His sins were so many: gluttony, impatience, anger, and stealth. Oh, he would pay for this. Melody would not tell Duncan, but God would know. Oh yes, God would know.

When she dug in the pockets, though, she found Robert hadn't been hiding food at all. She pulled out a little bottle filled with clear liquid. For a split second, she thought, perhaps, Robert had taken to drink, but these bottles were so small there wasn't enough in them to get anyone drunk. Curious, she walked across the kitchen and held them up to the dim light. She forgot about the water she had put to boil. She forgot to rinse the lye soap off her hand. She forgot Robert's coat and squinted at the tiny writing on the labels, but her eyes weren't good and the gloom didn't help. She would have to talk to Duncan about glasses. She unscrewed the top and smelled it. It didn't smell like anything.

"Melody, are you almost done?"

Startled by Teresa's voice, Melody wrapped her hand around the little glass bottle before she turned around.

"I just started. I'm cleaning Robert's jacket," she said.

Teresa nodded. Melody's heart beat faster and harder, the

vial burned in her hand. She imagined Teresa coming right across this room and prying open her fingers and calling her out in meeting for being selfish. Instead, Teresa was looking at the pot on the stove.

"Alright then, but I need to start dinner. Can you hurry?"

"I just need it hot. It doesn't have to boil," Melody answered. "As soon as it is, I'll call you."

"That's fine." Teresa took her jacket off the hook and put it on. "I'm going to get some tomatoes from the store. I hope we've canned enough to last the winter."

"I should be finished by the time you get back."

Melody let her go without showing her the bottle and now she thought that was ridiculous. Teresa wouldn't have been angry with Robert the way Duncan might have been. Later, after meeting, Melody would show it to her. Together they would decide how to tell Duncan so that he wouldn't think Robert was being dishonest when he had probably been forgetful.

Melody put the cap back on the bottle, went back to the washroom, and collected the other ones. Back in the kitchen, she put them up inside away from the regular spices and near the herbs she had dried and juices she had squeezed for her teas.

The water was boiling so she took it off the stove. She forgot all about the little bottles as she started to scrub the jacket. It was a hard job and by the time the stains on the jacket were gone, Melody was tired, Teresa was cooking, and the long night of meeting and *Hours* had begun.

By the time she fell into bed, she had forgotten about Robert's treasure.

10

I'm awake in a strange place. I don't know how I got here. I only know that the color of my world has changed. In Hermosa Beach, the color of the world was Cerulean blue: blindingly bright and seamless. When I was with Billy Zuni the color surrounding me was Mars black: dense, deep, and unending. Once after that, I saw gunmetal grey: cold, flat, a neither here nor there color. Now my eyes are wide open and the dark surrounding me is the deepest indigo. I've seen this color in the early morning and I've seen it in the night sky, so it could be one or the other.

I check my body, and it is seriously out of whack. The only things working are my hands and eyes, so I use my fingers to see. They work their way across a worn sheet and a coarse blanket. I can move my head a little, and when I do something bites me. I pull at it and find it's the nub of a feather in the pillow. I let the feather go, and it floats into the indigo.

That pretty much takes all I've got in me.

My hand falls to my side, my head lolls the other way. Pain shatters through the top of my skull like there's a rave going on inside it. I raise my hand again. This time I touch stitches angling down from the top of my forehead toward my eye. The skin around them is hot and swollen. The really strange thought I have is that I must be healthy if I hurt so much. When I was sick in my heart about my life and a little crazy in my head, it didn't hurt when I cut myself. Now I feel every bruise, and scrape, and cut, and stitch.

I clear my throat just to see if I can talk, but all I hear is a moan; all I feel is a golf ball size lump at the side of my mouth. I panic even though I tell myself not to.

I breathe hard to rally all that strength everybody is so sure I have but it's bled right out of me. When no one comes through the door my heart beats like a friggin' jackhammer in my ears; my stitches pulse; sweat falls from my brow and it stings where the needle went in.

With every thing I have, I push myself up onto my elbows, pause, pant and then walk myself back. I collapse. I regroup. Finally, I'm propped up at an awkward angle on the pillow.

One, two, three.

I throw my arm out hoping to find some light, a switch, something, anything to calm my terror.

I hate the dark.

I think I sob. I think I sob for Billy.

I hit a glass and it falls to the floor. It shatters. There is no carpet beneath me. Everything that happens is a clue, not an answer.

Where am I? In a room with a hard floor.

Who put me here? Someone who cares enough to stitch me up.

Where is this place? It's not Hermosa. It's cold.

I collapse. My body is bent, my neck is crooked, my ear is folded, and I have no strength left to undo what I have done. My eyes roll. I see faint outlines of things: a chair, a table, a door.

"Somebody! Somebody!"

No one comes. Not even Billy. He must be dead because he would never leave me alone in the dark for any other reason. My throat is thick and lumpy, and I am going to cry. If I cry I will hurt everywhere. I am already in too much pain, so I don't cry.

I fall deeper into the pillow all the while wishing I were dead, too, if he is. I grieve and grieve and feed my anger and when it is hot enough I forge it into determination. I want to know how badly I failed Billy. With one more huge effort, I get myself up on one elbow. My arm shivers and shakes. I strain and grab at the things on the table but miss them. My heart tries to beat itself to death under the fabric of the nightgown like a bird trapped in a glass house banging itself against the false sky.

"Somebody?" I cry.

With the last push of hysteria, the fingers of my right hand scrabble over the top of the table next to me. I lunge, I'm on fire, but I touch something slick and grab for it. I fall back and in my hand is a bottle. I hold it to my chest. My face is covered with sweat. My eyes burn hot holes behind my closed lids.

With a scream, I hurl the bottle as best I can. It hits something – the wall, a chair, the floor – and the shattering glass sounds like an explosion. But it was nothing more than shattering glass. Still, someone has heard this time. I think it's a girl. I think the door has opened and she is looking at me.

I hyperventilate, my head is about to split open, my eyes feel like pinballs whacking around the sides of my skull, and, then, strangely, a great calm comes over me. It doesn't matter who this is. It matters that I am not alone. I hear a click and trill that sound like the throaty call of a bird. I think she must have spoken, but I'm too sick to understand.

"What?" I ask.

Then I see that it isn't a girl standing in the doorway looking at me.

As Duncan came up the stairs he was thinking of what Pea had said the last time he visited her.

. . .

Samuel 2:1-10

The Lord brings death and makes alive; he brings down to the grave and rises up.

The Lord sends poverty and wealth
he humbles and he exalts. He raises the poor from the dust
and lifts the needy from the ash heap; he seats them with princes
and has them inherit a throne of honor.

This was the prophecy of the biblical Hannah and now there was a real life Hannah in this house and under his protection. Hearing this message from the lord, Duncan faced a conundrum that bothered him. Was biblical Hannah asking him to raise mortal Hannah? Or was the passage to remind Duncan to rise up and heal the congregation? Up from the ash heap? That might refer to them all. But a throne of honor? That might only be Hannah. Or Billy. No, Duncan rejected the idea that Pea was referring to the boy. Billy was not humble. He was not orderly. He was a pain in the neck. He was always after Duncan to let him see Hannah. Duncan would let him do that when the time was right and not before.

Duncan closed his eyes and leaned against the wall in the narrow hallway. He raised his face, giving in to his mystical senses. Thinking of these glorious messages felt like rain falling upon his skin, it was as if he saw the glowing letters and numbers of the passage dancing in front of his eyes, it was if the sound of Pea's voice pulsated in his mind, a mind that never got enough of her wisdom.

Standing alone, face raised, Duncan's contentment was spreading from the very core of his mind to the deep cavity of his heart when it was disturbed by the sound of something breaking. The sound came from behind the door in the room where Hannah lay and that, he believed, was the answer to his question. It was not the congregation but Hannah who was meant to be raised up.

"You are so blessed, Pea," he muttered and then bypassed his sister's door and went to Hannah's.

Duncan's heart beat slow and steady in his narrow chest as he prepared himself to speak with her for the first time, for the surprise of her voice, for the energy that would come from the woman awake. In the dark he could see the white of her gown and the sheets, he could see the spark of her gold colored hair.

The breaking glass was the cry of a baby newly born, the first crack of the shell as a chick fights it's way into the world, the blaze of a star escaping the hell of a black hole. Duncan's eyes, so accustomed to the dark, could see every twitch and strain of her struggle. He smelled her sweat and felt the tears welling in her eyes. The Lord had reached down to the grave and up she came. He waited to see what she would do next.

"What?"

She asked this as if he had spoken and that pleased him. Her first word, a question, had no answer and yet a host of them all at the same time. It was for him to interpret which it was. This was yet another sign that she had been delivered to him for some heavenly reason.

Duncan went to the stove and opened the grate. The wood had burned to near cinders and the light cast was no more than a shimmering trail of firefly dust. He walked through it, shoulders back, head high, his stride long and purposeful. The girl on the bed was twisted and turned. He well knew that her face was hardly a face at all, but swollen and stitched up like Frankenstein. The skin around the stitches was scarlet, her hair a mat of knots, her breath was foul, and her heart was fearful. It was up to Duncan to make it all right. But first he must find out what her sin was. That was the only way to understand her destiny. That was truly the only way to heal her.

Sweeping up a ladder back chair, Duncan lifted it easily. He set it down just close enough to the bed to reassure Hannah, and far enough away to show he meant no harm. One of her eyes was nearly swollen shut, but he could see that both of them glittered, sharp and piercingly green. They were stunning eyes; gorgeous eyes; mesmerizing eyes. Those eyes assessed him as no other person ever had, and he waited for her to make her peace with what she saw.

What Hannah saw was a man moving through the indigo darkness. She had seen old men carry themselves like they were twenty and twenty-year-olds bent down as if they were old men. Until she saw his face or his hands she could not tell which he was. Not that it mattered. He was a man and men had not done well by her. She couldn't sit up, she couldn't roll over, and she could not protect herself if he turned out to be a bad guy. All she could do was lie there and wait for him to prove he wasn't.

Hannah tensed when Duncan reached for her but all he did was pull the chain that turned on the lamp. Hannah's eyes went toward it. She had pushed it so far that it teetered on the edge of the table. One more lunge and it would have gone over the side along with the glass. The man adjusted it so that it was stable, and then he drew it closer so that she could see him better.

"You've got yourself into a pickle," he said. "Let me help you."

Duncan slipped his hands under her head and cradled her skull. Hannah pulled back. He was not surprised. He had once awakened in a strange place himself, hurt and fearful and young. He remembered it as if it were yesterday. He was about to reassure her when she whispered:

"Are you a maniac? Are you?"

Mama Cecilia made new curtains for her son's room. She took

down those of his childhood and put up yellow ones. The new curtains looked happy, but she didn't expect them to make her son happy when he came home. She didn't even expect him to pretend they made him happy, but she thought he would say that he noticed them. That would be enough for her. If he noticed that she had made curtains and mended his sheets and changed the pillow on his bed for the one from her bed that was a finer pillow then that notice would be good.

On the third day after she was alone, the mail came with another message from her granddaughter, Susan. Again, the girl asked for money. Mama Cecilia felt very tired when she read that letter. She sat down for a bit in her chair and looked out the window and into the purple/blue sky. She thought very hard about her life and how it had come to what it was. She put her head back as she thought. Soon she was asleep.

She slept a long while, and when she woke up she thought she was very much like her son who slept so he didn't have to look at his problems. Mama Cecilia didn't think she liked being like her son, so she got up and did some more chores. She thought about her granddaughter, waited for her son to come home, and for a sign as to what she might do when her house was clean.

"No. I'm not a maniac. You don't have to be afraid."

He straightened her head on the pillow and stepped back only to swoop down again. This time he put one arm under her shoulder and another under her hips. He lifted her up and set her right, before pulling up the covers and tucking her. She bit off her cries of pain; he talked all the while.

"It's easy to say that, isn't it? It's easy to tell someone not to be afraid. It's very hard not to be. I know. I truly do. I've been there."

He stepped back and put his hands in the pockets of his jacket.

"On top of that, even if you can make yourself unafraid, it's a whole other thing to believe there is no reason to be, isn't it?"

Hannah watched him as carefully as she could, which wasn't carefully enough for her liking. She started to speak, but her vocal cords were tight and unused. She tried a second time.

"Where's Billy?"

"Safe and almost well. I think he's with Glenn now." Duncan pulled up a chair and sat next to her bed. "You need to have faith, Hannah. That's pretty much it. When you have no information, when you find yourself in the most confusing circumstances, you have to let yourself go and believe that you are being told the truth."

Hannah stayed silent. What was there to say? Faith hadn't gotten her very far in her young life. Her mother told her things would be fine. She was eight when she realized that was always a lie. The court told her things would be fine. They weren't. It was only with Josie that Hannah ever had faith and that turned out to be a good call. One out of three wasn't a great track record. Now here she was, sitting with a guy telling her to take him at his word.

"I'm telling you the truth, Hannah, you don't have to be afraid."

He touched her again. His fingers rested on the back of her hand. She watched him do it and felt nothing bad when he did. Maybe that was the worst thing of all. Hannah had no faith in her own perspective. She was afraid to take her eyes off him in case he was lying, but she longed to know what he could tell her: What was this room? How badly was she hurt? How soon would he turn on her if she looked away?

"Are we good so far?" he asked and withdrew his hand.

She nodded once and clenched her hands. Her fingers

tapped against the inside of her palm. Her eyes never left his face.

"Billy?" she whispered.

"He's well," Duncan answered. "Maybe not well, but recovering better than you. You've been gone from us for days."

"How long . . . in the truck?" she asked.

"We don't know. Robert – my brother – found you. Bless the Lord." He shook his head and his fringe of fine hair shimmered in the half-light. "There are miracles. You were saved for some wondrous reason, Hannah."

"Where is this . . ."

A sudden pain cut off her question. Her fingers went to her head but Duncan caught her hand before she touched her stitches.

"Don't touch. You are in Clara's Landing. It's a very romantic name for a place that only has three buildings and a dock." Carefully, he lowered her arm to her side. He pressed her hand into the soft bed so she would know he meant for her to stay still. "Do you know what state you're in?"

"Alaska." Hannah licked her lips.

"Yes, that's great you remember. It's been quite a chore keeping Billy away from you. As for visitors, we've only let the women come in, and me, of course. Melody and Teresa. Do you remember seeing them?"

Hannah moved her head so slightly it would be hard to know that she was shaking it, but Duncan knew.

"That's alright. You'll get to know all of us," he said. "We've tried to keep you isolated because we don't have a doctor here. We have only the most basic medications." He opened his hands as if to show her that what he was saying was true, but to Hannah he only proved his hands were empty. "We have good intentions in abundance, though, but that's not going to help if you get an infection. Do you understand that?"

Hannah nodded, but just barely; Duncan smiled, but just barely. She looked so fragile with the white nightgown buttoned up to her chin, the little fringe of lace framing her battered face. Her green, oh-so-painfully expressive eyes were filled with such fear and caution that the look of them cut Duncan to the quick. Still, he had no doubt that if the occasion arose to defend herself she would. She would be truly unique in their little community.

"Yes, well, I didn't really expect an answer to that. My name is Duncan Thoth. I am the head of this little group. The spiritual head, I suppose you'd say."

"Cult?" Hannah whispered through her cracked and dry lips. The swelling on the side of her mouth made it impossible to form her words properly.

"A group of like minded people," he answered as he looked at the shattered water glass and over his shoulder to where she'd thrown the bottle. Yet when he got up, he went out of the room without even trying to clean it up. When he came back he had a wet towel, and he put it to her lips.

"It's not much, but it will help. I'll have Melody or Teresa bring another glass for water when they come, but they're cooking now."

Hannah took the towel and held it to her lips. It was cold and fresh as if it had been dipped in snow. Her eyes closed. She had never felt anything so wonderful. When her hand started to shake, Duncan reached for the cloth. She let him have it, and he put it against her cheek.

"You don't have a fever. That's the good news. But your face is pretty beat up. Your leg is in a cast. You have fifteen stitches in your head. Now, hold this against the side of your mouth. That's where the swelling is the worst." Hannah did as she was told and he took his seat again. "You've got a lot of questions, yes?"

Hannah nodded.

"I won't answer them all. It will just make more work for the women if I wear you out and you get sicker." He crossed his legs and sat back in his chair as if he came everyday to talk with her. "So, where do I start? There are eight of us here. We live off the grid as much as possible. We are Christian. I don't think that makes us a cult, but everyone has their own word for people like us. We are a commune because we all work for each other. We're a retreat because we all spend some time each day in contemplation. I think most of us are too young to be hippies. But, cult? No, Hannah. You'll find each of us is quite different. No lockstep here," he laughed softly. "If you're interested, we will tell you more. If you're not, it's our duty to take care of you."

"Want to see him. . .Billy."

"You two have one track minds. You must have a very strong bond." Duncan smiled but Hannah thought he sounded peeved. Still, when he spoke again it was with kindness. "When you're a little stronger we'll get you back together."

He leaned forward and lowered his voice.

"Billy told me an amazing story about what has happened to you. I wondered if Billy might not have a vivid imagination."

"He doesn't lie," Hannah said.

"No?" Duncan leaned back like an old woman at a coffee klatch who was disappointed that the gossip wasn't juicy. "Then I am amazed you made it this far. Everything happens for a reason, Hannah, so there must be a reason you are here. Believe that. Trust that."

Hannah reached for his hand, more to see if she could make her arm work than to actually touch him. She had so little strength and that hand fell on his knee. She touched denim and the feel of it made her want to cry. He wore jeans, not sackcloth; he talked about God but like a normal human being. He was not scary and he would not hurt them. Duncan pulled a small smile from his inventory and his eyes glowed like a candle flame. He took her hand, cupping it in both of his.

"There you go. That's what I'm talkin' about. Let yourself be. Trust in..."

Before he could finish there was the sound of thunder, but it wasn't coming from outside. Someone was pounding up the stairs like the house was on fire. Duncan turned, tightening his hold on Hannah's hand. Instinctively, she grasped him back. In the next instant, the door flew open, seemingly blown off its hinges as it smashed against the wall.

Billy Zuni filled the doorway. Hannah's name was on his lips. Relief filled his eyes. Then he saw Duncan and the change in him was lightning fast. Billy clenched his fists. His smile faltered, and faded, and a look of utter horror crossed his face. His horror turned to rage, and he threw himself at Duncan, grabbing his wrist, and yanking his hand away from Hannah's.

Hannah cried out. Duncan shot up and stood back. In the next instant he threw himself at Billy. Billy grabbed Duncan's lapels and shook the man who tried to fight him off. Billy was stronger and Billy was angrier. He pushed Duncan back again and again until he was up against the wall.

"She doesn't like to be touched, dude."

11

I tremble. That's all I can do. I don't know this man, Duncan. I only know what he's told me, and it all seemed pretty okay. I believed that he and his friends would take care of us, which I am grateful for. Now here is Billy fighting with a holy guy. There are only two things to think. This man lied when he told me we are safe and Billy knows it. Or, two, something's happened to Billy and he's the freaking crazy guy.

"Billy. Billy."

The word sounded like *Milly,* but it didn't matter what Hannah called him because he couldn't hear her. The two men kept shuffling and moving around the room in some weird guy dance. Glass crunched under their feet. They grunted. They breathed like bulls.

"Billy?"

This time when Hannah said his name it was a cry of disbelief. He heard it in his head, but his body didn't get the message. His hands were wrapped up in Duncan's jacket again, and Duncan's hands were on Billy's arms. Finally, with one huge shove, Billy pushed Duncan away. He was talking as he rushed to the bed.

"I'm here. Hannah. Jesus, Hannah. Jesus. You're awake."

"Billy. Billy." Hannah breathed his name over and over again.

"Ah, heck, Hannah."

Billy does what he didn't want Duncan to do. He touched her and then he stopped. His hand hovered over her head and to the side of her face as if he was afraid even the lightest touch would hurt her. Tears poured from his eyes, and wet his words, and Hannah laughed just a little.

"Look as bad as you?" she mumbled through her swollen lips.

"Worse, man. You look so much worse." He put his forehead on the mattress and let his hand fall onto her shoulder. The last time they touched, flying by one another as the truck tumbled down a mountain, she thought they were saying goodbye. This was a whole lot better. Billy lifted his head. He saw a tear course down her cheek and another hover at the corner of her good eye.

"Awesome, Hannah," he whispered and scooped up the falling one.

That was the same moment that Duncan's hand landed on his shoulder. Billy twirled, one leg up, the other still on the ground.

"Get off me, dude," he growled

Duncan held up his hands, but he didn't back away. He pointed to the floor. "The glass, Billy. You're kneeling on glass."

Billy looked down at the scatter of shards and chunks of glass. A piece had punctured his already swollen knee. He lifted his knee to see the damage done.

"I'll get Teresa to wash that out," Duncan offered.

"No, dude. No, I'm good." He pushed aside the glass on the floor. "Sorry, man. Sorry. I'm sorry for pushing you."

"Thank you, Billy. I appreciate that."

Hannah handed him her towel. He knelt on it to stop the bleeding.

"You just promised to tell me when she woke up," he muttered. "That's all I asked you to do. You know, talk to me dude."

"I heard glass breaking. I thought it was more important to check on Hannah first, don't you?" Duncan pointed to the floor again. "There's more near you. On the left. Do you see it? Billy? Do you see it?"

"I see it. I got it." Billy snapped, his temper barely under control.

"Duncan. That's my name," Duncan reminds him, "Say, 'I see it, Duncan'. I'm sorry, Billy, I've explained that's the way we do things here. We say our names and validate. . "

"I got, it," Billy said. "I'll clean it up – Duncan."

"That's great, Billy. It really is. We don't want anyone else getting hurt. Especially not Hannah." Duncan didn't back off as much as he proved to be the adult on the playground. He picked up the fallen chair and set it right. He pushed the hair out of his eyes. "Sit here, Billy. Sit down so you're not on the glass."

Billy looked at him and at the chair.

"Please," Hannah said.

For her, he sat on the chair. He put the towel over his knee. It hurt like the blazes, but he didn't want Duncan to know that. He was tired of all the help that didn't feel like help at all. Duncan was mightily pleased that everything had worked out.

"I'll leave you if that's alright, Hannah?"

She nodded. Billy smiled at her with his beautiful Billy smile.

"I'll leave the door open," he said. "Hannah, I'm so pleased you are back with us. Maybe now that you're awake, Billy will get some rest. Try to convince him to do that."

"Thank you, Duncan."

Hannah spoke to Duncan, but she was looking at Billy with his splinted hand, his mottled bruises, and skid-mark scrapes. He was pale, his eyes sunken and purple dark.

"I'm so sorry," Hannah whispered. "It's my fault. All of it."

She reached out and Billy scooted his chair closer until his knees were touching the mattress.

"I thought you were a goner," Billy said.

"So happy to see you. So happy," she murmured.

"We're going to get well, Hannah," Billy said. "We'll go home when you're better. I'll get you home. Don't worry. Don't worry."

He leaned ever closer to her. All she could see was Billy until Duncan startled them both.

"Dear Lord, thank you for delivering Hannah and Billy to us. Give us the strength to keep them safe. . ."

Billy stiffened. Hannah looked at Duncan and tried to smile. There is a ripple of pity in the smile Duncan gives back, but Hannah thinks it's directed at Billy more than her.

"I told you, we don't do religion," Billy said.

"There's been a lot of praying for you. Sort of a hard habit to break," Duncan answered.

"It's okay," Hannah said and that was all it took to make him smile and split his face into two happy parts.

"You're welcome." He was about to leave but he had one more thing on his mind. "You're just kids. Someone should have done something more to help you."

He's gone. Billy's shoulders fell, his forehead went into his raised palm as if Duncan's departure was a physical relief. Hannah closed her eyes, but the side of her lips that wasn't swollen tipped up.

Hannah Sheraton has waited a lifetime for someone to say those words. Here, in the middle of Alaska, is a man with half-mast eyes who looked at her, and saw that she was just a kid. That was as much a miracle as being alive.

The little plane dipped, vibrated and rose again, flying smoothly for as long as it took the wind to catch its breath and blow again. Nell took the roller coaster ride in stride. Beside her Andre Guillard, Alaska State Trooper, assigned to accompany the two VIPS from California to the site of the truck crash was out of sorts and didn't care about the weather. He was peeved to be babysitting these folks, unhappy that his supervisor had told him to get over it, and vexed to find himself in this plane.

Behind Andre, Archer looked out the window and gave no indication that the weather bothered him. Behind Nell, Josie Bates looked out the other window. Her lower lip was caught under her top teeth, and her brow was furrowed. She wasn't crazy about the turbulence, but that was nothing compared to the sick feeling she had as she looked at the land below. The Alaskan wilderness was a whole lot of nothing.

From the first call, Alaskan authorities had been clear. Josie Bates should accept the inevitable. Hannah and Billy would not be coming home. The driver of the rig was not only dead; he was dead and dismembered by the elements and animals. Hannah's duffle was found inside the truck, but there was no evidence that Hannah herself had been there at the time of the crash. Ditto with Billy Zuni. And, they were sorry to be blunt, if the teenagers had been inside that truck and miraculously survived, and even more miraculously gotten out of the container, they were most certainly dead by now. Their remains would never be found. That was how formidable the Alaskan wilderness was.

They were sorry.

They wish they could be more optimistic.

They would call if they found anything.
Stay home, Ms. Bates.

That was not an option she told them and then went on to share her plan. First, they would make arrangements for someone to accompany her to the crash site and, second, they would provide unfettered access to their reports. To make sure they did not mistake her intent, Josie pulled rank. The Hermosa Beach PD was the first domino to fall. They had seen the brutality Gjergi Isai was capable of, and they knew that there was a real possibility that others would come from Albania in search of Billy Zuni. No one wanted a reprise of what happened in Hermosa Beach, least of all the Alaskan authorities. When Alaskan authorities did not respond appropriately, The Hermosa Beach PD made contact with their FBI counterparts in the Eastern European Organized Crime Division. The FBI pinged back to the head of the Alaska Bureau of Investigation to inform them that the two missing persons were involved in an international incident.

They further informed Alaska that Ms. Josie Bates had been a government witness at the behest of Senator Ambrose Patri-ota, possibly the next president of the United States, and their cooperation with her would be greatly appreciated. It escaped Alaska's notice that the FBI did not open their own investigation nor did they offer to send agents to assist the Alaska Troopers. They did not offer to reimburse the state of Alaska for time and resources, but the fact that the FBI had taken an interest in this incident seemed to be enough to put Alaska on notice. Thankfully, none of these folks had been informed that Josie Bates was on Senator Ambrose Patriota's hit list and the federal government would probably be happy if she was left in Alaska as bear bait.

The result of all this strong-arming was a promise that Josie Bates could accompany Trooper Andre Guillard who was assigned to collect remains and secure the site. Ms. Bates and her investigator had forty-eight hours to get to Alaska or they would be left behind. Terms were agreed to and here they were in a plane that seemed mighty small in comparison to the never ending sky and the uninhabited land below.

Nell touched Andre's arm and gave him a signal. Andre swiveled and held up five fingers. Josie nodded, and as Andre turned away again Archer brought Josie's hand up to his lips and gave her a kiss for luck.

They both zipped up their jackets and put on their gloves as Nell started the descent. The wind picked up. The plane teeter-tottered and then the wings dipped perilously. Nell flipped switches, swore, swore again, and kept the plane on course through clouds and snow until touching down in a small clearing Josie hadn't been able to see in the never-ending carpet of trees. Nell cut the engines, took off her earphones, turned around, and looked at Josie.

"This is as close as I can get you. I have to leave by three. That gives you seven hours up and back. You good with that?"

Josie nodded. Nell gave Archer an optical prompt. He nodded, too.

"Okay, then. The only way out is the way you came in. Andre?"

The trooper opened the door and said: "Let's do it."

Three tall people piled out of the plane on one side, Nell jumped to the ground on the other. Archer, broadest of them all, squeezed out and hit the ground hard. He shook his head and snapped the collar of his jacket up so that it created a cuff around his chin. He put his hands out for Josie. She held onto one hand even after she was on the ground.

"Pretty unforgiving place," she said.

"I think it's safe to say we're not in Kansas anymore," Archer muttered.

"Don't let it get you down. Soon as we find Dorothy and Toto we're out of here."

Archer chuckled. He didn't think there was a snowball's chance of finding those two kids, but Josie didn't have the word defeat in her vocabulary. She was determined this would be a successful mission. What Josie didn't acknowledge was that success came in many forms. In this case, finding a couple of bodies might have to be considered a win. Archer gave her hand a squeeze and went to help Nell. Josie went to where Andre Guillard was doing the same on the near side.

"That's a lot of gear for a couple hours," Josie said.

"This isn't a sightseeing tour, Ms. Bates." He pulled a pack from the wing compartment. "I have a few things to do up there."

"I get that," she answered. "I just thought it might help if we divvy it up some. We could go faster that way. It's a lot for one man to carry."

"Ever walk in snow, Ms. Bates?" Andre checked the lay of the load inside the first pack.

"I've done my share of skiing," she answered.

"Skiing isn't walking." Andre pulled a second bag from the wing. This one clanked and through the fabric Josie could see the outline of chain links.

"I play beach volleyball," she said. "If I can run across the sand, I think I can handle a little snow."

Andre stopped what he was doing. He rested his weight on one foot and his arm on the wing. He wanted to dislike Josie Bates but it was hard. She wasn't at all what he expected. She had sharp eyes. She pretty much kept to herself and when she asked a question there was a reason. She was a confident and tenacious lady who believed she could handle anything without breaking a sweat. If he were a betting man, Andre would put his money on this trip taking her down a peg or two.

"I grew up on a coast," Andre said. "Florida. I've run on sand. It's not easy. Still, I think you'll find this a little harder."

He slung the larger pack onto his back and stooped to pick up the smaller, heavier one but Josie took hold of it at the same time. He stood up and so did she. The bag was between them.

"Look," she said. "I want to be really clear about why we're here, so you don't think this is some stunt. Hannah is my ward. She is one heroic, gritty girl. I can't begin to describe what she's been through, and not just because of this incident with Gjergy Isai. A lesser person would be dead by now or in an asylum. We're here because she deserves to be given every consideration. We are not here because we don't trust your assessment of the situation so don't take this personally."

"Understood." Andre kept his gaze steady and, though he would have denied it, Josie was sure she saw a wry glint behind his eyes, as if he had heard it all before.

"Yeah. Sure," she mumbled and pulled on the pack again. "I'll take it."

Andre seemed to smile, but it was hard to tell beneath the beard and mustache. She was getting majorly ticked off, but not as ticked off as Andre was getting. He pulled on the pack.

"Trust me. I'll carry it."

"I'd let her have it, Guillard."

Archer and Nell had come around the tail of the plane in time to see the stand off. They distracted Andre just long enough for Josie to take possession of the pack.

"Suit yourself." He stepped aside. "The one you have is the heaviest. If it was my lady, I'd lend a hand."

"Then she probably wouldn't be your lady long," Archer said.

Josie gave him a nod. There was a reason they were going to spend their lives together. He knew when to step back and let her carry the load. She threaded her arms through the harness.

"Which way?" she asked.

Andre started to walk. Josie fell in behind him and Archer pulled up the rear.

"Good luck," Nell called and Josie raised a hand in thanks.

Nell watched until they were out of sight before she set up her own camp. When she was done, as she sat in her small tent, she realized she wasn't wondering about what they were going to find out there. She was thinking how well Andre looked with that woman. She was also thinking how glad she was that he would never notice.

Andre didn't have to look at Josie Bates to know that he had been right about running on sand and trudging through the snow. She had gone further than he expected and done so without complaint, but she was struggling. Archer was the one to call a halt at the second mile mark, but Bates stayed upright, her legs splayed in the snow, her fists tight around the harness, eyes forward.

They rested in silence until Andre started them off again. Forty minutes later they were at the site, and Josie Bates was the first to toss aside her pack. She was already prowling the perimeter of the wreck by the time the men put their loads on the ground. She swished away snow on one of the boxes and noted Andre's markings. When Andre joined her he was efficient and professional, showing her what was left of the driver's body, the point of departure from the road, the chain, and lock on the back of the container, and filling her in on the details of the cargo. She asked about the trucker, and Andre ran it down. His name was Joseph Green. He owned the rig. It was uninsured. There was nothing to indicate who he was hauling for or what his destination was. Andre had someone tracking down the cargo. They had the manufacturer, but they were not showing paperwork for a shipment of those lot numbers.

"Inside job. Maybe a friend of this guy worked for the company and loaded for Green after hours," Archer suggested.

"Could be," Andre agreed. "If that's the case, no one's going to come out of the woodwork and admit it."

"Where do you think he would have been heading?" Josie asked as they all ambled toward the back of the truck again.

"I have no idea. That road up there isn't on any map. I'll have to drive it to see where it ends up. Nell can spot for a while, but we can't get the whole thing from the air. Pretty much it's a guess at this point where it dumps out," Andre said.

"And what about the cargo? What's it used for?" Archer asked.

"Liquid nicotine is used in insecticide. When it's super diluted, it's used in those e-cigarettes. Could be he was just taking this to wherever he lived to dilute it and resell it. He could send it anywhere once he did that. If he didn't do it right, though, he could kill a whole bunch of folks including himself. That stuff is three times more toxic than arsenic."

"Ouch," Archer muttered.

"The general public would never know. I wouldn't," Josie mused. "I just think nicotine is nicotine. They put it in gum, on patches, in cigarettes."

"Inhaling isn't the problem when it's in this form," Andre said. "Get it on your skin or ingest it, and you're in trouble. Vomiting. Seizures. Death. It's fast."

"I haven't heard about any big underground push for this stuff," Archer said and looked at Andre. "You?"

Andre shook his head. "There isn't any because there's no real benefit. You're not going to get high from this, just dead."

"Do you think it might be terrorism? Maybe meant for the water supply," Archer asked. Andre shrugged.

"Your guess is as good as mine."

Josie indicated the container. She was tired of the chemistry lesson. "I'm going inside. Are you good with that?"

"Sure. Just be careful."

Josie motioned to Archer. She was first in, grabbing the sides and hoisting herself up a lot easier than most would do. Archer followed. Andre raised his voice when he heard them head toward the back.

"Don't move anything. Don't touch anything."

While he waited, Andre leaned against a tree, put his hands in his jacket pockets, and watched the beams of their flashlight move through the interior. This little exercise in futility reminded Andre of first responders visiting a sunken ship or a blown up building. All Archer and Josie Bates would find would be twisted metal, tumbled cargo, and terrifying silence. There would be no bodies, and yet death was a certainty. Closure, in Andre's book, was a nice concept but never a reality. The promise of it gave survivors unreasonable hope that they would find something no one else could: words carved into the side of a box or etched onto the floor, a loved one buried but breathing under rubble, clinging to a piece of wood floating in the wide ocean, or hanging from a precipice. That's what survivors envisioned because they had such faith in their loved one's will to live. It was a waste of emotion and time. There would be no happy tears, no miraculous rescue. Even Josie Bates wasn't strong enough to raise the dead or find the lost and that was the only closure she seemed willing to accept.

Tired of waiting, not wanting to interrupt before they reached the only logical conclusion they could, Andre got a plastic bag and a small hand pick and went to collect what he could of the driver's remains. These would be sent to the State Medical Examiner's office in Anchorage for storage until they were claimed – which Andre doubted they ever would be. The rest of him would be collected when the truck was moved. Eventually the bones would be disposed of according to the law and Mr. Green would be forgotten.

Andre had just finished when he heard the sound of the container floor giving. He went to his pack and stored the opaque, zippered bag just as Archer jumped to the ground. Josie followed slowly, but only went as far as the door. She stabilized herself with the angle of her body and one hand that clutched the bent metal frame. Archer put up his hand to help her down. She and Archer locked eyes; Andre kept his on Josie Bates. Andre had to admit she was more than handsome. Few women could look good bundled up in winter clothes, but she did. Few women could handle their disappointment with such grace, but she did. And few women would remain as stubborn as she when everyone was waiting on her.

When Archer turned around and looked at Andre, the trooper shrugged. She was Archer's woman, and he'd have to deal with her until it was time to go. Andre dug into his pack again, and pulled out the things he needed, walked through the snow, over the uneven ground, and dropped the new chain and lock near the container figuring that might get her moving. Josie Bates couldn't take a hint. She scanned the terrain, finally focusing on a point over the men's heads. Archer dropped his hand. Andre made an impatient turn. The day was getting on.

"Ms. Bates," he said. "I've got to secure this site. We have to start back."

"Where's the closest town?" she asked, ignoring Andre's directive.

"There aren't any towns out this far. There's nothing out this far." He indicated the open door. "Do you mind? I've got to inventory and get those boxes back inside."

"Sorry." She moved aside. He climbed in and started counting, but Josie was still talking, and still standing behind him, and still bugging him. "Okay, so where is the nearest human being?"

"Hard to say." His voice came from deep inside the container. She peered through the dark toward the pool of light from his flashlight. He was bent over, pointing to the boxes, counting them off.

"Twenty-two inside." He made a note and walked back to the entrance, ignoring Josie and talking to Archer as he pointed to the snow-covered boxes on the ground. "You want to pass those up here?"

"No problem." Archer handed up the first one while Andre talked more than he had talked in the last three months. Lawyers would ask questions until they got the answer they wanted; Andre figured he would give Josie the truth in the hope that would shut her down.

"People carve spaces out for themselves in Alaska. The farther north they go, the less they want to be found. They live off the land. They don't get permits to hunt. They don't get married or divorced. They just say they're married or divorced, and that makes it so. There are kids up here who have never seen the inside of a school. There are people who come to challenge the great outdoors and disappear into it without a trace. There are cults and communes and whatever else you can imagine. There are no street numbers out here. No neighbors. Nothing."

"So why are they here?" Josie persisted.

Archer handed up another box. Andre took it and walked it back to a stack. The darn things were heavy. His breath blew white as he worked and talked.

"Sometimes they're fugitives. Most times they're just ornery or lonely or a little off their heads. They're folks that can't make it in the real world, so they hunker down behind some tree. For the most part, they are happy." Andre lifted another box and rested a minute. "If you're looking for a city or a town, you won't find it. You might stumble across some squatters settled into what's left of the old mining stations, but you're talking about tiny communities. Five, ten people at the most. They add to the census data when government types can find them, but it's finding them that's the problem."

Andre came back to the front of the container and waited for Archer to bring him the next box. Josie moved out of the way but not out of his face.

"Is that it? Just loners?" she asked.

"There are Inuit villages. The natives move to the river in the summer where they camp, fish, hunt, and stock in for winter." He turned to look at Josie who didn't move back a step as he thought she would. "But, if I'm reading you right, you're asking whether there's a logical place to start looking for those two kids. The answer is no."

Archer handed up the second box. The one Andre had opened on his first pass at the site. Andre checked it. Three vials were missing and now were in the custody of the Public Health Office for analysis.

"There's packing tape in that bag," he directed and Archer obliged. When he found it, he tossed it up. Andre caught it easily, taped the box closed and went to move it, but Josie was in front of him again. He raised an eyebrow as if to ask if she was really going to play this game. She was.

"So, how do you search for someone who is lost in this state? Or, if someone goes missing, do you just kind of chalk them off?"

"When it's called for – and there is a reasonable expectation of success – we alert the troopers to keep their eyes open. Believe me, if we had something solid regarding your kids, we'd be on it. We're not lazy, we're practical and we understand our juris-diction."

He hoisted the box onto a pile, turning his back on her briefly.

"There aren't enough troopers in all of the north to scour this kind of wilderness. We send up planes if we have a solid search area." He paused, and then called out to Archer. "Can you get those two over there? I didn't see them before."

Archer looked around, saw the boxes nearly hidden under the snow, dug them out and carried the top one over.

"Well–" Josie began but Andre was done with speculation. He rested his weight on one leg. He put his hand up on the broken metal. He looked right at her and told her what she needed to hear.

"Look, we don't have a search area, Ms. Bates. All we have is a duffle bag, a cellphone, and no proof that either of the kids you're looking for was in that container."

"There is blood in there," she insisted.

Archer lifted the box up. Andre stepped over, grabbed it, stacked it, and dusted off his hands.

"We don't know who it belongs to, or how it got there, or how long it's been there. Nobody knows because the driver is dead."

"The duffle has Hannah's clothes in it. I can tell you, those are her clothes," Josie insisted.

"The driver could have picked her up anywhere and let her off anywhere." Andre pushed the box to the side. "He could have stolen the duffle. She could have traded it to him for food. He had it. That's a fact." Andre put his hand on his hips wanting nothing more than to finish his work and be done with this exercise in politics. "You're a lawyer, Ms. Bates. You could explain away that bag a hundred ways from Sunday. I'm just a cop, but I can do the same. It's a fact that it was here; it's not evidence of anything."

They stared at one another, the look of determination in Josie's blue eyes was as hard as old ice and Andre's warm, brown eyes were drained of sympathy. It was Archer who broke the standoff.

"Guillard. Hey." Andre set his jaw and gave Josie one last warning look. Archer called again. "Guillard!"

"Yeah. Here." Andre went to the doorway. Archer handed up the last box.

"This one's open," Archer said.

Andre pulled back the flaps. Five vials were missing. He knew he had taken only three samples of the load. Andre located the first box and reopened it, confirmed that was the box from which he had take three vials and taped it up again. When he turned around, he saw Josie crouched down by the second box. He thought he detected a smile when she swung her head his way.

"Someone opened the lock on this truck. Someone besides you took a couple of bottles of this poison. Don't you think there is a good chance whoever did that found those kids, too?" She stood up, put a foot on the open box and pushed it his way. "Now tell me you're just going to let this go."

"Jo," Archer called, but she was in no mood to be messed with. Her head whipped Archer's way.

"Do you want to let it go, too, Archer? Really? All this is just so we can stand here and wonder what in the hell happened? Then what? We go home and stand on the pier and throw a couple of wreaths out onto the water, have a beer at Burt's, and get on with our lives? Or, maybe you think we should wait for them to show up? Is that what you think we should do? Because if you think that. . ."

"Hey! Take a minute," he warned.

Andre turned his back. This wasn't his fight. Even though Archer moved close, Andre could still hear every word.

"Jo, we're out of our depth here. There isn't much we can do with what we have. It would be better if we went back, talked to whoever we need to talk to, and get authorized to search. I'm just saying we need a plan."

Josie stormed back to the opening and held onto that door. She looked down on him, her face a play of anguish and anger.

"How far could they have gotten, Archer? Hurt? Bleeding? With only what they have on their backs? They couldn't have gotten far without help. I'm telling you, they are out there. If someone found them, they would have slowed down because they were hurt. Maybe there's a camp somewhere, or it's one of those people he's been talking about. We can find them. I know we can."

"We don't know how long this wreck has been here," Archer argued.

"It's been at least a week." Andre came up behind her, and Josie whipped around.

"I'm asking for a sweep. Five miles. That's what I want. We came up five miles easy, and we'll go back another route. We can do one leg today. We'll take our best guess which way to go. Two will do that, and one of us will get back to Nell. Archer, you could find your way back, right? Don't you think you could?"

"It's not like jogging on The Strand, Jo," Archer said. "We're in the middle of Alaska. It's dark. It's getting darker. What are we going to do in a few hours when we can't see our hands in front of our face? We don't have a tent. No sleeping bags. No food. Listen to the man. Listen to me. Now, come on. Get down."

Archer put both hands up and crooked his fingers. Josie eyed him as if he had just slapped her. Her chin quivered.

"It's Hannah, and if you don't care. . ." Josie began.

"Don't go there, Jo." Archer stepped back. She was making the ground rules, but he wasn't going to play by them. "Now, come on. I'll help you down if you want, but I won't beg, and Andre isn't going to stand there forever."

Josie's eyes slid to Andre Guillard. Young and handsome, he

was a dedicated trooper, but he had no real skin in this game. She appreciated what he was saying. He was warning her off in the same way she would warn a client away from uncharted territory. This was his truth and his truth was that to search was futile. Archer was offering something in the middle, and both men waited for her to choose one option or the other.

Andre jumped off the container, picked up the chain and lock from the ground. "I've got to close this up."

Josie didn't care what he had to do or that Archer was angry with her. The good news was that Archer didn't turn his back on her. She stood on her crumpled perch, looking into the gun metal-colored afternoon. The wind was stronger, and it pushed the cold through every exposed inch of her skin. What did that Alaska cold feel like in the dead of night? How dark was dark in Alaska? How terrifying was it to listen to things moving and be unable to figure out what or where they were? Worse yet was to hear absolute silence lying in absolute dark. Josie knew what that was like, and she wouldn't wish that kind of terror on anyone. Now she squinted into the distance and saw what the two men could not: a slim thread of hope running through the trees and across the snow.

Instead of stepping down, Josie went back inside the container. The flashlight beam bobbed, then stopped, and then start moving again. When Josie reappeared she had a ragged piece of bloodstained cardboard in one hand and in the other a piece of yellow material.

"I ripped one of your boxes," she said to Andre. "But I didn't do anything to the bottles inside. I found this fabric. There's blood on it. It needs to be tested. We have DNA from both Billy and Hannah to check it against."

She jumped down from the truck.

Archer asked, "Are you ready to go back now?"

"Sure. Why not." Josie grabbed the pack and put her evidence in the side pocket.

Archer picked up his gear. Andre pushed the metal door shut. It groaned and clanged. He threaded the new chain through the handles twice, secured the lock and posted the warning that it was a crime to tamper with the vehicle. When he was done, he picked up the pack with a bag of bones inside. Josie started to walk before either of the men and Archer spoke to her back.

"We'll talk to Andre's commander, and we'll get this figured out, Jo."

"You do that, Archer. I'm going to talk to Nell. I want to see a little more of Alaska than Trooper Guillard is willing to show me."

Josie paused, adjusted her pack, and let Andre go on ahead of her. He took the lead not liking her at his back anymore than he liked her walking ahead of him. The last time he'd seen a female act like this she was covered in fur, on her hind legs, and ready to devour the guy who was messing with her cub.

Yep, a mama grizzly was almost as ornery, single minded, and scary as Josie Bates.

12

Ham and bacon.

That was what Melody brought up the stairs every night. In the morning she only brought bacon. She brought the blue plate because that was what Pea preferred. Melody had tried to make Pea eat a bit of vegetable or sweets, but Pea would have none of it. Melody tried to talk to Pea, but the most she got was a trill or a pretty burp. Though it was well known that Pea spoke only to Duncan, Melody was sure if she were kind enough, nice enough, patient enough, Pea would speak to her, too. If that happened then she would be worthy of Duncan. The circle was obvious. She would be a good servant, atone, be blessed for her efforts, and healed by Duncan who would then take her for his own. It was so simple, so long in coming, and now, seemingly, out of reach because Hannah and Billy had caught Duncan's attention – or rather Hannah had.

Melody made the turn on the second landing and started up the next flight of stairs, and thought about Billy. The sheets of his bed were tangled as if his sleep was always disturbed. She saw him looking out the window of Duncan's house where he stayed, watching the big house, waiting. She had seen him go to the river to look at the water and ask about the ice that had formed up against the banks. Robert said he had to chase him off the boat, and Glenn said he could hardly get his wood split with all the questions Billy asked. Teresa fed him, but he sat at the table with his head in his hand, watching them all. He especially watched Duncan.

It had only been a few days since Robert brought these two back from that wreck and already their world was tilted. It seemed to Melody everyone was leaning different ways trying to right it. She knew one way to make it right. Duncan should set a date for the healing.

Just as she thought she would like that interrupted conversation to begin again, Melody stumbled. The plate wobbled, the napkin slipped and the scent of the grease made her suddenly sick.

Twice a day she climbed these stairs and smelled this smell. She used to think Duncan had only chosen her because Pea was her temptation, but now Melody thought it was because she was the only one willing to climb this many stairs. On top of that, she was beginning to think that Pea wasn't really all that. It was Duncan who spoke to them. None of them ever heard Pea say a word; most of them forgot the woman even existed. Melody wondered what would happen if she didn't bring food. Would Pea come down when she was hungry? Would God feed her? Maybe she would starve to death.

Melody stopped thinking. Disrespect could send her back down the chute of forgiveness. She may have her doubts about Pea, but she had no doubts about Duncan's ability to heal her and that was what was important.

At the top of the stairs Melody paused, and listened. She heard nothing from Hannah's room. Melody's forehead was so furrowed, her jaw so tight, it hurt. She had only felt like this once before – rebellious and bloated with jealousy – and that hadn't turned out real well.

She put the blue plate down in front of Pea's door, twisted the knob so that it unlatched, and then picked up the plate again. She pushed the door open with her hip, went inside, and closed it with her shoulder as she had done every morning and evening for the last two years. And, as she had done since the first time she entered this room, Melody took a moment just to 'be' in this place.

In the far corner was a large bed covered with a quilt the color of marigolds. It was the largest bed of any in the house, and the softest, and the highest. At night, Pea's head rested on a down pillow. On the floor was a rag rug, a rich braid of brown and mahogany and black that looked like a native woman's hair. The hardwood floor was smooth and fitted tongue and groove unlike the rough-hewn boards in the rest of the house. There were pillows on top of the rug, and each was large enough to lie upon. At the other end of the room was a fireplace, but no fire ever burned there. It was a shrine to a sculpture of a beating heart struck through with a sword. It was the heart of Christ that Duncan had carved out of wood. He set it in the hearth because it symbolized that such a heart was impervious to the flame. The room was heated by a potbellied stove, the grate hidden by a beautiful, intricately constructed tin cabinet that kept Pea from burning her fingers or catching her long hair on fire.

By the bed was a lamp with a stained glass shade. One of the panes was broken. When the light was turned on the lamp looked like a lighthouse with a single beam of pure, white light shining for those lost on the endless ocean of sin. There was a cracked pitcher and a flowered ceramic bowl atop a wooden chest that they had found in the attic. There was a hairbrush made of whalebone that Teresa used to brush Pea's long, long hair. Lace drapes faded to yellow covered windows that never opened. Pea's world was perpetually dark, and to keep the summer light away wooden panels secured by intricately designed iron hasps were attached to the sills. The wood and walls became an art gallery for Duncan's paintings: Christ on rivers, Christ on mountains, Christ melting under a desert sun, Christ rising from a mob of adoring people of all races.

And he drew women.

Women with beatific eyes turned heavenward or women with humble eyes turned toward the earth. Women with their hands crossed over their breasts and women with their arms open. Melody would live in this room forever if she could. If she had to die, she would like to die in this room. But this room wasn't hers, and if the only way to get a room like this were to be like Pea then Melody would pass.

When her arm began to quiver, Melody realized that she had been leaning against the closed door longer than she thought. It was hard to be as dutiful as Melody. Perhaps it was hard on Pea to be so *Within,* but Melody would bet it was harder to have her chores than to simply commune with God all day. She called out:

"I'm here, Pea. Come out now, Pea."

Melody was annoyed to have to say this silly nonsense, but she did it anyway. Nobody could be so *Within* that they didn't hear a door open. Even dogs knew when they were going to be fed. Still, Pea did as Pea always did: Nothing. Melody did as Melody always did: announced herself, walked to the middle of the room, knelt on the red pillow, and set the plate in the middle of the rug. When that was done, Melody took a deep breath.

"Come out now, Pea."

Melody's call was only an expression because Pea was right there in front of her. The woman knelt on the purple pillow as she always did at dinnertime. At breakfast, she knelt on the yellow pillow. All this was done so that Pea was never upset.

Looking at her, it was hard to imagine she could be upset by anything.

Pea was on her knees, her arms spread wide, her hands flat on the rug, her head bowed, and her long black hair hanging straight over her face. She wore a white gown that covered her from shoulder to toe. And Pea was always and forever *Within* which meant that Melody could amuse herself any old way she liked and never bother the woman.

"Did Duncan tell you about the girl and boy, Pea?"

Melody took the covering from the plate of food.

"Robert thinks they are like you and Duncan. I don't think so. They don't look alike. Not that they would have to, of course. But she's dark, you know."

Melody arranged the bacon straight again since it had been jostled on the way up the stairs.

"I think they are lovers. Duncan says no. Teresa says they are running away from something awful. She says someone is trying to kill them. I can't imagine what they did that would make someone want to kill them. I don't think they did anything bad, really, but Teresa says they must have done something to be locked in the back of a truck and left for dead. Oh, and they came all the way from California. From the beach. Who would do that if they hadn't done something awful? I'd love to go to the beach. If I looked different, that is."

Melody pushed the plate forward, not expecting a response but hoping for one. Just once. Just to make things a little more interesting. She nudged the plate forward again.

"You have to eat now, Pea. I have things to do. There's more work with two extra people. Please, Pea. Eat now."

Melody tried not to sound irritated, but she did. What she didn't know was whether or not Pea understood or cared. Teresa said Pea knew everything. Teresa said Pea's every sense was a thousand times greater than any human being. Teresa said that

Pea was so *Within* and content that she could not bear to come out and into the world. But that was Teresa talking. Teresa said that Pea used to speak to her, but Melody didn't believe it.

"Pea? Please."

If silence was golden then Pea was cast in 24 karat. Melody suffocated under the weight of her silence. When she thought she couldn't stand one more second in the presence of this woman, Pea's right hand twitched, and Melody's heart quickened. She was not immune to the magic of Pea as much as she would like to think she was. Melody leaned forward as she always did; her eyes went to Pea's right hand as they always did.

The woman's thumb moved and then the pointer and the middle finger. Finally, all the fingers on that hand arched until the hand itself resembled a spidery, spindle-legged thing with a life of its own. That hand walked over the rug at a right angle but before Pea touched her hip, the hand moved at another right angle and spider-walked toward the plate. One finger touched the pottery tentatively as if expecting it to be hot. When it was not, another joined it and then another until three fingers skittered over the plate and took up a piece of bacon.

The bacon disappeared under the long fall of black hair. Back came the fingers. Up went the bacon. Five times this happened and then the two rounds of ham. Melody strained to catch just a glimpse of the woman's face.

The one time Melody tried to part her hair so Pea could see who brought her food each day, the woman lashed out. She was crazy strong, slapping and biting at Melody. All the while, her head hung down, and her face remained hidden, and the only sound from Pea was a brutal belch followed by snake-like hiss. By the time Melody got help, Pea was *Within* again, and Melody was in *Hours* where she prayed that her sin of trespass against Pea would be forgiven. Now Melody sat and watched Pea eat.

When the last piece of bacon was gone and Pea was still

again, Melody washed Pea's fingers with the little cloth she carried in her pocket, picked up the plate, and started to leave the room. In a few hours Teresa would bathe her, dress her, and lay Pea down to sleep. In the morning this would start all over again.

As she turned her back, Melody heard the click and the whirl and trill of noises that signaled Pea was back in whatever world she inhabited. Melody put down the plate, opened the door, picked up the plate, and was almost through the door when she heard something different.

Melody listened more closely. When she was sure the sound had not come from Hannah's room, she bent her knees and put the plate down. Slowly, she turned and opened the door wider. She peered through the gloom. Pea was as Pea always was: hands on the floor, white gown cascading around her prone figure, dark hair covering her face.

"What, Pea? What?"

Melody inched into the room. Though she didn't think it was possible, the house had become even more still: no clatter of Teresa's pans downstairs, no thump of Glenn's ax as he perpetually chopped his wood, no moaning from Hannah as she turned in her bed. In all her years, Melody imagined very little except how it would feel to be loved. Now she imagined she had heard Pea speak. Melody tilted her head and took another step toward Pea. She shut the door with the greatest care.

She prayed that Duncan would not disturb them because the import of this moment was not lost on her. If Pea had spoken to her then didn't it follow that Melody was blessed? Didn't it follow that if Pea spoke to Duncan, and Pea spoke to Melody, then Melody and Duncan were joined in blessedness, bound together for eternity in the service of Pea? Melody's heart, so dried up and unused, could accept no other logic; her brain, so single minded and hopeful, could entertain no other explanation.

Careful not to move too quickly, Melody slid across the slick floor, lowered herself to the ground, and was on her knees in front of Pea once again. The woman was clicking like the tick of a second hand and then she trilled a scale. Melody pulled back, confused and disappointed. They weren't heading in the right direction. Still, she had heard something, she was sure of it.

Melody put her hand on the floor, ready to push herself upright and run to get Duncan. If Pea was going to speak, she should speak to Duncan. But Melody didn't push herself up. She didn't leave the room or run lightly down the stairs to get Duncan because this could be nothing more than Melody's wishful thinking. Or it could be a little trick of the silence. Possibly it was nothing more than the wind in the eaves or the house settling. Duncan disliked hysteria. He would not think more highly of Melody if she ran to him with tales, and that was why she leaned closer to Pea. Not close enough to touch her, but close enough to hear if she decided to say a word again. Melody's breath was almost gone; her heart was nearly beaten to pulp; her brain was filled up with as much anticipation as it could handle.

"Come out, Pea," she whispered.

Pea trilled.

Melody licked her lips. Ten seconds. That's what she would give Pea.

One second. Two. Three. Four. Five.

Melody could feel the hardwood beneath the pillow where she knelt waiting on Pea.

Six. Seven.

Melody felt the warmth from the stove turn to heat. She began to sweat. Still Pea said nothing.

Eight seconds.

Melody put her hand on the floor, ready to rise and leave.
Nine.

Her heart fell. She was no more special in this moment than she had been when she walked through the door. Melody stood up and looked down on the girl/woman's finely shaped head and counted the last second.

Ten.

Melody turned toward the door. Before she could take a step, she heard:

"Numbers 12:1"

Melody stopped. Her shoulders slumped. Her head fell back. She listened.

"Numbers 12:1"

Melody turned, sank to her knees, placed her hand flat on the floor and bowed her head. She listened to the seconds marked not by Pea's click and whirl, but by the voice of God himself.

"Numbers 12:1"

Mama Cecilia ate Cheerios. On the yellow box there was a picture of a little boy holding up a spoon filled with Cheerios, and in front of him was a bowl filled with more Cheerios. It seemed to Mama Cecilia that Cheerios made the boy very happy. Perhaps, she thought, she did not feed her son enough Cheerios and that was why he had been so unhappy. She doubted the wisdom of this, but that was how her thoughts went since her son had left and was now away for longer than ever before.

Mama finished her Cheerios and closed up the box. She washed her bowl, and put it to dry. Then, as she had done each day since her son had gone, Mama put on her *amaut* and her good moccasins. Usually, she would go to look for him, but this was not daytime. This was evening, and it was too dark to look for anything much less a son. Still, she had a place to go and a plan. She would go to Oki. The *Angakoqus*. The shaman.

Before she left, Mama Cecilia looked in her drawer and found a very sharp knife with a white handle. The knife looked like ivory, but it was not. Still, it looked like ivory and that was better than not looking like ivory. She put the knife into her deep pocket and left the house.

One small foot was put in front of the other, her plump hands hung at her sides, her back was straight, and her hair braid was so tight it did not even swing with her walking. It was a long while and far away, but eventually she was at Oki's house. He was old, so one would think he would not work any longer yet he did. One did not simply stop being a shaman any more than one stopped being a mother.

Mama Cecilia knocked on the door of his house. It was a nice house, bigger than Mama's and painted only five years earlier by a man with a camera that had come to make a film about Oki. The man never sent the movie to Oki, so no one was sure if he was in it or not. Still, his house had been painted a beautiful blue. Blue like the ocean and not like the river. Eventually, Oki came to answer her knock. He opened the door, not too fast or too slow. He was not surprised to see her, or at least it did not sound like he was surprised when he said:

"It is you, Cecilia."

"Yes, Oki. I have come for your help, please."

"I have my program." He opened the door wider so that she could see the television. People were dressed in funny clothes and seemed to be yelling at one another as well as at the man with the microphone.

"I see, Oki, but perhaps you might make an exception. I have brought you this."

Mama Cecilia took the knife from her pocket. It was best to bring something to the shaman to show your gratitude. She held the knife on the palms of both hands for him to take. He inclined his head this way; he cocked it that way. Finally, he took her gift.

"It is a fine knife, Cecilia."

When he motioned to her, she followed him into his house. The room where he spent his time was full of things: books and papers, an easy chair, a bench, a couch and a table. On the table there were Oki's things: cigarettes, a lighter, a glass to drink from, and glasses for his eyes. There was a lamp carved like an eagle that Mama liked very much.

From the small table by the easy chair, Oki picked up the remote and pointed it at the television. The screaming people in strange clothes disappeared. He sighed a little as if he missed them. Oki put the remote on the table and the knife in a table drawer.

"You wait a little," he said.

Mama did just that. She did not sit. She did not touch his things. She did not look at the pictures on the wall. She did not unfasten her *amaut*. When Oki called, she went to the back room.

This was a small space with two chairs and a table. There was a curtain and Oki was behind the curtain. Mama Cecilia sat down and put her hands in her lap. On the table was a large stone. It had a name and that name was Labradorite, but Mama did not know that name. She only knew that it was frozen fire fallen from the Aurora Borealis, and it was very precious and important to Oki's work. There were also two carvings: one of the wolf and one of the bear; one made of wood and the other of stone.

Suddenly, Mama Cecilia heard a moan and a cry. The curtain shook and in only a moment Oki appeared. On his shoulders was a cape of hide and needles. There was a hat upon his head. His old face was streaked with red.

"The spirits are warring," Oki exclaimed. He pointed to his face. "Is this not the proof that there is war?"

Mama Cecilia nodded but only in her brain. It was not her way to answer questions that had obvious answers. She saw the red upon his face. That was proof of the spirit war although Mama Cecilia knew this was not truly spirit blood. Oki had rubbed something red on his face. Mama also knew the brain was a feeble thing; it was the heart that was the center of all knowledge. She believed the spirits were at war because he said so, and because bad things had been visited upon her house, and because her heart hurt. She blinked once as Oki turned in a slow circle. When he came back, he rose up a bit, raised one crooked old finger, and narrowed his crinkled eyes.

"The bear says to the wind, 'can you not blow the other way so I can smell who it is that hunts me?'" Oki turned full circle. He raised a crooked finger on the other hand. "And the wind says to the bear, 'I can blow but one way, the way I am meant to blow. You must wait until you can smell the hunter. Until then you will use your eyes and your ears to find the one who hunts'."

Oki sang a bit and danced a little, and when he was done with his trance, he sat across from Mama Cecilia and picked up the frozen colors fallen from the Aurora Borealis. The stone helped him see into the future.

"I know what you wish to find, Cecilia," Oki said.

"Yes, I am looking for my—"

"Do not name the person you are looking for," he admonished.

For a moment, Mama Cecilia's motherly longing interfered with her good sense. She knew that it was wrong to name the thing you wanted to be told about. The bad spirits were all around. Some were looking to harm that thing that should not be named. She did not want her son harmed. She did not want anyone harmed. Mama put her lips together tightly so the bad spirits would not hear her ask for her son.

"I will tell you this. In the war there are survivors, Cecilia. As with all wars, there is a victor and one who is not a victor. Even in the spirit world. There are the deer and there are the wolves. Sometimes the victor is swift and other times the victor is strong."

Oki sat back. He slipped the hat from his head and slowly took away the cloak of hide and needles. He looked very tired as if he had just traveled a great distance. His old face was lined deeper for the spirit war, his black hair seemed dull but the silver in it still shined. He was a shaman for a while, but now he was once again a man who liked to see the people on television. That was fine. He had told Mama Cecilia what she needed to know.

"Thank you, Oki, for showing me the way. I will use my eyes and not just my nose. I will not worry about the wind and which way it blows. I think I will win the war."

"I think, Cecilia, you did not need me to tell you that," he answered.

"Still, it is good to know the spirits have spoken to me through you," she answered politely, with gratitude and respect.

"Not many believe any more," he lamented. The stuff on his face no longer looked like battle wounds but like rivers of red tears.

Mama said nothing. Oki spoke the truth and when the truth was spoken there were no extra words that would make it truer.

Mama Cecilia left the house that was painted the blue of the ocean and walked toward her own house again. Even though the evening was gone and it was now dark night, even though there were no lights to guide her way except for the moonshine, even though the snow had started to fall again, she did not hurry on her long way.

The walk home was easier than the walk to Oki's house because she did not walk in sadness. Mama Cecilia had heard in her deepest heart Oki's words and understood them in her deepest brain. She did not lift her head to the wind in the hopes of catching the scent of her son. Instead, she used her eyes and started to look closely at the forest and trees and dirt and mountains. She listened for their spirits to tell her if he had passed their way. If she did not find him that day, she would look again tomorrow and the next day because her moccasins could take her a long way.

Now she knew that looking and listening was what she must do.

13

I don't feel like myself in this place. I don't know who I am. I smile and that bothers Billy, but it makes Melody happy. Duncan and Teresa, too. Funny, I think of them as my friends. I've been wondering why I feel this way. I think it's because I didn't have to save them, or follow them, or watch them get hurt. It's not like being with my mom who was always a train wreck waiting to happen; it's not like being with Josie whose goodness brought the train wreck to her.

This is like something new just for me and Billy. We are outsiders, but they don't think we're weird because we don't do the religious thing and we don't think they're weird because they do. Nothing is better than being with people who just are what they are.

But I don't think being here makes Billy happy. No matter how much I want him to be, he isn't. He should be, but he isn't.

"What do you think?"

Hannah held her arms out and kicked up one leg. The other one was a rock of concrete from knee to ankle. The thing was ugly and rough as a potholed road. Billy had freaked when he first saw it, but Hannah wasn't upset and that freaked Billy even more. It was like she went into the truck one person and came out another. She wasn't guarded, or suspicious, or looking for options and ways out. She was just grateful that the people who found them knew what to do about her leg; Billy was worried that it would be seriously screwed up by the time they got to a doctor. These were just regular people no matter how much they talked about God, and what did they know about broken legs? That, Hannah pointed out when she was awake for more than fifteen minutes at a time, was exactly the point: there was no doctor, there was no way out of this place, they were stuck for the duration. They had done what they set out to do. They had reached the ends of the earth. The fact that they arrived smashed to pieces hadn't been in the plan, but they had survived.

"Billy? Billy? What are you looking at?" Tired of holding out her arms, tired of trying to distract him, she flopped them down.

"I hate the cold and it always feels like it's midnight around here." His forehead was against the window, and his good hand was flat on the wall. Billy wasn't really thinking about the weather. He was thinking about her. "I thought you were going to, you know, die."

"I know," she answered. "I do know."

"What would I have done if you died, Hannah?"

"But I didn't. You kept me alive. That was incredible, Billy." Hannah said this too quickly, too brightly, as if she were giving the dirt on the floor a quick flick under the rug so she could pretend everything was tidy. "So? Come on. What do you think of the stuff Melody lent me? Billy, look. Please, look."

Hannah put her arms out again. Billy looked. He smirked. She tried to smile, and that was funnier still. He planted his butt on the windowsill.

"You look like that lady on the pancake mix box."

"Aunt Jemima is a hundred years old," Hannah said.

"Naw, they drew a new one. She's really good looking. I mean, she still looks like Aunt Jemima but she's maybe twenty." Billy hooked his good thumb in the front of the old pants he was wearing. They were too short for him and too wide, but he didn't seem to mind. "We ate those pancakes all the time at home."

"Do you miss your sister?" Hannah asked.

"I try not to think about her. The way she was the last time, you know, wasn't really a good memory." He drifted away to a terrible place and then pulled himself back again. "Anyway, you're like the new babe Aunt Jemima."

Billy shook back his hair. The shadows under his eyes, the furrows on his forehead, and his bruised skin, made him look older, exhausted, and despairing. He couldn't be still unless he was sitting beside Hannah's bed. Now that she was starting to move, and he couldn't find a comfortable place to be. He pushed off the sill and plopped himself on the braided rug beside the bed, stretched out his legs, and leaned back on his elbows. He used to sit like that in Josie's house. In the old days, Hannah tried to ignore him. Now she couldn't imagine being without him.

"What do you think the girls at school would say if they could see me like this? Not that it matters. That was a thousand years ago anyway. All that stuff... Stupid...." Hannah laughed a little and realized she didn't want to think about home either. Going back was never, ever good. "What's with all the high necks and long sleeves?"

She pulled at the material in the full skirt that fell below her knees. She plucked at the cuffs on the purple blouse printed with tiny yellow flowers. She missed her flowing tops, her bling, her jeans that fit like a second skin, but she appreciated what Melody had done for her. The kindness of giving so much when these people had so little did not escape Hannah's notice.

"Everybody here is really, like, modest and stuff," Billy said. "They're Amish, I think."

"No. They're kind of born again but with their own religion," Hannah said. "Duncan told me they believe that if you face your sins head on and resist the temptation to sin again, then you earn being healed by God. So, I guess my mom would have to stay with me twenty-four seven if she wanted to get into heaven."

"My sister didn't have any sins. She's in heaven."

"I was just saying what these people believe." Hannah took a deep breath and walked herself back to a safe topic. "Melody said my clothes were trashed. Did you see them?"

"She's going to try to sew up your jeans, but she's still trying to get the blood stains out. She didn't think you'd want to see the blood stains."

"That's nice of her," Hannah said. "And I'm not laughing at these clothes, you know. I'm not laughing at anything. I'm really grateful."

"I know." Billy's head tilted to one side as he mirrored her. "They saved your boots, but it's going to be a while before you can put shoes on. Well, one at least."

"No kidding. This thing is tight. I think it's cutting off my circulation," Hannah laughed. "The socks aren't bad. They're warm."

"Teresa knit those. She can do anything."

"You like her." Hannah tired to find a bright spot for him.

"She's okay," he admitted.

"So, can we go now?" she begged. "Please, Billy. I have to get out of this room."

Billy curled himself up, got to his knees, and walked on them until he was at her feet. He smoothed the wide, shapeless skirt and then put his hands on Hannah's knees. He looked her in the eye.

"We should go home. We need to go home."

Hannah's spine stiffened. His touch felt intimate and that wasn't good. Billy was her history. Their boundaries were set so long ago that Hannah didn't want to blur them. She could count on his affection, but she couldn't count on him to keep her safe. That was why she wanted to stay. They were both safe here.

"If we go home, then what was all this for, Billy? Really, what?"

"I don't know anymore, Hannah. I really don't."

"It was for you. I mean, I know it was for me, too. I do know that, but mostly it was for you." Hannah moved his hands away.

He fell back on his heels, defeated and then Billy pushed himself off the floor. The window drew him back time and again. But he wasn't seeing what he wanted to see. The perpetual night was a solid wall to him while Hannah thought of it as a cloak. He had never been moody, but now he was. He had never whined, but now he did. Hannah didn't know what to say, so she struggled to stand up instead. Her first step was for balance. Her second step was a 'thunk' of a heavy foot as her casted leg came down hard. Billy whirled around and reached for her.

"Hannah. Don't–"

"It's fine."

She had taken more steps without him in her life, and been more injured than this, but he looked so horrified now that Hannah took his hand. When she was beside him and looking out the window, he said:

"Why do you think you can do everything by yourself, Hannah?"

"Because there never was anyone to help?"

"I don't think you look very hard for people to help you," he answered.

They stood side by side and Hannah wondered if he was right. Not that it mattered now. They didn't have to look for people to help, they had a whole bunch of them waiting just outside the door. This minute, though, they only needed each other. The snow sparkled in the moonlight. Hannah didn't mind that Billy's little finger was petting hers. He always needed to be tethered, and maybe she did, too. Just the littlest bit.

"Josie would come for us if I could call her," he said.

"But there isn't any way to do that. Duncan says we're here for the winter." Hannah reminded him. "Besides, we should let her have some peace."

"You really think that's what she wants?" Billy asked.

"Maybe she deserves it." Hannah glanced at him and even she knew that was lame. Next thing out of her mouth was the truth. "We deserve it. It's been a long run. If it was easy to get out of here, then it would be easy to get in. It isn't and that means Gjergy Isai will give up."

"I think he already has."

Billy faced her, but Hannah couldn't look him in the eye. She could barely breathe with him so close and the night so quiet, but Billy was on a roll and didn't notice.

"I think we got kind of hysterical. Nobody would chase us that long. And I'm just so tired, Hannah. If we can't go home, I want to go somewhere with you. All these people creep me out."

"We have a long way to go before we're strong enough to be on our own."

Billy shook his head. Hannah caught the swing of his hair out of the corner of her eye but then his hands were on her, turning her, squeezing her arms until she paid attention to him. Hannah's eyes dropped and then her chin dipped. She stared at his chest and thought it was strange to feel so small beside him.

"Hannah, listen. It's more than the accident. I can't sleep. I don't sleep."

He gave her a little shake. When he did that, her head snapped up. Not because she was feeling that familiar anger but because she felt so sad that he didn't understand they had fallen in a soft place. She wanted him to rest with her. Here. For a little while.

"You've been worried about me too much and not about yourself," she said. "You have to–"

"No, No. You're not getting it." He let her go. He put his hands to his face and rubbed as if it would wake him from a dream. "It's something they're giving me. Medicine, or something in the food, or – "

"No, they're not." Hannah put her hand on his arm, her fingers hooking into the open work of the old sweater he was wearing.

"We're just on another planet, that's all," she insisted. "We've got to get used to the atmosphere."

"Maybe you're right."

Billy shook his head. He didn't know where he should look. He couldn't look at Hannah without his heart breaking. He was tired of the window because there was nothing to see. He was tired of closed doors, because even if they opened there was only another room beyond the one he was in. If he started to run, he wouldn't know which way to go. Instead of sand, Billy saw snow; instead of being warm, he was freezing; instead of days that give up the ghost in a golden haze over a green/blue ocean, the night never ended and the day never began. Instead of the sweet familiarity of Hermosa Beach where he wandered at any hour, he was surrounded by forests and boxed in by mountains.

"I liked it better the way it was." His sad smile took a lot of effort. "Just us, Hannah, until we get back to Josie and Archer. That's the way it should be."

"I always thought I was the one who didn't like people." She gave his sweater a little tug. Billy frowned.

"What's with you, Hannah? You're like, just. . . I don't know. You're just like all given up." He waited for her to change back to the person he had followed to the ends of the earth. When she didn't, he said: "I don't want to get buried here."

"We can wait out the spring. I like it here, Billy. Please. It's just a few months."

"It's Duncan," Billy blurted out. "He gets up. He prays. He moves around and I'm afraid to close my eyes."

"What do you think he'll do?"

Billy shook his head. He had no answer. "I just can't sleep with him around."

"Well, that's all I do," she muttered. "We're a pair, huh?"

"Yeah, I guess," he mumbled.

"We're both awake now, so can we get something to eat?"

"I want you to tell Duncan I should move in here with you. I'll sleep on the floor. I could sleep if I was near you," Billy insisted.

Hannah was going to tell him that she didn't think that would be a good idea. The rules of the house were clear: men didn't go into women's room. Then another thought crossed her mind. Billy was too concerned about sleep, too concerned about being separated, too concerned about Duncan.

"Did someone do something to you, Billy?"

"Naw, nothing like, man." His shoulders dropped. She missed the point. "It's like I'm alone all the time and never alone. I don't know how to explain it."

"Then maybe we should just go have some dinner." Hannah did a quarter turn. She stumbled before she could take her first step. Billy caught her.

"And I'm not making stuff up," Billy insisted. "Duncan's an ass. Everyone does whatever he says."

"You do everything I say," Hannah answered and Billy went cold.

"I always thought we worked together, dude."

The blood that flooded Hannah's cheeks was hot, and her

shame was instantaneous. What happened to his sister had given him good reason to follow whoever was willing to lead, and she was the one who volunteered. Hannah thought she was noble; now she knew she had been arrogant and cruel.

"I'm sorry." Hannah leaned into him and put her cheek on his chest and her arm around his waist. "I'm so sorry. I didn't mean it."

Billy closed his eyes, hardly hearing her. She was nestled against him, and he wanted to put his arms tight around her in the worst way. Instead, he held her away.

"Forget it. Let's go downstairs. Just remember they aren't all like Melody and Teresa."

Before Hannah could ask him what he's talking about, Billy swept her into his arms. She threw hers around his neck and put her stitched head against his bruised jaw. When he opened the door, Hannah saw the world was bigger than the attic room again and she was happy.

There was wainscoting and faded cabbage rose wallpaper. The stairs creaked beneath their weight. The house's scent was layered like food in a pantry: toasted stuff, syrup, spice, soot, and sweat all closed up too long together. The finials on the bannister were carved to look like pineapples; the carpet runner was ancient. Patches of wood shined through it like a hint of a baldhead under a deceptive sweep of once luxurious hair. The smell of food and burning wood rose to meet them. There was a pop and snap of a crackling fire, and better than anything, the sounds of conversation rolled their way when they reached the ground floor.

There was no door to the dining room, just a huge opening in the plaster wall that was framed by stained lumber. Billy walked through it like he was taking a hill; as if he feared he would retreat if he hesitated. The conversation stopped.

Hannah looked at the people looking back at her. She

started to smile the way a person does when they're the new kid at school – tentatively, hopeful that she would be liked. Then, like the new kid at school, the blur of excitement was gone, and Hannah saw everyone clearly and what she saw took her breath away.

These people around the table – each and every one of them – were broken.

14

Duncan stood up and the others put their hands in their laps.

This was the first time Hannah had seen him in living color instead of through the shadows of her room. He was artist-pale and slope-eyed, but she could see that his eyes were hazel-clear like topaz. He smiled that fantastic smile and the more he did it, the tighter Billy held her.

"Well, well. This is wonderful," Duncan said. "Truly. Wonderful to have Hannah with us. Everyone stand. Everyone."

Everyone stood up but Hannah kept her eyes on Duncan, the most normal person in the room. He wore a plaid shirt and skinny jeans and cardigan. Downstairs the house was chilly and warm in waves depending on the proximity to a stove, so it didn't surprise Hannah that he was layered up. It was the rest – the style of Duncan – that was kind of cool. His hair was short in the back with a long fringe of soft, dark, blond-streaked hair hanging across his forehead. It covered one artistically arched eyebrow. His lips were wide and strong but stained by nature to a beautiful rose color. His skin was as translucent as alabaster. He looked like a young man in a medieval painting. Back home he'd be a hipster. Here, he was leader of the pack, the choir director, the warm and welcoming host who acted as if nothing was wrong.

Which it wasn't.

Not really.

Now, though, Hannah understood what was wrong with Billy. The beautiful, golden beach boy was in an alternate universe and not just on another planet. Everyone in this house was flawed and it made him feel guilty that he was not. Not that Duncan noticed Billy's discomfort or Hannah's surprise. He just kept on keeping on.

"This is wonderful to see you downstairs."

Duncan was still enthusing and when he raised his arms everyone around the big table clapped. Some of them didn't do it as well as others. Melody didn't do it well. Duncan lowered his hand and that was a signal, too.

"Sit, everyone. Sit down. Hannah and Billy, we've saved you these places. Here, sit next to me. Come on now. This is such a wonderful moment. We hoped you would come down tonight. You look wonderful, Hannah."

Duncan held out a chair to the right of his own. Billy hesitated, and then carried Hannah down the long room. She didn't make eye contact with anyone but then again no one made eye contact with her either. They looked at her cast, her face, her stitches, her swollen eye, the bruises, and the lump on the side of her mouth. They looked at the tattoo that was peeking out of the high neck of her blouse. They looked at her dark skin. She didn't know how she knew they were looking at the color of her skin, but she knew.

Hannah sought out the most familiar face and that was Melody's. The woman dipped her head the way she did when she was pleased. Hannah hadn't noticed that one of Melody's arms was shriveled and useless. Her hand was a claw that twitched of its own accord. Hannah thought she had a light touch, but now she knew that Melody couldn't do more than drag those fingers across her skin while she nursed her.

"Hello, Hannah," Melody said.

"Hi," Hannah answered.

Teresa was next to Melody. Her silver hair was neat and tidy as always, skimming her chin, long bangs at her brows. Her guarded expression was no surprise. Teresa wasn't a fawner, but she had leaned over Hannah's bed for days as she cared for her. Hannah had seen her back more often than she could count and yet she never noticed that Teresa wasn't just stooped, her spine was deformed.

Next to Teresa there was a middle-aged man with melted hands. Three fingers were stumps. His body was stiff. As Billy passed, he turned it like he was rolling a barrel so Hannah knew his torso must be patch-worked together, shrunken and tight like hide on a Kettle Drum.

Hannah's lashes fluttered. They were almost past him when she looked at his face. That was a mistake. Whatever catastrophe befell this man it spared his face. If it were a beautiful face, saving it from the fire would have been a lovely miracle; if his face were ugly the fire would simply have evened things out so that his body matched it. But this was just an unmemorable face.

She looked away so she wouldn't stare only to find herself eye-to-eye with a mountain of a man. If the burned man's face was unmemorable this man's was the stuff of nightmares. Half of it was covered with a port wine stain so deep and dense that it looked like it was fashioned of leather. The other half was all pink, white, and round – cheeked. He smiled – sort of; Hannah smiled back – sort of. Beside that man was a child, a dwarf.

Beside that child were a man and a woman who were also small people. There was another man ...

"Right here, Billy. Just put her here. I guess you're still moving sort of slow, Billy. That's okay. Put her here, whenever you can manage." Duncan directed them but when they didn't move any faster, Duncan bypassed Billy. "Hannah? Is this fine? Hannah?"

Startled, Hannah looked at Duncan. It had taken no more than thirty seconds to walk the length of the table and yet the journey seemed endless. They had passed faces that were blank and bright all at the same time. They had looked at bodies put together in the right order with the wrong tools. Duncan, garrulous host of this party, was old world mannered and conciliatory. He held out a chair like he was a suitor on a first date. He was out of place in this room because there was nothing wrong with him.

"Gently, Billy. Right here. Can you do it, Billy? I can do it if you can't, Billy."

"I got it, dude." Billy put her down. His lips brushed her ear. He whispered, "You're doing good."

Hannah turned her head to whisper back: *Why didn't you tell me?* Before she could say anything, Hannah saw Duncan staring at Billy, looking through him as if he didn't exist. When Duncan noticed her, the two happy parts of his face were back.

"Help me, Billy. Let's get her a little closer to the table." In the next second, Hannah's chair was airborne. When they set her down, Billy asked:

"You okay, Hannah?"

Before she could answer, Duncan called out:

"Lord!"

Heads snapped toward him. Eyes sparked. Broken bodies seemed to realign. Only Billy and Hannah were immune to the call: Billy because he just didn't like Duncan and Hannah because she didn't know what to make of it. In all the times he visited her, Duncan never sounded like he was leading a revival. He sounded like a friend.

"Lord." Duncan hit the 'd' really hard. "This is just so cool that Billy and Hannah are at our table, safe from everything and everyone that could do them harm. We all look forward to hearing what your purpose is in bringing them here. We hope you will speak through our sister, Pea, sooner than later, but we are patient people. Until we hear from you, we will watch over these two wonderful young people and I know they will live with us in peace and harmony. Amen."

Amens weren't mumbled, they were shouted out like high fives to heaven, their words slammin' and jammin' like God's backup singers. It was a lot of noise for a small gathering, and Duncan grinned as he surveyed the room. Finally, his hands pumped and he shut off the worshipful spigot. The broken people helped the other broken people adjust their chairs until everyone was settled in two neat rows. Duncan looked over his congregation as if trying to decide who to pick for his playground team.

"Melody, will you do the honors and introduce everyone?"

She blushed and bloomed under his attention. She stood up and lifted that withered, useless arm of hers. The fingers fluttered but didn't really move as she touched Teresa.

"Teresa cooks all our food and helps Robert in the store. Or maybe he helps her. We can never really be sure." Everyone laughed a little, and the tiny boy reached for a piece of bread. His mother stopped him. Hannah made a sympathetic face, but he didn't smile, so she nodded at Teresa while Melody talked. "Teresa's our doctor because she used to work for one before she came here. She made your cast."

Melody turned to her left and to her right as she went

around the table. She picked up a fork with her good hand and used it to point at the burned man.

"That's Glenn Gallo. He cuts all our wood, cleans the flues and makes sure the fires are always burning. We're all really happy to have him be our friend in the winter," Melody leaned toward Hannah. "He helped carry you up stairs."

"Thank you," Hannah said even as she wondered if she was the only one who saw the irony in a burned man being in charge of cutting wood and stoking fires. But Melody was merrily off again.

"And that's Robert." She indicated the huge man with the leather face. "Okay, so you know he helps in the store. It's his job to get supplies. Our food and clothing and things. That's what he was doing when he found you. He was coming back from his last trip to the city for the season. He carried you to the boat and then helped Billy get there. Then he helped carry you upstairs."

"That was amazing, Robert," Duncan broke in. "Truly, truly amazing that you were able to get both of them on the boat. Well done."

Duncan put his hands together and clapped. Glenn of the burns tapped his hand on the top of the table and Melody clasped her own in front of her heart. Teresa didn't move and the others sat quietly. Robert's tiny little eyes blinked – one working more efficiently than the other.

"Billy told me you were really brave," Hannah said.

It was getting easier to look at all of them. It was probably getting easier for them to look at her, too, so Hannah figured they were even.

"God told me where to find you. Duncan helped, but it was God that talked to me." Robert's expression didn't change. His high, nasal voice had no inflection, and was made unique because of it. He pursed his lips and added: "You are heavy. You didn't look heavy. You were dirty, too."

Everyone laughed as Robert blinked and blinked. Even Billy was laughing, pushing his long hair behind his ear, looking at her, and sparkling like Billy did in the old days. Hannah's dread was starting to fade. These were just people. Melody was trying to get everyone's attention, but nobody gave it to her until Duncan frowned.

"That's Connie and Paul and their son Peter," Melody went on. "They tend the gardens when it's warm, and Paul repairs things."

Hannah nodded at them but Melody was already on Foster, a trembling man who stuttered something. He was the teacher and Peter his only student. He could barely get hello out of his mouth, and Hannah could only imagine what it must be like trying to learn a lesson from him.

While all this was going on, Teresa went to the kitchen and came back with a platter. Hannah thought that this must be what Thanksgiving felt like if you had a big family. But when Melody was finished and people started talking she decided this was more like Thanksgiving and Christmas and Easter all rolled into one. Questions came at her like confetti and she scooped them up and sent them back in a flutter of answers.

Tired.

Fine.

Tired.

My head hurts.

I didn't feel the needle.

Yes, I'm hungry.

We came from California.

Teresa offered chicken and pasta, and everyone took a small portion. Hungry as Hannah was, she took the same. Even Robert didn't take more than his share. Teresa went away and came back with tea. She filled each glass by half. The bread was passed, and there was exactly one measured piece for each of them. When everyone was served, they all picked up their forks at the same time.

"This is so good. Thank you, Teresa," Hannah said and she meant it.

She glanced at Billy. There was barely enough food on his plate for a snack but he didn't seem to mind. He stabbed at his food and smiled at her. She went back to talking to Duncan about books and painting. To Billy the guy sounded like a dweeb, but Hannah was happy. The more he listened to her, the more Billy understood that this whole thing – their journey together – may have started with him, but in the end it was all about her. It always had been.

Hannah had been running through the dark forever and now she was seeing some light at the end of the tunnel. Billy couldn't see it, he didn't even believe it was there, but if Hannah could then that was cool. Maybe a few months here would be okay. Hannah might decide she didn't like it. Or maybe she wouldn't want to leave. Whatever happened, they would each have to choose whether to stay or whether to go.

He ate a piece of chicken but admitted he was kidding himself if he thought he had a choice when it came to Hannah. He would never leave her, not even if she told him to go away. He was thinking he could pretend everything was cool for the next few months, when Melody stood up. One by one, the people around the table got quiet as they noticed her. Duncan was so involved with his conversation with Hannah he was the last one to look at her.

"Melody?" Duncan said.

"Duncan." She clasped her hands to her breast and looked around the room. "Everyone."

Beside her, Teresa reached up and put a warning hand on Melody's hip. Billy put his fork down. Robert's mouth fell open, and Glenn asked 'what's going on?' even though it didn't really sound like he wanted an answer. Foster stuttered and the two little people exchanged a look that wasn't good. Melody was oblivious. She only had eyes for Duncan now. He started to rise but what Melody said next kept him in his chair.

"Oh, Duncan," she breathed. "Pea spoke to me."

15

Hannah sat on her bed with her legs up and out in front of her. Billy sat on her bed, too, but his feet were on the floor, his head down, and his eyes on a knot in the wood that was black with age. Melody had been up to fill the water glass and put something on Hannah's stitches, but she was silent and looked sicker than her patient. Billy and Hannah hadn't spoken since she left, partly because they weren't sure what to say and partly because there was a shared sense of caution. When Billy figured no one else was coming to check on them, he said:

"That was weird."

"No kidding." Hannah hitched her skirt up and over her cast. She popped the top buttons on her blouse and rolled up the sleeves.

"That's better," Billy said.

"What's better?"

"Those clothes look better now. You look like yourself. Kind of like you're cool Amish."

Hannah shrugged. She didn't know what 'herself' was anymore. Before they went to dinner she was all in to spend the next few months in this peaceful place. It wasn't so peaceful anymore.

"He was so mad." Billy put his hands behind him and rested on them. He kicked out one leg and then the other and then got tired of that. He scooted back, crossed his legs, and faced Hannah. "It would have been better if he yelled or something, but it was like his guts were kind of all over his face. Did you ever see that movie where there are these huge cocoons, and people get duplicated in them, but they have all this slime all over them and they can't really talk or anything? Body Snatchers! That's the movie I was thinking about." Billy was pleased with himself for remembering, but he couldn't help shaking his head. "Duncan was so mad at Melody. Man, she looked like she was going to puke."

"It wasn't her fault. I mean, if that Pea person said something to her then she did," Hannah said. "Do you think it's a rule that she can't talk to anyone else but Duncan?"

"No, I think Duncan was the big cheese because that lady talked to him. Didn't I tell you he was weird? Didn't I, Hannah?"

"Maybe Pea is weird," she shot back. "I mean, what kind of person only talks to one person?"

Hannah looked at her nails. She had broken them all over the last few months. In the last week while she lay in bed, they had started to grow back. Funny how seeing those little white half moons made her feel well. She dropped her hands.

"Do you think he's keeping her a prisoner?" Hannah asked.

Billy shrugged. "I don't know. I don't think so. Maybe. I mean he locked the door when he left me that first night. He said it was an accident, but maybe not. Maybe he's locked her in."

"Nobody locks my door," Hannah said.

"Like they couldn't hear you coming?"

"Good point," Hannah said.

"We would have been able to tell if there was something

really bad like that going on, don't you think? I mean, we would have felt it, wouldn't we?"

"Yes. I suppose," she said. "Do you think they'll let you stay in here, tonight?"

"No choice." Billy moved around again, trying to get comfortable on the narrow mattress. "I'm moving in. That's just . . ."

Billy stopped talking. He put his finger to his lips. He inclined his head toward the door. Hannah looked, but there was nothing to see. She listened and that's when she heard the doorknob jiggle. Billy got off the bed slowly, and Hannah sat up straighter. She threw the skirt down over her knees and buttoned up her blouse again.

"Billy. . ." she whispered.

"Shhh," he hissed.

Tiptoeing across the room, he stopped long enough to take the pitcher off the dresser and emptied it into the bowl where it was nestled. For a second it seemed whoever it was had gone away but then the knob jiggled again. Billy scooted the last few feet and flattened himself against the wall. He held the heavy pitcher high with one hand and reached across his body for the doorknob with the other. Counting to three, he threw it open, ready to strike.

"What? What?"

Outside the door, a horrified Glenn dropped the pile of logs he was carrying and stumbled back. His scarred hands went across a face so plain even terror couldn't make a mark, and his saddle-stitched body jerked as he tried to move away from Billy.

"Don't hurt me," he called. "Don't. . ."

"Oh, man, I'm sorry. Sorry, man." Billy pulled back. He put the pottery on the floor and scrambled for the logs, apologizing as he scooped them up. "We didn't know who was out here. Sorry, man. We just didn't know."

"Isn't it just me? Isn't it time for the fires?"

"Yeah. I forgot. Come on in."

Billy held the door. Glenn came in looking as if he'd prefer to be going out. He nodded at Hannah, but still gave Billy the eye.

"You want me to do it? I can do it if you're not up to it?" Billy offered as Glenn let the wood roll off his arms and onto the floor near the stove.

"No. I have to do it," Glen said. "That's the way it is. That's the rule."

Billy gravitated back to Hannah's bed.

"Why can't he help you?" Hannah asked.

Glenn hunkered down and opened the grate as if he hadn't heard her.

"Dude?" Billy nudged him. "Why can't I help you make the fire if it would be easier all around?"

Glenn put the first log in and then the second, and still he didn't speak. Hannah and Billy exchanged a look. When the third log went in he swiveled on the balls of his feet and looked at them from behind the rise of his shoulder. His eyes glinted and in that second his face was one Hannah would never forget.

"Because that's how I got burned. Starting fires."

Duncan pulled his scarf up over his lips and his nose. The cold in the hidden room was almost beyond bearing, but he was in too much of a hurry to warm it. All he needed was light. Yes, he needed light to see the word of God so he could make some sense of this. . . this. . .blasphemy.

Never, not in all his life, not even the first time Pea had spoken, not even when he realized what his mother had done, not even when he had first understood his gift, not even when he had been entrusted with the first of his broken, battered, doomed flock had Duncan felt such horror. He had lived his whole life with a grace that allowed him to meet each test and trial calmly.

Until now.

Until Melody announced that Pea had spoken to her.

Until Melody looked at him as if she were his equal.

Which she was not.

Which she would never be.

Duncan was so upset that he started to upset everything in his ordered room. He banged his legs and his pen fell off the table. He lunged to get it and the table jolted. That caused the blessed book to fall to the floor, face down, pages bent and scored.

Duncan nearly wept when he picked it up and saw the damaged pages. He lifted the book and put it back on the table. He smoothed the pages knowing he could never look at it again without thinking of this night.

Damn Melody.

She must have done something to cause Pea to betray him or, perhaps, Melody was lying. But that made no sense either. Melody would not jeopardize her healing with such a grandiose lie; with any lie for that matter.

Duncan settled himself back in his chair. He pressed the scarf to his face. He must be calm. There could be no emotions as he put Melody's revelation to the test. He waited, and waited until he was as *Within* as he could make himself.

He was not, after all, Pea.

Just then, thinking about his sister and her gift, Duncan understood that there might be another explanation for what happened in that room: What if Pea were *Without*? What if Pea was becoming one of the flock? If that happened then he would be alone among them all and that thought was crushing.

His head fell forward the way a condemned man's will when the executioner tilts it to bare the neck.

How could he live if Pea were *Without*? How would God speak to him? How would he know when the time was right to heal them all? Did it follow that Pea would have to be healed? How oh how would he find the answers?

It was only when Duncan felt a tear run from the corner of his eye, when he heard it drop onto the book, when he opened his eyes and saw the spot it made on the blessed page, that Duncan righted himself. He was the brother and he was strong. If he had not been, none of them would have come this far.

Pulling the scarf from his face, Duncan wiped his tears. He needed to see clearly, think clearly, and act decisively. If the connection between Pea and God was broken, Duncan needed to know.

He opened the Bible.

He turned the pages.

He came to the passage Melody had so proudly – even arro- gantly – announced to the stunned congregation.

Numbers 12:1

Duncan read the passage once.

He read the passage again.

He read it once more, using his finger to follow each word so that there would be no mistake. When he was finished, Duncan sat still for a very long time. He was warm despite the cold, filled with purpose, awed by the glorious simplicity of it all.

"Thank you," he murmured, and he had no doubt that God heard.

He closed the book. Pea was blessed and still *Within*. He was the brother who was *Without*. He was the man who interpreted God's design and Pea's words led him on the right path as always. Nothing had changed except one thing; this time Melody had received the message because the message was for him, Duncan.

The tears of despair he had shed were now tears of joy. They spilled from his lazy eyes and ran cold down his cheeks. He had been waiting so long for this. Now, no matter what, even long after the healing, he would not be alone. He would be blessed beyond his wildest dreams.

Everyone, including Duncan, would be at peace.

———

Josie sat cross-legged on her sleeping bag and Nell lay on the other side of the tent, her head cradled on her upturned palm, watching the tall woman pour over a map.

"You're not going to find anything else. You know that, don't you?"

"Maybe," Josie muttered. "Maybe not."

Nell rolled onto her back and looked up at the dome of the tent. It was close quarters, but she didn't mind. What surprised her was that Josie Bates didn't seem to mind either.

"I wouldn't be able to make heads or tails of some lawyer thing so you'd probably tell me to give it up if I kept trying. I'm the expert here, and I promise you won't be able to tell anything by that map."

Josie picked the map up, folded it part way, and floated it toward Nell. The woman caught it and opened it up as Josie scooted over and got on her knees.

"Look over here." Josie poked the map. "What are these Xs? They have to represent something."

"Native summer camps. They stock up for the winter and then go back to their villages until the ice breaks up again and they can get back to the river."

"Do they do that every year?" Josie asked.

"Every year since the beginning of time. Now the government gives them all sort of paperwork, permits for subsistence harvesting. Stuff like that makes me mad. It used to be so easy, so natural. Boy, we screwed them up."

Josie took the map back and folded it in half. "It's the law. You've got to follow the law."

"So you say."

Josie laughed, "It's not me. People vote, politicians make the law, and there are courts to hear cases. There are cops to enforce laws. Look at Andre."

Nell barked a laugh, "I love to look at Andre."

"He is easy on the eyes," Josie admitted. "Still, he enforces the law."

"That he does. But the law he enforces can sometimes be a little different than what's on the books. So can justice, and politics, and religion, and the whole ball of wax." Nell turned on her side and cradled her head in her upturned hand. "Look, Alaska isn't California. We don't have the population you do for one thing. People aren't living on top of each the other. That alone creates a whole new dynamic. Frankly, we're all happy to get away from people like you."

"How do you really feel about us?" Josie asked.

"Honest to God truth." Nell raised her fingers in the Girl Scout salute. "We do pretty good on our own. The only thing we get all hot and bothered about is when you all come in and tell us we've got to do something different when it's been working fine the way it is."

"Like looking for Hannah and Billy?"

"Yeah, like that. Want a drink?" Nell sat up and reached for her pack and took out a flask.

"What have you got?" Josie asked.

"Scotch."

Josie shook her head and Nell kept talking.

"It's not that we don't care, it's just we know the lay of our land. When you went over Andre's head, you might as well have just kicked him in the gut. So much for his expertise; so much for his authority. I'd like to see what you'd do if someone walked into your office, went to your boss, and said you didn't know what the hell you were doing."

"I don't have a boss," Josie pointed out.

"No one would hire you, huh?" Nell chuckled. "Can't blame 'em."

"They didn't know what they were missing," Josie answered. "But what about you? You didn't get all bent out of shape about helping me."

"Me?" Nell took a swig directly out of the flask since she wasn't sharing. "I'm a businesswoman. You're not wasting my time if you pay me, and if you're paying me, you can't hurt my feelings. Andre is a cop. He's a man. What he told you was the truth. You're not going to find your girl. You're not going to find her friend. Andre doesn't like to waste his time. He really doesn't like people to get their hopes up."

"If it was his daughter he'd be doing just what I'm doing," Josie said.

"Probably," she finished her drink. "But she's your daughter, and I think you'd be out here by yourself if no one else would go. I couldn't let you do that."

Nell screwed the top back on the flask and lay down. She threw the top of her sleeping bag over her body and zipped it up. Josie did the same, but she took the map to bed with her.

"Time to get some shut eye. Night," Nell said.

The lantern went off. They lay in the dark, zipped into bags, under the shelter of a small tent.

"She's not my daughter, you know," Josie said.

"Might as well be," Nell answered. "That's why I'm assuming you want to start again in the morning."

"I didn't think that was even a question," Josie said.

"Figured I'd be polite and ask. Now go to sleep." Nell turned over in her bag.

Josie just stared into the dark, her mind still working. "So, do you think the natives are still at those camps by the river?"

Nell sniffed, but that was all the answer Josie got. The other woman went to sleep knowing that tomorrow they'd be headed to the summer camps.

Josie arranged her backpack and used it as a pillow. She slid the map underneath it, closed her eyes, and listened to Nell's breathing. She also thought about how cold her nose was, and then drifted off to sleep aware that her last thoughts were to wonder what Hannah and Billy were doing at that very moment.

That was how great Josie Bates' faith was. That in the demonic darkness, wandering in the wilderness, lost and without direction, Josie Bates believed that Hannah Sheraton and Billy Zuni were alive and able to do anything at all.

16

I should have known. There had to be a crazy in this group, but Glenn wasn't the one I would have figured on. I look at Billy, and he's looking at me. He's pale as a ghost. I feel like I might be, too. Every bit of blood feels like it drained from my face and all my stewing pot of genes isn't enough to leave my skin the color of toffee.

I check out Glenn. He doesn't even notice that I'm staring at him like he's the monster that just climbed out from under my bed.

He's happy with his logs and his fire.

He's really happy – with his logs – and his fire.

Hannah spoke up, and Billy thought it was cool that her voice didn't even shake because it should have.

"What kind of fire were you starting when you got burned? In your fireplace? In your house?"

Glenn shook his very ordinary head. He picked up a poker and the flames flared. His hand looked like melting wax in the gold/red light. Seemingly satisfied that it would burn well, he put the poker down, and started stacking the wood.

"Sort of. I mean it was at my house, but we didn't have a fireplace." He chuckled a little, and it was an almost merry sound. "I think about it now, and I realize how really terrible it was. I was mad at my wife and my children. I don't think any of them liked me very much. My wife, well, she really loved our house. So I thought, you know, I'd scare her a little, and so I burned the house down. But they were in it."

"You knew they were in there?" Billy asked.

Glenn took the small log off the stack and replaced it with a larger one.

"Isn't that what on purpose means? I didn't do it very well, but I guess you could tell that. I mean will you look at me?"

He did a mechanical quarter turn, paused, and did it again as he poked at his chest.

"Do you want to see?"

Hannah shook her head, "No. No."

"We're good," Billy agreed.

"It's pretty ugly, even if I do say so myself. It's amazing I survived at all. A real testament to medical science. They said I was nuts and sent me to a hospital instead of jail. I told them that I wasn't nuts." Glenn finished his stacking and brushed off his hands. "I was really honest about the whole thing. I told them I meant to do it, and it wasn't the first time. I've always thought fire is amazing. It just can get out of hand so fast. Still, there are so many things to really like about it."

His drum body rolled around. He picked up the poker and used it again. Cinders sparkled, flames flamed, wood blackened. Reluctantly, he closed the grate, struggled up, and trotted over to Duncan's chair.

"Can I stay here for a little? It's awful downstairs. Melody is so unhappy and Teresa just has her mouth all clamped shut. Robert's crying. The rest went to *Hours,* but I think they just don't want to be around when Duncan comes back. Nobody gets disturbed in *Hours.* Ever. I used to hate that. There are times I would just pray for someone to disturb me. *Hours* can be so long and lonely. I sure hope this doesn't interfere with the healing."

Glenn didn't seem to like the position of his chair so he got up again and carried it closer to the stove.

"Anyway, it would be sad if this screwed up the healing."

"What's with the healing thing?" Hannah asked. "Do you think Duncan is going to lay on hands or something? I mean, do you believe that he can make your scars go away or Melody's arm okay? Is that it?"

"Oh, okay. I guess nobody really had a chance to explain it to you, did they?"

"No. It would be good to know." Billy moved closer to Hannah.

"Well," Glenn answered, "It's really pretty simple. We believe that Pea speaks to God. She is perfect and *Within. . .* "

"What's that?" Billy asked.

"Oh, that just means there's nothing wrong with her. Duncan is close but she's perfect. When you're perfect, you live all alone inside yourself because you just don't need anything else. That's what we all strive for. Pea was born that way. That's what I hear. I've never seen her myself because Duncan is the only man who can see her. Melody told us how beautiful she is, though, and how *Within* is amazing. That's how it is when you're perfect. Anyway," Glenn waved his hand. "Pea's got nothing wrong with her, and she's so perfect that nothing in this world can touch her. She doesn't have to be with other people, or move, or look at anyone. She and God talk in their brains. Then Pea tells Duncan what God says, and he looks in the Bible, and he tells us all what it means. That's how we are guided, and that is how we will know when the healing time is on us. It's going to be pretty soon. Or at least it was supposed to be."

"Duncan interprets what she says? Like Bible study?" Hannah asked.

"He's more than a study person. He is blessed with the gift of interpretation."

"And the rest of you?" Billy asked.

"We're chosen. We're the people who God told Duncan could be healed. Not everyone can be, you know. It's not easy to earn it. When Duncan first told me what I had to do, I didn't think I could manage but here I am. I haven't set a fire since I've been with him. Except in a stove, of course."

"So, dude, I'm totally not getting it." Billy said. "What do you have to do?"

"Face our sins head on, of course. I burned down my house, so I tend the fires. That's how we prove we won't sin again. We are tempted and we resist. Melody tends Pea – and now Hannah – Teresa has to care for everyone like they're her own children, Robert has to help Teresa as if she's his mother."

"Do you mean everyone did something as bad as you?" Hannah asked.

"Oh yes." Glenn raised his hands and made a little box with them. "I set a fire and killed my wife and my kids and burned down my house. I did it once before with someone else's house. My sin is hurting people with fire." He made a box-like gesture in front of him. "Then I got arrested and sent to the hospital where I met Duncan while he was doing ministry. We talked about how to be healed and he said–" Glenn moved his deformed hands to another imaginary space to the other side of his body " – if I faced what I did, if I could resist temptation, if I lived by God's word, I would be healed and released from the pain of this world. That's what he said. Released from the pain of this world and be whole and happy."

"And so he makes you be the fire guy so that you have to resist temptation all the time?" Billy asked.

"Yep. Works good, don't you think?" Glenn said brightly. "If I can be responsible for the fires around here, God will see that I have conquered temptation and atoned for my sin. I will be released."

His hands came down on his thighs. He was smiling. Hannah wiped the sweat from her head. It was getting hot in the room. Clearly, Glenn was good at his job.

"What about the others?" she asked. "What did they do?"

"Melody had a twin sister who was very pretty and not damaged at all. When Melody was younger, she slashed her pretty sister with a knife."

"Did she die?" Billy asked.

Glenn shook his head. "No, but she looks pretty bad as I understand it. Melody cut off her nose and part of her ears and lips. That's why she has to tend to Pea. Pea is beautiful so Duncan tempts Melody with Pea. Then she saw your arms," he pointed at Hannah. "Sorry, but she told us about your arms. Duncan said that proved she had to care for you. You would be pretty when you got better and the scars would remind Melody of what she'd done to her sister. So now she has to look at both you and Pea. I thought she was handling things very well, but maybe not. I mean considering what happened tonight. Maybe she went off the deep end."

"Hannah," Billy said. "Jesus, Hannah."

She held up her hand. They would talk when Glenn was gone. Right now he was on a roll and she wanted to hear the rest. Glenn happily ran through everyone in the house but they barely heard about the little people, and they just caught the end of Foster's tale. They tuned back in just in time to hear about Teresa and Robert.

". . .And Robert. He beat up his mother because she laughed at him and told him how ugly he was. He's huge – as you saw – so it didn't take much to hurt her bad. She's a vegetable, I hear. So he has to take care of Teresa no matter how she treats him.

And Teresa has to take of him like he is her child. You know, mother and son squared off every day."

"What did Teresa do?" Billy asked.

"She tried to kill her children and herself. She gave them sleeping pills." Glenn adjusted in his chair, warming to his subject. "That's an interesting story. She couldn't take care of them, and she didn't want to see them given away because they were so special. Teresa thought she was doing it out of love. Duncan says it doesn't matter why things were done, it matters that they are done. He says a mother's sin is the greatest of all. Sometimes I wonder if Teresa's going to be healed. Sometimes I think Duncan hates her. That would only be normal except that he's, well, Duncan and so close to God. I don't think he can hate if he's the one God chose."

Hannah lifted her casted leg closer to the edge of the bed. She wanted to be on her feet if anything happened. She glanced at Billy to see if he was thinking about running. His head wagged. He brushed his long hair behind his ears, flipped it back, and did it all over again.

"Why would Duncan hate her so much?" Billy asked. "I mean, isn't he like the go to guy for all of you? Shouldn't he want to heal you all the same?"

"He should, but I can see where it's difficult for him. I mean, it was Duncan and Pea she tried to kill," Glenn said. "Those are her real children. Duncan and Pea."

Duncan trudged through the snow. It was late, but the lights still burned in the house. Usually, at this hour, everyone was asleep except for him. This was the time when he sat by Pea's bed and listened to her breathing. He had no idea what it was like for Pea to sleep. He assumed she was removed from heavenly grace, but one never knew for sure. He was truly curious about Pea's state of mind tonight. He wondered if she felt the same joy he did. He hoped so because he was fairly drunk with it.

He danced up the three wooden steps. Snow had piled up on the porch. It was snowing so hard, it might actually be up to the top stair by morning, but right now the white stuff looked like a festive garland around the house.

Duncan threw himself at the door and burst through like a favorite uncle arriving just in time to open the Christmas gifts. He whipped the scarf from his face. He pulled the gloves from his hands. He unbuttoned his jacket and threw it off his body as he called.

"Everyone. Come everyone! Come down. Come out! Come here!" He looked down the hall to the dining room, he looked in the living room, and then he looked up the stairs. "God will forgive if you're in *Hours*. Come now. Off your knees!"

The flock appeared as they had when Robert called them from the river: one by one, in their own time. Unlike that day, they were not curious about why they were being called. They were fearful. The order was disturbed. Duncan had not been Duncan at all when he left them behind to fend for themselves. Melody was stricken that he had not embraced her.

Terrified that Duncan would take Pea to task after Melody's revelation, Teresa had rushed after him and thrown her wretched body across the stairs to stop him from trying to see Pea. She collapsed on the bottom step, relieved when Duncan dressed himself and went out into the snowy night.

Foster stumbled into the living room to have a conversation with himself about what he would do now. It was all mumble and stutter and no one bothered to try to understand him. He took his conversation to a closet and closed himself in.

Glenn poked at the fire and rearranged the wood in the downstairs room, unnerved by the sudden pall. When he was done, he went off to tend the fires in the other rooms and had not returned.

Hannah and Billy had gone up to her room, determined to wait out whatever was going on. It was, after all, none of their concern.

Now Duncan was raising his voice and it carried throughout the house. Slowly they congregated in the front room: Teresa and Melody came from the kitchen, Robert from the corner of the dining room where he tried to hide by turning his chair to face the wall, Foster from the closet, and all the rest. They glanced at Duncan like good dogs waiting for the whip. Duncan didn't notice them cringe or that they gave him wide berth.

"Wonderful. There you all are. Where is Glenn? Oh, and little Peter is asleep, of course, but where is Glenn?"

"He took wood upstairs," Teresa said, eyeing him closely.

She had seen him like this before. In the hospital when he had awakened from the deep sleep the doctors had induced. Pea woke as she always did, silent save for her verses.

Within the young Duncan had called it.

Autism, the doctors called it. Biblical savant. That's what Pea was. Prophetess, Duncan insisted and that's what these people believed.

Now here they were and history was repeating itself. Duncan was waking when she hadn't even known that he was asleep. He stood before them gripped by a new and frantic fervor, waiting to share some Godly revelation. Teresa felt a shiver run through her. If this was the healing and Duncan failed, she couldn't bear it. Not just for herself and the others, but for him and Pea. They had all believed so long that she wished they could simply go on doing it.

"Teresa. You sit there. There in the big chair," Duncan chirped "Oh, Melody. Blessed, Melody! Come here."

He took the young woman's hands in both of his and kissed

one and then the other. Melody made a nervous little sound; the kind a woman makes when she isn't sure if her man is going to beat her or love her.

"Melody, you sit over there. On the couch. Yes, yes, near Teresa's chair." Duncan eased everyone into the room and then dashed into the foyer to call up the stairs once again. "Glenn and Hannah and Billy! Come . . . oh, there you are, Glenn. Where are the others?"

"Aren't they behind me?"

Duncan laughed. "Yes, actually. They are."

Glenn passed and Duncan waited as Hannah and Billy came slowly down the stairs. This time Hannah walked on her own, her casted leg goose-stepping, making her progress slowly. Billy was squeezed beside her, his arm around her waist.

"Let me help." Duncan started up the stairs, but Billy pulled Hannah back and held her tight.

"I got her, dude."

"Of course you do," Duncan answered, but the brightness in his voice dulled.

He hurried away having grown tired of waiting for them. Hannah and Billy could hear him in the living room settling people, asking after their welfare, throwing a compliment here, there, but oh-so-eager to get on with whatever it was he wanted to get on with. When Hannah and Billy arrived, all eyes went to them. No one smiled except for Duncan.

"Hannah. Please. Sit there on the other side of Teresa. Please. In the other comfortable chair."

Out went Duncan's hands. Up went his palms. His long fingers were extended as he guided her to her seat. Billy stood beside her.

"Billy, why don't you sit next to Foster there. Please," Duncan said.

"I'm good here, man."

"Of course. Sure. Whatever works." Duncan's smile faltered, but didn't disappear. When it came back it was better than before. "Great, now. Here we are. First, I apologize. I wasn't prepared for what happened tonight. Melody." He turned toward her and she almost jumped out of her skin. "Melody, God has blessed you through Pea. I confess to my sin of arrogance. God has spoken through her to me for so long that I never thought he might choose another soul. What happened tonight is proof that you are, indeed, worthy of healing."

Melody gasped. Teresa started. Foster mumbled at Glenn who asked an unanswerable question in return. Robert waddled in just as Duncan made his proclamation. Duncan looked at the house-of-a-man.

"Robert. Oh, Robert. How could we have begun without you?"

"You're going to heal Melody?" Robert asked.

"No, not tonight. But soon."

Billy looked at Melody. The guy might as well have shot her. Stupid idiot, making her believe like that.

"But she is worthy. As you all are." Duncan slapped Robert on the back. "Go sit in your chair. No tears. This is a celebration. This is a sign. God has sent a message for me, specifically. That is why Pea spoke to our beloved Melody," he circled around to her again. "I could not hear the message myself for fear it would be dismissed. God and Pea are wise to have chosen Melody."

Amens were murmured, some a bit more enthusiastic than others. The only one who didn't speak was Teresa. Something bad was coming, something cataclysmic, and she was powerless to stop it.

Duncan opened his hands, and he raised them not to heaven but toward Hannah. Billy tensed, ready to step between them if necessary.

"Numbers 12:1," he said. "Numbers 12:1, Hannah. Miriam and

Aaron spoke against Moses because of the Cushite woman whom he had married, for he had married a Cushite woman."

Ecstatic with the importance of his announcement, Duncan's lazy-lidded eyes were bright as stars as he moved closer to Hannah. When no one responded, he paused. He pivoted. He looked from one incredulous face to the other. Billy had enough. His voice sounded like thunder when he spoke.

"What the heck does that mean, dude?"

Slowly, Duncan turned on him. His eyes no longer sparkled and his lips no longer broke his face into two happy parts. Those lips were twisted in a disdainful grimace as he looked at Billy Zuni, the beautiful, disrespectful, ignorant boy.

"Cushite, Billy," Duncan drawled. "Moses married a black woman. That is why God sent Robert to find you. That is why God saved Hannah. I am to take a black woman as my bride."

17

Mama Cecilia could hunt and fish and she could travel long distances just with her feet. She could steer a canoe. Still, it had been many years since she had done any of those things, so she felt lost much of the time she was walking and looking for her son.

Thinking very hard about what Oki said helped to pass the time and calm her as she searched. She thought that he had been very correct. The wind could only blow the way it would blow and the bear must seek out what it needs. Understanding this, she decided she must take a journey and not just walk in the forest.

She walked back the mile and some steps to the lodge where Priscilla Wolf Skin continued making reports for the chiefs. When Mama told her of her plan, Priscilla did not offer to go with Mama but she took twenty dollars from her purse and pressed it into Mama's chubby hand. She also gave her the box that was her very own lunch and wished her well. Mama Cecilia knew that Priscilla Wolf Skin shook her head a good long while after Mama left to begin her journey.

Mama asked Thomas, the good and sober son of Sam

Starlight, to take her to where the bus would pick her up on the long road to Eagle, but Thomas ran out of gas half way there. She walked the rest of the long way and waited. Just when Mama Cecilia thought the night would come but not the bus, it arrived. She sat in the very back. The seat was quite comfortable. The ride was very long, she ate the food Priscilla Wolf Skin had given her, and she slept some.

When the bus arrived in Eagle, she found a boarding house. The owner was very kind but not kind enough to let Mama Cecilia sleep in one of the rooms for free. It cost more money than she expected. In the morning, the owner gave her food and sent her off with good wishes to find her granddaughter.

Mama did not find her granddaughter and the person at the place where the letter came from asked her if she would like to leave money. She had no money to leave, but she did not say that. She only asked again if she could have the phone number or the address of the girl who had sent the letter. The man shook his head and said 'no, it is the law', and Mama Cecilia knew she had failed. She would go home alone and that made her sad. She had dreamed that the girl would take her arm and together they would save Mama's son, the girl's father. It was a fine dream while it lasted.

Sometimes a bear found food and sometimes a bear stayed hungry.

That was the way.

Outside the shop where one left money for other people, Mama Cecilia realized she had made a mistake. She had not told Sam Starlight's son when she would return. She had spent too much money on the boarding. Now she didn't have quite enough for the bus ticket home. Mama stood with her back against the building, her small feet together, and her hands folded as she waited for her spirits to send her a sign about what she must do.

So great was her faith in her good spirits that they answered her in very little time. They sent her an old man who spoke to her politely and offered her a ride in his boat as far as he was going. It was not far enough, but it was better than staying where she was. He would not leave for another day or two but she was welcome on his boat until the time he went upriver.

Mama Cecilia accepted his offer saying she would cook for him and mend whatever he had which was torn and, therefore, pay for her passage. He did not object because it would be rude to do so. He also would like to have a meal cooked for him and his things mended.

While they arrived at the boat, the man handed her up to the deck. When she stepped onto his boat, the old man admired her moccasins and that made Mama Cecilia smile just a little.

Archer and Andre hadn't said much to one another in the time they had been together, but they accomplished a lot. They drove a couple hundred miles, stopping at every turnout where a trucker could get gassed up or find a bite of food. They flashed the dead trucker's ID and pictures of the crumpled truck. Archer took out his favorite photo of Hannah standing in front of one of her paintings, all dolled up in the way only Hannah could be. Those startling eyes of hers looked into the camera as if it were a person she wasn't sure she liked. All he got when people looked at the picture were head shakes. It wasn't until their fourth stop that they hit pay dirt.

It was a filling station with a store, public johns, and an ancient phone booth squatting like an outhouse in the back. In the middle of nowhere, the place looked like a veritable Wal-Mart and like Wal-Mart they got just what they wanted at the right price: a fairly positive I.D. on the driver, solid one on

Hannah, and confirmation the girl was with a boy with long hair. All that for the price of a cup of coffee.

The guy behind the counter looked twice at Hannah's picture. The first time it was to admire her. The second time to confirm that it was the same girl just without the earrings and nose ring and long black hair. She had short hair now. He also remembered it was blond.

"How can you be sure it's the same girl?" Archer asked.

"You kidding? Check out the eyes. She looks like she's ready to deck me if I look at her cross eyed, not to mention she's black and she's got green eyes." The man made change for their coffee and pushed the cash drawer shut with his hip. "I see a lot of 'em coming through here. Runaways, hippies, kids thrown out for one reason or another. Most of 'em have some kind of attitude. Little thieves, really. This one had an attitude but it was an honest one."

He rested against the counter while he reached for the cigarette he had going. The man took a long, deep drag of his cigarette and the smoke curled out with his words.

"I'm not going to make you pull it out of me. She bought a jacket. Yellow. Fleece. Looks like that one over there on the sale rack," he motioned to a rounder. "Men's large, but the boy wasn't a large. I was surprised she bought it since she counted the pennies on food. Still, the kid needed it. That was nice of her."

"Guess what the lab has?" Archer reminded Andre. "They've got some of that fabric." To the clerk he said: "Where did they go?"

"How am I supposed to know? They were just gone with some trucker. Those guys all look alike to me. It could have been with the guy in the picture. If it was a court of law I couldn't swear, but I'd say it's a good bet he was the one they went off with."

"Do you remember the rig?"

"I only remember the spit and shine ones. Those are beauties." The guy was almost done with his cigarette, but he wasn't going to stub it until the last drag.

"Thanks." Archer gave the cigarette a nod. "Watch your fingers."

The guy grunted and picked up a magazine as Archer and Andre left. Coffee cups in hand, they paused to take in the scenery. The highway was one long black ribbon that went from somewhere to somewhere. There was no forest here, no mountains, just a flat expanse of nothing. A tanker pulled up and they watched a bleary eyed driver get out of the cab. He nodded to them as he passed and went inside. It was late. It was snowing. Archer tossed his empty cup in the can beside the door.

"Damn cold here." He zipped his jacket up to the chin.

"You should be here in January." Andre threw back what was left of his coffee. He didn't wait for Archer to ask the question. "None of this is evidence your kids were in the truck when it crashed, but I'll give you that they were probably in the truck."

"Bet you're fun at parties." Archer's lips twitched. He stuck his hands deep into his pockets. "Look Guillard, I understand your reservations, but I think we're agreed that they were probably hitching with that trucker. Now the question is, what did he do with them? He could have abused them, killed them, whatever."

"He hasn't got a record." Andre pointed out.

"And I can give you a list of killers without records because they were driving rigs through remote areas or crossing state lines and there was no way to track them," Archer countered.

"True, but I would just rather not think the worst," Andre said.

"Me either," Archer agreed. "So we go down the list. He could have chucked 'em out for the fun of it before the crash. They could have been in the back of that thing when it went down. He might have picked up another passenger who let them out. So let's establish for certain that they were here. Then we'll figure out where they ended up."

Archer stepped off the raised porch and headed to the phone booth. When Andre joined him, Archer pointed to the glass door.

"Someone's been in here recently." He looked closer at the mess on the glass. "We've got prints. I don't know how good they are but we've got 'em."

Andre looked, too. He could get a partial and he knew from Archer the girl had been booked once, indicted on a false murder charge. That was bad, but then he figured all things happen for a reason. This, it seemed, was the reason.

Archer put the inside of his wrist through the opening and pushed on the door. It only went so far. He pushed harder and got another inch that allowed him to squeeze in. He was out again a second later.

"No number. Think you can track it down for me?" he asked.

"Yep," Andre said.

"Great. Hannah left a message at Josie's office. I'm betting we can trace that call back here."

"Okay," Andre turned away and started back for the car.

"You're going to dust it, right?" Archer called. Andre pivoted. Archer said. "For Josie. For me, too. To be sure."

"I'm going to dust it," Andre answered. "For myself, and just in case we do have a third hitchhiker. I just have to get my kit."

By the time they were done with the booth, it was late in the afternoon. The man behind the counter in the shop pointed them down the road and gave them the turnoff where they could find some home cooking. It was ten miles down and hard to miss. The place was small, but the sign screaming SLOW FOOD was big. They pulled into the dirt lot ready for some serious eating and maybe a beer, but before they could get out of the car the radio squawked. Andre picked it up.

"Guillard here."

Cressi's voice came back at him.

"We've got an ID on the prints on that key you found."

"Let's hear it."

"Looks like partial on your driver. We've got an intact index finger on one side and a thumb on the other. They belong to Robert Butt. He was arrested in Colorado. Beat his mother to a pulp. She's brain dead," the woman said.

"Where is he now?" Andre asked.

"No info, Andre," Cressi came back. "He served three years in the Mental Health Institute at Pueblo and was released when he was twenty-one. Want me to ask the Colorado authorities to look into it a little more?"

"That would be good, Cressi. And have a bulletin made up for him and our kids. Do you have a description?"

"Big as a bear. Half his face is covered with a birthmark. He'd be hard to miss even out here," Cressi said, and then she added. "We're talking real low IQ, Andre. If he's got your kids, it could go one way or the other with him."

Archer moved in his seat, sitting up a little straighter. This wasn't the kind of news he wanted to hear.

"Okay. Thanks. You have a good evening, now." Andre started to sign off and then thought again. "Cressi. You still there?"

"Yep," she came back.

"Nell is going to be checking in. She's got a Ms. Bates from California with her, and they're supposed to keep us apprised of their position. If she checks in, tell her we have a positive I.D. on the two kids we're looking for but that is all."

Cressi signed off. Andre stayed put with one arm slung over the steering wheel and the other hand still on the radio. His fingers drummed once and then again. A couple of guys tumbled out the door of the restaurant, checked out the trooper and his vehicle, and sobered up long enough to walk a straight line to their truck. Guillard and Archer didn't even notice them. Finally, Archer said:

"Are you ready to eat?"

"Sure."

The doors of the car opened simultaneously and slammed the same way. Andre threaded his nightstick through his belt as he walked. Archer opened the old door and punched it so it stayed wide enough for Andre to go through after him.

The place was warm and busy. A woman in jeans, a white t-shirt, and a grey sweater motioned them toward the back, pirouetted, filled two water glasses, and somehow managed to make it to the table before they did. She dropped the water glasses, pointed to the menus in a little silver paperclip thing on the table and told them to take their time.

Archer sat with his back to the door, Andre with his to the wall. Gloves were shoved into coat pockets, coats were shrugged off and flopped over the chair backs, hats were slid off heads, and fingers were run through hair. Archer tossed a menu Andre's way. Andre opened it and ran down the options – all of them fine on a cold, cold night.

"I'll have them expedite the prints I picked up from the phone booth," Andre said.

"Thanks," Archer muttered. The waitress came back.

"What are you boy's wanting tonight?"

"How's the steak?" Andre asked.

"Tough," she answered.

"I'll do the bison stew."

"You got it, baby." She looked at Archer, shifted her weight, and tapped the pencil point on her pad.

"What about you, sweet cheeks? What do you want?"

Archer looked up at her. He knew exactly what he wanted.

He wanted to know for sure if Hannah had picked up that receiver in that phone booth. He wanted to know if that was the place where she'd made a call and left the message:

We're still okay

Then he wanted to know if that was still true.

He pushed the menu aside.

"I'll have what he's having."

18

I don't know how we got up the stairs. I don't know how we got back to this room. I don't know what to say to Billy or what to think.

No, that's not true. I do know what to think. I think that we don't have to worry about Glenn anymore because all of them are friggin' maniacs. Every last one of them.

"Is the door locked?"

"Yeah, Hannah. A thousand times, yes. It's locked," Billy said, but he checked it again just to be sure. Then he put his hands flat on it. "It's solid, too. It's real wood. But I don't think anything's going to happen. I don't think these people actually do anything about anything. I think they just talk, you know?"

He turned around and went to the stove. He kicked at the small pile of wood, and moved it around with his foot.

"We've got enough for tonight, but I don't know how long we're going to have to stay in here."

"As long as it takes to figure out how to get out of this place, not just this room," Hannah muttered. She looked up at Billy.

"I'm so sorry. You were right about Duncan. I should have listened."

"It's okay." Billy sat down on the bed. "At least he's not going to hurt us. None of them are. I mean, they think they've got to be super good until they're healed, right? Duncan says the healing is after you guys get married, right? So that means everybody has to be super good until then. That means we're okay. We just need to figure out what to tell him about why you can't get married and, you know, put him off 'till we can make a plan."

Hannah snorted. Billy almost smiled. She must be okay if she could still snort like she thought the whole thing was a crock. Now he had to keep her thinking that way.

"Anyway, we just stay away from them or we make something up about you being a Druid. He can't marry you because God would be ticked at him if he married a Druid."

"Billy," Hannah warned, "It's not funny."

"I know." Billy sat back.

"Thanks for trying, though," Hannah mumbled and then they stopped talking.

They listened for sounds that would put them on their guard but they heard nothing. Not a footstep on the stair, not a spoken word, not even a creak as the old place settled. It was like everyone was in a mega time out. The silence made Hannah nervous.

"Even if we got out of here, we don't know where we are. I can't run with this thing on my leg." Hannah knocked on her cast.

Before she knew what was happening, Billy was kneeling on the mattress and cupping his good hand around her instep. His bandaged hand was pressed on the ball of her foot.

"What? What are you doing?"

"Hannah. What if they're messing with us?" Billy asked. "What if your leg isn't broken. I mean, maybe it's like cracked or something, and they didn't really know what to do so they put a cast on it. Don't you think if it was broken you would be in a whole lot of pain?"

"I don't know. I never broke anything before."

"Well, are you in pain?"

She shook her head. "Not really. My leg throbs."

"Okay. So, remember biology and the way all the muscles and bones look in the leg? Remember?"

Her head went up and down again.

"Yeah, me too," he said. "If I press your foot back then I should really hurt you, right? Like you won't even be able to stand it if I do that. So, can I do that? I don't want to hurt you, Hannah. I never want to hurt you." Billy's voice caught. He cleared his throat. "I don't want to, but I think we've got to try. I think we need to know how bad it is."

"You're right. You are, Billy. It's okay. Let's do it."

Hannah propped herself up on her pillows. His hands quivered. The sock covering her foot was scratchy and the cast on her leg was a rock. Billy sniffed and took a couple of deep breaths before he started to count down.

"One," he said.

"Wait," she whispered. "We don't want them to hear."

Hannah looked around, saw the towel on the bedside table and grabbed it. She stuffed it in her mouth. Her green eyes filled with fear. Billy held her gaze. He was scared, too, but this had to be done. There was no one to do it but him.

"Two," he said.

He took the next breath, but Hannah never heard him count three. All she heard was her own muffled scream.

Josie woke with a start. She was sweating even though it was freezing inside the tent.

Next to her Nell was a lump of a body buried in her sleeping bag. Josie's brow beetled. Obviously, Nell hadn't called to her. She tugged at her cap, ran her finger underneath the edge to wipe away the sweat, and then put her head back on her pack hoping she could get to sleep again. She nestled her chin against her chest and wondered what had awakened her. She was sure she hadn't been dreaming. She was equally sure that whatever woke her wasn't in her head but in her ears. The only other person around was Nell and she hadn't uttered a sound since closing her eyes. Then again, maybe it wasn't someone calling to her; maybe what she heard was more like a grunt.

Josie tried to roll over which was an impossibility given the sleeping bag and all the clothes she was wearing. She scooted up again and freed her arms. She felt around her pack until she found the side pocket and pulled out her cellphone. She turned it on. The bars were nonexistent, and the battery not exactly full. It was four in the morning.

She put the phone away and settled in once more. It was going to be a long couple of hours until they got going again. Instead of counting sheep, she ran through the hundreds of scenarios she had been thinking about on their long hike. Funny, how many situations she could imagine Hannah and Billy in. Lost in Alaska was not one of them. Just when she had boiled down her options to waking Nell and having a gab-fest or seeing if she could locate that bottle of scotch, Josie Bates heard the sound that had awakened her.

It wasn't a call or a scream or a grunt.

It was a rumbling, a snorting, a growl and it came along with the sound of the tent ripping under a paw with claws the size of machetes.

"Oh my God. Oh, Billy. Oh, my..."

Billy's name rolled out of Hannah's mouth along with a tidal wave of swear words. She had ripped the towel out of her mouth and her hands were pumping her chest like that was the only way she could keep breathing.

"I'm sorry. I'm so sorry." Billy grabbed for her leg and ran his hands down her cast. "You okay? I didn't mean it. What? What?"

It was hard to see her even as close as they were. The fire had burned down and the light didn't make it all the way to the bed before it petered out. But then he saw the glint of her teeth and heard her laugh as she put her fingers to her lips. She pumped those fingers against her mouth, suppressed her laughter, and shushed him all at the same time.

"I'm sorry." Hannah put her hands over his and held them tight. She whispered but loud enough for him to know she wasn't hurt and she wasn't afraid. "Stop. It's okay. I thought it was going to hurt so bad that I screamed before you even pushed. I'm sorry. I'm sorry."

"You mean it didn't hurt?" Billy whipped himself up onto his knees. He teetered on the soft mattress, but steadied himself when he took her face in his hands. "Oh geez, Hannah. That's great. That's great."

He threw himself at her, gathered her up in his arms, and kissed her hair and her cheeks. Her arms went around him and they clung together in the dark, snickering and laughing like children until Hannah pulled back. Billy stopped laughing. For once Hannah's lips weren't tight with worry, or anger, or frustration. They were the most beautiful lips he had ever seen even though one side was knotted and swollen.

"Billy." Hannah put her hands on his chest.

"I know. I know."

He sat back on his heels. His hands slid away from her and he felt like he had lost a part of his soul. But it wasn't his soul, it was only Hannah who he loved more than anything; loved her too much to mess it up now. He put one leg over the side of the bed.

"That's good. That's good you didn't feel it when I hit your foot."

"I didn't say I didn't feel it. I just said it didn't feel like anything awful."

"Okay. Okay," Billy got up and walked the floor. "We've got to figure out what to do."

"This thing isn't super hard." Hannah bent over her leg. "It's water heavy. I've done paper mache sculptures that were dense, and that's kind of how this feels. But there is other stuff too. Concrete maybe? Plaster? I don't know but we should be able to get it off."

As he listened to her, Billy tiptoed to the door, put his ear against it and tried to hear if anything was happening in the hall.

"I think they all went to bed." Billy put his back to the door. He laughed once and then again. "Man, this is weirdly awesome when you think about it. I mean we should have been dead a couple days ago, and then I was going to be your maid of honor, and now you'll be able to walk down the aisle 'cause your leg isn't really broken."

"Shut up." Hannah's relief had faded and reality was starting to sink in. "I'm scared. I really am."

"I know. Me, too."

He checked out the room. The high window offered no escape. There was nothing that could be used as a weapon. Then again, nobody had threatened them. Duncan and his troops were just Loony Tunes. Still, Loony Tunes could morph

real fast, and Billy didn't want to be around when that
happened.

"I'm going downstairs," he said.

"No, don't leave me." Hannah reached for him as if she could
pull him back from across the room.

"I'll be back. I promise."

If he touched Hannah he wouldn't go, so he unlocked the
door and slipped out. It was as black in the hallway as it was in
her room so Hannah didn't see him go. The only reason she
knew she was alone was because she couldn't hear Billy
breathing anymore.

Josie screamed and rolled, but she was caught in the sleeping
bag. Above her, around her, inside her she heard the roar of the
gigantic animal. She felt the swipe of its claws tear through the
sleeping bag like it was tissue paper and scrape her ribs. She felt
the animal's hot breath. She smelled the damn thing. Up was
down and down was up. Nell was hollering, scrambling inside
the tent that wasn't a tent anymore. Josie's screams and groans
mixed with the bear's roar. Nell's voice rose above the hellish
sounds of the attack as she threw out orders and food. The food
went outside; the orders shot right at Josie.

"Dead. Play Dead. Don't move," she called. "God dammit,
play dead! Fetal position. Now!"

Nell's voice muffled and Josie knew that she was following
her own orders: tucking her head down, pulling her knees up,
and holding her elbows tight. She jeopardized her own life every
time she spoke, so Josie tried to do as she was told. Her body,
though, had a life of its own. It struggled against the confines of
the sleeping bag, her legs and shoulders jerked in opposite

directions. Her brain was misfiring with thoughts, ideas, and plans.

If only she could. . .

If it would just. . .

If they hadn't. . .

"Dead. Now."

Nell's voice had dropped two octaves. Her breathing had calmed. She believed with everything in her that playing dead was the way to stay alive. Josie's brain heard that conviction. One part of her argued that all she needed was a fighting chance. The other part of her insisted she have faith in the woman who was curled up beside her, playing dead.

Finally, Josie pulled her knees up and rolled her shoulders forward. She tucked her head into her chest and didn't fight anymore. The bear roared and snuffed, but it had grown tired of the attack. She could hear it trolling. At one point – surely a hundred hours after the assault had begun – its nose came so close to Josie's head that it touched her hat. Behind her eyes was a slideshow of every image she had ever seen of a bear: the yellowing teeth, the hinged mouth that was wide enough to wrap itself around her head, its hind legs as big as trees. The whole package was majestic. Beautiful. Deadly. Deadly.

Play dead.

Play dead.

Play dead.

Play. . .

"You did good. You did good. Josie? Josie? It's over."

Nell's voice, sounded far away. Nell's touch was too soft to comfort her. The snow drifted lazily, like the angels were sifting flour for a heavenly cake. Josie Bates lay very still and waited for Nell to convince her it was okay to move. She didn't want to play dead anymore, but that's all she could do. She wanted to speak, but her vocal chords didn't work. When she could speak, she would tell Nell this: Even though she looked dead, Josie felt more alive than she ever had. When she could speak again, Josie would tell Archer how death came at her in the dark, how she felt its claws and smelled it's breath. It was a giant thing covered in fur, a roaring thing that pulled sounds from the very depths of hell. She knew that and yet she hadn't seen it. She would say to anyone who would listen that there is more than one way to survive and we are not cowards when we choose to play dead.

19

I feel like I'm ten years old because the first time my mom left me alone a whole day and a night was when I was ten years old. I watched the door of that terrible apartment and wished her back minute-by-minute-by-minute. It wore me out wishing her back. When she finally came, I thought my wishes worked. A few years later I figured it out: she came back because she had nowhere else to go. Now, watching the door of this bedroom, I wish Billy back in the worst way. I know there is nowhere else for him to go, but you never know about things like this.

You just never know.

Billy paused at the top of the stairs, torn between going down them or going through the door behind him. Behind that door was where Pea lived. She seemed to be the one causing all the trouble, so maybe it was time to have a talk with her. He decided to take the stairs because he didn't want to talk. He wanted something else, and what he wanted was in the kitchen.

The top flight of stairs was short. The second floor landing opened onto a long hall. There were four doors, two on each side. All were closed. He paused, heard nothing, made the jog and went down the stairs to the first floor. There was a creak and a snap. His boots were heavy and the woodwork was old, but he knew that each groan and crack was magnified in his mind. Anyone sleeping probably wouldn't give the noise a second thought. He took the last three steps quickly and crouched behind the banister when he got to ground. Peering through the rails, he looked toward the living room and through the picture window. Duncan's house was dark. The happy bridegroom was dreaming of wedded bliss.

Billy scooted over and looked the other way. He swung around the staircase, flattened himself against the wall, and inched toward the dining room. The heating stove in that room glowed faintly, the fire had burned down to embers and was ready to be stoked in the morning. They wasted nothing here, especially precious fuel during the darkest hours when blankets and quilts would keep them warm and there was nothing interesting to see.

By the time he reached the dining room, Billy was breathing easier. He pushed open the kitchen door and checked out the interior. Satisfied that it was empty, he went in. There was enough moonlight coming through the window that he didn't need more light.

There was a cabinet to the right of the stove. He opened the first drawer and found tableware. He took a big spoon. He opened the next drawer down. It was deep and cluttered with odds and ends. He went to the next drawer. Towels. The next one had what he wanted: knives.

Billy touched the blades like a blind man. They were sharp, thank goodness, and sturdy, but he had no idea what kind he might really need. He settled on a short, thick bladed one and a longer serrated one. Just as he closed the drawer, he heard a creak of wood and behind him the door started to open.

Stashing the tools under his shirt, Billy turned around expecting to see Duncan. Actually, he expected to see Duncan like maybe ten feet tall and his eyes all glowing red behind those stupid eyelids of his. Instead, Teresa, the human question mark was standing in the doorway.

"Are you alright?" she asked.

"I'm good. Yeah. Thanks," he answered. He even managed to chuck his chin up a little like he was cool with everything.

Which he wasn't.

It would be stupid to feel relieved just because it was Teresa who had found him. He and Hannah had no friends in this place. Every single one of them drank the same Kool Aid. Still, if he was going to be found out, Teresa was probably the best one to stumble in here.

She walked into the room. In in the moonlight, her silver hair sparkled and her expression was softened by weariness. She wore a thick robe curled up to her neck and long in the sleeves. It had some sort of embroidered thing on it that looked like Mickey Mouse.

"Are you hungry?" she asked.

Billy shook his head. "Hannah can't sleep. I was going to try to fix her something to help sleep."

"I just came to do the same thing. We're not supposed to, you know. Not after dinner."

Teresa puttered while Billy crossed his arms over his chest, feeling the knives and the spoon under his shirt. He hoped that she didn't turn on the light and see the hilts of the knives through his shirt or the guilt on his face. If that happened, he would have to do something bad to keep her from telling Duncan. If the choice was Teresa or Hannah there was no contest. Still, he would hate to hurt Teresa. He would hate to hurt anybody.

But Teresa didn't light a lantern, and she didn't seem much interested in him. She got the kettle, filled it with water, found a match and lit the stove. The sudden flare of the flame startled Billy. Teresa stared at it a minute and then put the kettle on.

"I used to do this every night after my husband left me. I thought a cup of tea would help me sleep. It didn't. Some worries are too big for a cup of tea." She looked over her shoulder and smiled. "Nobody should have worries that big when they're young."

"I don't think old people should either," Billy answered.

"You're right. It all should be easier, shouldn't it?" Teresa mused. "Or at least fairer. Maybe that's it. That was Duncan's dream to lead odd people to a place where they would be accepted. He believes he is blessed, and a prophet, and that together they can heal sad and broken people. Poor boy. It's going to be so hard for him when he realizes he can't heal anything and he can't make life fair."

"I think it's going to be kind of hard on the rest of them. I mean, they're the ones that need to be better," Billy pointed out.

"True." Teresa watched the pot as if she didn't expect it to boil. "And they need to be better in a different way than they think. That's the biggest problem."

"Are they really your kids?" Billy asked, wanting to leave but knowing he had to play it through with the tea.

"Oh, yes." She turned around and looked at him. "Duncan was a beautiful little boy, but shy and unsure of himself. I tried so hard to get him to come out of his shell. His father had no use for him. It was such a pity."

"What about the lady?"

"Penelope? That's her name. When Duncan was little he

called her Pea. She's beautiful and special. That's what they call people like her. Special."

"Is she a prophet like Duncan says?" Billy asked.

"No." Teresa shook her head. "At least I don't think so. She's a biblical savant. She knows every verse in the bible. I don't know how that happened. Me, a nurse's assistant from San Dimas gives birth to a biblical savant. Craziest thing. Can you imagine?"

Billy shook his head, but Teresa didn't notice. Billy was just the sounding board she was bouncing her memories off.

"And, yes, before you ask, I tried to kill them. And me. That was the only way I could figure out how to save them. I couldn't get help, you see. My husband was gone. I had no family. Every government agency passed me off to another one. Charities told me that I had a job, and that I should be grateful I could provide for them. I didn't have two cents to rub together. How was I going to pay for the kind of help we needed? Pea could get violent. I had no idea what she would do if I left her alone with Duncan. He should have been in school. What a mess. Me. Alone with these two odd children who I loved so dearly.

"Anyway, I did leave them alone. Duncan learned all sorts of things even though he didn't really go to school. I went to work. Duncan cared for Pea. Pea talked to him in verse and he figured out what it meant. We had a beautiful big bible at home. I don't even know where I got it. Anyway, I guess that's how Duncan came to believe that was his job in life – to interpret the Bible."

"How does he know what everything really means?" Billy asked.

"Oh, he doesn't. He never did. He just takes what he wants and fashions it into directions that seem to make sense. He contrives stories to justify what he wants and how he thinks life should go. I think it comforts him. I think it makes him feel useful in the world."

Teresa brightened. She was happy to have someone interested in what she had to say.

"The way he talks is so convincing that people believe him. Desperate people. Lonely people. People who just don't fit in anywhere. You can't blame them. It's a lovely thought that our lives are directed by a beautiful young woman who talks to God and a handsome, happy young man who brings the message. Who wouldn't like that?"

"Me. Us," Billy said. "Hannah and me."

"I know." Teresa shrugged but the hump on her back didn't move, only the shoulder in front of it. "It was quite hysterical tonight. I got caught up in it myself. But I know Duncan can't marry that girl. We'll figure out a way to put it off. Spring will come, and you'll go away."

"We want to go now," Billy said.

The kettle whistled just then. Teresa took it off the stove and brought it to the counter. She opened a cabinet and took down two mugs.

"Do you want some, too?"

He shook his head. "No, just Hannah."

"Alright." She reached in the cabinet again and took down a tin of tea bags as she talked. "You can't go now. That is one truth from Duncan. The river is bad."

"But if we could go, which way would we head?"

"If you could?" Teresa dipped the tea bag and thought about that. "I honestly don't know, Billy. I've been here too long. Robert goes off in the boat and comes back. People come to the store, but I don't know where they live. I don't know their names.

"Just stay here. We'll take care of you. Duncan will calm down. Pea will say something else, and he'll forget about getting married. He might even try to heal us all. I might suggest that to him. You know, the healing before the wedding. That would be just like a sign, wouldn't it? That's a thought, isn't it?"

"Yeah, good idea. Maybe that would work," Billy agreed.

"There, that should do it." Teresa took the tea bag out and offered the mug to Billy. When Billy reached for it, she pulled it back. "Wait. Melody keeps some special things in her cabinet. She's very good with herbs and such."

Teresa turned around, opened another cabinet, tiptoed up and felt around. When she found what she wanted, she unscrewed the cap and put a little into Hannah's tea. She was smiling when she turned around.

"Tell Hannah it will be fine. This will help her get some rest. You should sleep, too."

She pressed the mug into his hands and then patted his face. Billy put his shoulder to the swinging door. He looked back to see her cleaning up the kitchen, putting things away. He wanted to say something to her, but Billy couldn't think of much so he just said:

"Night, Teresa. Thank you."

"Goodnight, Billy. It will all be better in the morning."

"Sure."

He carried the mug of steaming tea in one hand and took the knives and spoon from inside his shirt with the other. He saw no one on his way upstairs. He opened the door of Hannah's room and locked it behind him.

"Here. Teresa said this would help you sleep." He handed her the tea and showed her his tools. "And you'll sleep a whole lot better when we get that thing off you."

An hour later the cast lay in pieces around the bed and the tea was drunk. Her bruised and swollen leg was examined and both of them decided it was hurt but not broken. When Hannah was tucked in for the night, Billy sat at the foot of the bed watching her until he couldn't keep his eyes open another minute. He was so tired he couldn't even be afraid anymore. For the first time since he'd been in this place he was in a quiet room. No prayers, no weird hours for him to be awake or asleep, just silence and dark and Hannah.

She was turned on her side, one hand under her cheek, her high-necked blouse all buttoned up. Dragging his blanket with him, Billy lay down behind her. He didn't think twice when he put one arm under his head and the other over her hip. He pressed his body gently against hers. When she didn't wake up, Billy Zuni closed his eyes. Sleep came so fast the only thought he had before he drifted off was how right it felt to lie close to Hannah Sheraton.

"Guillard?"

"Yeah?"

"I was thinking?"

"Yeah?"

"What was with the glove?"

"What glove?"

"The one you found at the scene," Archer answered. "Did you ever figure out if it was the truck driver's? Was he wearing gloves when you found him?"

"One," Andre said. "His other arm was gone, remember?"

"Yeah."

Archer put one arm behind his head. The bed in the six-room motel was too soft, too narrow, and too unfamiliar for him to fall asleep easily. The information they had received about the prints on the key that opened the back of that container was not exactly soothing.

"Think you could have someone take a look? You know, check the size, the manufacturer, stuff like that. Just a look to see if there's anything interesting."

"Sure, Archer. I'll call Cressi in the morning. The glove should be in the locker."

"Thanks. 'Preciate it."

"No problem."

"Still. I appreciate it."

"Archer."

"Yeah?"

"Just so you know. I'm with you until we find out what happened to them. One way or another"

"'Preciate that, too, Guillard. Night."

20

"He did a number, didn't he?" Nell said.

"I think it was a she," Josie drawled.

"Funny." She looked Josie up and down. "You know, I really hate your guts right about now."

"For bringing you out here?" Josie asked.

"No. I hate you because a bear mauled you and you look like you had your beauty sleep and then some. You and Andre are cut out of the same cloth. Ticks me off royally."

"Yeah, I'm sure I'm a sight to behold." Josie started to laugh, but like the old joke she stopped because it hurt when she did. "Did you find the satellite phone?"

"Not yet."

Nell bent down and grabbed what was left of the tent shell and held it up for Josie to see. The material was shredded on one side. Five slashes had destroyed it, three of which made contact with Josie. Nell took the stakes out of their sleeves and folded the whole thing up as best she could. She picked up the bottle of scotch and tossed it at Josie.

"You need more of that."

"You are cruel." Josie said.

"Do it," Nell ordered.

Since Nell had been right about everything so far, Josie did as she was told. She took the bottle of booze, opened it. Gingerly she brushed the snow pack away from her torso. Nell had applied it to stop the bleeding and reduce the swelling. The slash marks were red and raw, but not deep enough for stitches. They ran from her side to the middle of her back.

Josie picked up the bottle of scotch, breathed deep through her nose and before she let it out, she poured the alcohol onto her wounds to clean them. She let out a yelp, and then bit it off with her lower lip between her teeth.

"Damn, that hurts," she muttered. When she could unclench her teeth again, she said, "I don't think I've ever been so scared."

"Nature is a scary thing."

"You're telling me? I'd rather tangle with a shark at home. At least we have lifeguards in civilization. And we have hospitals and cars to get you there." Josie struggled to her feet. On her right side, her jacket, sweater and shirt beneath it were cut to pieces, but she'd have to make do. "I'm good now. Let me help."

"Just see if your stuff is together."

Nell tossed the pack toward Josie who let if fall at her feet rather than reaching for it. She was mobile, but she wasn't going to risk making things worse. Nell had informed her in no uncertain terms that if Josie was in a bad way, Nell would be hiking out alone to get help. Josie wanted none of that, so she bent her knees and unzipped the pack. There were no claw marks on the fabric, and it was still bulging with her belongings.

"Hey, I found an extra sweater. Can you help me get out of this one?" Josie unsnapped her jacket.

Nell was by her side in three steps, easing the parka off Josie's shoulder. The ruined sweater was more problematic.

"Bend forward," Nell directed. "Put your arms out in front of you. That shouldn't hurt as much as it would if we tried to get this off with your arms up over your head."

Josie did as she was told, taking her own sweet time to do it. Finally, she was in position and they got the ruined sweater off. Nell had the fresh one rolled up and ready to go.

"Okay," she said. "Here it comes."

Josie looked up, ready to tell Nell to take it a little slower this time, but she never got the words out. Her sudden silence had less to do with the fact that she was standing half-naked and freezing in the middle of Alaska than with what she was looking at standing at the edge of the clearing.

Hannah bucked and the sound she made while she did it was as close to someone strangling as Billy figured he'd ever heard. He bolted out of his sleep, and sat up against the wall in case she was ticked at him for being in bed with her. She wasn't. In fact, it was doubtful Hannah had any idea he was there. Her eyes were rolled back, her mouth was open, and her hands clawed at the blankets. Her head whipped one way and then the other.

"Hannah! Hannah! Hey, wake up!"

He screamed at her. He grabbed her shoulders and pulled her close, wrapping her in his arms. The seizure was so violent he could hardly keep ahold of her. He pushed her down into the mattress and held her there as best he could. She was out of control, so he threw himself off the bed and dashed for the door. He stopped when he heard a crash.

Hannah's hand had hit the bedside table hard and everything on it jumped. Billy rushed back and put the lamp and glass on the floor. Hannah groaned, and moaned. She was spread out on the bed in the most improbable contortion of limbs. Her chest heaved and her eyes stared sightlessly at the ceiling. When she started to roll again, Billy had no choice. He ran for the door, threw it open, and went screaming into the hall.

"Help. Help me. Someone. Anyone. Help!"

He pounded down the stairs taking two at a time. On the second floor he ran up and down, banging on each door.

"Help! Hannah's dying! Help!"

Foster stuck his head out to see what the commotion was, and then he ducked back inside again.

"You freakin' freak," Billy screamed at him. "Teresa! Melody! Anyone. Help! Help!"

No other door opened. He took the final flight of stairs, jumping the last three steps and skidding on the rug. He turned toward the living room. It was empty. He threw open the front door. Glenn was where he always was, chopping wood. It was day, not night. He called to Glenn:

"Glenn! Glenn! Hannah's sick. Hannah's. . ."

"Billy. What's happened?" Teresa hurried from the dining room, wiping her hands on her apron. He grabbed her and pulled her.

"Come up. Hannah's dying. Come now."

Teresa went as fast as she could, up the stairs, calling down the second floor hall for Melody before Billy pulled her on and twirled her into the room.

"Oh my lord," Teresa gasped.

Melody rushed in and stopped in the doorway. Hannah had thrown herself around again. This time her legs were scissored and her head hung over the side of the bed. Drool dripped from the corner of her mouth and made spots on the floor. Her body jerked like she was being electrocuted, her fingers twitched, her face was chalky.

Teresa rushed to the bed. "Help me, Billy. Help me get her upright."

"What's happened? What's going on?" Melody rushed to the

bed, putting her good hand on Hannah as if that might help right her. Suddenly, Hannah's neck arched, her back jackknifed, and a second later she lay across the bed and vomited.

Melody cried out. Teresa stepped back. Billy wailed and took her in his arms.

"Hannah, what's wrong. What's wrong? Wake up."

"Get away, Billy. Go away," Teresa barked.

"I'm not leaving you alone with her. I'm not leaving you. . .you tried to kill. . ."

Before he could finish, Teresa drew back and struck him. His head flew back and his long hair snapped around his face.

"Get out of here," she ordered. "Get out of here now."

Melody took his arm and hurried him to the door. She shoved him into the hallway. "If you want to help her, go away. Let Teresa and me see to her."

Melody slammed the door and before he could open it, he heard her throw the lock. Billy slammed his open palms against the wall. He slammed them again and again and downstairs Duncan heard the commotion as he came into the house.

He didn't want to go upstairs. He wouldn't go upstairs. Waiting was what he did best.

"Nell, put my sweater on. Now, Nell," Josie said. "We have a visitor."

Nell looked over her shoulder, raised an eyebrow. She put Josie's sweater on, picked up the ruined parka, and helped her put that on, too. All the while she kept an eye on the man leaning against a tree watching them.

He didn't smile. Then again he didn't frown. He wasn't exactly checking out Josie's bod. Then again, he wasn't exactly looking away either. He was just standing there holding a couple things: a towel that belonged to Nell, a hunk of plastic that looked suspiciously like part of a satellite phone, a rifle, a .44 Magnum, a quiver of arrows slung across his back one way and a bow the other way. On his head was a dew rag made from the American flag. On top of that was a cap that looked like he had stitched it himself and on which was affixed a ptarmigan head that appeared had not spent enough time at the taxidermist.

His clothing was equally interesting: a down jacket, puffy at the chest but worn out at the arms and making him look like a partially deflated Michelin Man. He wore a sweater, jeans that were shiny with wear, boots that were dull with scuffing, laces in one and not the other.

"Neighbor." Nell moved back a step so that she and Josie stood shoulder to shoulder.

"Ain't your neighbor," he said, his mouth opening just enough so that Josie counted three teeth.

Since there seemed to be no response to that comment, they all waited. The women figured he would make the ground rules since he was the one with the weapons. It took a good five seconds before he threw back his head and laughed hard and loud. Josie could see she had been wrong. He had eight teeth, and it wouldn't take long before those fell out from the looks of them.

"Had you ladies goin' didn't I?"

Josie and Nell looked at one another. When Nell shrugged and pulled a face, Josie relaxed.

"That you did." Nell stepped out in front. She didn't put out her hand but she raised one, and their new friend was happy enough with that. He held up her towel.

"You had a visitor last night looks like. Found a little trail of your belongings. I was looking for something that might want killing afore winter really sets in when I stumbled across all this."

"Did you see it?" Nell asked.

"Naw. Saw the slashes in the trees by the river, but that's about it. Stood maybe seven feet. Not the biggest I've ever seen, but good size." He checked out the tent, looked at Josie's jacket, and took a long look at Nell. "Figured I'd be finding me a body or two. Just didn't know they'd still be breathin'. Happy to see you ladies up and about. Too bad though."

"You'd rather we were dead?" Josie asked.

"No ma'am. But if you were I could scavenge me a few things, you know. I'm the lazy sort. Don't like to go get my supplies in any store less I have to. Besides, haven't got any country money to speak of. Well," he pulled his bushy brows together, "that ain't exactly true. Might have some. Got a disability check the government's always telling me I'm supposed to get. Must be at my address."

"And where would that be?" Nell asked.

"Don't remember. That's my disability. Don't remember much of anything important." He prowled around the campsite, checking things out, seeing if there was anything he liked. The only thing that seemed to catch his interest was Josie's pack.

"Want to sell that?" he raised his chin toward it.

"Not if you don't have any money," Josie said.

"You could take it out in trade," he answered.

He waited a few beats, threw back his head and laughed again as he wilted to the ground. The bow pushed up behind him nearly knocking the ptarmigan hat off his head. He moved his butt until it settled in just right. He put his rifle on the ground. But he kept his gun in his lap. He laughed so hard he had to wipe away a few tears.

"Don't worry. I ain't no pervert."

"Great. We'd hate to have to beat you to a pulp and leave you here to freeze." Nell sat down across from him. Josie put herself back on her log. Nell pointed her thumb her way. "Josie." She pushed it at her own chest. "Nell."

"Stu. Nobody calls me that, though," he said.

"What do they call you?" Josie asked.

"Nothing. Ain't nobody out here but me, and the damn grizzlies don't care what my name is."

There was that laugh again. Josie sighed but before she could suggest to Nell that they take off, Stu made them an offer they couldn't refuse.

"I'm serious, there, about trade. I mean you ladies gotta be out here for some reason, and looks like you're not making a real fine go of it. So, what can old Stu help you with? Trade you that fine pack you got there for a little guidin', maybe a warm place to sleep? Got me a little cabin I built myself. Got some food laid in and such. What is it you need and old Stu will make sure it happens. All I'm asking is that fine pack of yours."

Josie smiled. This kind of trade was right up her alley. "Well, Stu, here's the thing. We're looking for people."

"Any specific people?"

"Yes, but we'll settle for a little map of where we'll find any people. Then we'll take it from there."

Stu smiled, reached in his pocket and pulled out something brown. It could have been a plug of tobacco or moose droppings. It didn't matter what it was, he put it in his mouth and it made him happy.

"Well, now, that's a trade I can certainly make. I know where all the people are. Good folk, crazy folk, lost folk, sad folk. . . "

"Great," Josie said. "Let's get to it."

He stuck out his hand. "Pack first."

21

Billy slid down the hall wall, knees bent, arms resting on top, hands hanging, and head back. He stared at the ceiling and listened for sounds coming from Hannah's bedroom. The minutes went by. Thoughts and plans ran through his head and disappeared through some trap door in his brain before he could catch hold of them.

His head rolled to one side. He looked at the floor. The edge of his lip tipped up and he found himself thinking about Hermosa Beach. He was weird when Hannah met him and he was a kid. A stupid kid who thought a cloudy day was about the worst thing that could happen. Childhood still clung to him like sand on wet feet and like that sand it had become bothersome and itchy and hard to get rid of. This day wasn't just cloudy, it was storming and it was time for him to grow up for good.

Billy swung his head the other way. He looked at the stairs, and the faded wallpaper. Hannah said whoever built this house was an artist. All Billy saw was old stuff and that's why he needed Hannah. He needed her to see the world with her artist eyes and she needed him to see. . .

To see. . .

Billy closed his eyes. He wasn't quite sure why Hannah needed him, but Billy was almost positive that she did.

His chest rose with one deep breath. He pushed his butt up against the wall and let his hands drop to the floor. His eyes stayed on the bedroom doors. There were only two: Hannah's and Pea's. Pea, the prophetess. Pea the one who ran the place according to God's will. If she could talk to God then it was time she started having a conversation with Him about Hannah.

Billy got up and went to that door. He put his hand on the knob. He thought to knock. It was a lady's room after all. But what if it wasn't? What if it was, like, some kind of angel's room?

Billy turned the knob.

If this was an angel's room then he definitely had to go in.

Archer and Andre had made two stops by the time the call came. One stop was back at the diner for a breakfast so good that it almost made Archer forget why they were in Alaska. The other was at a small cabin where a guy who maintained the road in winter lived. He also ran a first aid stop, was on call for stranded travelers, and basically was the only guy around dedicated to waiting for disaster to strike. He hadn't heard of any kids hitching who were having problems. He hadn't seen them. It had all been pretty quiet around his parts for a good long while. He was hoping it would stay that way. His plow was ready, though. It looked like the snow was going to be bad, but trucks still had to get through. It wasn't like everyone just sat around the fire knitting when the winters were bad.

As soon as they got in the car the radio lit up. It was only eight in the morning.

"Guillard. Good morning."

"Morning Andre," came the now familiar voice. "Hope you two slept tight."

"Bugs in a rug, Cressi. What do you have for me?"

"A little something. Might not help you out too much, but it can't hurt," she answered. "That glove had a sales ticket on the inside that someone didn't remove after they bought it. Also, the glove is huge. Don't know if you noticed that when you bagged it. I checked with the morgue. It was two sizes too big for your driver. If he was wearing it, that could have contributed to the accident. He might not have been able to get a good feel for the wheel. If not, it belongs to someone about the size of a mountain."

"Where's the ticket from?" Andre asked.

"It's a thrift shop over in Taylor. Want me to call over there and ask them about it?" she offered.

Archer shook his head. Andre answered:

"No. That's okay. We're only a couple hours from there."

"Suit yourself," Cressi said.

Archer put out a hand to get Andre's attention. He mouthed 'send a picture' as he held up his cell.

"Cressi, can you shoot a picture of that glove to a cell phone? Good. Yeah." He provided Archer's cell number. Before he signed off Andre asked, "Have you heard anything from Nell?"

"Nope. Should I?"

"No reason. Just thinking she might have checked in."

Andre signed off and started the car. As he pulled out onto the road and headed the opposite direction they had been going, he said:

"Those two have been awful quiet."

Guillard was right, so Archer didn't bother to respond.

———

God didn't strike him dead when he opened the door to Pea's room, and Billy figured that was a good sign. Still, he kept one hand on the knob after he closed it just in case he had to dodge a thunderbolt or some lightning or something.

"Hello?" he whispered.

He was standing in some kind of Goth freak church. Every inch of the walls was painted with pictures of Jesus doing stuff like cracking open an eggplant or wearing a crown of thorns that was really made out of pencils and pens and hypodermic needles. In between the paintings were papers all neatly printed with poems and stories. Each of the paintings had a little sign next to them with the title and price.

Billy couldn't imagine who would buy these things but he also couldn't figure out who would see them. Not only did no one come to Clara's Landing, only the congregation came inside the house. Most of them didn't go into Pea's room.

"Hello," he called again.

This time his voice was stronger and he ventured further, checking out the great bed, the beautiful cover on it, and the fluffy pillows. He started for the bed, and that's when he heard it: a trill, a burp and a trill. He whirled around and peered into the corners of the room looking for Pea.

"Where are you?"

He wished there was more light, but he'd been wishing for more light since that stupid fishing boat where they had to sleep below deck. That felt like a coffin; this room felt like a mausoleum.

In the stove the fire flared and threw golden light through the intricately molded grate. It cast a pattern of flowers and swirls on the far wall and that's when he saw the woman kneeling by the window. Her arms were bare and beautiful. Her hands were splayed over the heavy wooden window shutters. He could see the soles of her feet, pink and pretty as if they had never been walked on. The rest of her was covered in a white dress that was spread out around her like a wedding gown. Her head hung between narrow shoulders and her hair hung over her face. Billy inched his way across the room, talking all the while:

"Hello, Pea. I'm Billy. My name is Billy Zuni, and my friend is Hannah. Do you know Hannah? She said a lady was looking at her when we first got here. Was that you? Is that how you knew she was black? Is that why you told Duncan about that black woman thing and Moses?"

He was standing right behind her and still Pea didn't turn around.

"Hey, so I'm sorry for just coming in here, but here's the thing..."

Billy's voice caught again. He rolled his eyes. He was like a little kid afraid to talk to the teacher. If he was going to be a little kid then he better be the kind that didn't run away crying. He tried again.

"Here's the thing. My friend, Hannah, is really sick. She needs a doctor. She needs to get out of here. And I was thinking, since everyone says you talk to God you must be really special."

She didn't move. Her hands were still against the wood. Her arms didn't even shake. Billy cleared his throat.

"I'm not asking you to talk to God, but maybe you could tell Duncan to help us. I don't think the river looks that bad. I think we could make it on the boat. I think we've got to try. You know, to get Hannah back home. To save her. So, could you please?"

Billy stood behind Pea and waited, but he waited in vain. She didn't move a finger. She didn't make a sound. The wood in the grate shifted and the fire inside cast its pretty patterned light over her white dress once more.

Suddenly tired and defeated, Billy couldn't stand up a second longer. He stepped around her. He knelt beside her. He was so close to her that she should have at least looked at him or told him to go away, but she didn't. Billy wasn't even sure Pea knew he was there. That was okay because he knew she was there, and he felt safe right then. He understood the whole *Within* thing now, and he was happy for her. This time, when he talked, his voice didn't catch. He talked to her the way he would have liked to talk to Hannah.

"You know, Pea, it's just that I love Hannah. I think I'd die for her, but I don't want her to die. You should help someone who feels like me because there aren't many people in the world who love someone the way I love Hannah. That's why you should help me. If you can, I mean. I'm just sayin', I love her."

Since that was all there was to say Billy stopped talking. They knelt together, looking at the wall until he heard a trill and a pretty burp and a trill again.

22

I saw a movie called What Dreams May Come. *It was about a man whose children die in a car crash, and his wife kills herself because she can't bear her grief. Killing herself is a sin and she goes to hell. But this man loves his wife so much that he travels down to hell where she is living in a place that looked like their house, but it was all rat infested and gross. She has to live with the ruin she believes she caused. He tries to save her soul because it wasn't her fault that her children died, and it wasn't his fault. It just was.*

I don't think anyone will be at fault if I die. I know what's happening to me is so bad that whichever way the scales tip is the way they will stay. I can't do anything about it. That's just what I know. My body is awesomely broken because it moves by itself. I am thrown around this bed like that girl in The Exorcist, *and I want to bite my tongue off, and I am choking on whatever comes up out of my stomach.*

It won't be anyone's fault if I die.

At least I don't think so. And I don't think I'm going to hell because I tried real hard to do the right things on earth. Then again, I've ended up places I didn't deserve to be before.

But I wouldn't expect anyone to come get me in hell.

. . .

Duncan sat at the head of the dining room table.

Hours had been suspended so that everyone could be in the meeting, and they were starting to wonder why *Hours* were ever sacred if Duncan dismissed them so easily. No one was happy, least of all Duncan. But this was different than the night before. The congregation wasn't afraid of him now; they were sad and baffled. The Cushite woman was sick, perhaps dying, when just a few hours ago she was Duncan's intended. A few hours ago there was not only going to be a wedding, but Duncan had confirmed there would be a healing for them all on the night of the wedding. That was the plan. The plan wasn't any good anymore because Hannah was upstairs dying or maybe possessed.

"Teresa," Duncan said. "What do you have to tell us?"

"She's quiet now, but she's still convulsing. I don't know what's wrong. Her stitches aren't infected. There's no fever. She was healthy last night."

"Then it's God, isn't it?" Glenn asked his question. Robert tried to give him an answer.

"I would deduce that it's the devil because she's like throwing up and writhing." Robert wiped his nose on the back of his sleeve. "That's right, isn't it, Duncan? That writhing people are from hell. But then. . ."

Robert's brows beetled. He turned his massive head one way and then the other way. His tiny eyes looked at the people around the table. He scratched at the leather-like mound of red flesh on the side of his face.

"Then why would Pea say God said for you to marry her, Duncan?"

He swung his head back to Duncan.

"Are you like the devil? Is this a trick? Are you going to heal us for the dev. . ."

"Oh, no!" Melody's lips rounded and her face became an mask of pure horror.

"Enough, Robert. That's enough out of you," Duncan snapped. "Hannah is not the devil. I am not from the devil. Pea was not wrong. Something else has happened. Perhaps, the devil has tried to interfere with our happiness, but it might be something else. Melody, you looked in on her last night."

"She was fine like Teresa said. She and Billy were talking."

"He didn't come to his bed last night," Duncan said.

"Did he stay the night with her? Duncan?" Glenn said. "Isn't she supposed to be your wife? How could he stay with her?"

"He's her friend. I didn't think there would be any harm in him staying one night with her," he said, but everyone was uncomfortable with yet another rule broken.

Duncan knew that nothing short of hog tying Billy Zuni would have kept him from Hannah last night. He wouldn't let Billy disrupt the order further. He and Hannah had already upset everyone with their reaction to Pea's revelation. That Billy was shocked was understandable; that Hannah was appalled was unfathomable. God had sent her; Pea had confirmed it. There could be no other interpretation of the passage. There should have been joy.

Duncan's fingers went to his lips. Those lips weren't splitting his face into two happy parts anymore. His expression was grim. The people around the table were looking at him all wrong. He felt their confusion, and he knew what they were thinking. If he could heal, why didn't he heal the girl who was supposed to be his wife? From the kitchen came the sound of the kettle. Teresa rose, but Duncan got up first.

"I'll get my own tea."

He left the room, and behind him anxious looks were exchanged. Duncan never got his own tea or food or anything. Melody put her hands in her lap, the fingers of her good hand stroking the back of her withered one. Teresa kept her hands on the table as if she was ready to rush off. Glenn's burned hands went up and down, touching his nose, his chin and his cheeks. Robert swiped at his perpetually running nose. Foster muttered, the family of little people whispered to one another. From the kitchen they heard a cup drop and shatter. No one spoke for fear Duncan would hear them; they stopped thinking for fear that God would hear their thoughts and tell Pea. A cabinet opened and then they heard nothing until the swinging door between the dining room and the kitchen opened. Duncan stood there, his face tight with anger. He didn't have a cup of tea. He had a question:

"What is this?"

Everyone looked at him and then they looked at the vial of clear liquid he was holding between two fingers.

Stu's place brought a new definition to the word cabin. It was four walls made of logs, and a roof made of wood and tin. The windows had no glass, but were covered with crucified hides to keep the cold out and the warm in. He had a needle stuffed mattress made of sacks, a table with three legs and a stack of rocks for the fourth one. He had a blanket that looked like a bearskin, a bowl fashioned from wood and two cups made of tin. He had some books. *Madam Bovary*, which he hadn't read, three books in a series called *Spooky Things*, which he had, and a cookbook with recipes to be made over an open fire.

"Got 'em from all over the place," Stu opined. "Amazing what people leave behind when they come around here. You're supposed to clean up after you, you know. Yeah, but you two know that. Damn fine you carried all your gear out. How you feeling there, Miss Josie? Feeling okay 'cause if not, the hospitality of my bed is all yours. I'll be respectful, especially with Ms. Nell standing around here, but you just lie on down if you're feeling faint."

"I'm good, Stu," Josie said. "Thanks though. That's really nice of you."

"Been a while since I entertained a lady, but I still remember how to be polite."

Josie didn't dare look at Nell for fear she would laugh. Even though she would kill to lie down, Stu's bed was not the most inviting prospect.

"So." He rubbed his hands together. "What's it going to be? I got coffee. Made it fresh day before yesterday."

"We've got water." Nell tossed a plastic bottle at Josie who caught it easily. Stu shook his head.

"Hate those things. People leave those things everywhere. Made me a duck blind out of a bunch of 'em once. Figured I'd put 'em to good use. The ducks could see me clear as day, so it didn't work. That blind is probably still there."

"So," Josie pulled out a chair and put her map on the table. "Can you show us where there are people around here? That's what we really need to know. We're looking for two teenagers who were in an accident over here." She pointed to the area where she and Nell had started. "We think someone found them and probably took them in. It would have to be remote otherwise they would have called us."

Nell sat down, too, and Stu found another chair in a corner and pulled it up. The seat was so bad that he sunk to eye level with the table when he sat down.

"This won't work." He stood up and pushed it with his foot so it slid over the hard-packed dirt floor. "Move over there, Miss Nell."

She did and he sat down beside her. Nell put her hand to her nose. Josie turned the map so he could look at it right side up.

"So, you're looking for somebody who has a good heart. Well, that limits things some." His finger came down on a spot near a lake. "Colonel Mustard's over there."

"Is that his real name?" Nell asked.

Stu shook his head. "Naw, I call him that 'cause the guy got gassed over in the Middle East somewheres. I thought it was funny. He nearly blew my head off when I called him that. We don't socialize much anymore. I don't think he'd have your kids. Not the friendliest person in the world. Take us about a day and a half to get to him, anyways. Now, way over here you've got the Bensons. She's a native – handsome woman – he's retired from something. I don't know what. They're sort of normal. They've got a septic tank and everything. Can't imagine they would have been up there with your wreck. Show me again where?"

Josie pointed to the spot on the map.

"Nope. They're old folk. There's no reason for them to go that far. He's got a bad heart. Now here, maybe you've got something here." Stu tapped hard on the map at a place near the Yukon. "That there's a real Inuit settlement. A pretty little town. Well, it's sort of a town. One street. Well, it's a sort of street. They have a council lodge. Course, there's almost no one left to go there, but you've got a few families. I've been over there – it was a long time ago – but they had some kind of festival. Pitiful turnout. Lots of their young folk are gone. Still, they would take care of your kids if they found them."

"Do they have communications?"

"Damn straight! One of 'em even has a satellite dish. Big stuff over there. Poor as church mice, but one of 'em got a dish."

Nell looked at Josie and shook her head. "If Billy and Hannah were with them and could talk, they would have given them your information."

"We could check it out. They might have heard something," Josie said.

"Worth a shot. We've got nothing else," Nell agreed.

"I didn't say that, did I? I didn't say you got nothin' else," Stu barked. "You gotta let me finish. You gotta give me a moment to gear up my thought process and such."

"Sorry." Josie pushed the map closer, doubting they would get any useful information. Stu was a happy hermit who, now that he'd found some people to talk to, wanted the tea party to last a little longer.

"Here," his finger circled a spot right on the river. "This is where you can find a bunch of do-gooders. Don't have much truck with them, but they got a little store and they don't mind trading. But they might . . ."

Before he could finish, the room was filled with the sound of tinny voices. The women sat up. Nell looked over her shoulder. When she turned back, she was grinning.

"You've got a radio."

"Damn straight. I don't want to be alone out here. That would just be plain nuts."

———

"What is this? Where did it come from? Melody? It was in the cabinet with your remedies."

"It's. . .oh. . ." Melody shot a frantic gaze Robert's way. He rubbed and rubbed his nose and then his face. From behind his hand he looked at her. It was hard to tell if he was pleading with her or threatening her. Not that it mattered. She had to tell the truth. "It's . . . I found it in Robert's jacket."

Robert tried to jump up to defend himself, but his stomach got caught on the table so he pleaded his case sitting down.

"I didn't mean to keep it. I just forgot it, Duncan. I forgot.

Can't a guy forget?" Robert wailed and threw his head back. His leather face was paralyzed and his pink, baby face was screwed up in a tantrum. "I wasn't stealing, and if Melody didn't give it to you then she was stealing."

"No, really, I wasn't." Both her hands went up, one waving and the other flapping. "I found it when I washed his jacket, and put it aside to keep it safe until I finished that chore. There are four more. They're way in the back. That's all I did."

"It was in the truck," Robert screeched. "Boxes and boxes of it. I was going to show it to you for the store. I was going to get it and. . . "

". . .Then there was Hannah and Billy and everything," Melody talked over Robert.

Around the table, the others cringed. Peter hid his face against his mother. Foster made sounds. Teresa's head hung down. Melody tried to explain.

"I just didn't get around to giving it to you Duncan. I'm sorry," she sobbed. "There hasn't been anyone at the store. We didn't miss out on a chance to sell it. . ."

"Stop! Both of you." Duncan ordered.

He palmed the vial. His jaw was so tight it felt like it would shatter. Sell it! The fools didn't know what they had. They hadn't even looked at the label. It was just a shiny little thing. That's what they liked. Any shiny little thing. Except for Melody. She was intelligent. She was also hurt by the prophesy of Duncan's wedding. She'd been restless and unhappy waiting for the healing. Perhaps she was also a good little actress. That might be it. She might have failed in her penance. She had tried to kill her sister, why not try and kill Hannah?

"It's not full? Why is that? Look, there's some missing."

He pushed the little bottle toward her. Melody looked at it. It had been full when she found it. She shook her head and shook it and shook it.

"I don't know. I don't know," she said. "Maybe I spilled some. I mean, I opened it, but I put the top right back on and . . . Brother. . .Duncan. . ."

"Melody, do not lie," he roared. "God will know. Pea will know. Tell me the truth. It won't affect your healing. I promise."

"But I didn't lie. . ." Melody sobbed. Her withered hand began to tremble and her good one covered her face. "I didn't. . ."

"Stop." Teresa stood up and all eyes turned her way. She raised her chin. "Melody didn't do anything. It was me, I used it. I will confess, Duncan. Privately."

Duncan stared at her, dropped his hand, and put the vial on the table. He should have known. Teresa was trying to ruin his life once again.

"Everyone go to your rooms," he muttered. "I'll talk to Teresa now."

Chairs scraped. People struggled to get up and when they finally went single file out of the room, Duncan called to Melody.

"Look in on Hannah. If she's not quiet, come back and get us."

"May I do my *Hours* with her?" Melody pleaded. Duncan nodded. When she was gone, he sank into his chair and held the glass bottle between his fingers.

"You are so deceitful, Teresa," Duncan said. "I thought you were ready to be healed, but here you are up to your old tricks. Trying to kill a child, a child who would be my bride. You can't help yourself, can you? You'd do anything to harm me."

"You can think what you want, but I didn't try to kill her. I don't know what that is. I only know that I must have put it in her tea by accident. Billy was in the kitchen last night. Hannah couldn't sleep, so I fixed her tea, and thought I was putting in Melody's sleeping potion. That's all it was."

"You expect me to believe that?" Duncan snapped.

235

"I don't care what you believe anymore, Duncan. All these years I've served you and Pea and tried to make up for what I did. That should count for something."

"If you are poisoning people then I have every right to doubt you." He slapped the glass bottle in front of her and turned it so she could see the label. "Liquid nicotine. This will kill you if you drink or even get it on your skin. You put half a bottle in that tea."

"Lord, forgive me." Teresa hung her head. "I didn't know, Duncan. I didn't."

"You just couldn't stand for me to be happy. I found a bride and you try to kill her. I have a sister, and you try to kill her. I . . . "

"I didn't try to kill that girl upstairs and this was never about hurting you." Teresa's hands came down hard on the table and she turned her tortured body so she could look at him. "I've reached in that cabinet a hundred times. There has never been anything in it except Melody's remedies. The one for sleep is on the right. I took it and poured this in the tea. It was a mistake."

"Teresa. Teresa." Duncan shook his head. "If anyone finds out about this they will put you away for murder. It won't be like last time. No institution for you. I will testify to anyone who will listen that you attempted cold blooded murder."

"And you will be an accessory. I'll tell them that you intended to keep that girl prisoner. I will tell them that when she didn't want to marry you, you hurt her. The rest of them will be thrown out into the world again. I know that's not what you want, so don't you threaten me, Duncan. You're the one who is evil. You have preyed on these people's hopes and fears. It sickens me. And why did you do it? To make yourself important? To keep from being alone? To punish me? You just can't stand being overlooked."

"I helped them," he shot back. "They came willingly."

"They did not," Teresa countered. "They were so sick and helpless. They were all disturbed. And you came with your ministry, scooping them up when they were released and had nowhere else to go. I should have stopped it then. I should have told someone, but I didn't because I wanted to atone. For a while I even believed that you and Pea and God had a plan. I was so wrong."

"I am what I say I am, and I'll prove it to you. You don't even understand healing. There is more than one way, and I will heal. . ."

"Oh, stop it," Teresa said. "You can't heal anything. You make things up. Hannah's leg wasn't broken and they know it. They took the cast off last night. They were going to hightail it out of here. Hannah wasn't going to marry you. No one would marry you. Duncan," Teresa begged, "tell these people the truth. I'm going to take Pea. I'm going to get her to a good place. I'm going to– "

Duncan shot up. He towered over Teresa, his face was red with anger, his eyes flashed, and his fists clenched.

"Blasphemy!" Duncan's lips curled. "Go away. Go to *Hours*. You failed God's test. You tried to kill again. You will not be healed. You will be left behind and you will weep that you were not granted everlasting release from your afflictions. You will. . ."

As he ranted, Teresa stood up. She pulled herself as straight as her body would allow. She looked at Duncan, not the conduit between God and his flock, her son. She said:

"Shut up, Duncan."

23

Duncan sat alone in the house for a long while. He bit his nails to the quick. He picked up the little bottle of poison and put it down. He thought and thought about what Teresa had said – that she had poured this stuff into Hannah's tea by mistake. Duncan didn't believe in mistakes. He believed in confession and penance and the ultimate peace. He believed in a higher power, and he believed that no one should get a third chance.

Teresa had the heart of a killer. Oh, she tried to pretend that she had a mother's heart. In heaven, she had explained to the doctors, she and her children would be safe from pain and fear and want. She insisted that it took incredible strength for a mother to hurt her children. Duncan knew better. Teresa preyed on the weak. First it had been him and Pea, and now it was Hannah. She was the perfect victim, and Teresa proved herself to be the monster Duncan knew her to be. Yes, God had put Hannah here for so many reasons and the greatest of which was that Pea and Duncan were now strong.

Duncan gnawed at this thumbnail as he thought about all this, and it wasn't until he tasted blood that he stopped, stood up, and wiped his thumb on his favorite jacket. He stuck the bottle of liquid Nicotine in his pocket and went to look in on Melody and Hannah. Half way up the stairs, he changed his mind. What he really wanted was to find out more about this poison. Teresa and Melody could own Hannah's death if it came to that; he would, however, take credit for her resurrection if he could find out how to manage it.

He opened the door to Pea's room and walked in without his usual ritual. He did not admire his paintings or breathe in the scent of her. He did not bother kneeling on one of the colored pillows. Instead, he set himself down, crossed his legs and rested his arms on his knees. He almost doubled over as he tried to see under Pea's curtain of hair.

"Pea. Come out, Pea. Come out." She remained as she was, kneeling on her pillow in the middle of the rug, her arms out, her fingers tented, her head hanging down. "Damn, Pea. Come out. I need you. I need you now."

He leaned very close as he took the vial out of his pocket. He put it under her curtain of hair.

"Why? Why do I have this? Why is this in my house?"

He waited. And waited. And this time the waiting was unbearable in the stillness of the room that, for the first time, felt stale.

"Come out, Pea," he snapped.

There was the burp and trill and then she spoke.

24

Revelations 21:5
John 1:5
Deuteronomy 33:27

Duncan sat back on his heels, and buried his face in his hands. God still spoke to Pea, and Pea spoke to him. His gratitude was so great he almost wept.

His hands fell away, his lips opened to thank his sister, his legs started to unfurl. He was so overwhelmed with gratitude that he didn't notice the man coming out of the corner of the room. He had no warning before an arm went around his neck and he was pulled upright against a broad chest. Duncan's hands went to that arm, but the man's grip was as strong as steel, and the voice that spoke was as cold as ice:

"We're going to find a doctor, or I swear I will kill you, dude."

On the floor, Pea trilled and burped and trilled.

Teresa and Melody kept watch over Hannah who lay shivering and shaking, her system overloaded by the nicotine she had ingested. Teresa hadn't bothered to explain what happened to Melody. What good would it do? All Melody wanted to know, all any of them wanted to know, was whether or not what had befallen Hannah had to do with the devil.

If the answer were yes, then would it hold that Teresa was the devil? If Teresa were the devil, it stood to reason that she could possess all of them. If she possessed all of them they would fall back and sin again as Teresa had. They would hurt people, betray people, kill people. They would never be healed.

If the answer was no, then the world would be upon them soon. Outsiders would come looking for Billy and Hannah, or God would send something else to test them. They were not strong enough for that. Already they were falling apart as the promise of healing slipped away.

Teresa understood how human they all were. That included Duncan who, as she saw him leave the house, had to put his shoulder into the wind and keep his head down against the slant of the snow just like everyone else. To her surprise, he didn't go to his own house but past it on the path that led to the store. If she'd had any curiosity about him any longer, she would have followed him. Since she did not, she looked back at the poor, poisoned girl.

She was about to tell Melody to go to bed when Billy opened the door. He ignored the two women and went to Hannah's side, looked down at her, and then sat on the bed. Without hesitation, he took up the sick girl's hand and held it tight as if by sheer force of will he could stop her body from torturing itself. He winced with every shudder that ran through her, bit his lip when she bucked, wiped away the froth that came from the side of her mouth. He moved the pail closer in case she threw up. She didn't. Twice she opened her eyes. Twice she called 'Billy', and twice he assured her he was there. And then he told her something else.

"We're going to get you a doctor tomorrow. We're going to get you out of here."

When Hannah went back to her fitful sleep. Billy talked to the women but didn't bother to look at them.

"Duncan is taking me to find a doctor tomorrow. Tell everyone that if I come back and Hannah is sicker, or she's dead, or anything, then I'm going to kill all of you.

Now, get out of here."

Duncan slipped. He fell.

The snow blinded him. His breath was hot beneath his scarf. His nose and mouth were wet with his own sweat. He had managed to dress for the short walk – gloves, parka, sweater, hat – and still he was freezing.

He got up, slipped, and got up again. He was shaken by how quickly things had turned. Teresa's betrayal, the others with their fear and uncertainty and even anger, Billy Zuni's threat, and Hannah's illness had turned his world upside down. Pea had seen an upheaval months ago, but this was a catastrophe. Pea had not told him it would be like this, like the end of time. Or, had she? Perhaps he had missed it. Maybe he was the one who had been lazy and not interpreted the passages correctly.

He slipped once more but this time he was close to the rock wall and he caught himself before he fell. Duncan struggled, made it over the wall, pushed through the brush, dug out the small pile of snow in front of the door and finally got inside. He ripped the scarf from his face. He shook his head to clear his eyes and finally found the latch on the hidden door. Duncan threw himself into the narrow room and shut the door behind him. He flipped on the overhead and fell into the chair in front of the table.

The Bible was still as he had left it. To read that God meant him to take Hannah as his bride had been thrilling, but now his bride was near death and her friend was ready to kill. That simply could not stand. His congregation could not survive without him. If Hannah needed to be taken, so be it. But Duncan? Impossible.

Duncan took off his gloves. He put his hands on the desk. He looked at his binder and thought he should go back to the list of prophesies Pea had uttered before Robert found Hannah and Billy. He would re-read the passages. Duncan would see if the fault was his. Then again, he needed to take care with what was happening that minute. Billy was a problem; perhaps he was a priority. Yes, he needed to start there.

Revelations 21:5

Duncan took up his pen and scribbled the reference in his log with one hand and turned the pages of the Bible with the other. He forgot the order and couldn't find the right place. Genesis. Deuteronomy. Ephesians. The pages were snapping. Where was Revelations? He riffled them so fast, so ineptly that he almost ripped the pages from the spine.

There it was. There it was.

He pursed his lips and blew out an icy breath.

Revelations 21:5

He who was seated on the throne said, "I am making everything new!" Then he said, "Write this down, for these words are trustworthy and true."

Duncan wrote the words: *Make everything new.*

He scribbled John 1:4-5 and then looked at the book. His fingers weren't shaking now. He was warmer, and he was calmer. He found this passage more easily.

John 1:4-5

In Him was life, and the life was the Light of men. The Light shines in the darkness, and the darkness did not comprehend it.

He wrote down: darkness does not comprehend.

What? What was the last? There was another verse! He bit his lip. He tugged at his ear. He put the heel of his hand to the side of his head and pounded. What was the other verse Pea had told him? What?

Deuteronomy 33:27

That was it! He had it. Pages flew and fluttered and Duncan leaned closer to the book and read aloud:

The eternal God is your refuge, and underneath are the everlasting arms. He will drive out your enemies before you, saying, 'Destroy them!

He wrote down: Drive out your enemies. Destroy them.

Duncan sat up. He closed his eyes, but before he could open his heart and his mind and interpret the word of God, the radio spit and sputtered. The radio on which Duncan relied to enhance his interpretations was crackling now. Duncan slid the chair to the ancient piece of equipment and fiddled with the dials. He put headphones on.

"We've got Nell. . . down river. Says to tell you . . .injury. . . Stopping at. . .then onto . . . two days. . .Copy that Trooper Guillard? "

25

Duncan went to see them, one by one. They were so afraid of the terrible things that had befallen them that no one opened their door until they heard the sound of his voice assuring them it was, indeed, Duncan knocking and not a demon. He sat with each of them and listened to the same litany.

Hannah was possessed by some devil, brought down even as she was to become the wife of Duncan.

Billy Zuni was stalking through the house threatening to kill people.

Duncan was running into the night, leaving them at the mercy of the boy with the long hair and the bandaged hand.

Teresa was not cooking food.

When it was his turn to speak, Duncan reassured them. Had he not returned? Had he not made peace? Wasn't he going to drive out everything bad? He was taking Billy away. Hannah was not their enemy; she was a victim, too.

Robert lay down upon his bed and Duncan stroked his face, the part that felt like leather, and the skin that not even his mother wanted to touch. Duncan listened patiently to Foster try to put two words together. Duncan took Glenn's pitiful hands in his and held them while they talked, and he looked into his unmemorable eyes as if he, at least, would remember them. Duncan stroked Melody's toothpick arm, and held her claw-like fingers, and told her that she would be worthy of being hand-maiden to God. Boldly, Melody said she only wanted to serve him.

Duncan just smiled.

Duncan laid his hand on Peter and reassured his parents there was no need to worry about their child.

He spoke to Teresa, also. He called her mother. He almost made her believe that he had forgiven her. He touched Teresa's misshapen back and promised her life and healing, but he could see that she had closed herself off completely and felt nothing for him or Pea or the others.

Now it was morning. Duncan had not slept and it would seem neither had Billy Zuni. But Duncan, walking in the light of the lord, was energized; Billy, whose companion seemed to be hatred and despair, was tired and edgy. That's what Duncan thought as he watched Billy come down the long flight of stairs after spending the night watching Hannah.

"Did she know you, Billy? Did you tell her where we are going?" Duncan asked as he waited at the foot of the staircase.

"She didn't understand, but I think she's better. She's not throwing up."

Duncan put a hand out. Billy stopped. Duncan said:

"I'll ask you one more time, let us pray for her. Let us heal her on our own. We don't need to bring outsiders here."

"Don't go there, dude." Billy pushed past him.

"You understand that we are using up the last of our fuel for you," Duncan called after him and Billy slammed open the door and called back:

"We'll get more when we get wherever we're going."

Melody watched all this from the living room where she

was sitting with the mending, not mending at all but looking at Billy as he stood by the snowmobile. She looked at Duncan who still stood by the stairs. Setting aside her chores, she went to him.

"Will you be alright, Duncan?" she asked.

"Thank you, Melody. I will."

"Are you sure you shouldn't take the boat? It would be faster."

"No. The boat wouldn't make it. This is the only way."

Duncan turned toward the door and opened it. Together they looked at Billy as he paced and scowled.

"I hope he'll be warm enough. He's wearing the things he had on when Robert found him. It's so much colder now."

"He'll be fine. Take care of Hannah and Pea."

"How long will you be gone?" Melody asked.

"Not long. If I don't stop, we'll make good time. Perhaps I'll even be back tonight."

"Will he really kill us if Hannah dies?" she asked.

"No. Billy won't kill anyone. I promise you."

With that Duncan walked out of the house, down the steps and swung himself up on the snowmobile. He started the engine, but Billy Zuni had one last thing to say to Melody. He walked up to her; he towered over her.

"Make sure there's a light, for Hannah," he said. "She's going to be afraid if she wakes up in the dark. As soon as she can understand, tell her I'm going to get her home. Tell her that, okay."

Melody nodded, afraid to speak to the man who had threatened her life.

"Billy," Duncan called.

Billy swung his head and looked behind him. The guy looked like an idiot in his huge helmet. He looked back at Melody.

"Tell her I promised everything will be okay. She'll believe you if you say that I promised."

"Alright," Melody whispered.

"Billy!" Duncan gunned the throttle. The engine sounded sick. When Billy got close Duncan said: "Swing up behind me. I know it's tight quarters, but it will keep you warm. Body heat will do that."

Billy swung on behind Duncan, hesitated, and then put his arms around the man's middle. Melody backed into the house, but didn't shut the door. Teresa came down and put her arm around the young woman. Glenn stopped his work to watch and Robert peered out of his window upstairs. Duncan leaned into the machine and they were gone.

Behind them, everyone held their own thoughts. Some wondered when they would return, others wondered if a doctor would truly come all this way to see Hannah, and some of them wished that they would never come back at all. The only people who didn't think about Duncan and Billy or where they had gone were Hannah Sheraton and the prophetess, Pea.

Andre and Archer found that they were going to have to wait for proprietor of the Moose Tangle Thrift Shop to appear. A sign in the window announced that he would be back soon. In Alaska, that could mean an hour or in spring. Andre and Archer split the difference and gave it overnight, passing the time in the local bar where they had a burger and Internet access. Archer caught up on a few clients, checked in with Faye, and pretty much tried to keep his mind off Josie. If he had understood the communiqué correctly Josie was hurt, not dead; she was safe, not comfortable; she was hoping they would meet up soon; given their traveling companion soon was relative. Best of all, she had a lead she was hoping would pan out. The men slept well and in the morning the proprietor of The Moose Tangle Thrift Shop showed up at ten-thirty. He opened the door in his pajamas and unaffected by the cold that blew in with Andre and Archer.

"Well ain't this special." He took in Andre in all his glory. "Been a while since we seen any troopers up this way. I'll tell you right now, I won that jackhammer free and clear, so if George Putnam up there said I stole it, that just ain't so. It was mine to sell, and I sold it."

"No, we're not here about a jackhammer," Andre assured him.

"Don't tell me Maria's been calling you guys. We were never married proper and I'm not buying that stuff about palimoney. I ain't got no palimoney for her and that's the truth."

"Palimony." Archer corrected him.

"That's what I said. I ain't got none of it. You think money grows on trees? Business ain't good, and I got robbed not too long back and–"

"We're not here about any of that," Andre interrupted. "Do you want to put on some shoes or something? It's kind of cold in here."

The man shook his head, "No, I'm good. Can't think of anything else I might have done, so just tell me what you want and then you can get out of here. You're bad for business."

Andre raised his chin to Archer who took out his cell and brought up a picture of the glove.

"We're looking for some kids. A boy and a girl. We think they were in a wreck about a hundred miles north of here. They would have been with a trucker named Green."

The man shook his head, "Don't know the name."

"Have you seen two teenagers traveling together in, say, the last three or four weeks."

He shrugged, "Not that I'd remember. I don't pay real good

attention to people. They come in and sometimes they buy stuff. Most times they come in to see if I want to buy their old trash. Sometimes I do. Most often I don't. Money doesn't grow on trees. You can tell Marie that. She's the one who sent you, right?"

"Do you remember this?" Archer put the phone in front of the man's face.

He stepped back and grumbled: "Don't need to shove it in my face, there, partner."

He tipped his head. He pulled his mouth to one side and then the other. He took one finger and rubbed the side of his nose.

"You know what? I do remember that. Well, not just that one glove, but a pair of 'em. Sold 'em about three months ago."

"Did you sell them to a young man? Blue eyes, blond hair. He would have called you dude?" Archer asked. "He would have been traveling with a light skinned black girl with short hair dyed blond."

"Nope, don't recall anyone like that. Besides, those gloves were big. That's one of the things I remember about them. Paul Bunyan gloves. I told that joke to the guy who bought 'em. He didn't get it. Dumb shit. Just kind of stared at me. Blinkin' and blinkin' and wipin' his nose on his sleeve like a little kid."

"That's not the trucker," Andre noted. "He was small."

"What else to you remember about this guy?"

The man snorted. "What's not to remember? He was something. Big as a house. I'm not kidding. A house. And his face was scary."

"Mean scary?" Andre asked.

"No, weird-scary. Like the whole of one side was all deformed or something. Red. Like a big red scar but real thick. Looked like he'd been tanned, I tell you. And then the other side looked all smooth like a baby's butt. I sure wouldn't want to wake up and see that face staring back at me."

"Does he live around here?" Archer asked.

"Naw. He passes through now and again. Seen him maybe twice in the last year. He comes down to get supplies and clothes. Sometimes he gets clothes for women but he's not all funny that way. The clothes he gets wouldn't fit him. He always had a set amount of money. No more and no less. He doesn't know to haggle. Told you, dumb as a rock."

"Has he got a family?" Archer asked.

"Kind of. He told me that he lives with a bunch of other folk up the river some."

"Do you have any idea where?" Andre asked.

"What do you think I am, the census taker?"

"Just thought I'd ask," Andre pulled out a card and handed it to the man. "If you remember anything."

"Yeah, I know the drill," the man said. "We done here?"

"We are unless you have anything else for us."

"Not me, buddy." The two men were almost out the door when he called after them. "Might try down at the landing. He comes in by boat. Someone down there might know where he hails from?"

"Thanks," Andre said and held the door for Archer.

Ten minutes later they had the information they wanted. Archer was going to see Josie sooner than he expected because they were both headed to the same place: Clara's Landing.

"Are you okay back there?"

Duncan knew the answer even before he asked Billy the question. An hour earlier Billy's grip went slack, and his head fell so that his cheek rested against Duncan's back. Now with this last bump of the snowmobile Billy's entire weight shifted so Duncan hockey-stopped the big machine. Duncan shut down the engine and the silence was deafening. He caught Billy just before he fell off.

"Get off me, man," Billy pushed him away.

"Not doing too good, are you?" Duncan swung off the snowmobile.

"I'm okay, dude. Just tired. Where are we?" Billy did a three sixty, checking out the surroundings as if he expected to find something familiar.

"The middle of nowhere," Duncan said. "Stand up. Come on. Get off, and get the blood flowing."

"No. Get back on, man. We've got to go." Billy motioned to him. "What do you think? Another hour or two or what?"

Billy was pale as a ghost and almost frozen solid. Pity they hadn't thought to get him a hat before they left. Cold could befuddle even the sharpest mind, and Billy's was not in that category.

"No can do, Billy. I'm the one driving. I need a breather," Duncan said. "Come on, come on. Up and at 'em. Five minutes won't kill you."

Duncan laughed a little. Billy was annoyed, but he also knew Duncan was right. They had been on that sorry excuse for a snowmobile way too long. Billy swung off bent over and pounded on his thighs. His jeans were stiff and crusted with cold, and his muscles were so cramped they were painful.

"Does it ever stop snowing?" Billy asked.

"I think it's pretty. You probably didn't get much snow there in California."

"That's stupid, dude."

"Yes, I suppose it is. Just trying to lighten the mood," Duncan said as he paced. "I guess I misjudged how far we had to go. It's so much easier in spring, but spring isn't just around the corner, is it? Maybe I should make a fire. Just to warm us up a bit. We'll take an hour or so."

"No, man, I'm telling you. We're going," Billy insisted.

"Okay, okay. I've just got to check the oil. Sometimes I have to add some when I've had it going too long. It will be harder with you sitting on it. Go sit over there."

Billy looked around. Duncan was motioning to a tree stump that looked like it had been hit by lightning. He went over, sat down and massaged his legs while Duncan whistled and dug into his pack and then fiddled with the engine.

Billy couldn't look at Duncan without thinking about the night he said he was going to marry Hannah, or the fact that her leg wasn't broken at all, or about that night at dinner when Hannah had acted like she was happier with those people than she was with him. He couldn't get past the fact that when he left her, Hannah didn't know who he was.

"I thought you said there was a doctor pretty close."

"Have some faith, Billy. I'm doing the best I can." Duncan got up from his crouch and dusted off his hands. "Yes, I'm just doing what I can to make sure you're taken care of."

"The sooner we go the sooner you're rid of me," Billy said.

"That is the truth," Duncan answered. "A pit stop and we'll be on our way. Do you have to go?"

"No. Just hurry, dude. I'm freezing."

"We wouldn't want you to freeze to death." Duncan muttered as he walked into the woods. Billy waited. He looked over his shoulder, but he didn't see Duncan. He raised his voice:

"You sure you know what you're doing, dude?"

"No worries on that score, Billy," Duncan called back.

Duncan pulled on a tree branch, testing its strength with his weight. It was solid and it wasn't going to come down easily. He kicked at the snow and uncovered a mass of fallen tree limbs and rocks. He picked up a branch that was dead, brittle, and hollow. He tossed it aside and picked up another that was stunted and knotted and heavy. He bent one more time and picked up a stone. It was smooth and pleasing in the hand. He tossed the stone, pulled down his zipper, relieved himself, and then walked back using the tree branch as a hiking stick.

Duncan high stepped through the snow and got to the place where he had left Billy. It was a beautiful day really, dark and crisp and quiet. The fact that Billy had shut up made it perfect. Then he saw why Billy had stopped talking. He was hunched over, his arms crossed as he slept sitting up. Duncan hunkered down in front of him, steadying himself with the big branch.

"That's a good trick," Duncan muttered.

He stood up and stepped away. He hated to do it but he really had to wake Billy Zuni and get on with it. Duncan planted his feet. He held the heavy branch with both hands and pulled it back over his shoulder and barked:

"Billy!"

Billy shot upright and turned toward the sound of his name. Duncan swung away. The wood made contact with a sickening thud and the force threw Billy off the stump. Billy was crumpled on the ground, unmoving, his blood ruby red against the beautiful white snow.

Duncan stood there, breathing hard, stunned that he had actually done what he had done. He laughed a little. He giggled thinking that maybe he should hit Billy again. Or, perhaps, that would be overkill. He laughed harder because that truly was funny. Yeah, he was a funny guy. So, if you kill someone in the forest and they are never found is that someone really dead? His face fell. His eyes hooded. That was no riddle. The answer was yes.

Duncan tossed aside the branch, bent down and stripped the jacket and shirt and sweater and pants off Billy Zuni's body. Waste-not-want-not out here in the wilderness. He left the shoes because they weren't worth much. He rolled Billy's clothes into a ball, and tucked them under his arm. Billy looked so peaceful that Duncan believed he had done him a favor. The poor guy had never had a moment's rest if the story he had told about the murderous man from Albania was true. Now he would have an eternity of it thanks to God and Duncan.

Deuteronomy 33:27. *The eternal God is your refuge, and underneath are the everlasting arms. He will drive out your enemies before you, saying, 'Destroy them.*

Done and done.

Driven out. Destroyed.

Duncan went back to the snowmobile and put Billy's clothes in the saddlebag. He was about to leave when two things dawned on him. First, he really shouldn't take the yellow jacket back to the compound. It was too identifiable. It also occurred to Duncan that he should say something over Billy Zuni. Everyone deserved to be sent off with a few words from a holy man.

Duncan pulled the yellow jacket out of his saddlebag and walked back over to the body. Already, Billy's skin was taking on the blue-purple tinge of frozen flesh. He tossed the yellow jacket on the ground and then crossed his hands low, bowed his head, stared straight at Billy.

"You should never have said you were going to kill me – dude."

26

Mama Cecilia enjoyed her time on the boat with the old man. He told her stories of his life and his children. They talked of Mama's son and her granddaughter. He was kind, but eventually he told her the truth. They would not come back to her home unless they had nowhere else to go. Mama was not angry because it was good to hear someone be both honest and kind.

When they reached the place he was going, the old man started to worry about leaving her alone. She assured him that she would be fine, but now she realized it was a long way to her house. There was nothing to do but begin to walk, so that is what Mama Cecilia did. Her old fingers grew tired from carrying her small pack with her extra sweater. Eventually, she sat on a large rock and ate the food the old man had given her. She looked straight ahead at the trees. There were so many of them and each one more beautiful and stronger than the next. She took another bite of her bread and thought that she was perhaps a few miles from Oki's house and that meant she was only another few miles more from her own. It was a pity to have to think so hard about where one was, but that was what an old mind must do.

Mama raised her feet to look at her good moccasins because it pleased her. In her mind she told them it was time to walk again and she thought that they agreed. She put her hood on her head and began to walk.

She had not taken more than a dozen steps when she heard someone speak sharply. Quickly, she swiped the hood from her head so that she could hear more clearly. Whoever had called out did not call out again. Instead, Mama heard the sound of a motor. It was a snowmobile motor, and Mama Cecilia went toward it. She walked as quickly as she could, but she couldn't go fast enough. The sound of the engine was fading.

"Hello!"

She called out even though she knew she could not be heard over the noise and the distance. When she came to the place where she saw tracks, Mama Cecilia saw that the driver was going the opposite way of where she wanted to go. Still, it would have been good if she had said hello, and if the driver had offered to turn around and take her home.

She took a deep breath and looked toward her home as she thought about this missed opportunity. That's when she saw the other thing – an almost naked person lying in the snow that was red with his blood.

Mama went to the person to see if he was dead. She dropped to her knees and brushed the snow off his face and saw it was a very young man, younger than her son. His eyes were closed and his skin was blue/white. On his head was a wound. Mama reached her hand out but before she could touch him, the man sprung up and clasped her arm.

"I'll kill you. I'll. . "

The boy looked at her with great anger, but when he saw that she was not the person who hurt him he didn't hold her so tightly.

"I will help you," Mama said.

"I won't kill you," he promised.

The boy's arm shuddered and his eyes filled with tears. He fell into Mama's arms. This was not her son, but the spirits had sent this person to her because he was somebody's son. Mama Cecilia opened her small pack and gave him her extra sweater. She took off her coat of three furs and put it around him. It was a long coat, but it did not cover his legs. She had nothing for his legs, but she put his boots on his feet. In the snow she found his yellow jacket and she put that on herself. When all that was done, she helped this boy out of the snow and decided to do what a mama bear would do with her cub.

"My name is Mama Cecilia."

"Billy," he said. "My name is Billy."

Mama Cecilia smiled and she took his hand.

Melody and Glenn sat on the sofa in the living room. Robert stood behind them. The others were in *Hours*. Pea, of course, was *Within*. Teresa was with Hannah but those in the living room knew that she was upstairs doing exactly what they were doing: looking at Duncan's house.

"When did he come back?" Glenn asked and this time he did want an answer.

"Late," Melody answered.

"Did you see him?" Robert asked.

Melody nodded. She crossed her arms on the back of the couch and rested her chin on top of them. She hadn't taken her eyes off Duncan's house since he'd returned.

"I saw him walk from the store and go into his house," Melody said.

"But it was really dark then, Melody. Are you sure it was Duncan?" Robert said.

"Who else would it be?"

"I deduce a demon." Robert coughed and wiped his nose.

Glenn shrugged, "Billy? Maybe it was Billy who came back."

"Then where would Duncan be?" Melody asked. "I'm almost sure it was Duncan. He went right into the house."

"Teresa didn't make dinner. He didn't come to see us," Glenn said. "I think one of us should go talk to him. Melody, you should go."

"No, I don't think so. Teresa should go." Melody sat up and turned away from the window. "I'll go get her. Somebody needs to know what's going on. Hannah is asking for Billy. I told her he'd gone to get the doctor, but now there's no doctor."

"I could go talk to him," Robert offered.

"No, Melody is right. Teresa should do it," Glenn said. Half of Robert's face fell. The other half of his face never moved.

Melody got up. "You watch the house. Come tell us if you see him."

Melody went up the stairs, but instead of going to get Teresa she opened the door to Pea's room. It was as it always was except for Pea. She was not on her pillow. Instead, Pea was on her knees facing the shuttered windows with her hands flat upon them. It wasn't time to eat so, perhaps, this was where Pea always was at this time. Or else she was watching Duncan, in her mind, in her soul, facing his house and praying that he would make himself known. Melody stood behind her and said:

"Come out, Pea. Come out now."

The woman didn't move, not that Melody had expected her to. Melody looked around. She walked across the room to the bureau. There was a small chair in the corner, dainty enough for Melody to pick up with one hand. She put it beside Pea and sat down. She was so tired. Not just because she had kept watch all day and night but because she had been watching for years one way or another.

"Pea, Duncan needs you. I don't know if you can come *Without,* but if you can, now would be a good time."

While she waited, Melody looked at the kneeling woman. She had beautiful hands and her bare neck was lovely, too. Her skin was smooth and pale. Then Melody had the strangest thought. She wondered if Pea would feel it if Melody took a knife to her? Would she run like Melody's sister tried to do? Would she put her hands up to protect her face? Would she be strong enough to protect herself? Melody's sister hadn't been. Funny how wonderful it felt to be stronger than her beautiful sister who had two good hands. Melody shook away those thoughts. She didn't look at Pea's beautiful neck. She tried not to think about Hannah's scars, crisscrossed on her pretty dark skin.

"Pea!" Melody snapped.

When Pea didn't move, Melody stood up and reached over her head. She worked the latch, but couldn't get it to move. She wanted the window to open in the worst way. She wanted to have this woman see the world outside. Melody wanted Pea to understand that Duncan was in trouble.

When she couldn't manage the latch, Melody leaned on the wood and pounded it with her fist. She sniffed and tears came to her eyes. She swiped them away and looked down on Pea.

"Do you hear anything? Do you care? At all? About anything? Do you?"

27

James 2:10

Melody just stood there, looking down at Pea's black hair and the pink soles of her feet. Her shoulders slumped in resignation and disappointment.

"What good is it without, Duncan, Pea?"

Melody left the silent woman to commune with God and went to the next room where she hoped she would have better luck with Teresa.

Oki opened his door even though it was late. This time the television was turned to a show about animals.

"It is you, Cecilia."

"We need your help, Oki."

"I see that Cecilia," he answered. "But this is not your son."

"No. But if this boy were my son, I would want another mother to help him."

Oki opened the door and took the boy's arm as Cecilia

handed him inside. Oki guided him to a large chair. He looked at the parka.

"This is your *amaut,* is it not?"

It seemed to Mama Cecilia that there was no need to answer his question. Did she not stand there dressed in a yellow jacket and didn't the boy lie there covered in a fine coat of wolf and seal and fox? Still, if Oki asked then she should be respectful and answer.

"Yes."

"He is still very cold." Oki was on his knees. He took off Billy's shoes and he put his own slippers on the boy's feet. "Can you get him coffee, Cecilia?"

Mama Cecilia went to the kitchen that was part of the room where Oki watched his programs, and she could see the old man doing what he could to warm the boy. She brought the coffee and gave it to Oki who gave it to Billy.

"He does not speak." Oki stepped back to look at the boy.

"He does, Oki," Cecilia said. "His name is Billy."

"Billy." Oki spoke the name as if he were trying to decide if it was a good one. Then he nodded and pulled up a chair that he offered to Cecilia. He turned off his program and sat on a chair himself.

"Will you speak to me?" Oki asked.

Billy nodded.

"Then tell me what has happened to you."

"He is a shaman," Mama said by way of reassuring Billy when he didn't speak.

Billy swallowed his hot drink and he thought while the two old people waited patiently.

"Do you know the devil?" Billy asked.

Oki closed his eyes and nodded. Mama Cecilia felt her heart grow faint. She did not think she could take another boy into her heart who had devils, but then he made it right.

"I've seen him, man. I've seen the devil, and he tried to kill me."

"He is gone now," Mama Cecilia said, and she told the truth. The devil had gone off on a snowmobile so it was fine.

"Teresa?" Melody touched the older woman. Teresa opened her eyes. "Duncan didn't bring a doctor. He hasn't come in the house."

"Then he hasn't, Melody. Leave me alone."

"But–"

"He'll come when he's ready. He'll go see Pea. That's who he cares about." Teresa looked over at Hannah who slept quietly. Melody did the same.

"What about the doctor?"

Teresa sighed. "There was never going to be a doctor."

"But Duncan said that's where they were going," Melody insisted.

"Go to bed, Melody. Duncan will come when he's ready. Or he won't come. Just go to bed."

"Pea spoke to me again."

"That's fine." Teresa closed her eyes.

Melody stood there, not knowing what to do. Without Teresa, Melody was lost. She didn't know how to put Pea to bed. She didn't know how to do anything but her chores. Teresa was the one to say what they cooked and when they cooked it. Teresa set the hours for the fires to be stoked and Glenn had not even brought the wood in from the pile. They were all waiting for something, and that was not the way it was supposed to be. It always had been Duncan who waited. Now he was hiding even from Pea and that frightened Melody more than anything.

Melody gazed at Teresa who, it seemed, was not waiting for

anything at all. Melody clasped her withered hand. It was a brittle and useless thing, like her; like all of them. How stupid she had been to think it could be any different. She turned her eyes away, unable to look at Teresa any longer. But when she looked away, she caught Hannah's gaze.

"Billy?" Hannah whispered.

Melody bent her knees and got down beside her.

"He's not here."

"Where is he?" Hannah asked.

"Duncan took him to find a doctor," Melody said. "For you."

"When will they be back?"

Melody shook her head, "I don't know. I'm sure it won't be long. You look better."

Hannah nodded. Melody put her hand on the mattress and started to get up but Hannah tried to grasp her hand. Melody got down on her knees again.

"We're going home when he gets back."

Melody nodded. "Yes, I know."

Melody stood up and when she turned away from the bed she saw Teresa's eyes were open. She was half smiling, daring Melody to be the godly girl she professed to be and tell Hannah the truth. Duncan had come back; Billy had not.

Instead, Melody left them and when she got to the living room nothing had changed. The men were still watching the house across the way. Connie and Paul had left the *Hours* and Peter asleep to huddle with the others. They were all silent except for Robert's sniffing and Foster's muttering. Glenn's mutilated hands went from his face to the couch and back to his face again. He rolled his body left and then right, unable to find a place that felt comfortable.

Melody looked at each of them and saw the truth. They were sad, sad specimens: a burned man, a wordless man, a giant man with half a face, small people. There was Teresa, a woman who had given up hope long ago, was just now showing her true colors. Or, perhaps, Teresa knew what all of them did not. She knew that their faith had been misplaced.

Melody went to the couch. She knelt upon it and leaned over so that she could put her good hand on the cold window. She waited to feel Duncan's energy. When she didn't, she raised her palm to heaven. She wanted to feel God's love. She didn't. She put her hand out to Glenn, but he didn't see her anymore than anyone in the real world had seen her. She was walking through the shadows while everyone else in the world walked in the sunlight, and she was so tired of it.

Without a word, Melody got off the couch and walked to the front hall. There she took the first things she found on the rack: Glenn's coat and Robert's scarf. She dug in the pocket of the coat and found gloves. She took a hat and didn't know who it belonged to. When Melody was dressed, she went out the door without acknowledging the people who had gathered in the entryway to watch her. As she walked into the cold, it was Glenn and Foster who rushed back to watch through the big window in the living room. They saw her put her head down and bury her hands in the coat pockets. They saw her go to Duncan's house. To their horror, Melody did not knock before she went inside.

28

Pea was kneeling. Duncan lay on his stomach clutching one of her beautiful pillows as if it were the last plank of a sunken ship bobbing in a quiet and endless sea. He looked at his paintings and his writings, gaining no inspiration, simply lost in the stunning images he had created of a Christ that bore a surprising resemblance to him. It was too dark, and the writing too small, for him to read his poems or his prophesizing, but he knew each and every word by heart if he chose to remember them. Which he did not. In fact, the only thing Duncan Thoth had chosen to do since returning to Clara's Landing was to lie in this room. It reminded him of his childhood: The silence, the dark, the warmth, Pea and him, him and Pea. And God, of course. If Duncan were truthful, he would admit that he resented that Pea always brought God to the party. Today, He was absent and Duncan, lazy in the mind, wished Pea would remain silent forever. That would mean Duncan's work was done. There would be no prophesies, no interpretation, no need to heal. Nothing for Duncan to do; nothing for Duncan to explain.

Duncan turned his head and let his eyes rest on Pea. Now he knew why her head was perpetually bowed. She bowed it not because she was in awe of the Lord but because there was nothing worthwhile in this world to see. His head had been up for years and all he had seen was the worst of humanity, the cruelty, and the hopelessness that people refused to acknowledge. It would be so much easier if people embraced the thing that made them freakish, or slow, or unworthy. Hope was not just a bitter pill; it was a horse pill, so big you could choke on it before it did any good.

Still, he would have liked Pea to look at him once. If she did, he would know what kind of man he was: a savior, a killer, a man of God, or simply a man. It would be a pity if he were simply a man. Duncan willed Pea to look at him, because her gaze would be honest. Unlike Melody's. The minute she walked into his house unannounced and saw him clutching his pillow and cowering under a blanket, her eyes had changed.

She knew what had happened to Billy Zuni. In his eye she saw the kaleidoscope of pride, and delight, and horror, and guilt. She saw his honesty and his humanity. It was that – his strength and frailty – that at once disappointed and elevated her. He knew she would no longer fear him or beg him.

And Pea's gaze would not be like Hannah's.

He saw her distrust; he felt her wariness. No matter how eloquently Duncan spoke, nothing could convince her that Billy refused to return to Clara's Landing. Her faith was in that boy when it should have been invested in Duncan.

Pea's gaze would not be like Teresa's.

Her old woman eyes stared through him as if he was the one of no consequence. She used to desire his absolution more than anything in the world. Now that she had forgiven herself, his forgiveness was insignificant.

Duncan rolled onto his back and brought the pillow with him. He sighed. He put one hand over his face as he closed his eyes. He was very tired, very content to just be, and very annoyed when Pea chose the moment he was nodding off to trill. She burped and trilled again. His hand fell to his side and the other hugged the pillow tighter. He took a deep breath and rolled himself up until he was sitting.

"What, Pea? What do you want to tell me?" he asked, his voice soft with weariness and the love he had for her.

29

Mark 1:14
Matthew 10:8
Luke 13:32

She burped and trilled. Her fingers twitched and then were
quiet again.

"Pea. . ."

His reached out for her, his palm upward, his fingers
extended. He wanted to touch her chin, to raise her head, to see
her eyes. Only Teresa could touch Pea that way and knowing
that gave Duncan a revelation. He did not keep Teresa because
he wanted to heal her or guide her to God's good grace; he kept
her because she was Pea's handmaiden.

With that knowledge, Duncan's soul lightened. Tonight, he
would have Melody attend to Pea. If Pea allowed that, Teresa
would be sent on her way. She would be doomed to live the rest
of her life in the world that had shunned her. She was as

unworthy of being a handmaiden in the same way she was unworthy of being a mother.

Problem solved. He put his hands gently on the side of Pea's head and put his lips atop his sister's soft black hair.

"Thank you, Pea."

The healing had begun and it had started with him.

Mama Cecilia watched through the night. She may have slept a little because the chair in which she sat – the very chair in which Oki watched the people on the television – was soft and comfortable. She had a blanket Oki had given her and she wore the yellow jacket. Oki said it would be better if Billy slept covered by her *amaut* so that he would sleep with the spirits of the seal, and the fox, and the wolf. The yellow jacket had spirits, too. She could feel that there was goodness in it.

Mama Cecilia also watched over Oki's blue house because Oki was gone. Not his body, of course. She saw him lying on his bed, his hands crossed, and his eyes closed. He even snored as if he was sleeping, but he was not. He was *Journeying* and conversing with ancestors as he made his way through the Otherworld. She hoped he would come back with wisdom for both the boy and her. Still, if he only brought a message for the-son-of-another-mother that would be fine, too.

It was early in the morning when Mama realized that Billy was not sleeping under her *amaut* any longer. He was moving quietly in Oki's house, opening drawers and looking at the things on the tables in Oki's house. He still wore the sweater she had put on him, but he also wore some pants that Oki had found for him to wear. She thought to cry out when Billy seemed to find something he liked and took it in his hand. If he was stealing from Oki then Mama Cecilia should say something, but it seemed that he was not.

Billy went to Oki's bathroom and shut the door.

Mama Cecilia watched that room and thought perhaps he would climb out the window, stealing whatever he had taken from the drawer. That was a possibility, but then she must have slept because when she woke Oki was standing in the room. He was not watching television; he was looking at Billy, who did not look like the son-of-another-mother any longer.

He looked like a warrior.

30

I am better, but I am not well.

Whatever happened to me was worse than the truck accident because it left me hollow and wrung out. I'm lying in this bed, watching outside. I know that this change in darkness is simply the passing of the day and not a storm coming. I can't hear anything, not even Glenn chopping wood. This room is like a sensory deprivation chamber. I am neither here nor there. I don't want to stay like this, but there is nowhere I'd rather go. I think this place has made me feel this way.

This was what frightened Billy.

This is what he was trying to warn me about.

This is why he left, because I wouldn't listen and he didn't want to wither away here. I can't blame him.

I think he's gone to find the sun. Or maybe he's gone to call Josie. All I know is that he's gone and most of me is gone with him. Josie faded away in that container; Billy has melted away with the snow. Duncan must not want to marry me anymore because he doesn't come to read to me or show me a drawing. That's not a bad thing. I wasn't going to marry him anyway, but it's strange to be here alone *and not caring that I am. I could do something about it. I can walk. I can talk. I just don't.*

I'm hollow.

Without Billy, I have no reason to fill myself up again.

So I lay here. I watch the dark.

I wonder what everyone's doing.

I don't care.

Duncan stood before his congregation wearing the jacket he preferred. His dark hair with the blond streaks fell over his brow. There were shadows under his hooded eyes, but he did not seem tired. He smiled at those gathered in the living room. No one smiled back. They were worn out and worn down.

Robert had stopped crying and fretting, but he was unable to hold himself upright any longer. He was a pile of a man made of donuts of flesh and a sad mask of a face. Teresa seemed to have gone deaf, dumb and blind. Melody served Pea, who ate her bacon and ham, she looked in on Hannah, but mostly she sat in the chair in the corner, mending and darning and watching the stairway for Duncan. Foster did not teach, Peter did not learn, Peter's parents did not fix things, and Glenn did not chop wood. He simply sat and stoked his fires and added the wood that was already cut. Of all of them, it was Glenn who seemed most content.

"I know how hard these last hours have been," Duncan said when they were all settled. "But I want you to know that the upheaval is over. In our midst was a devil–"

Teresa snorted. She put her chin in her palm and looked away from Duncan. Eyes darted her way, back to Duncan, and back to Teresa again. Only Melody looked at Duncan and he met her gaze head on. Hours ago he thought Melody was challenging him, now he realized she was showing the way. He needed to regroup and find his strength and faith as she had. He nodded to her; she nodded back.

"There was a devil," Duncan reiterated. "His name was Billy Zuni. His presence tested us and we prevailed. He is gone."

"Where did he–" Foster stuttered and everyone looked his way. "Where didd–" and once again. "–go."

"He went on, Foster. He went back to the faithless world."

"He left Hannah?" Robert piped up. "I deduced he liked Hannah."

"Yes, Duncan, tell us why he left Hannah?" Teresa mocked him without doing him the courtesy of looking his way.

"He left because he was not recognized. God only spoke of Hannah, not Billy."

"Then why didn't he leave right away?" Glenn asked.

"Because he thought he had his hooves on Hannah's neck. When Robert found them the evil came with the good."

"I let out the devil?" Robert scrunched up his eyes and the tears came again.

"But you also let out an angel, Robert," Duncan assured him. "That is why Hannah remains, and that is why Billy has gone. Our faith was too much for him." Duncan clapped his hands and grinned. "Everything is now in order. We are blessed in God's eyes. Pea has spoken and I have read the passages. And I do not need to interpret them, my friends. The message from heaven is clear. Clasp your hands. Open your hearts. I share God's word."

Everyone sat up a little straighter. Someone murmured something. Melody's withered hand jerked and she covered it with her good one. Even Teresa looked at him. He raised his chin. He looked down on her.

"Mark 1:15. The time has come. Repent and believe the good news." Duncan's Goldilocks voice hung over each of them as if he had laid hands upon their heads. "Believe the good news."

We believe

I believe

Good news

Duncan's eyes closed and he swayed to the music of their affirmations. There were tears in his eyes, warm and happy tears.

"Matthew 10:8." Duncan raised his face to a heaven that was somewhere above the roof over his head and the dark sky above that. "Heal the sick, raise the dead, cleanse those who have leprosy, drive out the demons."

The collective breath went out of the men; there was a sweet gasp from Melody. He opened his eyes – his hooded, private, topaz eyes – and lowered his chin and whispered.

"Luke 13:32. I will keep on driving out demons and healing people. Today–"

His voice became stronger.

"And tomorrow."

And stronger still.

"And on the third day I will reach my goal."

His eyes met Melody's and his words seemed only for her.

"This is from God to Pea. This is from Pea to me. This is from me to you. The healing is upon us. The healing will begin today, and by the third day you will all be risen, perfect in God's love, whole in his heavenly grace."

Duncan raised his arms. The fire crackled. The congregation wept quietly and called loudly to God. They touched themselves: a withered arm, a fingerless hand, a leather upholstered face, broken vocal cords and legs that did not grow tall enough. Teresa, hunched in her chair, watched their ecstasy but all she felt was pain and disappointment. She looked at her son and tried to remember the little boy, so unsure of himself, safe only with his sister who spoke to God. She remembered the day she made her decision to release them from their pain and suffering.

She had felt much like Duncan: blessed and invincible and so righteous. And when she woke, none of them were dead or in heaven. That was the saddest day of her life. Duncan would fare no better than she.

Teresa looked out the window again, unable to stomach the ridiculous devotion he inspired. Slowly, she sat forward, hardly believing what she was seeing. Duncan's best-laid plans were about to change. She swung her head back. As the congregation gathered around her holy son, Teresa said:

"We have visitors."

Billy stood in the living room. He held the white handle knife that Cecilia had brought to Oki; the one that was sharp enough to cut his hair and shave his head. He looked frightening with his white scalp and his cuts and bruises and his bandaged hand. He looked more frightening because he wore no shirt and there were bruises upon his body, too.

Mama Cecilia got up and stood beside Oki. She blinked at the son-of-some-another-mother. He looked back at them as if he didn't quite know where he was. His eyes were filled with hurt, and determination, and courage, and cunning, and knowledge of the underworld. But that was to be expected since he had worn Cecilia's *amaut* and slept under it. Surely the spirits of the fox, and wolf, and the seal had shared themselves with him. The hurt, though, was his. No spirit had given him that; only people could give that.

"What are you doing?" Oki asked.

Billy walked past them and picked up the fur coat from the couch and held it out to Mama Cecilia.

"Thanks for lending me this, but I need my jacket. I have to go back for my friend."

"Where did you leave your friend?" Oki asked.

"Clara's Landing. Do you know where it is?"

The two old people nodded, but Oki spoke. "It's not far if you know where you are going."

"I'll find it," Billy pushed the beautiful *amaut* at Mama Cecilia. "Can I have my jacket, please?"

Mama Cecilia looked at Billy and said, "You cannot find this place."

"You can tell me. I can figure it out." He put down Mama's coat and picked up the shirt that Oki had laid out for him. He put it on. "How long will it take?"

Oki's shoulder's came up. "You are hurt. You are not from here. I am too old to go with you."

"Please, just tell me how. The guy who did this to me has my friend. She's sick. Please."

Oki nodded. A woman. Of course, a woman.

"Why did you cut your hair off?" Mama Cecilia asked.

Billy's lips tipped on one side and for a moment there was no pain in his eyes. There was only affection, soft like the reflection of the trees in a still spring lake.

"It's just something we do," he said.

"Cecilia," Oki said. "You will fix some good food. I will go see what can be done in a short time. The spirits do not like to hurry, but this is an emergency."

Oki went one way, to the small room to talk to the spirits. Mama Cecilia went the other way to cook. Billy fought the urge to run through the door and finally sat down on the sofa. He put the knife with the white plastic handle on the table in front of him and then put his head in his hands. He was hungry. He would eat. They would tell him where to go, and he would get Hannah. If push came to shove he would die trying to get her, or whoever got in his way would.

Everyone gathered at the window and looked at the two men coming up from the dock. One was dressed in a uniform and the other was not. Robert panicked first, but before the fear spread Duncan sent them to their rooms and prayer. Teresa went to Pea. Only Melody stayed, sitting in her shadowy corner keeping her eyes on the men coming toward the house.

Duncan stood on the porch, his feet apart, his stance firm. He didn't like that these men traveled in such obvious companionship. He didn't like that one wore a uniform.

"Hello." Andre called out. He stopped a few feet from the porch with Archer a step behind. Archer was watching more than the trooper's back. He was checking the place out, looking for traps, looking for problems. Duncan hated people like him, the kind who immediately thought the worst.

"Hello," Duncan answered. "How can I help you?"

"My name is Trooper Andre Guillard. This man's name is Archer, and we're looking for some people. We have reason to believe one of them lives here. Maybe the other two are here, also. The man we're looking for is Robert Butt. He is a big man with a birthmark on one side of his face."

"Why are you looking for him?"

"We want to ask him some questions about an accident a ways from here."

"What kind of questions would you like to ask him?"

Andre smiled his brilliant smile. "We would like to ask him those questions directly. Does he live here?"

"A few people live here. We are a religious group," Duncan answered. "Has this man done something wrong?"

"No. In fact, he might have done something very good. We think he might have helped this girl and her friend."

Archer passed the photograph of Hannah to Andre who

held it out to Duncan. Duncan couldn't believe he was looking at the same girl. Hannah had deteriorated since coming to Duncan's house when she should have thrived; Melody and Teresa had come broken and become stronger.

"Sir? Sir," Andre called.

"She's very beautiful," Duncan muttered.

"She would look different now. Her hair would be shorter and probably dyed blond."

Archer added: "She would have been traveling with a young man. About six feet tall. Long, light colored hair."

Duncan said nothing. Andre tried again to get a rise out of him.

"We found Robert's glove at the scene." Archer held out his cell phone with the picture of the glove. "We also found his fingerprints on a key that unlocked the container. We know he was on site, sir. We believe he might have taken something from the truck besides these two people."

"So you believe he is a thief? Or a kidnapper?"

Andre shook his head, "No, sir. I know how it is out here. I understand that what a body finds is sometimes critical to survival. In this case, the cargo is lethal if it isn't used properly. I'd simply like to recover it. Our main concern, though, is the two teenagers who we believe were in the back of the truck."

"So you don't have a warrant for his arrest?" Duncan asked.

"I'm just hoping for your cooperation, Mr. . .," Andre answered.

"Brother Thoth. Duncan Thoth," he answered.

Andre smiled, but Archer didn't bother to play the game. That was Guillard's job. Archer was busy cataloguing the area and there was a lot he didn't like.

The compound was spread out. On the way up they had passed a shed stuffed with tools: axes and shovels, a scythe and a wheelbarrow. There was a sharpening wheel. By the huge pile of split wood there were two sledge hammers and more axes. None of it was unusual for a place in the wilderness, but all of it could be turned into weapons. There was another structure about fifty feet from the main house. Its front door must face east because Archer couldn't see a backdoor and there seemed to be only two windows. There was a path that intersected the one he and Andre had taken. Something important must be down that way since it was well traveled.

Then there was the main house. Duncan was guarding it like there was a harem behind those walls. Three stories. Old. Dry as tinder. There was probably a root cellar and an attic. There were also people inside. At a minimum there was one woman and two men. Archer could see the woman through the picture window on the first floor. It wasn't Hannah. On the second floor a man had looked through old drapes only to pull away when Archer looked up. He saw the man's silhouette behind the lace curtains and it was big enough to fill the window. That was probably their man, Robert Butt. The other guy looked straight at Archer, but Archer couldn't have given a description of him for a million bucks.

"Excuse me," Duncan called. "You. What are you looking at?"

"Just admiring the house," Archer said. He didn't mind that this man was a little annoyed. Archer was getting a little annoyed himself and it was with Andre's soft sell. It wasn't getting them anywhere, so Archer took a chance. "Are they here or not? We'll take any or all. Maybe we can start with Robert, but Hannah or Billy will do, too. Just one of them."

Archer started walking, stopping only when he reached the stairs. Since Duncan hadn't moved and was giving him a stinking, lazy-eyed look, Archer forced the issue. He put his foot on the bottom step.

"This is a private residence," Duncan said. He looked toward Andre. As much as he hated the man – his good looks, his uniform, his false authority – Duncan was happy to use that authority to his own benefit. "Trooper Guillard, I feel threatened by this man. I would appreciate it if you would remove him from the property. And yourself, if you don't mind."

"Archer." Guillard called, but Archer didn't move. Andre raised his voice. "Archer."

This time Archer listened. His foot landed back on the ground. There wasn't much to be seen in Duncan's eyes: some arrogance, not as much confidence as Duncan pretended, but not as much stupidity as Archer would have liked.

"Thanks for the hospitality," Archer said and turned his back.

"I just want to protect my people. I'm sure you understand that," Duncan answered. "Come back tomorrow. After we've prayed."

Archer went back to Andre who gave him a clap on the back as he passed. Andre tipped his hand to Duncan.

"Thank you for your time. We've got a boat just down–"

Before Andre could finish making nice, Archer spun around and bellowed:

"Hannah! Billy! Hannah! We're here!"

"Damn!"

Andre was on him, taking his arm, moving him out. Archer tried to shake him off but Andre had a good hold of him so he walked backward, calling out until the trooper forced him to silence. The only thing Archer saw before the Trooper turned him around was Duncan's back just before he closed the front door.

Hannah rolled over.

She opened her eyes wide.

She thought someone was calling her name. She thought

Archer had been calling her name. She rolled out of bed and onto her knees. Breathing deep, gulping air, she pulled on the bedclothes, got herself upright and, hand-over-hand, managed to get to the window. Once there, all she saw was outside: grey sky and white snow, the trunks of the trees brown and black, Glenn's woodpile, Duncan's house. Her head was spinning. She put it against the old window glass. Her stomach heaved. She draped one arm at her waist and closed her eyes. The icy cold glass felt wonderful on her forehead, but it wasn't enough to make her feel well. She wanted Billy to come through the door and get her downstairs and out into the snow. She wanted to breathe fresh air. But he wasn't there. She didn't know where he was. She didn't know if he was coming back. When the door of her room opened, Hannah shut her eyes. She didn't want Melody to fawn over her; she didn't want Teresa to check her stitches.

"I'm fine. I don't need help," she said.

When no one answered and the door didn't close, Hannah lifted her head and opened her eyes. She straightened up, intending to show Melody that she didn't need help. Instead, Hannah looked out the window again. She caught only a glimpse of two men walking into the forest and they weren't a part of the congregation. She knew one of them. She knew his walk and the breadth of his shoulders.

"Archer," she whispered.

If Archer had tracked her all the way to Alaska, Josie couldn't be far behind. They would help her find Billy. Hannah turned around to tell Melody of this miracle but her smile faltered. It was Duncan, not Melody, who stood behind her.

"There's someone you need to see, Hannah."

Then Duncan's face split into two happy parts that to Hannah's eye, if she'd bothered to think about it, looked a little cruel.

Oki wore his cape of hide and needles and the shaman hat. Cecilia sat in the chair and waited for good words. The shaman had none to give her. He shook his head.

"I journeyed to the fifth level and the spirits have all hidden themselves. This is not good business."

Mama Cecilia was sad. If a shaman could not figure out what should be done then the situation was troubling, indeed. She wondered if her spirits were bad and the failure was not in Oki's abilities. Perhaps she was not meant to have a son. And yet her spirits told her that this one, Billy, was kind of heart and in need of her attention.

"He is troubled," she said.

"His soul is lost." Oki sat back and waved his hand wearily. "If I had known, I would have requested assistance when I was journeying. I would have called out the spirits of his ancestors, but I did not know his soul needed retrieving. I should have guessed, Cecilia. All the signs are there."

"Can you restore his soul just a little? If you could do that, then perhaps he could find his friend and that would restore the rest of it," Mama Cecilia suggested, but Oki shook his head. He was so sad.

"It takes much strength and power to go to the otherworld. I cannot go back again." Oki sighed. "I have been a shaman all my life, Cecilia. Even if I could restore this boy, how do I know that he would not cause hurt and harm anyway?"

Mama Cecilia thought about the questions Oki raised. Finally, she said:

"Oki, if he has done as you told him – waiting to allow us time to discuss him – and he has not stolen from you, or hurt you, or said bad things even about the devil who hurt him, he must be a good person."

Oki nodded.

"If he is going to return to where the devil is to help his friend, does this not prove that his spirits are good even if his soul is harmed?"

Oki nodded again.

"Oki," Mama Cecilia said. "If I have found him does that not mean I must journey with him as I did not journey with my own son? Perhaps, this journey would show I am a good mother, and for Billy to prove he is a good man. Could it not be as simple as that, Oki?"

Oki shook his head, "No, Cecilia. I don't believe so. However, you have said wise things. But you are old, also. Perhaps, we should stay here and send him on his way."

Cecilia stood up. Her arms hung at her sides. She felt the warmth of her good moccasins.

"If he got lost and died, Oki, then why should I have found him at all?"

"This is true, Cecilia."

And it was settled. When they went to the room where Billy sat with his head shaved and his hurt hand hanging down between his knees, Mama Cecilia spoke to the boy.

"I will take you where you need to go."

31

Andre talked to his captain on the Satellite phone and gave her an update while Archer watched the river for any sign of Nell and Josie.

It was now two hours past their anticipated time of arrival. Despite Andre's assurances that, one way or the other the two women would get to Clara's Landing, Archer didn't like it. He didn't like the fact that there was no way to communicate with Josie. And he sure didn't like the fact that Andre wanted to do things by the book; Archer wanted to sit on Duncan's holy doorstep. A little intimidation never hurt anyone. Andre pointed out that in Alaska a little intimidation could get you dead. While he stewed, Archer watched the river. Finally, he said:

"They're here."

Up river the canoe slalomed across the wide water. There were three people in it: two were paddling and Josie Bates, taller than both, was in the middle.

"She's upright," Andre noted.

"She'd be upright in a body bag," Archer said.

"Good point."

The two men stood on shore watching the strange progress of the canoe. To pass the time Andre went over what he had.

"Robert Butt was released, clean bill of health, no probation. No warrants in Alaska or Colorado. Duncan Thoth has no record, but he did ministry at the hospital."

"Same year Robert Butt was there?" Archer asked.

"Yes."

"And what about getting in the house?"

"They suggested charm. We have no cause to pull rank or use force," Andre answered as he broke away from Archer when Nell called to him.

"Are they checking if Thoth owns the house?" Archer asked while he followed the trooper to the bank as the canoe drifted to shore.

"They'll look at land records tomorrow," Andre said and then he didn't want to talk about Duncan Thoth anymore. The canoe had made it across the water and through the ice and was now at the riverbank. He pulled Nell up and out of the canoe. Nell passed the paddle back to Josie who stowed it before she reached for Archer.

Just as he took her in his arms and she said, 'good to see you', the guy in the canoe with the bird on his hat hollered:

"Watch it fella! No bear hugs for Miss Josie."

Billy walked behind Mama Cecilia even though he would have preferred to run ahead. He had the weird idea that Hannah's spirit would lead him back to her. He thought Duncan's evilness would be like breadcrumbs dropped along the way. But neither Hannah's goodness or Duncan's wickedness were anywhere to be found. There were only trees and cold and an old woman in front of him. Without her, he would be lost.

In Billy's boots, scraps of leather covered the holes in his soles. Oki had put a scarf around Billy's neck. He found mittens that didn't match and he put them on Billy's hands. He gave them food and worried that they would not have a place to sleep, but Billy said they would not need a place to sleep. When they were close, he would send Mama Cecilia back. Billy had thought it would be easier if she just brought him to the river and he could follow that but Mama Cecilia said it was too far. A straight line would get him where he was going sooner.

They walked a long way and it was only when Mama Cecilia stumbled that Billy realized he had been lost in his own fantasies about what he would do and say to Duncan when he saw him again. He skipped ahead a few paces and took her arm.

"You should sit down."

Mama did not disagree and they sat together on some rocks. He took out some food to give her, and some water. They ate and listened to the nothing until Mama said:

"Is your friend a good person?"

Billy nodded. "You are, too, Mama Cecilia."

"My son has left me," she admitted.

"Sons do that sometimes," Billy said.

"Did you leave your mother?"

Billy shook his head and his sadness was so great that Mama Cecilia did not ask about his mother. Instead, she said:

"Will you come see me? You and your friend?

"Yes," he said. "I promise."

They ate some more and rested longer than Billy wanted to. But that was how he thought it should be. Worrying about Mama Cecilia instead of only about Hannah made Billy think that maybe Oki had retrieved just a little bit of his soul after all.

Nell was on the big boat Andre and Archer had rented. Andre was on the phone yet again. Stu had gotten himself off somewhere. Josie and Archer had tired of waiting on them and walked up the path so she could see the house. Now they stood at the edge of the forest looking at it.

"There are at least four people inside. Two upstairs in separate rooms when last I saw them. I saw one woman. She looked like she was probably young."

"Young like Hannah?"

Archer shook his head, "No, babe. Chin length hair. Bigger than Hannah. She was watching Duncan from the room downstairs. I assume that's a living room."

"So what's up on the third floor? One of the dormers is boarded up."

"Your guess is as good as mine," Archer said. Josie took his hand. He turned her so they were facing one another. His hands hovered around her waist but he didn't touch her. "Do you hurt?"

"Yes," she said and then she kissed him. "I want to go home. I want to go home with Hannah. I want to get married on a warm beach."

"I'm with you, babe," he said.

"I know. You always are, always will be." Josie kissed him lightly. "Watch my back, will you?"

Archer laughed as she slipped away and walked across the clearing. No one looked out the windows. No one came to the door and Josie wouldn't have slowed down if they had. She took the steps, knocked, waited what she considered a decent amount of time and then looked over her shoulder at Archer as she turned the knob and walked into a time warp.

The place was at least a hundred years old if it was a day. Upstairs, all was quiet. She looked down the hall to the side of the staircase and saw a dining room table. To her left was the living room where Archer thought he had seen the woman. The room was empty.

Josie walked into the room and looked at every inch. There were chairs, a couch, a low table, but no television, magazines, or books. There were pictures on the walls, beautifully, gruesomely executed pictures of religious suffering. As she passed the window, she looked to see if Archer was where she left him.

He saw her and raised a hand. She turned to the far corner of the room. There were more pictures on the long wall and one that was particularly well done over a deep-seated chair. It was a cozy corner with the painting, the chair, a standing lamp and two baskets. The small one on the side table was a basket of threads and buttons and even a darning egg. The other one on the floor was filled with clothes.

Josie figured to push her luck and try upstairs, but she changed her mind, bent down, and balanced on the balls of her feet. Carefully, she folded back the clothes on top of the mending pile until she found the pair of jeans that had caught her eye. They were small, narrow in the hip and boot cut at the hem. They had recently been washed, but the bloodstains on them were forever. They were ripped up the left leg. Josie took the other clothes out of the basket, set them aside, and then looked at the label in the jeans.

Size 2.

7 For All Mankind.

"What are you doing in here?"

Josie pivoted. In the doorway stood a young woman dressed in a high-necked shirt and a long full skirt. In one hand she held a pair of gigantic scissors. Her other hand was empty, deformed and twitching. On her face was a look of utter hatred. Still holding the jeans, Josie stood up.

"Where is Hannah?"

"She's not here," the woman replied.

"Is she dead?" Josie advanced but the woman did not retreat. Her good hand clutched the scissors like a dagger.

"Don't try it," Josie warned.

"God is on my side."

"Then he better step up his game, because I'm coming through."

32

I thought I had seen Archer out the window. I thought Duncan was taking me to see him. I was wrong – at least about where he was taking me.

He put his arm around me and I leaned against him. We walked out of my room but instead of going down the stairs, he opened the door of the room next to mine; the one where the prophetess, Pea, lived.

When he locked the door I knew three things. One, Archer was here, two Duncan was pulling a Flowers in the Attic *trick to keep me right where he wanted me, and three, I was screwed.*

Hannah's eyes adjusted to the darkened room and the first thing she saw were the paintings covering every inch of every wall. The next thing she saw was the bed with its beautiful quilt. It wasn't until she looked at the room a second time that she saw the woman kneeling with her hands against the shutters, her head down, and her white gown puddled around her bare feet. Hannah twirled out of Duncan's grasp and tried to run. She didn't get far. Duncan twirled her back into his body and held her tight.

"You haven't met your sister-in-law."

"Let me out of here," Hannah whispered.

"Un-huh, Hannah. That would be against God's wishes."

"Not against mine, Duncan. You don't want me if I don't want you."

"It isn't a matter of want, Hannah," Duncan said. He yanked her toward him and clamped a hand on the back of her neck. "Stop fidgeting. Stop."

Hannah stared at his chest and tried to calm herself. Her strength was limited. She needed to wait for her moment.

"That's better," he said. "As I was saying, my life has never been about what I wanted. Now, God has been very clear about why you are here. You are to be my wife. I have followed God my whole life, and I will follow him in this. Okay? Okay?"

"Yes, Okay," Hannah answered.

"Okay, Duncan." He pulled her tighter.

"Okay, Duncan. I'm sorry. But I can't breathe. You're holding me too tight."

"I'm sorry. You have had a bad time of it," he relaxed his grip a little. "It was so unfortunate what happened with the tea. I had no idea that poison was in my house."

"What poison?"

"It doesn't matter. None of it has anything to do with you except that you have survived. Another sign, Hannah. Twice you survived the unsurvivable. I can see why you were chosen. We will still have trials ahead, but nothing compared to what you've been through."

"I guess. Sure – Duncan."

Hannah pulled back. She had never been this close to him before and she didn't want to be this close to him now. He was stronger than her but not smarter. But smarter didn't matter because he had the conviction of his faith. Dark and twisted as that faith may be, it was his and she hoped reason could penetrate that wall.

"My family is here," Hannah said. "They will be your in-laws and–"

Duncan pulled her so hard and tight the words were pushed out of her.

"They aren't your family. That is a State Trooper and he has no jurisdiction here. We've done nothing wrong."

"My friend Archer is here, too." Hannah eased back a bit more. "That hurts, Duncan. Really. It does. Please. You're holding too tight."

"Alright." He loosened his grip. "Sit on the rug. If Pea chooses to talk with you, she'll do it if you sit on the rug."

"Thank you." Hannah sat down but kept her knees up and her hands on the floor.

"You're welcome," Duncan said. "You are safe with Pea. No one will harm you in here for sure."

"Archer wouldn't hurt me," she said. "He won't leave until he knows I'm okay. I don't want you to get in trouble for helping me and Billy–"

"Get it through your head!" Duncan screamed and Hannah cringed, startled by his explosive anger. It took everything he had to calm himself, but when he did Duncan said. "Billy is gone and he won't come back." He worked his jaw. "I'm getting a little tired of people talking about him."

That was it. Hannah had no choice. She stopped trying to make nice.

"Yeah, well get used to it because I'm not going to stop talking about him," she said. "I know you did something to him, and I'm going to find out what it was. I am going to, Duncan."

Hannah got to her knees but that was as far as she got. Duncan took a step forward and looked down on her.

"It's God's will that he is gone. That's all you need to know."

Hannah smirked. She couldn't play this God game as well as Duncan. But she would play another one; one she had learned watching the cool girls in school. She would play one against the other.

Hannah's eyes narrowed, and she raised her voice. "Hey! Hey! Pea. Turn around."

"Stop it," Duncan ordered. Hannah ignored him and started to crawl toward the woman in white.

"Pea. Hey, Pea! Look at me. Your brother hurt Billy! Do you know Billy? That's not very godly, is it? Hey–"

Duncan moved faster than Hannah thought possible. He swooped down and grabbed her, pulling her up until she thought he would pull her arm out of its socket.

"Pea," Hannah screamed, but Pea paid no attention. Not when Hannah screamed her name one last time, and not when Duncan hauled off and backhanded her. Hannah's head snapped back. Her body went limp. Duncan Thoth dropped Hannah Sheraton onto one of Pea's pillows and then pushed his hair away out of his eyes.

"The Lord works in mysterious ways does he not, Pea?"

With that, Duncan stepped over Hannah and left the room.

"Guillard!"

Archer called for the trooper at the same time he ran for the house. He'd seen enough to know that Josie wasn't having a nice little talk with the lady of the house. Behind him, Andre called for Nell to stay put. A man came out of the shed and yelled, "Stop." Archer didn't stop.

He was up the steps and in the house with Andre closing in fast. There was a woman on the floor of the living room and a pair of scissors on the other side of the hall. Archer reached for her, but she jerked away.

"Don't touch me. Get out of here," she screamed, but Archer grabbed for her again. This time he got a good hold of her arm only to pull back when he realized he was holding bone as delicate as tinder wood. Then he grabbed her hard and pulled her up. If he broke that arm, so be it.

"Where is Josie? Where's the woman who was in here?"

"You will burn in hell–"

Archer let her go just as Andre stormed into the house. Archer was about to tell him to check the back of the house when both men heard Josie calling Hannah's name. Archer and Andre hit the second floor landing running. Josie was at the far end of the hall, throwing her shoulder against a door.

"Jo," he called.

"Archer. She's here. She's here. Somewhere. These are hers."

Josie waved the jeans at him like a red flag at a bull. Archer barreled down the hall and pushed her back. He put his shoulder into the door but the old wood was solid and all he got for his effort was a whole lot of pain. He was about to go at it again when he heard the lock engage. Andre had come up beside them and together they watched the knob turn. The door stayed closed.

"Open up. Whoever is in there, open this door," Archer said as Josie called out Hannah's name. Archer looked over his shoulder. "Guillard. You're a cop. I want this door opened. You have cause."

Before Andre could do anything, Duncan stormed toward them.

"What is going on here? This is private property. This is a church. Get away! Get out!"

Andre wasted no time. He turned on his heel and met Duncan half way, blocking him. "Stay back. Stay back."

Duncan pushed at him. "I will own you. I will sue you. All of you get out of here now."

"Hannah! Hannah! Where are you?"

Josie's voice sounded above all the rest and she pounded her hand, flat palmed against the door only to stand back when it finally cracked open. Everyone fell silent. Andre took Duncan's arm and pulled him against the wall opposite the door. Archer stood beside Josie. The door opened wide enough for them to see Robert Butt cowering there. He was massive, wider than the door itself and almost as tall. His face was a mask, red and tough as raw meat on one side and baby-bottom pink on the other. He blinked at them. When he raised his arm, Archer tensed. Robert Butt put his sleeve to his nose and wiped it. Josie was the first to recover; she was the first to speak.

"Do you know Hannah?" she asked.

"Robert," Duncan warned but it was too late. Robert was not quick. He blinked.

"Yes," he said. "Hannah's an angel."

33

I've never been hit like that before. Not backhanded. It felt like every-thing that ever ticked off Duncan in his whole life was behind that smack. This doesn't bode well for a happy marriage.

The one good piece of news is that he shut down my pity party pretty well. I'm still not feeling great, but I've got my legs working and I'm totally motivated. Now all I have to do is figure out how to get out of here, and I've got to do it before Archer leaves.

If he hasn't already.

If he hasn't given up, too.

Like Billy.

And then I hear it. That sound I heard on the first night. A trill. A burp. I say:

"What?"

The pillow Hannah was lying across felt really good. It was filled with down and covered with fine cotton and she was tempted to lie there and take whatever was going to come. Then she heard the bird-like trilling sound, the one she heard the first time she woke up in this house. She propped herself up on her elbow and hung her head. Her right eyeball felt like it was keeping a drum beat in its socket. Hannah wondered if Billy could tell her what muscles in a wrecked jaw connected with an eyeball. Not that it mattered. He wasn't there. It was just her and Pea.

Finally, Hannah sat up and checked out the room. It was darker than dark in the corners but the fire cast shadows through the tin box that surrounded the stove. She got up slowly and stumbled over to where Pea knelt by the shuttered window. She knelt down. It didn't take long to figure out Pea wasn't going to say anything, so Hannah began to talk. She said the first thing that came to her mind

"My name is Hannah. I'm just a kid. . ."

"She's not dead. She's in that house, Andre. An angel," Josie spat. "That is such bull. We've got to go in now. Warrant or no warrant."

Josie paced back and forth in front of the fire Nell had built. She moved out of the light and into the dark, out of the warm and into the cold. Archer, Andre, and Nell sat close to the fire and listened. They had stopped exchanging looks of frustration an hour earlier and were simply waiting for Josie to run out of steam. When it was clear that was not going to happen Andre put a stop to it. A man could only take so much talk.

"We'll have a warrant by morning."

"Josie, sit down," Nell begged. "Their snowmobile and boat are right here. From the looks of that boat, they aren't going anywhere in that thing."

Josie stormed back to the fire and planted herself. She looked like some kind of an ancient goddess about to annihilate nonbelievers. "Listen to who's talking. All I heard from you two was how Alaska was different. Nobody follows the rules. So what are we waiting for if there aren't any rules?"

"Jo, that's a stretch," Archer said. "Andre's a sworn officer."

"Fine. He stays here. Nell, you stay, too. Archer and I'll go. There's got to be twenty ways to get into that house."

"And they'll hear us coming a mile away," Archer pointed out.

"He's right," Andre agreed. "And all that Alaskan independence could get you filled with buckshot. They'd have every right to defend themselves if you break into their place."

"They're Christians. They aren't going to do that."

"You must have flunked history," Nell mumbled. Josie turned toward her.

"I figured you'd be on my side," Josie said.

"We're all on your side," Andre said. "When we get that warrant, I will go in. Me. The law. I will search the premises. If your girl is in there, I will find her. If she's not there, we'll figure out where she is. It won't take much to get the big guy to talk as long as he's not around Duncan."

Andre reached for his coffee cup. He was glad they'd been able to requisition a boat with a heater. Archer and Josie would sleep onboard; he and Nell would sleep in the open. That way he would have some quiet. Tomorrow he would have a warrant. Until then, he wasn't going to speculate, buy into Josie's hysteria, or be bullied.

"That's it then?" Josie asked.

"That's it," Andre said.

"Archer?"

"Sorry, Jo. I'm with him."

"Okay. Fine." Josie turned on her heel. "I've got to pee."

"Don't go far," Nell called and all they heard was a grunt of disdain. Nell looked at Archer. "You guys should think of moving up here."

"Why's that?"

"To give civilization a break."

Billy stopped Mama Cecilia when he saw the store building through the trees. Billy did not want Mama Cecilia going back to Oki by herself in the dark, and she didn't want to hold him back so they struck a pact. Billy would settle Mama Cecilia in the forest far enough away that no one could see her campfire, and Mama would wait until Billy came back with his friend.

Billy made her a campsite, assured himself that she would be warm enough and that she still had food to eat. She made him eat some, too. They sat quietly together for a while and Mama knew that his spirits were troubled.

"I'm afraid," he said.

"All things are afraid of something," she answered.

Josie caught her zipper on one of the shreds of her coat. She cursed, worked it free and finally got herself back together. Peeing in the forest in single digit weather was not the most pleasant thing in the world. It ranked right up there with getting yourself lost a few hundred feet from a campfire that seemed to have been as bright as a Klieg light when she was standing in front of it.

Stuffing her hands back into her gloves, Josie pulled her hat down and looked around. Trees and more trees. Snow. More trees and undergrowth. She had a couple of choices. She could give a shout out and admit she'd got herself lost, she could hope Andre or Nell would come get her, she could act on her best guess, or she could sit down, mope, and freeze to death. There was one other option. She could stand really still because there was something moving through the trees just off to her left.

Josie closed her eyes. She slowed her breathing. She did not want to play dead again but she might not have a choice. Whatever was out there was circling. She could feel it. She could smell it. And then she could hear it:

"They're doing something weird in that house, Miss Josie."

34

Josie stayed on Stu's heels and then scooted in beside him when he ducked behind a boulder. They were close to the south side of the main house, had a decent view of Duncan's place, and a clear opening to the shed.

"Where have you been?" Josie whispered.

"Out and about. Too many folks around your fire," he answered. "Keeps us out of trouble if we don't talk to each other."

"I'd be out of work if everyone thought like you," Josie said. "What's going on in there?"

"They're having a big meeting. Everybody's all dressed up fancy. Want to go see?"

"Sure."

They were off again and made it to the side of the house without notice. They kept close to the wall as they ducked around back. Stu hurried to a structure, lifted one side of an old wooden door that acted as a roof and went inside. Josie followed, feeling her way down a short staircase.

"Stu? Where are you?" she whispered.

"Here."

Josie heard a match being lit and the next thing she saw

was the mantle of a lantern glowing. They were in an old root cellar, but Josie wasn't seeing anything good here. Among the bins of potatoes and onions, there were boxes of ammunition and more guns than anyone in their right mind should have.

"Wow," she said.

"Nice stash," Stu agreed. "Come on."

The cellar was low ceilinged and rambling. Josie stooped to keep from hitting her head and followed him to the far end where it was particularly cold and dry and the ceiling high enough for her to stand up. Stu set the lantern to the side and pointed to a hole in the wall. Then he pointed to a box. Josie stepped up.

She could hear Duncan speaking but couldn't quite make out his words. She could see various parts of other people. She heard the kitchen door open and a woman passed by the peephole, moved around the table, paused and then moved on. Finally, Josie could see her in full. She was serving piles of food and people were digging in as if it were their last meal. Josie dropped down to talk to Stu.

"That's not the same woman who was upstairs," Josie whispered. "This one is older."

"There's a young one there. Something's wrong with her arm. I saw her."

"I see Robert Butt. He's the man I want to talk to," Josie said. "The big man."

"Maybe we can arrange that," Stu chuckled.

"You've been inside, haven't you?"

"I wasn't in all of it."

"We can't go in now. This time they may shoot first," Josie mused. "If they've got an arsenal down here, what do you think they have up there?"

"I didn't see nothing too interesting, but we don't want trouble. You don't worry, Miss Josie. We're going to figure this all out and get your girl back."

Josie slid down and put her back up against the wall and said: "Thanks, Stu."

He did the same, laying aside his gun and tipping his hat forward.

"I mean, we'll get her back if she ain't dead."

Duncan looked around the table. Every bit of food was eaten, nothing was wasted. It was a fitting end of the evening. When Duncan stood up, his flock was happy.

"My friends," Duncan began. "The Lord gave us three days for the healing. He did not say it had to take three days. The people who have come here want to take away our way of life. I won't have it. The healing will begin and it will end tonight. We will be made whole, and they will leave this place, and there will be peace."

Duncan's face broke into two happy parts. His soul filled up with joy as he watched their expressions transform from happiness to ones of ecstasy.

"Robert, Foster, and the rest of you who have no chores to finish up go to your rooms. Get them in order. Spend the time as you would in *Hours*. I will visit each of you in turn."

"I deduce this will be a wonderful night," Robert said as he helped little Peter down from his chair.

"Di...tt...di..." Foster stuttered.

Melody smiled and so did Glenn. Chairs were moved, congratulations made, and hugs were offered. When they were gone, Duncan sat alone at the head of an empty table. He picked up a fork that Teresa had left behind when she cleared the table and mindlessly let it thread through his fingers. He had one last decision to make: what would he do with Hannah and Pea. He was so lost in thought, he didn't realize that Melody was standing in the doorway watching him. He wondered how long she had been there. Not that it mattered. She couldn't read his thoughts, but he could read hers. He knew her question before she asked it.

"Robert will be the first, Melody."

She nodded. "Do you need me to do anything for you?"

"No. Thank you."

"I went to your house. It's already clean. It looks as if nobody lives there. You'll still live there after the healing, won't you?" Melody's good hand clasped her withered one. If those hands could wring, that's what they would be doing but only one moved. When she saw Duncan looking, she dropped her arms to her side.

"I will be here until you are all healed," he assured her.

"Duncan." Melody took a step forward. "Will you marry Hannah?"

Before he could answer, the door to the kitchen opened. Teresa stood there, wiping her hands on her dishtowel. Her eyes cut from one to the other.

"Will you need anything else tonight? Should I see to Pea?" Teresa asked Duncan.

"No. I'll see to Pea and Hannah." He answered Teresa and then said, "Melody, go on now. Get your things in order. Say your prayers."

Melody left and Duncan looked after her. When she was gone, he asked, "Is there something else, Teresa?"

"Will you heal me, too, Duncan?"

"I haven't decided," he answered.

"And Pea?"

He pushed back his chair and got up, "I haven't decided that either."

Teresa let the door go and finished up her chores. As much as she hated to admit it, she hoped, she believed, she still had a kernel of faith that Duncan, her flawed and angry son, might be able to heal her. She would welcome a second chance. She would do things differently. She would prove to her children that she loved them.

She opened the door again, ready to tell Duncan that she believed in him but the room was empty. The sideboard door was open. She went to close it because Duncan said everything must be in order. The small glass decanter was missing and that seemed odd to her, but not odd enough to concern her.

Teresa went back to the kitchen and while she washed and polished and shined things, she wondered if it would hurt as much to heal as it had hurt to be alive?

Billy dashed from his hiding place to the store. His heart was pounding so hard he was sure they could hear it all the way to the main house. He closed his eyes and concentrated.

One breath. One beat. One long breath. One slower heartbeat.

When he was ready Billy ran on to Duncan's house, let himself in, fell to his knees, and crawled to the day bed. He scrambled up and put himself against the wall. When Duncan walked through that door Billy's yellow jacket would be the first thing he would see. It might take him a minute to figure out that Billy Zuni was back from the dead, but when he did the dude would be scared. Billy's very sharp knife with a handle that looked like ivory was the second thing Duncan would see. Then he would be terrified.

"Nell? You want to go see if you can find her?"

Andre poked at the fire. It was burning down and it was about time for everyone to turn in, but Josie wasn't back.

"Boy, when she gets a pout on she really gets a pout on, doesn't she?" Nell muttered.

"I'll get her." Archer got up and dusted off the back of his pants. He zipped up his jacket, adjusted his hat and looked around.

"She went that way." Andre pointed in the last direction Archer would have gone.

"Maybe you should go, Nell." Archer conceded as he walked toward the boat. "I'll make sure the heater's going onboard."

When Archer was gone, Nell said, "I wish you were turning on the heat in that cabin."

She rolled a shoulder against Andre's before she went on her way to find Josie Bates to tell her to pull up her big girl pants.

35

Like nocturnal animals, everyone in Clara's Landing was moving in the dark. Nell looked for Josie. Josie waited for Teresa to finish in the kitchen so she and Stu could go through the pantry door and into the house. Teresa put away the now clean dishes. Duncan was upstairs healing his flock. Hannah was in the room with the ever-silent Pea working at the latch that locked the shutters nailed over windows that opened out onto the roof.

There was one moment when each of them had a personal epiphany and they all had them at just about the same time.

Nell figured out that Josie was gone.

When she told Archer, he knew she wasn't lost.

When they told Andre, he was ticked and that wasn't something Nell saw too often.

Teresa's moment came when she put away the last of the dishes and pulled out the trash bag to tie it up. She heard the sound of glass. When she opened the bag and saw the empty vials that had held the poison, her blood ran cold.

Robert Butt convulsed and threw up. He was deducing that he didn't particularly like healing when the final convulsion threw him off his bed and he landed on the floor with a massive thud.

Duncan heard the sound and crossed himself. Melody opened her eyes when he hesitated. He smiled at her – not a face splitting smile – but a gentle, loving one.

"Duncan?"

"It's time," he said.

"I love you. I always have," she said.

"I love you, too." He kissed her. Melody raised her arms but only the fingers of one hand touched his face. The other fluttered, and stuttered, and dragged down the side of his cheek. That was the hand he took. That was the hand he cupped. With the greatest of care, he poured the healing liquid into her hand. He put the glass to her lips. She drank.

"Close your eyes. All is well."

Now there was only Glenn, Teresa, Pea and Hannah. There was just enough left in the bottle to see them all to heaven.

Easy Peasy as Robert would say.

———

It was a best guess, but Hannah figured about ten minutes passed between the time Pea had crawled on her knees to the middle of the rug, planted her hands, and froze again. In those ten minutes, Hannah ransacked the room and came up with a narrow band of plastic, a narrow metal rod, and a length of knotted rope she found piled underneath the bureau. She forced the rod between one of the shutter hasps and rocked it back and forth against the old wood. The nails gave at the same time she heard someone at the door. She hid the rod behind her full skirt, moved away from the window, and held her breath. It could be Duncan. It could be Melody. How she wished it would be Archer, but she was beginning to have her doubts that the man she had seen was Archer at all.

Then the door opened and she breathed easy.

"Come with me." Teresa held out her hand to Hannah. "Come now."

"What about her?" Hannah whispered.

"I'll come back for her."

"No, she needs to come with us," Hannah insisted.

"Alright. Alright." Teresa hurried toward Pea. She knelt in front of her and whispered. "Come out, Pea. Come out now. Please."

Hannah rushed forward, "Maybe if we take her arms. Both of us."

"Alright. Be careful she might hit you if you go too fast." Teresa stood up and Hannah positioned herself as Teresa pleaded with her daughter. "Pea, come out. Please, please."

"Yes, please, Pea. Come out."

Hannah and Teresa looked toward the door. Duncan was there, smiling at them. Hannah and Teresa let go of Pea. The older woman moved between the young ones. She put her hands on Hannah's arm and Pea's bowed head as Duncan ambled into the room.

"I'm glad you're all together," he said.

Billy couldn't imagine what was keeping Duncan. It was well past time he should have come back to his house and Billy was antsy. He got off the bed and prowled around Duncan's house. There was nothing to find. Literally. Nothing. No clothes in the closet. No shoes. Then he found out why. Everything Duncan Thoth owned was packed into a suitcase under his bed. Billy looked out Duncan's window toward the main house. The front door was open. Glenn was bringing wood inside. That was odd since they let the fires burn down at night.

Billy went back to his place and sat down in the shadows again. He wondered how Mama Cecilia was doing and if her fire was bright enough and warm enough. He smiled thinking about her. She would like Hannah and Hannah would like her. Once Billy had Duncan, he and Hannah would have a passport out of this place. When he and Hannah were safely gone, these freaks could have Duncan back. Hannah was all Billy wanted.

Glenn put wood in the stove in the dining room and stood back to admire his work. The whole house smelled so good. He closed the grate and went back to the porch to get the wood for upstairs. He hummed under his breath and he hadn't done that since the night he had set fire to his own house. It was wonderful to hum a little tune and carry wood and stoke a fire and not want to kill anybody.

He picked up enough wood for Robert's room and maybe Foster's. He would have to make a few trips, but that was all right. These fires would be his gift. Everyone would be warm and cozy during the healing. Duncan was sure to doubly bless Glenn for this kindness.

He climbed the stairs but stopped humming the moment he opened the door to Robert's room. The stench was foul and Glenn dropped the wood he was carrying so that he could put his poor burned hands over his nose. He blinked. He took one step in and then two out. Robert was dead and he had thrown up so much before dying. He was dead and his face was still red like leather. He hadn't been healed at all.

Glenn closed the door to Robert's room and ran for Foster's. The smell wasn't as bad but the result was the same. Foster was dead. His mouth was open as if he was trying to say something important.

Melody was half on her bed, her poor little arm out like she was reaching for something. She looked so pathetic. She was so dead.

Connie and Paul dead. Little Peter dead. Dead. Dead.

Glenn's very ordinary face transformed as he realized that Duncan had pulled a fast one. Glenn walked back down the hall, chose just the right pieces of wood for his chore, and went into Melody's room.

It was just about to get a little hotter.

36

I'm watching a mother fight for her child. Maybe she's fighting for both of her children. It's hard to tell. I've never seen a mother do that. My mother never wanted to save my life. She just wanted to save hers.

It's cool to see a mom like Teresa.

It's not so cool to know that one way or the other, she's going to lose.

"Put the bottle down, Duncan. I know what it is. I know that you killed them."

"Are they gone already?" Duncan asked.

"Yes. Robert and Melody and Foster. I saw them. It was so fast," Teresa said.

"I had hoped it would be. I'm just sorry that Hannah's resurrection wasn't a miracle after all," Duncan pouted. "I would have loved to have had a miracle."

"What are you talking about," Hannah asked.

"Oh, this." Duncan held up the decanter. "This is what was in that truck with you. Liquid Nicotine. It's lethal in its raw form.

Teresa accidentally mixed yours with tea. That's why you only felt like you were dying. When this is diluted, you get sick; undiluted, you die."

"And you gave it to everyone? Why would you do that to these people?" Hannah put her arm around Teresa and pulled her close. "They loved you. They believed in you."

"Their faith wasn't misplaced. I have healed them," he said, well pleased with himself. "I promised they would be whole in the eyes of the Lord, and that they would be freed from their trials. They are exactly that. In heaven they are whole in the eyes of the Lord, and free from their trials."

"That's bull," Hannah said and let her arm slide away from Teresa. She moved a little left, a little more right. She kept her eyes on Duncan. Whatever was going to happen, it was going to be between him and her and she needed to be ready.

"You know that's not what they believed. They believed you were going to make them whole in this world. All Melody wanted was to have a regular arm."

"Do you really think a new arm would have made Melody happier?"

He shook his head at Hannah's naiveté.

"You're quiet now, aren't you? Okay, I'll tell you the answer. The answer is no. Melody would always lead a withered life. She would be haunted if not by the memory of her beautiful sister, by the memory of how she mutilated her. And Robert? He would always be a misanthrope. Even without the birthmark, he would be an oddity. Slow of mind, giant of body. Where would he find people to love and care for him? Would you? Would you have done what I did for them? All of them lived because of me. Now they live with God because of me."

Hannah took a breath. She laced her fingers through Teresa's, ready to run with her.

"And what about Glenn?" Hannah asked. "Is he just a useless piece of crap, too?"

Duncan chuckled. "That isn't very poetic, Hannah, but it is the truth. Poor Glenn. He's a simpleton, a child who plays with matches. That's all Glenn is."

Hannah's green eyes refocused to a spot over Duncan's shoulder. She said:

"Is that true, Glenn?"

Slowly, Duncan turned around. There stood Glenn with the saddest look on his unmemorable face. In his nearly fingerless hands he held two branches, both burning nicely, perfect torches lighting up the hallway. Glenn had such a way with fire.

"I didn't mean that, Glenn." Duncan held his hands out to the man with the torches as he walked toward him. When he got close enough, Duncan pulled one arm back and threw the last of the poison at Glenn's pitiful face. Glenn screamed and dropped his torches just as Duncan ran for the stairs.

———

"Oh my God!" Nell cried. "Look."

Flames licked out of the second floor windows and the ones on the third floor glowed yellow bright.

"Let's go."

Andre, Archer, and Nell took off at a full run, charging up the outside stairs just as Stu and Josie were coming down the hall.

"Out. Now," Andre ordered as he took the first staircase two steps at a time.

Archer grabbed Josie and Nell took Stu's arm.

"What are you doing? What's happened," Josie asked, pulling away from Archer.

"Fire, upstairs," he said and yanked her to the door.

"Come on Miss Josie," Stu hollered. "This old place is toast."

"Not without Hannah." Josie broke away and Archer dashed up after her. The second floor was burning, driving Andre back for a minute. He regrouped, took off his coat and put it over his nose and mouth as he dove through the first door.

"Andre!" Nell screamed, but Josie held her and dragged her back.

"Hannah? Hannah!" Archer bellowed but it was Andre who answered.

"Archer! Here!"

Coughing and wheezing, Andre came out of the smoke with a child in his arms. Nell rushed forward and took the boy.

"I got him," she hollered. Her eyes went to Josie who was starting for the third floor. "Josie! We've got to go."

Josie looked behind her. The fire was spreading fast. The old wallpaper was licked with flames and the threadbare rug had caught cinders and was starting to burn. Andre shoved Nell ahead of him. She stumbled but kept her feet, holding the little boy close to her chest as she hurried down the stairs to the first floor. Outside, she put him on the ground and fell on her knees beside him. She pressed on his little chest; she put her mouth over his and tried not to look at the house that was half engulfed in flames.

"I got it, Miss Nell." Suddenly, Stu was there. Without missing a beat, his hands replaced hers on the boy's chest. "By the shed. There's a pump-a ladder–"

Before he could finish his direction, the shutters on the third floor window cracked and Nell saw someone clawing at the boards.

Billy had been staring at the wall where the door of Duncan's house was for so long that it took a while for him to realize that he could actually see the door. It took him another minute to realize that the outside was bright. For the craziest second, Billy thought the sun was shining. He scrambled off the bed and looked outside and that's when he saw two things: the main house was burning like an inferno and Duncan Thoth was headed his way.

37

There is nothing to think about except surviving, and you can't really think much about that. You either do it, or you don't.

"Teresa, help me. Help me."

Hannah pulled the lace curtains off the rods. One was already burning and Hannah stomped on it, blessing the heavy knitted socks that Teresa had made. She tossed that panel away and went for the next one but Teresa was already there. She pulled and pulled. It took two of them to get the last one off. Teresa threw it in the corner of the room. Hannah looked up. It sounded like rain on the roof and she knew the fire had gotten into the attic.

"Hurry. Teresa, Hurry! Come help me!"

But Teresa didn't go to the window to help Hannah. Instead, she ran to the bed, grabbed the quilt, threw it over Pea who knelt as she always knelt, unaware and unconcerned. Hannah attacked the shutters again while Teresa went for the water pitcher on the dresser. Hannah dropped her whole weight onto the metal bar while behind her Teresa doused her daughter with water. It would do nothing to save the woman so Hannah pulled harder against the wood.

From outside and the floor below she could hear voices calling out. One board broke in half and Hannah fell back when it snapped. Above her, a piece of the ceiling fell in. Teresa screamed. Hannah rushed to it and kicked it out of the way. She ran back to the window and through the grimy pane she caught sight of Josie rushing toward the house only to be driven back by the flames.

"Josie!" Hannah cried.

She tried to pull out the metal rod, but it was stuck on the splintered wood. With nothing left to loose, Hannah drew back her fist and put it through the small square of exposed glass. It shattered. She didn't even feel the pain. She tried to push the shards out with her fingers.

"Josie! Josie!" She screamed but didn't wait to see if Josie saw her. Instead, Hannah pulled on the metal bar, putting all her weight on it. She heard the wood crack again. She felt it splinter. She clawed at it with her hands and called Josie's name over and over and over again until her voice was hoarse with smoke and terror.

Hannah threw herself up against the shutter. She put her face against the part of the window she had been able to break. The hell if she was going to die without Josie Bates looking her in the eye just one more time.

Billy crouched by the door, but Duncan didn't come through it. Billy ripped it open in time to see Duncan running toward the store. With one last look at the burning house, one moment of mourning for Hannah who surely must already be dead, Billy Zuni ran after Duncan Thoth.

When he reached the store, he slowed down and held the knife high and close. Duncan's footprints veered off the path and stopped at the low rock wall. Billy followed them, pushed through the bushes, saw a thin line of light through a crack in the back door, opened it, and went inside. Boxes were piled in the middle of it. Behind those Billy could see another room. Light spilled out of the doorway and he could hear a hiss and a crackle.

Billy Zuni stepped around the boxes. His hand was beginning to sweat and the knife felt heavy. He pushed the door open wide. Duncan Thoth looked up. He looked like he was seeing a ghost. Billy Zuni saw something even worse than that. He saw the headphones Duncan was wearing. He saw the radio. Then he looked at Duncan and his hand tightened around his very sharp knife.

Hannah worked harder and faster. Teresa had taken a pillow and was trying to beat out the patches of flame on the rug, but it was a loosing battle. Soon the rug would catch in earnest. Pea had to move or she would burn to death.

"Get her over here. Further back," Hannah screamed as she finally yanked the metal rod out of the wood and smashed it against the window, breaking out even more. She gulped in the raw fresh air but that same air fueled the fire and the smoke thickened. Hannah got low and called: "Drag her if you have to. Teresa. Her hair. Drag her."

Hannah shot up again and put her face out the window, not caring that the shards of glass cut her cheeks and sliced through her fingers.

"Josie!" she screamed, but the name was lost in a fit of coughing.

Hannah took the rod to the planks again and this time the bottom half broke off. She punched at the glass. Putting her face up to the broken window, she gulped the air. The smoke stung her eyes, but through it all she saw a miracle. Josie was looking at her, calling her name, rushing toward the fire. That was all Hannah needed. If Josie was willing to die trying to save Hannah, then dying trying to save herself was the least Hannah could do. Staggering to her feet, she grasped the metal bar and attacked the window with all that she had left.

Nell moved as close to the burning house as she could get and tossed a pitiful bucket of water on the flames before running back to the pump by the shed. She was on her third run when Andre stumbled out the front door, his beautiful face black with soot and singed by fire. Nell dropped her bucket, ran to him, and took him around the waist. They only got a few feet before he collapsed in the snow and Nell fell with him.

"Lay back," she said. "There's nothing you can do now."

"They're still up there. Still alive," Andre insisted as he tried to roll onto his side. Nell pushed him back.

"Stop. Stop. Archer and Josie have a ladder. Look!"

Andre put his hand up to guard his face from the heat as he looked where she was pointing. Archer had an aluminum extension ladder and was trying to figure out where to put it. Finally, he made a choice. Josie rushed to hold it and Archer started to climb. On the ground, Nell and Andre watched the girl with the blond hair reach out of the window as if she believed Archer would get to her in time.

"You have a radio." Billy's voice was flat and cold. "A god damn radio."

Slowly, Duncan took off the headphones and set them aside. "I only listen."

"You could have called for help. You could have called when you found us," Billy said.

Duncan stood up slowly, eyeing the knife. The room was so small it was barely big enough for the both of them.

"No. I couldn't. I speak only to Pea who talks to God–"

"Cut the crap, Duncan. You are a worthless piece of–" Billy's voice caught. The terror of the last weeks fell in on him, the loss of Hannah was like a sword in his side. His shoulders fell, the hand holding the knife dropped and his eyes filled with tears. "You murdered Hannah, you tried to murder me, and you still talk about God?"

Duncan reached for his notebook and Bible.

"It is here. I did what I was told to do. See? There? All the prophesies. See the notes? Drive out your enemy it says. Destroy him. That's what it says. You were my enemy."

"No, dude, I was never your enemy. None of us were."

"Okay. Okay, you're right." Duncan moved again. He had almost managed to turn Billy Zuni full circle. He was close to the door. In another second he would have the advantage. He would also have a gun. He always thought he would have to use it against an animal. As he looked at Billy Zuni, he decided maybe that was exactly what he was doing.

"You weren't my enemy, Billy, but you weren't my friend."

"You're right. I wasn't your friend. But you're wrong about the other."

"What other?" Duncan asked.

"The part about being your enemy. I am now. I am your enemy now, dude."

With that, Duncan bolted and Billy Zuni lunged. It was a

battle of the spirits and had Oki been there he would have been hard pressed to decide who would win the spirit war: Duncan who fought for his life or Billy Zuni who fought to avenge his love.

Hannah watched Archer climb the ladder. The heat was agonizing, the smoke searing her lungs, unbearable. Still she kept her eyes on Archer. The ladder was old and Archer was a big man. It didn't go as far as the third floor window and the fire on the roof was advancing fast. Hannah dropped to the floor, fumbling with the thick hemp and eventually tied it around the legs of the dresser. She yanked it tight, pulled herself up to the window and threw the rope onto the roof. Behind her she heard the crash of the ceiling falling in the hallway. Hannah ducked instinctively. Behind her, Teresa cowered with Pea. Hannah scrambled up again. She threw herself at the window and saw Archer had missed the rope. She pulled it back and tried again. Archer lunged for it. The ladder wobbled but he had it. He held on with both hands and Hannah rushed to Teresa.

"Come on. Come on. He caught it."

Teresa shook her head, her arm tightened around Pea. The doorway was now blocked by flame; fire was skittering over the ceiling. Hannah threw her arms around Teresa and tried to raise her. Tears poured down Hannah's cheeks.

"You go first."

"I'm not going," Teresa said.

"You'll die," Hannah screamed.

"I died a long time ago."

"What about her?" Hannah screamed.

"She never lived."

Teresa turned her head and tightened her hold on her

daughter. Hannah stood up. The heat was intense, the light blinding, and there was no time left. Teresa had made her choice; Hannah had to make hers.

"I'm going," she sobbed. "I am. I'm going, Teresa."

The older woman nodded and in that split second, the marigold quilt slipped and Hannah found herself looking into a face more beautiful than any she had ever seen. Pea's skin was porcelain, her eyes were black and bright and they were looking straight at her mother without seeing her.

Hannah dashed for the window, took hold of the rope and climbed over the broken glass. The dresser slid across the room as she put her weight on the rope. It crashed against the wall at the window but it held. The last thing Hannah heard was a trill. God was close to Pea. When Archer grabbed her leg, Hannah knew God was close to her, too.

38

I am looking at this girl in the mirror and I remember her. I remember me.

Tiny gold earrings stuttering around my ears, the small diamond stud in my nose, hair that is chin length, black save for the golden tips. Josie asked if I was going to cut the dyed ends now that it's grown out, but I'm not ready. The gold reminds me of so many things, but mostly it reminds me of Billy. I wonder what he would say now. I wonder whether I look like a black chick or a girl from India. I think I look like neither. I think I look like Hannah.

I lean forward and draw a cat eye with black eyeliner and green shadow. I pluck at the wavy curls that cascade across my brow and down my cheeks. I twirl them into corkscrews and still I am dissatisfied. Then I realize why I'm not happy with my hair. It's not the length or the gold tips, it is that I'm trying to use it to hide the crescent scar that starts high on my brow and ends at the edge of my eye. I take my hair and pull it back, fasten it with a comb made of rhinestones and shells, and let it show. It is the ugliest scar ever, a stair step of raised places where Teresa's unschooled hand stitched me up, and yet I don't think it makes me look ugly. It is simply a part of me like the scars on my arms and in my heart. Those scars are reminders of how I survived my mother; this one is my homage to Teresa and Pea and Melody. I am done with hiding and there is more to life than worrying about what I look like. I learned all that from living with people who so longed to be made whole that they put their faith in a man who was fractured himself. I'm not sure what I think about God, but I learned a little. I learned that you don't have to do religion to have faith. I think faith is a thing you choose to have and you can have it in whoever or whatever you want. If you believe it, it is so. Like believing that Archer could get hold of me, that Josie was holding the ladder, and that I would survive. That was my faith. Someday I will ask Archer if his faith was in God that night. I have a feeling he'll say it was in the lady holding the ladder. Then I will have to ask her if God was behind her. I think I will be asking questions about that night and about God for a long time.

I stand up to put my clothes on, but I see the report Josie brought me lying on the bed next to my dress. I push it aside and pick up my dress. Then I put down the dress, sit on the bed and pick up the report. I've read it three times now, but I want to read it again.

Peter has survived, but everyone else is gone. Most of them were poisoned by Duncan. Glenn burned up. They say he stood in the flame. I am glad I didn't see that. Pea and Teresa died of smoke inhalation. I will always wonder if Pea was *Within* as death came for her. In my dreams she spoke to Teresa. She told Teresa that she loved her and she spoke the word mother. That is my dream, and I'm sticking to it.

Duncan is dead. Stabbed to death. Only his blood was at the scene, but there were fibers under his nails and on the floor of the storage room. Yellow fibers determined to be fleece and consistent with the jacket I bought Billy at a truck stop. No hair was collected except for Duncan's. No bodily fluids except for Duncan's. Investigators could not be definitive about the manner of death. They couldn't tell if the wounds were a result of someone killing him deliberately or made by someone fighting Duncan in self-defense. Billy's name, of course, was brought up but there was a snag in the theory that he had killed Duncan. The clothes Billy had been wearing when he left the compound with Duncan were found in the saddlebag of the snowmobile. If Billy had been left in the wilderness without clothes, he was surely dead. Of course, the authorities had been sure that we were dead before, so I kind of found it interesting they went to that place again.

There was another theory. They wanted to speak to a recluse named Stu who had disappeared during the course of events. They would like to know if he had a fleece jacket or if there was someone out in the wilds of Alaska who had possibly found the jacket Billy Zuni was wearing since it wasn't in the saddlebag with the other clothes.

It was, they all agreed, a mystery. Except to me but no one asked me about Duncan's death so I didn't volunteer anything. I know Billy killed Duncan. When I was clinging to that rope, shimmying down a melting roof, crying to Archer, I turned my head. I saw the flash of yellow disappearing into the forest. What I saw wasn't moonlight. It wasn't fire. It was Billy Zuni walking to where he would be safe and hopefully happy. He was walking away in the yellow jacket that was as precious to him as the Golden Fleece and would always remind him of me.

I knew he had come back for me, and I knew that he could see the inferno from the store, and I knew the way Billy thought. If the house was engulfed in flames that meant I was gone. If he didn't think that, he never would have left. I also know that whatever happened in that store was righteous. Maybe not by the law's standards but certainly by Duncan's own. I didn't have Pea to guide me, but I knew what Duncan's thing was. I looked up the bible verse about an eye for an eye.

Matthew 5:38

You have heard that it was said, an eye for an eye, and a tooth for a tooth

I believe that was what happened. Duncan had tried to do something awful to Billy, Duncan had done something awful to me, and Billy had come back and done something awful to him. But then I read the rest.

Matthew 5:39

But I say to you, do not resist an evil person; but whoever slaps you on your right cheek, turn the other to him also....

The old Billy would have turned his cheek; the Billy who came out of the truck with me, who saw me almost die from poison, who believed me dead in a fire, that Billy couldn't turn the other cheek. He did what he had to. Since I'm done with what happened in that house, I set the report aside, pick up my dress, and put it on.

I pull up the zipper and as I look in the mirror to make sure everything looks right, I realize that we came full circle. Gjergy Isai came to kill Billy because someone he loved had been killed at the hands of Billy's grandfather. Billy had taken a life for my life. I guess he was more Albanian than even he knew. Blood feud was his to embrace and all the innate goodness that was in him could not resist the burn of vengeance. And that brings me to another thing I heard from the Bible. Vengeance is mine sayeth the lord. It's a bummer people keep forgetting that. If only the lord had done his thing, Billy and I would never have had to run from this place we love, his sister would be alive. 'If only' are huge words, but they don't belong in my head today.

I smooth my dress. It looks good. I am home. I am safe and today I am happy. I open the door of my bedroom and there are Archer and Josie waiting for me. Archer is smiling. I want to tell him to stop. I don't recognize him when he does that. Then I can't help it. I smile, too.

"Ready?" Josie asks.

I nod. I am ready. Archer takes Josie's hand and they go out the door while I take the flowers off the hall table and tie them to Max's old pink leash. I put my cheek against his head and feel his tongue flick out to lick my cheek.

"Go for a walk?" I whisper and he gets to his feet. He is so old. It is so hard for him to stand, but he does it for all of us. I think he is smiling, too.

We walk out the door, down the brick walk and go past the little gate. Josie and Archer are holding hands. Max and I follow behind, and I think I have never seen anything more beautiful than Josie Bates in her simple white dress. She is mistress of her universe, sure about herself, unaware of her beauty, comfortable in her strength, content now that her family is together.

We cross The Strand, step onto the warm sand and head to the shore. The beach is nearly deserted. The sun hangs low but even in December it is a bright ball in the ever-blue sky. When we are almost there, Archer and Josie pause. They wait for me to go ahead with Max. I stop to hug Archer, and then I linger in Josie's embrace. I want to say something profound. I can't think of anything profound. I'm just a kid so I say:

"Thank you for finding me."

She hugs me tighter. I know she will always hold onto me, but I also know she will let me go when it is my time. Today she lets me go because we have to get on with things. Max and I walk on. Josie holds Archer's arm and now they walk behind me and Max. I feel them melting into one another. They are more one person than any two people I have ever seen. There is no music for this small processional except for the sound of gentle waves lapping at the shore.

I lift my head and look at the people waiting for us. Faye and Burt, Josie's volleyball friends, cops Archer used to work with, a smattering of lawyers and judges. Stephen Kyle and his girls and Amelia have come from Hawaii. They have brought Josie's mom who doesn't know this tall beautiful bride. She is smiling at Josie like she knows something good is happening.

When we get to where we're going, I stand aside. Max plants his rear in the sand. We all watch Josie and Archer stop in front of the minister and face one another. They are holding hands. The minister invites them to recite the vows they have written. I don't listen. I know what they are saying: simple words about honoring and respecting one another. Love is private and they will talk about that later. Nobody needs to hear talk about love anyway, because everyone feels how much of it there is between them.

I raise my face just a little to feel the sun on my cheeks. I look out over the sparkling blue ocean. I hear the waves lapping at the shore and see the water tumbling toward us and dancing away again. It is so bright and so warm and I think how much Billy would have loved this day. He would have taken my hand and I would have let him. He might have even kissed me, and I would have let him. He would expect me to say something dry or sharp, but I wouldn't be able to because there would be a lump in my throat and tears in my eyes. That's how it would be if he were here. But he isn't, so I close my eyes because he wouldn't want me to waste tears. I swallow that lump in my throat. In my heart, I hear Billy talk to me. He says:

"It's okay, dude. It's okay."

BEFORE YOU TAKE A SNEAK PEEK AT
LOST WITNESS
I NEED YOUR HELP.

I would like to ask you to write something for me - a review. It only takes a moment to jot a few words about why you liked this book and give it a star rating.

Reviews are an author's life blood. Booksellers' algorithms don't look at what you write, they look at the number of reviews. In fact, many book sites will only show readers books with many reviews and star ratings. I appreciate every word, every star, every minute you spend reviewing my work. Just click the title below to get back to the bookstore where you purchased this novel, click on 'reviews', and write about what you liked about
DARK WITNESS
Thanks for helping other readers find me!
Rebecca

NOW TAKE A LOOK AT **LOST WITNESS!**

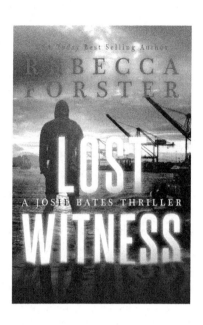

DAY 1, 2:00 a.m.

The man in the mid-ship cabin had sailed 6,300 miles on the
Faret Vild, and no one onboard save for the captain knew he was
there. It was the captain who brought him his meals, the captain
who made sure the man's linen was clean, and the captain who
had chosen the large, long unused cabin for this passenger.
When the man ventured out at all it was in the dead of night
when only the watch on the bridge was awake. Even then he was
cautious. If he was noticed at all his presence seemed no more
than a shadow on the deck, a spirit near the rails, a thing unde-
fined but sensed by those who knew the *Faret Vild* well. Now, on
the last legs of the voyage, he had cabin fever. The Port of Los
Angeles was within sight, the weather was clement, the hour
late, and the crew was busy preparing their cargo, so the man
took a stroll.

He breathed deep of the sea air, stretched his legs a bit,

turned his body, and heard the bones in his back crack. He took out a pack of cigarettes, lit one, and rested his arms on the deck railing. He would enjoy a moment before returning to his cabin to wait for docking and debarkation. At that time he would blend in as if he were an inspector, or a supervisor, or any number of men who worked on the ships or at the port. When his business was done he would return to the *Faret Vild* in the same manner, and he would come back richer.

But that was tomorrow and tonight was beautiful. Above him the heavens were as black as the water upon which the ship sailed. The sky sparkled with stars; the ocean illuminated by a moon that was bright enough to read by. A fresh, cool breeze caught the smoke from his cigarette and swirled it around his head before blowing it away. The man was raising the cigarette for one last drag when the back of his neck prickled. He had caught someone's attention. Being an old hand at watching and being watched, he gave no indication that he knew he was not alone. Instead, he allowed this person time to pass on or to return to where they had come from. When that didn't happen the man swiveled his head, chin tucked into his shoulder, and saw that it was a person of no consequence staring at him. He shook his head, stood up straight, took the last hit off his cigarette, and flicked the butt into the ocean. He started to walk past the watching person who did not stand aside and who looked at him brazenly.

The scum.

If he were at home he would teach this one a lesson. But he wasn't at home, and the last thing he needed was to make a scene at this late date.

Yet, now that he had been seen, the man realized how ridiculous it had been to hide all these days. It was boldness that had gotten him where he was, not timidity. Then again the stakes were higher than usual, and caution had served its purpose. His business in Los Angeles would be brief and lucrative if handled correctly. Then it was on to Panama. After that the route would be firmly established, and he would never have to travel in this low manner again.

"Move," he said, annoyed by this person's impertinence.

When that didn't happen, the man showed his knife, its blade shining in the moonlight. That should have been enough, and in the next moment it was. That person, that lowly being, moved aside, but only far enough for the man to pass. He put his knife in his pocket and went on his way only to stumble, missing his footing when he thought he heard the mate speak.

Tala.

The sound of it was not so much whispered as choked.

Tala.

The man righted himself. He tugged at his shirt and raised his chin. He did not look back, positive that it was a trick of his brain that made him lose his footing. Yes, this was his imagination working overtime, brought on by the affront of being scrutinized in such a manner. Perhaps he was unnerved by the solitude of the last many days. It could have been the sound of the ocean breeze bringing up the memory of that name, whispering as it followed him through the heavy door. No matter what it was that made him think of that time so long ago, he resented being put in such a position by someone not worth spit.

The man turned to unleash his fury on the brazen snake that dared address him, but the mate was gone, disappeared into the old, creaking hulk of a vessel. The mate had gone so quickly, so silently, that the man wondered if he had imagined the meeting. Perhaps all this was nothing more than a rare itch of conscience.

Putting a hand to his eyes, he pressed his fingers against the sockets to quell the pounding behind his lids. Undone by what had happened, the man considered that this encounter might be a bad omen. Then he laughed. Such thoughts were folly. He had a diamond in his ring after all. Everyone knew that diamonds kept evil spirits away. Yet here he was worrying like an auntie; acting like an amateur. That person was nothing but an ant in a hill, moving things about without knowing why, doing what was expected and unsure of how to handle the unexpected. He on the other hand made things happen with a snap of his fingers: big things, frightening things, deadly things.

Stepping through the heavy metal door, he turned left and not right toward his cabin. He would inspect his cargo once more, count the boxes, and check the lashings. He would visit each container, even the one down in the very bowels of the ship because tomorrow was important; tomorrow some of that cargo would be delivered, tested and accepted and he would arrange for the next shipments. All would be well. What just happened was nothing. He would move forward as he always had. He would come out on top as he always had.

The *Faret Vild* was a very large container ship built in 1990. In 2002 it was sold to Libier Knox, and then it was acquired by North Jutland, Boldsen Enterprises in 2004. The vessel sailed, as it had since 1990, under a Liberian flag, but it was no longer the pride of the fleet.

The massive ship's captain, Adeano Bianchi, was Italian; the first mate, Nanda, was Indonesian. The engineer was a man of mixed heritage whose papers indicated that he came from New Zealand. The crew was sparse - as crews tend to be on such vessels - and numbered seventeen seafaring souls. Of the crew there were four Chinese, one African, nine hailing from the Balkans (two Serbs, three Albanians and four Croats), two citizens of the Philippines and one - well one who was a mystery of sorts.

The Italian captain, needing another hand at the last minute, merely shrugged at this young man's poorly forged U.S. passport. He ignored his reticent, wary manner, and the distrustful darkness in his blue eyes. The young man was possessed of a quiet that made his fellow mates steer clear and the captain feel as if he were somehow lacking. Still there were worse types on board. Not to mention there was another mate who would not sign on without this strange young man. To get the refrigeration engineer Adeano Bianchi had to take the second mate who was not an engineer. That was fine because they both came cheap.

The young man - this boy - was not angry or cruel or even a little insane, he simply made it clear that if people kept their distance it would be for the best. Men like him were ocean swells, apparent and unsettling but of little consequence once they moved on. The first mate assigned the quiet man to the lower hold to monitor the temperature on the refrigerated units, and the captain thought no more about him.

Now it was zero two hundred hours and the *Faret Vild* lay off the coast of Southern California. Having been advised by the port that a berth would not be available until zero eight hundred at the earliest, the crew made the ship ready to anchor. They did their work quickly in anticipation of the 'love boat' the captain had promised. It would bring ladies who would help them pass the time in a happy way while the ship remained in the queue.

On the bridge, the first mate was on the radio walking through the anchor checks: brakes on and clear of the voyage securing devices, hydraulic power of the windlasses was checked, and the anchor crew was appropriately dressed for safety. The latter was a matter of faith since the first mate did not think it necessary to check on the crew's dress, nor had the Indonesian thought it necessary to send more than one crew to discharge the task. This was a violation of the company's safety regulations, but it had been done before and it would be done again. Finally the first mate confirmed there was no craft or obstacle under the bow.

Simultaneously the captain ensured that the vessel's GPS speed was near zero before he specifically identified the ship as the *Faret Vild* to those on shore. He did this to avoid misinterpretation should any outside person pick up the transmission. The ship, after all, was old and the communications were by radio, so the identification was necessary to avoid possible confusion with another vessel. This procedure was also necessary because Captain Bianchi wanted no curious eyes on the *Faret Vild* for any reason. By the book. No mistakes. For a captain who was more than willing to cut corners this was telling to Nanda, but the first mate asked no questions. That was how he stayed employed and healthy. Finally the Italian gave Nanda a nod and he, in turn, gave the order to drop anchor.

It was more than a minute before the first mate realized that he had not received confirmation from the anchor crew. He palmed the radio once again, but before he could speak the bridge vibrated with the telltale shimmy of the hydraulics engaging and the giant anchor being lowered by the enormous chain. Satisfied, the first mate turned away. The captain looked up, pen at the ready, in anticipation of verbal confirmation of the lowering of the anchor for the log. Before the Indonesian could speak, the shimmy stopped and all went quiet. In the next second a warning light blinked green on the bridge.

"Nanda."

When the captain had the first mate's attention, he moved a finger to indicate the walkie-talkie. Nanda picked it up and muttered *'omong kosong apa'* before depressing the talk button. The captain laughed.

"*Si*, but she is our piece of crap."

As Nanda tried to raise the anchor crew, the captain left his log and went out to the bridge wing. He called to Lito, one of the Croats working below, and ordered him to see what was what. The man dropped the heavy hose he had been using to wash the deck, and leaned over the railing. When he stood upright again, he waved his hands at the bridge and signed that the anchor was stuck, dangling against the side of the ship.

"*Che Casino.* Such a mess." The captain muttered as he went back to the bridge. "Nanda, send someone to check."

The Italian went back to his log, making meticulous notes, taking little notice as the first mate called to the lounge where the crew smoked and ate as they waited for the ship to be secured and the love boat women to arrive.

"Bojan will go," Nanda said when all was arranged.

The first mate went back to work. There had been a change in position that needed to be reflected in the log since the anchor was not yet in place. This he relayed to the captain.

While the men on the bridge monitored the drift, Bojan, one of the Serbs, rose from his dinner, stubbed out his cigarette thoroughly, downed the rest of his coffee, and made a joke at the expense of the Albanians. Only then did he go on his way, down into the bowels of the ship, keeping a more leisurely pace than he should have.

He navigated the narrow passageways and ladders with a light step, ignoring the cold that became frostier the deeper he went. He whistled a song from his youth and chuckled as it pinged a merry echo in his wake. He drummed a beat or two on the massive containers stacked high on either side of him.

As he approached his destination, the whistling stopped and his steps slowed. Despite the groans of the ship, despite the grinding of the hydraulics, the *Faret Vild* seemed suddenly, eerily silent. The only light came from poorly spaced industrial fixtures attached to the walls. These were encased in metal cages and cast ghostly shadows in the hold. Bojan inched forward unable to imagine what was wrong since he was a man of limited imagination. Not that it mattered. No one could have imagined what he found in the anchor room.

First he saw the dead man caught between the hydraulics of the windlasses and skin of the vessel. One of his arms was woven through the massive links of the anchor chain. It had been cracked in so many places the thing didn't look like an arm any longer. Part of his shoulder was crushed, too, and his neck was tilted at a ninety-degree angle. The man's body was being dragged back and forth on the floor, and his face was crushed flat where it rhythmically hit the hull as the chain strained against the obstruction. The Serb knew the man was dead without touching the body. He had seen enough dead men to know this. He also knew that men didn't wind themselves through chains to commit suicide, and that meant whoever had done this must still be about.

Knees bent, fists held at the ready, eyes narrowed as he peered through the shadows, Bojan pivoted slowly. The anchor room was not a large space, so it wasn't long before he saw the other one propped up against the wall, bloodied, glassy-eyed, and unmoving. Carefully Bojan righted himself and went over to take a closer look. This one had been beaten badly, cut in places; perhaps a bone or two was broken. Unsure of what to do next, knowing there was no help for the dead man, Bojan backed away. Keeping his eyes on the person against the wall, he called the bridge, and told the first mate what he had found. The first mate told the captain who said:

"Shit. Shit." Bianchi often swore in English when he was angered or upset so as not to soil his own language. "Who is it?"

When Nanda shrugged the captain ordered him to get two more men to the anchor room. The Chinaman, Guang, and the African responded, leaving the rest to wonder why the ship was not at anchor and what could be the cause of such urgency. The captain himself roused the engineer and then left the bridge to Nanda. The sound of men running could be heard from different quarters of the ship before it funneled into the bowels and converged in the hold. The captain was first to arrive. The engineer was next, but the Chinaman and African were hot on their heels.

Once there, they fanned out into a semi-circle. Stunned by what they saw, they fell mute. The engineer was the first to act when he came to his senses. He lunged for the windlass and shut off the hydraulics, silencing the groaning of the chain, the churning of the motor, and the banging of bone against metal. When that was done he stood back with his mates. All were more angry than distressed. The love boat would be cancelled for sure. Instead of the big bosomed American prostitutes it would be the U.S. law swarming the *Faret Vild*, and he did not like that at all.

Guang, the Chinaman, and the African were not happy either, but they weren't worried about the women; they were worried that they would be called upon to bear witness to the authorities. On this vessel, as all others, none of them were without fault and many were on the wrong side of the law. They preferred to come and go unnoticed. To make much of the dead at the expense of their living and their freedom was viewed as a ridiculous exercise. Besides, the dead man was unknown to them. If he were a stowaway, then he had taken his chances and lost. If he were not, then he was bad business that belonged to someone on board. In that case, the only law that mattered would be the captain's. The other one - the not quite dead one - they knew. It was not unexpected that this had happened. That one had simmered with anger from the beginning of the voyage, and that sort of thing always came to a bad end.

It seemed a long while that they waited for orders. Perhaps the captain was waiting for the one in the shadows to die.

Perhaps he did not know what to do. The crew was aware that the Indonesian often helped the captain to make decisions, but this time Adeano Bianchi surprised them. He took command, snapping his fingers at Guang.

"*Infermeria. Pubblicare una guardia.*"

There was no doctor aboard, but Guang was certified in first aid and there were supplies in the infirmary. The man was trustworthy which made him the best one to put on guard, but he was also slow moving. The captain waved him on.

"*Rapidamente. Rapidamente.*"

Forgetting English was the universal language of the ship, the captain fell back into Italian. Not that it mattered what language he spoke. Everyone understood that speed was necessary if for no other reason than to allow the anchor to lower. The swells from the north could change the ship's position for the worse if they were not secured soon. Repositioning would waste precious fuel and raise questions from the Port Authority; questions Adeano Bianchi did not want to answer.

"Now!"

The captain's roar finally set them to work. Guang took the bloodied one and the African and the Serb were left to the man caught in the chain. They jockeyed for position, arguing quietly about how best to extricate him before beginning their grisly task. The Serb slipped on the bloody floor once. When he righted himself, they found their rhythm.

The captain watched, tight lipped and solemn. He tilted his head when it seemed the dead man's own would fall off as he was pulled away from the anchor chain. When it remained attached to the torso, Adeano Bianchi seemed relieved. Seeing that the crew was better than he had given them credit for, he offered some encouragement and praise while he considered what else must be done before anyone from the outside stepped aboard the *Faret Vild*. Checking his watch, Adeano noted that time was short so decisions must be made quickly. When the dead man was finally freed, the engineer stepped in and reset the windlasses. As the anchor chain unfurled, Adeano Bianchi directed the two men carrying the body.

"*Contenitore quarantasette.*"

Container number forty-seven was nearly empty, and the temperature change needed to preserve the body would make no difference to the cargo it carried as far as the captain knew. Not to mention it seemed fitting to put the man in one of the containers he had watched over so carefully. Forty-seven was due for Panama, so that would give the captain time to think what to do.

The men heard Adeano Bianchi but remained where they were. Their eyes still on the chain, they held their collective breath and waited for the massive anchor to hit bottom. Only then did they re-adjust their load and go on their way with the body slung between them. When they came to the narrow ladder, the Serb passed the body up to the African and then joined him to carry the dead man toward the stern where they found the container.

Left alone, the captain looked at the mess on the floor and the walls and contemplated the problems that might lie ahead. It was possible that the Port Authority would question why it took so long to anchor, but that was a simple fix. He could adjust the log or point to the slack of the chain and the natural drift it would cause. He would tell them that the ship was old and the hydraulics needed work. The company would pay a fine and there would be no more to it. The authorities were all about business, and a fast turn around was all they really wanted. No, the discrepancy of anchoring was not a problem, but the dead man was another matter.

The dead man was Adeano's special guest. They had done business once before, a test run to see if the captain was a proper partner. Adeano had passed with flying colors and been awarded this job. He had been told what he needed to know about the cargo and no more. It was illegal, it was worth a great deal of money, and there was a ready market among Americans. Adeano understood. He did not need the man to draw him a picture. He also knew that the people waiting for this cargo had a strict time schedule and would not simply be disappointed with this turn of events, they would be vindictive against those who disrupted their business. It was possible that he, Adeano Bianchi, would be held accountable even though he only had control over the transport. Then again, was the dead man really of such consequence? It was the cargo that mattered, not the one who delivered it. Yes, the Italian decided, this was an inconvenience and nothing more. He would search the man's quarters. Certainly he had records, contact numbers, and an inventory list. Surely there would be something that would help Adeano show his good faith to whoever was working with this man. With that information, the captain would fulfill the order in Los Angeles as well as the one in Panama and all would be well.

Satisfied that everything that could be done was being done, he ordered the engineer to 'clean this up', and started down the length of the ship meaning to go to the man's cabin first thing. He didn't get far. There was a niggling worry in his head like an earworm; a tune playing endlessly, the lyrics of which he could not make out. The captain swung himself up onto the first rung of the ladder and as he began to climb he thought that, perhaps, the unpleasantness of a body on board his ship was bothering him. Yet that didn't seem right. He would simply dispose of the body once they were out to sea. If asked at the next port, he would say the man left the ship of his own accord. Let anyone prove that he had not.

No, the body did not seem to be a bothersome thing to Adeano Bianchi. What niggled at him, he realized, was the one who was still alive. It would be best if that one was dead too. He might have to encourage such an outcome. As sad as that would be, Adeano consoled himself with the thought that a quick confession to the monsignor and a heartfelt penance would take care of his soul while the deed itself would secure his job. The captain was, after all, a practical man.

By the time he thought all this, Adeano was on the upper deck, looking at the blinking lights of the port on one side and the grey/black darkness of the early morning on the other. It was then that he understood what was amiss.

The problem was not the dead man, nor the near dead.

The problem was not the crew who he trusted to keep their counsel.

The problem was not the state of Adeano Bianchi's eternal soul.

The problem was the one who had not been in the anchor room, or on the deck, or anywhere else that Adeano knew of. If he had come upon the bloodbath in the anchor room, he would never have left his mate's side. If he didn't know of the incident, then Adeano wanted to be the one to tell him what had happened to his friend.

Changing course, the captain went to the crew lounge instead of the bridge. The men sitting around the narrow table looked up. Each was somber. The news of what had happened traveled fast. The captain counted heads. Five mates were missing. Four could be accounted for. The one who was not there was Adeano's earworm.

"*Trova il ragazzo*," he said. And then in English, 'find the boy'.

BOOKS BY REBECCA FORSTER

THE WITNESS SERIES

HOSTILE WITNESS

Book #1

A prominent judge is brutally murdered. The accused killer is a 16-year-old girl with shocking secrets. Josie Bates takes her case, a decision that will change both their lives forever.

HANNAH'S DIARY

A Spotlight Novella

A free gift exclusively for subscribers to Rebecca Forster's mailing list.

Unsure of where she belongs and what the future holds, Hannah strikes out on her own only to find that dreams can become nightmares and the road home is treacherous.

SILENT WITNESS

Book #2

Josie Bates is blindsided when Archer is accused of murder. Reluctant to come clean about his stepson's suspicious death years ago, Josie finds her faith tested as she defends the man she loves.

PRIVILEGED WITNESS Book #3

The wife of a senate candidate falls to her death, his disturbed sister is accused and a critical election is at risk. Josie Bates must face her ex-lover to fight for justice in a world corrupted by lies, power, and abuse.

EXPERT WITNESS

Book #4

When Josie Bates disappears without a trace, Hannah and Archer must pull together to connect the dots between the woman they love, the ruthless attorney she used to be, and all the people who want her gone for good.

EYEWITNESS

Book #5

Three people are massacred in a California beach house; a latchkey kid Josie cares about is accused. The justice she seeks is brutal, barbaric and buried in a blood- soaked past half a world away.

FORGOTTEN WITNESS

Book #6

A madman's ramblings put Josie Bates on the road to find the teenage runaway she loves. But Josie's journey puts her on a collision course with the United States government that wants to keep the truth top secret at any cost.

DARK WITNESS

Book #7

In a remote wilderness, in an unforgiving land, Hannah's life hangs in the balance. To save her, Josie Bates invokes the fierce, primal law that she knows the girl's captors will understand: survival of the fittest.

LOST WITNESS - NEW!

Book #8

In the hold of a cargo ship off the Port of L.A., a powerful man is dead and the woman who killed him is mortally wounded. On shore a man staggers from the surf, a man once thought dead, a man whose plea for help Josie Bates cannot refuse even if it means hers might be the next life lost.

FINN O'BRIEN THRILLERS

SEVERED RELATIONS

Book #1

Two children and their nanny are slaughtered in the home of a rich young attorney and his beautiful wife. Detective Finn O'Brien follows a trail of bodies and shattered relationships only to be faced with a choice that could be deadly

FOREIGN RELATIONS

Book #2

When a woman hurtles from a freeway overpass in Los Angeles, Finn O'Brien discovers she is not what she seems. More than one person wanted her dead, two countries want her forgotten, and Finn O'Brien won't rest until justice is served.

SECRET RELATIONS

Book #3

They're illegal. They're undocumented. They're disappearing. Fighting a system that wants to turn a blind eye, Finn tracks a serial killer who preys on the most vulnerable and navigates a shadowy world where life is cheap - even his own.

MORE THRILLING READS

BEFORE HER EYES

A mountain grocer is executed and a fading model is missing. Sheriff Dove Connelly embarks on an investigation that drags him into a twilight world where nothing is at it seems, life and death hang in a delicate balance and his very thoughts could tip the scales toward hell.

THE MENTOR

When homegrown terrorists bomb an IRS building, fledgling U.S. Attorney Lauren Kingsley looks to her mentor to guide her through a prosecution fraught with peril. Little does she know that those closest to her are the most dangerous people of all.

BEYOND MALICE

When beautiful, arrogant Nora Royce is accused of murder, her sister, Amanda Cross, is the only one willing to defend her. Outgunned and outmanned, Amanda peels away the layers of entitlement and political protection surrounding L.A.'s legal elites to uncover a truth that could end Amanda's career and both their lives.

KEEPING COUNSEL

Attorney Tara Linley takes on her best friend's lover as a client and gets more than she bargained for. A killer smile and smooth talking ways can't hide this psychopath's insanity as he pushes the boundaries of client privilege, sexual desire and the limits of friendship.

CHARACTER WITNESS

(A stand-alone thriller, not a Josie Bates novel)

Kathleen Cotter, junior partner at a past-its-prime Beverly Hills law firm gets a doozy of a first case. A dead man's ex-wife says its murder; the insurance company says suicide. Kathleen thinks everyone is nuts until she uncovers a trail of lies and corruption that threaten to make her first case her last.

Yes, you can still **SIGN UP** for my spam-free mailing list and I'll send you HANNAH'S DIARY, an exclusive Witness Series Spotlight Novella, FREE.

ABOUT THE AUTHOR

Rebecca Forster started writing on a crazy dare. Now with almost forty books to her name, she is a USA Today and Amazon best-selling author. She lives in Southern California, is married to a superior court judge and is the proud mother of two sons.

FIND OUT MORE ABOUT REBECCA
or follow her on any of these sites

Made in the USA
Columbia, SC
19 June 2021

40567786R00202